THE
DO-OVER

OTHER TITLES BY T L SWAN

Stanton Adore

Stanton Unconditional

Stanton Completely

Stanton Bliss

Marx Girl

Gym Junkie

Dr. Stanton

Dr. Stantons: The Epilogue

Mr. Masters

Mr. Spencer

Mr. Garcia

The Italian

Ferrara

Play Along

The Stopover

The Takeover

The Casanova

Our Way

Find Me Alastar

THE
DO-OVER

THE MILES HIGH CLUB

T L SWAN

Text copyright © 2022 by T L Swan
All rights reserved.

Published by Montlake, Seattle

www.apub.com

Amazon, the Amazon logo, and Montlake are trademarks of Amazon.com, Inc., or its affiliates.

ISBN-13: 9781542034593
ISBN-10: 1542034590

Cover design by @blacksheep-uk.com

Printed in the United States of America

GRATITUDE
The quality of being thankful;
readiness to show appreciation for and
to return kindness.

I would like to dedicate this book to the alphabet,
for those twenty-six letters have changed my life.

Within those twenty-six letters, I found myself
and live my dream.

Next time you say the alphabet,
remember its power.
I do every day.

Chapter 1

CHRISTOPHER

The deep buzz of my alarm cuts the silence, and I stretch out as I wake.

"Fuck, it feels like I was asleep for three minutes," I murmur.

"I think we were," Heidi whispers as she throws her leg over me.

I keep dozing with my eyes closed, and I feel lips on my neck from the other side. "Morning, Nicki," I mutter.

She smiles into my neck as she cuddles in closer. "Good morning, Christopher."

The three of us lie in comfortable silence for a few minutes more, and I know I have to make a move. I have a board meeting at nine. "Up." I sigh.

The girls both grumble with resistance.

I sit up and look around the room. Clothes are strewn everywhere, and a bottle of wine and three glasses are still by the sunken spa in my bathroom. I bend and kiss Nicki's hip. "Get up, wench."

"Go away." She rolls over.

I smile and slap Heidi on the behind. "Party's over."

"Ow," she cries.

I climb out and stand at the end of the bed as I look down at the view. Seeing two beautiful women in my bed will never get old. "Come on, out." I flick the blankets off them. "I have to go to work."

It's very easy to get them to come over, not so easy to get them to leave.

"What's happening tonight?" Nicki asks.

"Nothing," I reply as I walk around naked, picking up their clothes. "I'm busy."

"Doing what?" Heidi asks as she leans up on her elbows. Her blonde hair is wild and messy.

"I have a date." I throw her panties at her head. "With a good girl." I widen my eyes to accentuate my point. "The exact opposite of you two hobags."

They both laugh. "You love hobags," Nicki says.

I lean down onto my hands and kiss them both; then I grab a handful of Nicki's hair and pull it toward me so I can kiss her longer. She's my favorite. "That's true. I do."

I lean over and kiss Heidi's breast. She grabs a handful of my hair, and I feel a throb between my legs. When they grab my hair, I'm done for.

Stop it. I don't have time for this. I pull out of her grip.

"So . . . you'll call us on the way home from your boring date, then?" Heidi asks.

I smirk as I continue picking up their clothes. They know me well. "Probably." I pull back Nicki's bra like a slingshot and fire it at her head. It flicks her hard.

"Ow, cut it out." She snaps it up.

I walk into the bathroom and turn the shower on. I look back to see them both still lying in bed, and I march back out there and put my hands on my hips. "Get up before I make you both do unspeakable things," I demand.

"What's new?" Heidi smiles playfully up at me. She's all crumpled and just fucked.

Tempting . . .

"I have a board meeting at nine."

I shower and minutes later walk out with a white towel around my waist to see them slowly dressing as I disappear into my walk-in wardrobe. I put on a navy suit and white shirt, a Rolex watch, black shoes, and a belt and walk back into the bathroom.

As usual, the girls both come in and sit on the vanity to talk to me as I do my hair.

"What's on today, boss?" Nicki asks as she tightens my tie.

"Business stuff."

"I love business stuff," Heidi replies. "Say something boss-like to me."

"You're fired."

They both giggle.

"Say something boss-like to me," Nicki says.

"Bend over my desk." I turn her away from me and lift her dress up over her ass.

A thrum of arousal runs through me as I stare down at her tight ass up in the air . . . ready and waiting.

Go to fucking work!

"Let's go," I snap as I rush from the bathroom.

I hear a voice come from the kitchen. "Good morning, Mr. Miles."

"Good morning, Miss Penelope," I call as I collect my brief-case from my office. I walk back out into the kitchen, and she passes me my coffee in a travel mug.

"You are undoubtedly the best housekeeper of all time." I smile as I kiss her cheek.

"I know, dear."

I'm not even joking. Miss Penelope truly is the best house-keeper of all time. If she wasn't fifty-six years old . . . and already married, I would marry her myself.

The girls come around the corner. "Good morning, Miss Penelope," they chime in unison.

"Good morning, girls." She smiles. Her eyes come back to me, and I give her a playful wink.

Yeah, yeah, I know.

I'm bad.

We've established this a million times already.

"Time to go. Have a good day, Miss Penelope."

"I will, dear. You too."

We make for the door, and the girls chatter as we get into the elevator. When we get to the ground floor, I walk out the front of my building with them. Hans is waiting with my car. "Morning, Hans." I smile.

"Good morning, Mr. Miles." He dips his head.

"Can you take the girls home for me, please?" I ask him.

"Yes, sir." He smiles. "Of course."

"Morning, Hans." The girls both smile as he opens the back door of the limo. I kiss them each goodbye on the cheek, and they happily bounce in. I watch the limo pull out and walk back into my building and take the elevator down to the basement. I get into my black Porsche and pull out of the parking lot and into the long line of cars.

Ugh . . . London traffic. Is there anything worse?

Three hours later

"And this right here." He points to a line on the graph. "This trend is what we're following. See how the overflow of the population . . ."

I yawn, hardly able to keep my eyes open.

"Are we keeping you awake, Christopher?" Jameson barks.

You are, actually.

I clear my throat to stop myself rolling my eyes.

"Sorry," I apologize.

Two of my brothers, Jameson and Tristan, are here in London to meet with Elliot and me for our quarterly board meeting. The shit we have to talk about is seriously boring. Jameson begins to speak again and goes on in great detail about some spiraling trend, and I yawn again.

Jameson glares at me.

"Sorry," I mouth, trying not to interrupt him again.

For fuck's sake, focus.

I can hardly keep my eyes open. I glance at my watch. How long is this meeting going to go for?

Elliot begins to talk. "I've been watching the outcomes on this, and I've found . . ."

He goes on and on and on . . . I yawn again.

"Will you cut it out!" Tristan snaps. "You are not the only person in the room who's fucking tired."

I glance up to see the attention of all three men fixed on me.

"I bet Christopher's way of getting tired was more fun than yours." Elliot smirks.

"One hundred percent," Tristan mutters dryly. "I slept on the floor while the kids slept in my fucking bed."

"Why?" Jameson frowns.

"The girls have decided that they don't want to sleep anywhere but in their bedrooms at home." He fakes a smile. "Traveling is so much fun these days."

"More fool you." I give a disgusted shake of my head.

"What's that supposed to mean?" Tristan snaps.

"Just . . ." I cut myself off.

"Just what?"

"Just that I thought you were the parent," I reply casually as I sip my water. "Why on earth you would let your child sleep in the bed while you sleep on the floor is beyond me."

"Summer isn't herself; she has a cough," Tristan justifies himself.

I wince back from him. "Don't breathe on me, then, you germy prick."

"If you had kids of your own, you would understand," Tristan snaps.

Elliot chuckles. "As if that's ever going to happen."

Tristan laughs. "I know, right?"

"Can we focus on the fucking topic here?" Jameson taps the whiteboard.

"What's that supposed to mean?" I fire back as I look between them. "I'll have kids of my own one day."

"Nope." Jameson writes on the whiteboard as if remembering the next topic. "There's no chance in hell you'll have kids."

"What?" I shriek in outrage. "That's bullshit. You have no idea."

Tristan rolls his eyes as if I'm clueless. "It's you who has no idea."

"You're way too selfish to have a wife and kids. It's never going to happen." Elliot smirks.

"He'll still be gangbanging chicks when he's ninety," Jameson replies casually as he draws a graph on the whiteboard.

The boys both laugh.

"For your information . . . I do not gangbang chicks." I readjust my tie in annoyance. "I encourage group activities where everyone is treated equal." I square my shoulders. "There's a big difference."

The three of them laugh, and I begin to see red. "You three are awfully judgy, seeing you used to be exactly the same as me."

"No, we weren't," Elliot snaps. "Nowhere close. You're broken."

"I'm not fucking broken." I gasp in outrage.

"You are thirty-one years old and never had a girlfriend. Not one," Tristan says.

"You take nice girls on token dates to try and kid yourself into believing that they stand a chance, and that's beside the fact that you only fuck women in pairs so that there is no chance you can fall for one of them," Jameson replies flatly.

My mouth falls open in horror. "This is how you see me?"

"This is how you are," Jameson replies. He begins to tap the whiteboard. "Now . . . back to the tracking," he continues.

My angry heartbeat bangs hard in my ears as I look between them. I can't believe this. "I am *not* broken."

"Spoiled," Elliot adds.

"How am I spoiled?" I gasp in horror.

Jameson screws up his face. "Oh, please."

"I am *not* fucking spoiled."

"Yes, you are," Elliot replies.

"Name one way," I snap.

"You have never had a job interview but have your dream job. You have penthouses in New York, London, and Paris, staff all around the world. You have a sports car collection worth ten million dollars. Somehow people think you are stupidly good looking, and you only have to look a woman's way and she drops her panties . . . regardless if she's married or not," Jameson says calmly.

I open my mouth to defend myself, but no words come out.

"And . . . you won't date an average girl because they are below you," Tristan adds.

"Nobody wants to date an average girl," I cry, outraged.

Jameson looks me fair and square in the eyes. "Name the last time you had to work for something, Christopher."

"Fuck off," I huff.

"No, I'm being serious. When was the last time you set yourself a goal and didn't have it the same night?"

Elliot smiles as he rocks back on his chair, and I look between them as they all wait for my answer.

"He's got nothing. Not one single time." Tristan smirks.

"I have goals I haven't achieved yet," I stammer, embarrassed.

"Sleeping alone?" Elliot suggests.

They throw their heads back and laugh out loud, thinking this is the funniest thing they've ever heard.

Betrayal washes over me.

This is how they see me?

"Fuck you." I stand. "And fuck your stupid meeting. I'm not staying here and listening to this bullshit." I storm from the office and slam the door hard.

"Get back here, wimp," Jameson yells from behind me.

I hear them burst out laughing once more . . . *fuckers*.

I march past reception, and the secretaries all glance up at my angry demeanor.

This is probably a first. I'm never angry.

"Everything all right, Christopher?" Victoria frowns.

"No. It's not," I huff. "Those fuckers in there think that I'm spoiled." I throw my hands up in the air as I march past. "Can you fucking believe that?"

"No. Not at all." Victoria rolls her lips to hide her smile.

I narrow my eyes in a silent warning and continue marching for my office. I hear the secretaries all snicker from the reception area.

I see red.

The world's gone mad. I begin to pack my briefcase with force.

I.

Am.

Not.

Spoiled.

I take offense at this accusation. How dare they? Do they even know what spoiled is? I really don't think so.

I walk back out to the elevator, and the girls all look up, surprised.

"I'm leaving," I announce.

"To go where?" Victoria frowns.

"Wherever I want to." That sounded bad. I point at her. "Because I'm pissed off, not because I'm spoiled."

Victoria widens her eyes to accentuate the point.

"Shut up, Victoria," I spit.

"Yes, sir." She smiles.

"And don't patronize me."

"I wouldn't dare."

I fume some more.

The girls all drop their heads to hide their giggles.

"Stop laughing or I'm firing you all," I demand.

They all burst out laughing hard this time. I'm usually the funny guy of the office. Never the cranky one.

"That's it!" I explode. The elevator doors open, and I storm inside and push the button hard. "No Christmas bonuses."

They laugh harder again.

Witches . . . I take the elevator to the ground floor and walk out to the parking garage and look around. My car isn't where I parked it.

I march over to the parking attendant. "Where's my car?"

His eyes widen in horror. "Um . . ." He looks around nervously. "We weren't aware you were coming to collect it, sir. We put it on the bottom level to make room for other cars that are leaving before you."

What?

I raise my eyebrow, infuriated.

"When I park my car in a reserved parking spot, I expect that the fucking car will be left where I put it."

The attendant opens his mouth to speak and then closes it again before saying anything.

"What?" I bark.

"That's why we have your keys, sir, so that we can move cars around to suit the schedule. We do it every day."

"Does this look like it is suiting my schedule?" I bark. "What am I supposed to do? I need my car. Now!"

"There it is," I hear someone mutter. I turn to see Elliot standing to the side, listening.

What's he fucking doing here?

"Never mind," I snap as I march back toward the elevator. "I'll catch an Uber." I straighten my tie as I try to regain some control. "Because I'm *flexible*."

The parking attendant frowns and looks to Elliot.

"Flexible," Elliot mouths.

"Go back upstairs, Elliot, before I have my Uber driver run over you," I snap as I bang the button to close the elevator doors.

Elliot runs and gets in alongside me, and the doors close. "Calm down," he says. "We're just having some fun."

I clench my jaw as I stare straight ahead.

"You are not spoiled."

I lift my chin in defiance.

"You're entitled."

My eyes bulge from their sockets. "Entitled to knock you out, right now," I growl. The elevator doors open, and I march out through the foyer and onto the street. Elliot is hot on my heels.

We both stand on the curb, and he looks over at me. "What time is he coming?"

"Who?"

"The Uber."

I frown.

"You ordered it . . . right?"

"Of course I did," I snap.

How the fuck do I do that?

"I'm not catching an Uber," I announce as I go up onto my toes while looking around at the street. "I'm catching a cab. I support old school."

"Oh . . ." Elliot smirks. "Good for you."

I see the moment of horror as the doormen all notice me. "Mr. Miles." They run over. "How can we help you, sir?"

"I . . ."

Elliot cuts me off. "He's fine, thank you." He smiles at them. "Thank you, anyway."

The doormen slowly go back inside, and I glance over at Elliot, who is watching me. "Go on, then," he says.

"Go on what?"

"Catch a cab."

"Do you honestly think I can't get a cab on my own?"

"When was the last time you did it?"

"When was the last time you went to the hospital for being beat up?" I narrow my eyes.

Elliot holds his hands up in surrender. "I'm just saying . . ." He walks back inside, and I watch him as he disappears into the elevator.

11

I stare after him, and determination fills me. I will catch my own fucking cab. I walk out onto the street and see a cab coming down the road. I put my arm up.

It speeds past with a passenger in the back seat.

Hmm . . .

Another cab comes, and I put my arm up. He drives straight past me. "Fucker," I call after him.

For five minutes I stand on the side of the road. No cabs are stopping.

What in the hell is wrong with them? Don't they know I have somewhere to go?

This is discrimination.

I hear a voice. "Mr. Miles." I turn to see that Hans has parked the limo. "Is everything all right, sir?"

"Umm . . ." I glance around. No cab is stopping, and I could be here for eternity. I peek inside to make sure Elliot has gone. "Take me home, please."

Hans gives me a kind smile and opens the back door for me, and I climb in. He pulls out into the traffic.

"How did you know I was here?" I ask him.

"Elliot called me."

"Elliot called you?" I fume.

"Yes, said that I needed to rescue you."

Asshole.

※

"I had a wonderful time." She swoons.

"Me too." I fake a smile. It's all I can do not to check my watch as we stand on the street saying goodbye. How long is this going to take?

This has been the worst date in all history.

Boring . . .

So fucking boring.

Carly is beautiful, smart, and sweet, with a body to die for. She's everything I should want. And yet, as usual when I'm out with a girl one on one, I'm bored as fuck. I even considered asking the waiter to poison my food so that I'd have a legitimate reason to leave.

Tristan's and Jameson's words from today run through my mind for the millionth time.

You are thirty-one years old and never had a girlfriend. You take nice girls on token dates to try and kid yourself into believing that they stand a chance, and you only fuck women in pairs so that there is no chance you can fall for one of them.

Carly frowns up at me. "Is everything okay?"

I stare down at her looking up at me, all kiss-me-like. "I'm just . . . I have a headache. I'm sorry, I . . ." I cut myself off before I lie to her more.

"That's okay." She smiles. "Some people just don't click, do they?"

Intriguing . . . *I click with everyone.*

"Do you click with most people?" I ask her.

"I do."

"Why do you think we didn't click?"

She shrugs. "Lots of reasons."

"Name them."

She laughs. "I don't think you want to hear what I have to say."

"Trust me, I do."

"Well, for a start, you're too perfect."

I frown. "What?"

Her face falls. "Look . . . I didn't mean to offend. That came out wrong."

13

"No, please . . . ," I reassure her. "Explain it to me. How can I get better if I don't know what's wrong with me?"

"You don't need to get better. You just need to . . ." She pauses as if choosing her words wisely. "You have no substance."

"What?" I put my hand on my chest. "Me? No substance?" I gasp, shocked. "I am high-quality fucking substance!"

She laughs. "That's the problem. You will never understand what I mean, Christopher, and it's okay—you don't need to. It's not relevant to your life."

I frown as I stare at her. "Whatever do you mean?"

"Your life has been so perfect that you've never had to dig deep to find out who you really are."

I put my weight onto my back foot, affronted that this is the second time today I am hearing this. "I disagree. Why do people think that only hardship builds character? Why would I have to dig deep to find out who I am when I already know?"

She goes up onto her toes and kisses my cheek. "Because diamonds are made under pressure." She turns and begins to casually walk up the street.

"What does that mean?" I put my hands onto my hips in disgust. "I am a fucking diamond, Carly." I hold my arms out wide. "Do you know how many women would love to have a diamond like me?"

She laughs out loud and turns back toward me. "The women that you spend time with just want rich coal. They don't even know what a diamond is. It's coal meet coal."

My mouth falls open in horror.

She blows me a kiss and turns and walks off into the night. I run my hand over my stubble as I stare after her.

That was weird.

Hmm, and . . . I hate to admit it . . . interesting.

I walk down the street and into a bar and take a seat at the bench by the window.

"What will it be?" a waiter asks me.

"Scotch," I reply, distracted.

It starts to rain, and I watch it fall through the window. "Here you go," the waiter says as he places my drink down in front of me.

"Thanks." I sit and drink alone.

I've had a shitty day, and I hate to admit it, but it seems there's a part of my personality that others can see that I can't.

The women that you spend time with just want rich coal.

I drag my hand down my face in disgust. Is that true? I tip my head back and drain my glass.

You are broken.

It's been a weird day full of revelations. Are they right?

How will I ever find my diamond if I'm only rich coal?

𝕏

I hear a voice. "It can't be that bad." I glance up to see a waitress wiping down the table beside me.

"Why do you say that?"

"Well, you've been sitting there for three hours looking completely miserable."

"What?" I glance at my watch. One thirty a.m. . . . shit. "Sorry," I splutter as I stand and dig out my wallet.

She rings up my tab. "Did you get dumped?" she asks.

I frown, confused at the concept. "No, nothing like that."

"Did you dump someone?"

"No."

Mind your business.

"Fired?"

I'm not in the mood for talking, and I just want her to shut up. "Yes. Fired," I lie.

"Well, that's great." She smiles. "I love crossroads."

This woman's a bona fide idiot.

"How is being fired great?"

"Because you get to start again. You can design who you want to be."

I frown as I stare at her.

Design who you want to be.

"Like a do-over . . . ," I whisper to myself.

"Yeah." She begins to wipe the counter down again.

"What would you do?" I ask her. "How would you start again?"

She smiles dreamily. "I'd disappear and travel the world. See it through new, untainted eyes."

I stare at her as my mind begins to run a million miles per minute. Not the first time I've heard this. I thought of this concept years ago myself.

"I mean, not that anyone can realistically afford to do it." She shrugs. "But wouldn't that be something?"

"It would . . ." I pay her, and deep in thought, I walk around the corner to the taxi stand. There's one waiting, and I get into the back seat.

"Where to?" the driver happily asks.

I smile. See . . . I *can* catch a cab by myself. In fact, I'm sure I could do anything that I set my mind to. I'd show those fuckers what I'm really made of.

But no money?

Ugh . . . that's tough.

I lie on my back and stare at the ceiling of my darkened bedroom.

I have this sinking feeling in the pit of my stomach that won't leave me alone.

Ever since the idea of a do-over came to me, I can't stop thinking about it.

But do I really need to become invisible so that I can be seen?

Am I overreacting?

I don't want to fall into the trap of money dictating my life, if I haven't already.

I hate how my brothers see me. I hate how Carly thinks I'm coal. The worst thing is, I know that she's right. As I am right now, I'm 100 percent coal.

I don't even know how to find substance, and I hate the thought of it.

I'm better than this. I know I am.

There is more to me than my surname . . . but how do I find what it is?

If I lived a year without money, how would it feel?

I imagine the possibilities and the risks and the feeling of pride I would have at the end, knowing I'd done it.

I haven't been out this week; for the first time ever the thought of socializing isn't something I can stomach.

I don't want to be out there . . . I want to disappear.

Monday morning

After the longest sexless week in history, I've come to a decision. I step out of the elevator with purpose. "Good morning, girls." I walk past them.

"Good morning, Christopher."

I walk down the corridor and into Elliot's office. Jameson and Tristan are leaving for New York tonight, and I know that I need to do this now, while we are all together.

"Can I speak to you for a minute in my office?" I ask.

Elliot looks up from his computer and frowns. "What about?"

"Just get Jay and Tris and come down and see me."

"Okay."

I walk down to my office and turn my computer on. I have a lot to do.

"What's up?" Jameson asks. He walks into my office and flops onto the couch.

Elliot and Tristan follow. "What's going on?"

"I'm taking a year off Miles Media," I announce.

"What?" Jameson frowns. "What for?"

"I'm going off the grid."

"How?"

"I'm going backpacking."

Chapter 2

"You've got to be joking."

"Nope." I sit down at my desk.

"For how long?"

"Twelve months."

Elliot screws up his face. "Fuck off. There is no way in hell you would do that. You nearly had me there. What do you really want?"

"I'm deadly serious."

"You won't last one hour backpacking, let alone twelve months." Tristan huffs. "You're more precious than the rest of us put together."

Determination fills me. "I'm not useless, you know?"

"If this is about us teasing you last week, we were only joking."

"This isn't about you. It's about me."

"Being on a death wish?" Jameson replies dryly.

"What you said got me to thinking, if I don't change the way I am . . ." I cut myself off, unwilling to say it out loud.

"What?"

"I've had this idea in the back of my mind for years. I know that if I don't go now, I'm going to be too old."

"You're already too fucking old," Jameson snaps. "I never saw a thirty-one-year-old backpacker."

"Because you know *so* many." I widen my eyes.

"Why would you want to do this?"

"Because I need to. I need to get my shit together. I've always said I was going to do it, and I think now is the right time."

Elliot is pacing. "I mean, I guess . . . I could rearrange the staff . . . you could work in our offices abroad."

"No, no contacts. I want to find my own way and earn my keep. I'm only taking two thousand dollars. I estimate that will last me a month if I'm roughing it?"

Jameson bursts out laughing. "You . . . with no money?"

"You kill me." Tristan laughs. "You spend more money than that in a day."

"What job are you going to do?" Elliot stammers. His eyes are wide as he waits for my answer. I can almost see his anxiety rising.

"Well." I shrug casually as if this isn't the scariest thing I have ever done. "I don't know yet. Something will turn up. I'll work it out as I go."

"No," Elliot snaps. "No way in hell. You need a plan. Mileses don't work it out as we go. You'll turn up dead somewhere. I'm not having you out there alone in the world. There are some bad fuckers out there."

"You don't have a choice."

"This is stupid," Jameson warns. "And not to mention dangerous."

"I've thought long and hard about this all week, and I know that it's something that I have to do. If I back out now, I know I'm going to regret it." I shrug. "I mean . . . how bad can it be?"

"Bad," Elliot snaps. "Real bad. Coming-home-in-a-body-bag bad."

I roll my eyes. "Why are you so fucking dramatic?"

"This is dramatic," Tristan snaps. "Can't you just get a fucking girlfriend like a normal person?"

"Don't tell Mom and Dad," I add.

"What?" Tristan snaps. "How the fuck do you think they won't notice you missing for a year?"

"I'm going to tell them that I'm doing a course in France. I'll call them all the time, and I'll go back to Paris from Spain to meet them for a few days if they decide to visit."

"Spain?"

"I'm starting in Spain."

"Why Spain?"

"I don't know." I shrug. "I like paella, I guess."

"Oh, fuck me dead." Jameson pinches the bridge of his nose. "You don't go backpacking for fucking paella, Christopher. There's a kick-ass Spanish restaurant here in London somewhere, I'm sure of it."

"I'll call you all every day if you want?" I put my hands onto my hips. "But I am going. You can't stop me."

They stay silent.

"And I'll let you know wherever I'm going in case shit goes south," I add.

"You're taking a guard," Jameson snaps.

"I am not taking a fucking security guard."

"Why not?"

"Because it defeats the purpose."

"Is the purpose to get yourself killed?" Elliot gasps.

"Look." I try to calm him. I know that he's the one who will have the hardest time with this. "It's fine. This week you can help me, and we'll get ready so that I'm prepared for everything."

21

He stares at me, and I can almost hear his brain misfiring as it freaks out.

"When do you leave?" Jameson asks.

"Next Saturday."

"That soon?"

They all fall silent as they process.

"Well . . ." Tristan slaps me on the back. "It was nice knowing you, brother."

HAYDEN

I drive the tractor over the paddock. The large wheels bump as I go over the creek between the two paddocks and back toward the house.

I smile into the late-afternoon sun and reach over to pat Nev's head. He's one of our trusty cattle dogs and my personal favorite. He sits proudly up on the ledge beside me as we do a final round of the farm.

As usual, the day has been crazy. Three heifers are in calf, and we've all been running in circles. As the only child of a farming family, I work hard, helping to run things around here, and there's a lot to run. We have a three-thousand-acre farm with over five hundred Angus cattle. Thankfully we have staff, but the workload seems to never slow down.

I turn the corner toward the house to see my mom waving me over. I pull the tractor alongside her. "Hey."

She taps her watch. "What are you doing?"

I frown. "What do you mean?"

"We have so much to do. Remember we're going shopping?"

I exhale as I jump down from the tractor. "Mom . . ."

"Seriously, Hayden, you leave in two days. Stop worrying about the damn farm."

"You know, I've been thinking. I don't really need to go anymore."

"Hayden." She grabs my shoulders and turns me toward the house. "You booked this trip two years ago." She gives me a gentle push. "You are *going*."

23

"Yeah, but I was newly brokenhearted when I booked it. I'm not now. I'm going to call the travel agent and try and get my money back. The timing's not right now."

"You're just nervous," she says. "Stop talking yourself out of it."

I've been sick to the stomach for days. Traveling to the other side of the world alone when I've hardly left the house in two years seems utterly ridiculous.

Nervous doesn't come close.

I'm terrified.

"I don't want to leave you and Dad in the lurch. I'm needed here. What if something happens when I'm gone?"

"Honey." Mom smiles up at me. "What Dad and I need is for you to be happy."

"I am happy."

"Driving tractors? Birthing cows?" Her eyes search mine. "Most of your friends have left town and got married."

"So? I don't care."

"You don't even go out anymore."

I get a lump in my throat because I know she's right.

It doesn't make it any easier.

"Hayden." She smiles. "There are exciting things just waiting for you out there."

I nod.

"And you are going to be brave and go out into the big wide world and make new friends and laugh and live and not worry about damn cows."

My eyes well with tears, and I shrug. "I'm just . . ."

"I know, baby, you're scared." She gives me a soft smile. "But I'm more scared for you if you stay here through your youth without knowing what's out there." She pulls me into a hug. "This farm will always be here waiting for you, Hayden. But . . . he's waiting for you too."

24

"Who is?" I frown.

"Your sweetheart. He's out there somewhere. I just know it."

I roll my eyes. "Mom, I'm *not* going to meet the love of my life in a backpackers' hostel, I can assure you that."

"You never know. There's lots of good wholesome farm boys out there."

"I guess." I smirk. "We do need a vet."

"That's the spirit." She links her arm through mine, and we begin to walk to the house. "Or a diesel mechanic would come in handy. Those damn tractors are high maintenance."

I giggle. "True."

"A fencer would be great," she adds.

I laugh. I imagine bringing some poor unsuspecting man home and my father making him build fences for days.

"Let's go buy you some date dresses."

"What's wrong with my clothes?" I act offended.

We both look down at my tight jeans, checked shirt, and steel-capped boots covered in cow doo. "I'm the epitome of high fashion, Mom." I put my hands on my hips and do a little sashay.

She widens her eyes. "Not really Spanish, though, are they?"

"And this is it, the BlackWolf Nomad." The salesman smiles proudly. "The bees' knees of backpacks."

I stare at the huge oversize backpack.

"Thank you, we'll let you know if we need any help with it," Elliot replies.

The salesman walks off, and I unzip the pack. "Zipper works well."

"I don't see how anyone could possibly walk around with that shit on their backs," Elliot whispers. "What would it weigh when filled? Like, twenty kilograms?"

"Probably."

"See if there's one with wheels?"

"I don't want to look like a wimp, wheeling my bag when everyone else is carrying theirs."

"Everyone else is an idiot."

"I don't want to stand out."

Elliot chuckles as he stares at the bag. "Trust me, a bag is the least of your stand-out issues."

I go to another bag and pick it up. I start to go through all the little compartments. In the bottom there's a little tray. I take it out and hold it up as I look at it. "What's this for?"

"Hmm." Elliot takes it from me and turns it over as he looks at it. "A dish?"

"Bit shallow for a dish. Wouldn't be much of a breakfast, would it?"

The salesman walks back over. "That's the toilet."

I stare at him as my brain misfires. "The what?"

"That's the pan." He shrugs. "You know, for when you need to take a shit in the woods."

Elliot throws the pan back onto the bag as if it burned his fingers. "He's going backpacking, not feral."

The salesman laughs. "You two haven't been backpacking before, have you?"

Elliot and I glance at each other but remain silent.

"If you're stuck in a crowded place and you can't find a bathroom, go in this pan and empty it when you can. It's easy as."

I frown as I stare at this feral animal. "Nothing about that sounds easy as."

"What? You think he's going to put it back in his bag dirty?" Elliot snaps, horrified.

The salesman shrugs happily. "It's an option."

"That I won't be taking," I mutter dryly as I walk away from this animal.

For fuck's sake, what is the world coming to?

I need to get out of here. I can feel my blood pressure rising by the second. "What is your most popular backpack?"

"This one." The salesman holds it up. "Without a doubt."

"I'll take it."

"Do you want the black or the red?"

Red.

I narrow my eyes. Is this guy for real? Nobody wants a fucking red backpack. "Black."

"What else does he need?" Elliot asks.

"How long you going for?"

"Twelve months."

The sales assistant whistles. "Hard core."

Hard core . . . what the hell does that mean?

"If I wanted your opinion, I would ask for it," I snap.

He points to Elliot with his thumb. "He just asked for it."

I roll my eyes; this guy is getting on my nerves. "What are the essentials?"

"Comfortable shoes, good mini towels."

"What's a mini towel?"

He holds up a little pack the size of a deck of cards. "This has a towel in it."

"Oh." I nod. "Impressive."

"What other mini things do you have?" Elliot asks him.

"Apart from the obvious," I mutter under my breath.

"Stop," Elliot whispers.

"Compass." He marches over to retrieve a compass.

"Compass?" I call. "I'm going backpacking, not climbing Mount Everest."

This guy is a total fuckwit.

Elliot widens his eyes in a shut-up-now sign.

The guy returns and passes me a compass, and I pass it straight to Elliot.

"We'll take it," Elliot replies way too fast.

"We have these great water bottles," the salesman continues as he walks to the other side of the store.

"We are not taking the compass," I whisper.

"What if you get lost."

"I'll look on Google Maps like a person from the twenty-first fucking century." I roll my eyes.

"You're taking it," he whispers angrily.

"I am *not* taking it," I whisper. I snatch it off him and stuff it onto a shelf.

The salesman returns with a huge-ass water bottle. "This one here is great. It will stay hot or cold for twenty-four hours, and this long cord allows you to wear it around your neck. And look, it's camouflage."

"If you think I'm wearing a camouflage water bottle around my neck, you need to go to the hospital."

Elliot gets the giggles as he pinches the bridge of his nose. "Do you sell GoPros?"

"Why would I need a GoPro?" I frown.

"Because I want you to wear it strapped to your head at all times so we can watch this shit live as it goes down."

I roll my eyes.

"This would make great reality television, actually." He raises his eyebrows as if having an epiphany. "I should call someone; a network would defo want this."

"Shut. The fuck. Up." I widen my eyes. "You are not calling anyone."

"Sleeping bag," the assistant says as he marches over. "This is *vital*."

"I'll be sleeping in a bed."

"But you need to have a sleeping bag. There will be times when you can't get accommodation and have to rough it."

We narrow our eyes as we stare at him. "Define *roughing it*," Elliot replies.

"You know, have to sleep in the woods or in a train station or something."

Train station . . . seriously?

"Do you sell mini mattresses, something that folds up like the towel?" I ask.

The salesman throws his head back and laughs out loud. "You're hilarious, man."

It wasn't a joke.

"We'll take a sleeping bag. This kind here." Elliot taps the display.

"Yellow or black?"

"Are you color blind?" I stare at him deadpan. "The fuck is wrong with you? Nobody wants a yellow sleeping bag."

The assistant begins to take our things to the cashier station. He piles all our purchases onto the counter. "Will that be all?"

"Yes."

He begins to ring them up.

Elliot eyes the pile of things on the counter, and I can see something running through his mind.

"What?" I ask.

"How is all that going to fit into that pissant bag?"

Hmm, he does have a point.

"I mean, where do your clothes go?"

"That's a very good question," I mutter.

"You travel light," the salesman says.

"How light?" I frown.

"Just the essentials, like one or two pairs of pants, two pairs of shorts, like three T-shirts, and one jumper. The shoes you are wearing."

I stare at him as horror begins to fuck me up the ass . . . "I can't . . ."

"You can," he says.

My eyes meet Elliot, and he shrugs. "I don't know?"

How the hell can you live in five things?

Five hours later

"What fucking bullshit is this?" I cry.

Elliot scratches his head, completely perplexed. "We shouldn't have taken it out of the case."

30

"Oh. Great idea, Einstein," I bark. "Because finding this out in a crowded hostel would be so much fucking better."

"I just don't get it." Elliot spins the directions around as he reads them. "It doesn't say anything here about this. Is there a button or something you push?"

I search and search. "There is no button, and there is definitely no way this is happening."

"Jameson went camping. He will know." Elliot calls the boys while I struggle some more.

"Hey." I hear Jameson's voice.

"Hi there," says Tristan.

"We're in all sorts here," Elliot replies as he sets his phone up so they can see us. "I think the guy in the store pranked us."

"What's happening?" Jameson asks.

"How is this"—I hold up the giant, huge-ass sleeping bag—"supposed to fit into this"—I hold up the tiny sleeping bag cover. I begin to try to stuff it in again.

Jameson laughs out loud.

"You idiot. You roll it up."

"It's impossible," I cry. "It's like an elephant trying to fuck a cockroach." I struggle some more. "There is no way *this* is fitting into *that*."

"Have you heard of lube?" Tristan laughs.

"Obviously not," Jameson replies. "Have you seen the women he likes?"

"Fuck off. I'm not in the mood for your shit," I yell in frustration. "This is a complete disaster. I'm supposed to be on a vacation. I don't have a spare nine hours every day to fight with a disobedient sleeping bag."

"Lay it out flat."

"What?"

"Lay it out flat," Jameson snaps.

I lay it out flat.

"Now fold it in half and then in half again, and then roll."

"Roll?" Elliot frowns.

"Roll . . . you idiot."

"Why didn't that half-wit tell us this in the shop?" I grunt.

Elliot and I get on our hands and knees and try to follow the instructions. We huff and we puff and moan and use all our strength, and to the sounds of Jameson and Tristan laughing out loud in the background, after twenty minutes we finally get it in.

"Now, fuck off." I pick up the sleeping bag in its cover and kick it up the hall as hard as I can. "You're not coming with me after pulling that bullshit. I never want to see you again."

"You have to take it," Elliot snaps.

"No way. It's a four-man job, and I'm not a magician. I'll happily freeze."

Four days later

The plane touches down on the runway, and I blow out a long hard breath.

This is it.

In a moment, I will leave my comfortable first-class seat to find an Uber and travel out into the unknown with no money.

I don't know what to expect other than the knowledge that my accommodation costs eighteen euros a night, I have nowhere near enough clothes, and I hate my sleeping bag with a passion.

Forty minutes later I walk out to the taxi stand feeling very pleased with myself.

Collected my luggage without a hiccup, and all is good in the world.

"Hello," I say to the driver.

"Hello." He smiles.

"Can you take me here, please?" I show him the address on my phone.

"*Sí.*"

"Great."

He pops the trunk, and I put my backpack in, and I hop into the back seat.

He gets in and starts the car. I smile happily out the window.

Everything is running so smoothly. This is a walk in the park.

He puts the pedal to the metal, and we go zero to one hundred miles per hour in five seconds flat. He pulls out in front of a car, and they get on the horn.

"Ah." I grab hold of the seat in front of me. "What are you doing?"

He changes lanes, and the tires screech; my eyes widen in fear. "Slow down," I bark.

He goes across five lanes of traffic at high speed. "Relax." He laughs as he waves his arms around. "It's okay. It's okay."

"Nothing about your driving is okay!"

He speeds through a red light, and I scrunch my eyes shut as I grip the seat in front of me for grim death.

"Slow down," I demand.

He goes over a bump in the road so fast that I bounce high and hit my head on the roof.

"Ahh," I cry. I peer out the front window at the oncoming cars.

Get off the road. We're all going to die!

He takes a corner so fast that it feels like the car is going to roll over, and I contemplate jumping from the car.

Finally, after the most terrifying twenty minutes of my life, he pulls to a stop.

"Here you go."

I get out and slam the door. "Never pick me up again."

"Okay." He smiles.

Dickhead.

I take my backpack and walk up the stairs of the hostel. It's big and looks like a cheap and nasty hotel.

I walk in through the front doors and hear chanting.

"Drink, drink, drink."

I look through the double doors into what looks like an outdoor courtyard bar.

A large group of people are gathered around a giant beer bong.

A guy is lying on his back, just about drowning as everyone screams and laughs.

The smell of bad body odor roils my stomach, and my eyes widen in horror.

What fresh hell is this?

Chapter 3

HAYDEN

"This?" Mom holds up a bikini on a coat hanger.

I screw up my face. "Where's the rest of it?"

She chuckles.

I'm shopping for my trip with my mom and my best friend, Monica.

"This one?" Monica holds up a yellow bikini. It has white spots on it.

"It was a teeny-weeny, eenie-meanie yellow polka-dot bikini," Mom sings.

I roll my eyes as I keep walking around. "There is literally nothing here I like."

"Because you hate shopping," they both reply in unison.

"This one?" Monica holds up a G-string black bikini and a barely there top.

"No." I gasp. "That bikini gives out the wrong message."

"What . . . like . . . 'Hi, I'm Hayden, and I have a hot body; I'm ready to have some fun'?"

Mom giggles. "True, we're getting this." She snatches it off Monica and throws it over her arm.

"Listen." I keep walking around the store. "If you wear revealing clothes, you attract the wrong type of man."

Mom and Monica roll their eyes at each other. "And what type is that?" Mom sighs.

"The player kind," I reply. "I hate players."

"That's the fun kind." Monica widens her eyes. "I say have fun while you can." She rubs her pregnant stomach. "Trust me, Haze, you're a longtime married."

"Don't I know it." Mom sighs in the background.

Monica holds up a stretchy white dress.

"No, that's totally see through." I gasp.

Mom snatches it off her and throws it over her arm.

"What kind of guy are you trying to attract?" Monica asks. She picks up a lace underwear set. "Oh, this is hot."

Mom throws it over her arm.

"I'm not looking for a man."

"Will you stop being such a prude?" Mom snaps.

"Regi isn't coming back, Haze."

"I know that," I snap.

"So why are you waiting for him?"

"I'm not," I splutter. "I just haven't met anyone I like, that's all."

"Okay, so you're telling me that if Regi walked back through those doors tonight and asked you to marry him, you would say no?" Monica picks up a teeny red dress and holds it up.

"Of course I would say no." I snatch it off her and put it back where it came from.

Regi was my boyfriend of five years, my high school sweetheart. He went to college and never came back.

"So what kind of guy?" Mom prompts me.

"Hmm." I think for a moment. "Blond. Capable. Hardworking. Animal lover." I keep looking over the racks. "A virgin would be nice."

36

"Virgin?" Mom gasps, horrified. "You want someone who knows what he's doing at least!"

"What I want is a loyal man who loves me with all of his heart."

"A virgin isn't going to do that," Monica huffs. "He'll practice on you and then wonder what else is out there."

"Sloppy seconds aren't my style," I reply casually. "And besides, you two can stop planning. I've got this. I will know him when I see him."

"Oh . . . because a blond, animal-loving virgin is going to run right into you in Spain?" Mom rolls her eyes.

"I know." I smile broadly. "I can feel it in my waters."

CHRISTOPHER

"Can I help you?" A voice sounds from behind the counter.

"Umm . . ." I look around, wondering if I should run now while I can. "I have a booking."

"Hi," the guy says. "I'm Nelson."

"Hi, Nelson. Christo." The boys decided that I shouldn't use my real name in case someone recognizes it. No idea how they came up with Christo, though. I sound like a count or something.

"Let me look." He logs in to his computer and reads the screen. "Ah yes, here you are. You are booked for ten days?"

I nod as I peer back in at the frat party going on in the bar.

"You have paid in advance?" he asks.

I nod again. No idea why I did that.

"I'll show you your room." He walks out from behind the counter. "Come this way."

I follow him.

"You're in the fossil room."

"Fossil room?"

"It's where we put the oldies."

"I'm hardly old," I splutter.

"Anyone over twenty-five is considered old here."

"Oh . . ." I look around some more. That makes perfect sense: nobody over twenty-five is stupid enough to come to this shithole.

"Ta-da." He opens the door, and the blood drains out of my face.

Bunk beds, three sets of bunk beds. All in the one room.

"There must be some mistake. I ordered a single room."

"Yeah, they are all gone. You only get one if they are available."

I narrow my eyes at this fucker. "So . . . what's the point of booking in advance, then?"

"I don't know." He shrugs as he walks into the room. "This is your bed, here." He taps a bed on the bottom.

"You expect me to sleep underneath someone?"

"Yeah."

"What if the bed breaks and they fall right through and kill me."

"I don't know." He shrugs happily.

"You don't know much, do you?"

"I just work here, man." He walks back out of the room. "Here is your locker." He taps the PIN pad. "You set your own code to get into it. Put your backpack down, and we will come back to put it in. Lock everything up at all times."

I drop my backpack onto the floor, and I look at the lock. I hope he shows me, because fuck knows how I do that. I keep following him as I try to concentrate on what he is telling me.

"This is the laundry." He opens the lid of a washing machine. "Tip, don't leave anything here. It *will* be stolen."

"Right."

He leads me out to a large outdoor courtyard. "The kitchen is at that end. We supply three meals a day here, but you eat whatever is cooked. There are no choices."

"Right." I look around at my surroundings. Every wall is a different bright color. I feel like I'm in a kindergarten or something.

Kindergarten of hell.

"At the other end is a bar. It's cheap and nasty, but it does the trick. It closes at twelve every night, so it's not an all-night thing."

I peer down at the bar end to see the frat party. Beer bong is in full swing as feral people drink like it's their first time away from their parents.

"Got it."

"Come and I'll show you the bathroom," he says as he's already walking down the hall. He opens a door in the main corridor. "This is it."

I inhale deeply at the horror before me. "Charming."

Stall after stall, shower after shower.

"No sex," he says casually. "Condoms in the bin if you do."

I frown, disgusted. "Why would you need to tell me that?"

"You'd be surprised."

Gross.

"So there you have it." He puts his hands on his hips as if proud. "That's it."

"Thanks."

"Call me if you need anything." He saunters off.

I stare after him. *You're just going to leave me here all alone?*

"Drink it down, down, down." The voices echo from the bar area. Laughter and screams can be heard.

I look around, unsure what to do.

I walk back up the corridor and put my backpack away. I go into my room . . . only it isn't my room, and I realize that I've never felt so uncomfortable in my entire life.

I go to sit down but then realize that I can't even sit on the bed; I have to lie down.

Fuck this—I'll go for a walk.

With a sense of dread, I set out into the streets of Barcelona . . . now . . . what the hell do you do in a city with no money?

Three hours later I walk back into the hostel. I couldn't stomach the thought of dinner at the hostel. I had dinner in a restaurant.

I now have $1,800 left. I'm quite sure that $100 steak wasn't on my budget.

Tomorrow I'll budget better.

As I walk up the corridor toward the bar, a girl grabs my arm. "Oh, hi, you're the new guy in our room?"

"Yeah."

"I'm Bernadette."

"Hi, I'm Christo . . ." I cut myself off before I say Christopher.

Fuck, I hate the sound of Christo.

"You want to come out?"

"Um . . ." I hesitate. What, like a date?

I have zero attraction to this woman.

"There's a heap of us. We're going to a bar." Before I can reply, she links her arm through mine. "Come on, it will be fun. I'm not taking no for an answer."

"Okay." I shrug. I guess anything is better than being here. "Let me shower and change."

"Meet you in the bar."

〣

An hour later we walk up the street.

I read the sign over the doorway as I walk up the stairs.

SANTOS

41

"This place is amazing," Bernadette gasps as she runs up the stairs two at a time.

"Why is that?" I ask.

"Cheap-ass drinks and dick for miles."

"Right." I raise my eyebrow. "Not sure I'm after that, but . . ." Hell, that came out wrong. "Actually, I'm definitely not after that. Scratch that from your memory."

"You should try it," she says casually as she keeps walking up. "Dick is way better than hairy biscuit."

What?

Hairy biscuit . . . what woman says *hairy biscuit*?

This chick is fucking weird.

"I seriously doubt that," I mutter as we get to the top of the stairs. I look around at the blazing spectacle. Neon lights are everywhere. Things are twirling; signs are flashing.

"What do you think?" she asks as she smiles in wonder.

"It's great, for an epileptic's nightmare," I mutter. My eyes roam around at the bright strobe lights. There's a dartboard and pool tables and a karaoke machine. The place is all timber and done up to kind of look like a log cabin or something.

The crowd is around my age. Laughter echoes throughout the space. It has a fun kind of feel about it.

Okay . . . this isn't so bad. I feel a little of my equilibrium return.

"There's everyone." She waves and grabs my arm and drags me over to the large crowd of people.

She's overfamiliar, or perhaps just genuinely friendly. At this stage, I really can't tell anything. It's like all my senses are so overwhelmed that they've completely shut down.

We arrive at the group. "You came?" A man smiles; he sounds Australian. "Knew you would."

"Yep."

"Beer?" he asks.

"Yes, please."

He hesitates, and I frown. "That will be five euros." He widens his eyes as if I'm stupid.

Oh fuck, I am.

"Sorry." I dig into my jeans and find a note and pass it over, feeling stupid. "Thanks."

He nods and disappears to the bar.

"Who are you, man?" a guy asks. He's tall and has long black dreadlocks and olive skin.

I wince. Fuck . . . he stinks. The worst body odor I've ever smelled. "You need a shower," I snap.

"What?" He frowns. He lifts his arm and sniffs himself. "No, I don't."

"Yes. You do." I wince. "You smell so bad it's hurting my eyes."

Oh god . . . go away from me. This is intolerable.

"Oh, come off it." He rolls his eyes. "I'm not putting those chemicals on my body."

"By *chemicals* . . . you mean deodorant?"

"It's a government conspiracy." He nods as if totally convinced. "This is how humans are supposed to smell. You've been conditioned to like the smell of poison."

I frown at him. What the fuck is wrong with this guy?

"First day traveling?" he asks.

"How do you know?"

"You're all uptight and judgy."

"I'm not judgy," I fire back.

"Yes, you are. I bet you're looking at everyone and everything and comparing them to your safe little home." He chuckles into his beer. "You need to get over it. And quick, or you'll be on the first plane home."

I frown. It's like he's reading my mind. I open my mouth to reply and get a strong whiff of him once more, and I screw up my face in disgust. "Fucking hell. You smell so bad."

"Well, aren't you an uptight prick?" He shrugs as if not believing me. "Nobody else has ever told me that."

"I find that impossible to believe."

"It's true." He smirks.

"I'm guessing that you do abysmally with the ladies."

His face falls. "How do you know that?"

"Women like guys who smell nice, not garbage dumps."

"I'm happy with who I am," he announces, indignant.

"Okay." I shrug and hold my two hands up in defeat. "If you say so. I'm just being honest. No malice intended."

We stand in awkward silence for a moment. "So what do you suggest for me?" I ask.

"About what?"

"You said I need to get over being . . ." I pause while I search for the right word. "Uptight."

"You do," he replies.

"How do I do that?"

"Well." He smiles as if excited that I'm asking for advice. "You need to just get on with it."

I frown.

"Just live in the moment; don't think. Don't worry what anyone else is doing. Whatever makes you happy at home, just do it here . . . just because the location and settings are different, the same things bring you happiness. Your deepest inner self will appear without your possessions."

I frown as I stare at him.

"I'm telling you, man, if you want to have a serious crack at traveling, you just need to do it."

"Hmm . . ." I contemplate his words.

44

"Trust me. I've seen so many travelers. The ones who relax into it and take each day as it comes love the experience. The ones who compare every single thing to home go home in four to six weeks, and when they go home, they lie and tell everyone they had the best time of their lives, but the truth is they didn't even scratch the surface. Some don't even last six weeks—they go home earlier."

I exhale heavily. I can't admit that I was considering going home today after six hours.

"Hmm . . . interesting observation," I mutter, distracted.

Get on with it.

"What relaxes you at home? What's your favorite thing to do?" he asks.

"Sex," I reply without hesitation.

He laughs out loud. "Well, you came to the right place." He holds his arm out to the crowd. "This is the sex capital of the world." He looks me up and down. "Good-looking guy like you . . . you must pull the pussy."

And then some.

"It's not my looks that get me laid," I reply.

"Bullshit."

"I'm serious. The ugliest guy in the world can be attractive if he knows how to be."

"How?"

I widen my eyes. "Deodorant."

"You don't know what you're talking about," he huffs.

"All right." I smirk. "I'm sure your right hand feels just like big fuckable lips. You do you."

He looks at me deadpan, and I raise my eyebrow in jest.

"Get fucked." He sighs.

"I will be." I chuckle as I look around. Now . . . who will it be?

45

The Aussie guy comes back from the bar with a tray of shots of tequila. "Jackpot." He laughs. "Bulla is working behind the bar."

"Bulla?" I frown. "What's a bulla?"

"It's a girl who likes my dick. She gives me free drinks all night."

Dreadlocks guy laughs. "I like your dick, too, if it gets us drunk." He picks up a shot and holds it in the air. We all take one and raise them to his. "To new friends." He smiles.

"And deodorant," I add.

Aussie guy spits his drink out as he laughs. "I'll drink to that," he splutters.

"You think I stink too?" Dreadlocks guy gasps, completely shocked.

"Real bad," he mutters.

"What's your names again?" I ask.

"I'm Bodie," the Aussie guy says. He has sandy-blond hair and is tall and sinewy.

"Hey, has anyone ever told you that you sound like Chris Hemsworth?" I ask him.

"It's the accent." He shrugs. "Wish I had the prick's money."

"And wife," I add. "She's fucking hot."

"I'm Basil," dreadlocks guy replies.

"Basil?" I frown.

"That's right." He spits, all defensive. "You got a problem with my name?"

"Calm down." Bodie laughs. "It is an unusual name, that's all."

I take another tequila from the tray and chug it down. Basil is right: I just need to get on with it. Tonight, I'll get laid . . . and then tomorrow I'll be relaxed and start afresh.

I look around at the crowded bar. Who will it be?

Four hours later

Teeth graze my ear. "Let's get out of here," she whispers in the darkness of the corner. "Back to my place."

She has a place. I won't need to sleep in that hellhole.

Now we're talking.

I slide my hand down over her behind and pull her closer to my hardened cock.

What is her name again? *Fuck.* I need to remember this kind of shit.

She's utterly gorgeous, long dark hair and a body to die for, athletic and shapely. She may be just what I need to unwind.

No complications, hard and fast.

"Let's go, Christo," she says in her sexy accent.

I smile against her lips. "Let's."

I've got a lot of stress to work off tonight. *I hope you're in the mood for pain, baby girl.*

She takes my hand and leads me toward the door. I wave at Basil and Bodie on the way out, and Basil rolls his eyes in disgust and Bodie laughs.

Told you.

We walk out onto the street hand in hand, and my eyes drop down the length of her body.

She's fucking hot, all right, wearing a skintight black skimpy dress that leaves nothing to the imagination.

What is her name?

"Cab?" I ask.

"No, I live just around the corner."

"Okay." We continue walking hand in hand.

"You know, the moment I saw you tonight, I knew I had to have you," she purrs.

I smile at her delusion. "Really?" I play along.

47

We turn the corner into a street. It's cobblestone and dark. Uneasiness falls over me. This is fucking sketchy.

Stop it.

I stay silent as she chatters on and on. Not that I'm complaining; her accent is fucking luscious. We arrive at a door, and she unlocks it while I feel her up from behind. I pull her hair to the side of her neck and lick her there. I bite her earlobe and feel the goose bumps scatter up her neck.

My cock throbs in my pants, and I feel a little more like myself.

The door opens, revealing a winding timber staircase, and I peer up.

Huh?

"This way," she purrs as she begins to take the stairs. I run my hand over her behind as she walks in front of me, and then I slide her dress up over her ass so I can get a full view.

The muscles contract as she takes each step. We fall to the top floor, and our lips lock.

We kiss. Her eyes are closed, and mine flutter open as I try to focus in the room lit only by a lamp.

What in the world?

There are weird pictures all over the walls, a million things hanging from the roof. Baskets and fake animal heads.

Wait . . . are they real?

I pull out of the kiss and step back as my eyes wander all over the apartment. I put my wallet down on the table by the door as I try to get my bearings.

The walls are black. There are flags and animal skeletons, skateboards, surfboards, a wall that's covered in graffiti. A huge bong pipe thing sits front and center on the coffee table.

Dear god.

Alarm bells begin to ring in the distance.

There's purple shag pile carpet and in the corner a freaky-looking giant rocking horse that stands taller than me.

I swallow the lump in my throat . . . as I look around.

It's so cramped in here; there's enough furniture to furnish ten apartments. What is this godforsaken place?

I've stepped into the house of horrors.

"You like my house?" She smiles.

"Yes," I lie.

Focus.

Just get to the business, I tell myself. *It doesn't matter what her house is like.*

Fucking focus.

Right . . . I bend and lift her dress over her head in one fell swoop, and as she lifts her arms up, I'm greeted with patches of thick black hair under her arms. Long and stringy, sticking to her arms with perspiration.

What?

I look down, and her pubic hair is hanging out of her G-string. It's growing halfway to her knees.

No . . .

I begin to sweat . . . what the actual fuck is that?

"I've got a surprise for you." She giggles.

"I'm already surprised," I mutter, distracted.

She pulls her panties down. The hair is thick, black, and long . . . I open my mouth to say something, but no words will come out.

Abort mission.

Abort fucking mission.

She pulls me into the bedroom. A mattress is on the floor, and she lies down and spreads her legs.

My eyes widen in horror as my dick instantly shrivels. "Do you have a bathroom?" I splutter.

She sucks her finger and then slowly slides it through the lips of her sex. "Come here," she purrs.

This should be so hot right now . . . my dick is like jelly?

Focus.

"Bathroom?" I squeak.

"Up the stairs to the left."

I take the stairs two at a time and rush into the bathroom and lock the door. I stare at my reflection in the mirror. What the fuck is happening right now?

I splash water on my face. *Get ahold of yourself, man. You can do this!*

I open the vanity cupboard behind the mirror and peer in. There's a heap of tubes of cream. I pick one up and read the label.

LAMISIL.

I go through all the tubes. They are all the same. My eyes widen. Oh no. What the fuck is this?

Does she have something?

I frantically take out my phone and type into Google.

What is Lamisil used for?

It's taking forever . . . come on.

I hit refresh.

"Come the fuck on," I whisper.

Bad reception.

What's this fucking shit used for?

I dial Elliot's number.

"Hey," he answers happily. "Miss me already?"

"Help me," I whisper in a panic. "I have an emergency."

"What's wrong?" he stammers.

"I'm at this chick's house and I took her pants off and it's gorillas in the mist down there and her house is *Rocky Horror Picture Show* and now I found fifty tubes of Lamisil in her bathroom cabinet," I blurt out in a rush.

"Gorillas in the mist?" he repeats. "What do you mean?"

"Fucking full bush, man. You've never seen pubic hair like this. I need a fucking machete to chop my way in."

"Fucking hell." He gasps.

"Search Lamisil. I have bad internet."

"Okay."

I wait on. My heart is hammering hard in my chest.

"Christo?" I hear her yell. "Hurry up."

Fuck!

"Oh god," Elliot replies. "This isn't good."

"What?"

"Fungus. It's fungus cream."

My eyes widen in horror. "Are you fucking kidding me right now?" I whisper angrily.

"What are you going to do?"

"Run!" I hang up and take the stairs two at a time. "I've got to go," I call as I run for the front door.

"What do you mean?"

"It's nothing personal," I yell. I grab my wallet. "You're very hot, by the way."

For a gorilla.

I run out the front door and down the stairs. I burst out onto the street as if I'm being chased by an ax murderer . . . or in this case, a gorilla with fungus.

A cab is driving past, and I put my arm up. "Taxi." He pulls up, and I've never been so relieved. I dive into the back seat.

"Where to?"

"BB Backpackers."

51

"Sure thing."

Ten minutes later we pull up in front of the backpackers' hostel, and the driver turns to me. "That will be twelve euros."

I take my wallet and go to get out my card to pay and frown. It's not where it goes . . . huh?

It's gone.

The driver looks up at me in the rearview mirror. "Twelve euros."

"I heard you the first time," I snap as I search through all the compartments in my wallet.

Fuck . . . I have no other cards. How am I going to pay him?

What if I've lost it? I have no money . . . what the hell will I do?

I begin to sweat again . . . I know why every fucker smells around here. Everything about this place is stressful.

No deodorant is this powerful.

"My card is gone," I stammer in a panic. "Where would it . . ."

The penny drops, and I sit back in my seat, shocked to silence.

That hairy bitch stole my card.

Chapter 4

"I'm so sorry, my card has been stolen," I stammer. "Can you take me back to where you picked me up from so I can collect it?"

"No."

"No?" I frown. "What do you mean?"

"I not take you anywhere without money," he replies in his heavy accent.

"But my card has been stolen?" I gasp as I keep pulling my wallet apart. *Please be in here.* "I can't help it if my card has been stolen."

"You can come and pay me tomorrow."

"Yes," I gasp. "I can do that. I'll come and pay you first thing."

"Give me your license."

"What?"

"Give me your license, and I'll give it back when you come pay tomorrow."

I think for a moment. This doesn't sound like a good idea.

"Or I can call the police right now and have you charged."

"Fucking hell!" I stammer. "This is the worst day of my life."

"Going to prison will be worse."

My eyes widen. "I'm too pretty for prison."

He holds his hand out for my license, and I slam it in his hand. "Thanks for nothing."

"You're welcome." He hands me a business card. "Be at this address in the morning by ten, or I am calling the police."

"Fine." I get out and slam the door. I lean back down through the window. "Be careful with my license."

"Yeah, yeah." He drives off.

I take out my phone and instantly call my bank.

"Hello, this is banking online. How may I assist you?"

"Hi, I'm traveling, and I need to cancel a card that has been stolen, please?" I begin to pace on the sidewalk in front of the hostel.

"Of course, what is the card number?"

"If I had the card in front of me, I could tell you."

Don't mess with me, woman, not tonight.

"Do you know the account numbers?"

"I'll log in to my online banking and check. Hang on." I put her on speaker and quickly log in. I narrow my eyes as I stare at the measly one account.

BALANCE: 0000

"Um." I frown as I try to work out what is going on here. Where's my $1,800?

"What's wrong?" she asks.

"It's saying zero balance, but I know there's money in there."

"What's the account number?"

I tell her, and she types into her computer.

"There was a withdrawal . . . several withdrawals ten minutes ago in Barcelona. I'm sorry, sir, the account has been completely emptied."

"Son of a bitch!" I cry. I pace backward and forward in the dark.

"Put in a dispute, and we will try and get it back for you."

"Oh, thank god. How long does it take for the money to come back?"

"Twenty-eight days."

"Twenty-eight days?" I cry. "I'm in Spain. I have no money. What am I going to do?"

"You will have to get some money transferred into your backup card until we send you a new one."

"What do you mean, a backup card?"

"Everybody knows that when you travel you have to have a second card you don't use in case this kind of thing happens."

Damn it, I specifically didn't do this so I couldn't have spare cash. I didn't want to have a slush fund.

You idiot.

"Everybody but me!" I cry. This is the literal day from hell.

"I've canceled the card and ordered you a new one. Where do you want it sent to?"

I stare up at the hostel. I don't even know the address. "I'll have to call you back with an address." I sigh, utterly dejected.

"That's okay."

"Thanks."

"Mr. Miles . . ."

"Yes."

"It's a good thing you weren't hurt in the robbery, sir. A lot of travelers aren't so lucky. Possessions can always be replaced."

I stare into the darkness. "Yes, you're right."

"Good night, sir."

"Good night." I hang up and look around in the darkness.

It's quiet and still. The sound of laughter can be heard in the distance.

I feel stupid, and so alone.

What am I supposed to do now? Call my brothers so they can bail me out on my first fucking day away?

And tell them that they were right, that I really can't cut it without my family's money. That I'm a big fat failure.

No way in hell!

I'll starve before I ask them for a cent.

"You all right?" someone asks from behind me. I turn to see a boy. He's young and struggling to carry two large garbage bags full of trash.

"Yeah." I exhale heavily.

He walks over and unlocks a large bin and climbs up and throws the trash in and relocks the industrial bin.

"What are you doing?" I ask him.

"I'm on close."

"Close?"

"I work behind the bar."

"Behind the bar?" I screw up my face. "Aren't you like twelve?"

"Fourteen."

"Don't you have school tomorrow?"

"I don't go to school."

I stare at him. He has black curly hair and is of Spanish descent. He looks so young, but he has an old-soul feel about him.

"Why not?"

"I support my household."

"At fourteen?"

"Yep." He smiles with a shrug. "You coming back in?"

"Nah . . ." I keep sitting on my step.

He lingers. "What's wrong with you?" he asks.

I exhale heavily. "Have you ever felt like a complete failure?"

"Nope."

I look up at him, surprised. "Not once?"

"Nope." He shrugs. "I know where I'm going. I got this shit."

His optimism is contagious, and I smile too. "I bet you do." I look back out over the street. "My card got stolen, and now I have no money, and I really don't want to call home and ask them to bail me out."

"Oh," he says. "Who took your card?"

"A gorilla."

"A what?"

"A woman with a gigantic amount of pubic hair."

His lip curls in disgust. "Ew."

I widen my eyes. "I hear you."

"So don't call home," he says. "Sort it out yourself."

I look back over my shoulder at him. "And how am I supposed to do that?"

"Get a job."

I frown. "A job?"

"Yeah."

"Where would I work?" I ask him.

"Anywhere."

Hmm . . .

"Anyway, I've got to go clean the oven."

I stare at him; this kid is fourteen years old, and he's cleaning an oven at midnight.

"You're all right, kid." I smile. "What's your name?"

"Eduardo."

"I'm Christopher." Oh crap, I told him my real name. "Everyone calls me Christo," I correct myself.

"Night," he says as he disappears back inside.

"Good night."

I drag myself inside and get my tiny towel from my locker and take a shower.

The water pressure is shit and barely hot, and who knew drying yourself with a washcloth could be so unsatisfying?

The hostel is nearly deserted. Everyone is out for the night.

I walk into my bedroom and climb into my bottom bunk bed. I'm six feet three; my head and feet both touch the ends. I plug my phone in to charge and lie alone in the darkness. The rest of my roommates are still out partying. I wonder what time they'll be back.

I can hear doors banging in the distance and people talking. Strange smells, and this bed is fucking uncomfortable. And what thread count are these sheets? They're so rough I'll be exfoliated to the bone.

I roll over and punch my pancake pillow as I try to get comfortable.

Worst bed ever.

I sigh, defeated.

Not a great first day . . . pretty fucking shit, actually.

After what feels like forever, I drift into an exhausted sleep.

⋈

The bell rings over the door as I walk into the taxi head office just at 8:00 a.m. I'm dripping with perspiration, having had to walk here at the crack of dawn, six fucking miles.

"Can I help you?" the receptionist asks.

"Yes, I'm here to pick up my license. There was a problem with my card last night."

"Okay." She pulls out a drawer and picks up a stack of licenses held together with an elastic band. "What was the name?"

"Christopher Miles."

She flicks through. "Here it is." She puts it down on the counter. "That will be twelve euros."

"Yes." I fake a smile. "I was wondering if I could speak to the manager, please?"

"What about?"

"I'll let them know when I get a chance to talk to them."

"*I'm* the manager." She raises an unimpressed eyebrow. "What do you want?"

"Oh." I fake laugh. "My apologies, you're just so young."

She stares at me deadpan.

"So." I smile. This woman has the personality of a wet blanket. "Here's the thing." I smile goofily again. I practiced this speech in my head all the way over here, but somehow, it's already not going to plan. "My card was stolen last night, and it's going to take a few days to sort out my funds."

She rolls her eyes. "I'm calling the police."

"I can work it off."

"What?"

"I have an international license." I point to it as it sits on the counter. "I speak Spanish, and I can read Google Maps. I'm the perfect employee for you."

"You speak Spanish?"

"Uh-huh . . . ," I lie. "I could drive for you all day, and then I could pay you this afternoon with my wages."

She stares at me as if thinking.

"I'm very trustworthy." I hold my hands out. "See, I turned up and am offering my services. That's trustworthy if I ever saw it."

"Do you know your way around Barcelona?"

"Uh-huh . . . ," I lie again. I mean, how hard can it be? "Of course I do."

She picks up my license and stares at it. "I do have a few drivers off sick today."

"You do?" I smile excitedly. "That's great . . . I mean . . . not great that they are sick, obviously."

She stands and takes a set of keys from the keyboard and then points at me. "One scratch and you're dead."

I frown. "What does that mean?"

"You bring my taxi back to me in perfect condition . . . or else."

"Deal."

She passes the keys over. "It's parked out the back. Come and I'll show you."

I can't believe this plan is actually working. We walk out the back and over to a cab. "This is the brake. It's standard auto."

"Okay." I get in and start the car. "What do I do?"

"You can do the airport run."

"So I just go to the airport and wait in line?"

"That's it. Pick up the people, drop them off, and return straight to the airport." She looks at her watch. "Be back here at four."

"Okay, no problem." I grip the steering wheel as excitement runs through me . . . look at me, getting jobs on my own and shit.

"And remember the customer is always right."

"Gotcha."

"No speeding, and the credit card machine is tap only."

"Okay." I nod as I look around the cab. "Sounds easy enough."

"Good luck."

I smile. "Piece of cake." I drive out and put the blinker on to pull out into the traffic. I watch her back inside, and as I get to the first intersection, I laugh out loud. I look left; I look right . . . now . . . where's the fucking airport?

The taxi line moves forward at a snail's pace. "Come on," I mutter under my breath. It took me fifty minutes to find this fucking place, and now that I'm here, I have to line up for customers.

I don't have time for this shit. I roll my fingers on the steering wheel impatiently as I wait. I need to make some cash for that vinegar-tits taxi bitch . . . and on the double.

The double doors of the airport open, and a woman strides out. She has honey-blonde hair in a high ponytail and a spring in her step. She oozes happiness. I smile as I watch her . . . *hot*.

The line moves up, and oh shit, I'm next. I pull up next to the line and get out. "Hello."

"Hi," the guy grumbles as he throws his bag at me. He's in his late teens and all scruffy looking.

I catch his bag in midair and glare at him.

Don't piss me off, dickhead.

I go to put it in the trunk. Wait a minute, how do I open it? I look around on the dash, and the taxi behind me beeps his horn. "Hurry up," he yells out the window.

"Shut up," I yell back. "Wait your turn."

My eyes nearly bulge from their sockets. "Where the fuck is the open-trunk button?"

"Come on, man," the guy groans from the back seat. "What are you doing? I'm so not in the mood for this shit."

I turn to face him. "I have waited for twenty fucking minutes in the line to pick you up. Do not push me, asshole!" I get out and march to the back of the car and throw his bag into the front seat. It sits so high that I can hardly see around it.

"You can't drive with my bag in the front seat," the guy gasps.

"Whose cab is this, motherfucker?"

He stays silent.

"Just as I thought." I pull out in a rush. "Where to?"

He mumbles something.

"I beg your pardon?" My eyes flick up to him in the rear-view mirror.

"I said . . . 123 the Boulevard!"

I narrow my eyes. "If you speak to me in that tone, I will drop you off right here."

"Sorry . . . ," he mumbles.

We stop at some traffic lights, and I quickly type in the address.

It's forty minutes away . . . ugh. The lights change. I take off once more. We've been driving for a few minutes when I make a wonderful discovery.

I can actually do this.

※

Half an hour later we are stopped at a set of traffic lights.

He moans from the back seat, and my eyes flick up to him in the rearview mirror.

He's wet with perspiration, and his face is contorted.

"What are you doing?" I ask.

"I don't feel so good . . ."

"What do you mean?"

"Oh no . . ." He moans.

"What's oh no?" I begin to drive faster. I want this fucker out of my cab.

"I think I'm going to throw up."

My eyes widen in horror. "Don't even think about it!"

HAYDEN

I walk out of the airport and am met with a surge of heat. "Oh, it's hot."

People are rushing past, and I struggle with my oversize backpack. Damn, this thing is heavy.

I see the cab line and take out my phone and bring up the address of the backpackers' hostel.

Nerves bumble around in my stomach. *Just walk over there and get a cab.*

That's easy.

Right . . .

I steel myself and walk over and get into the back of the line. I feel sick with nerves. Damn, I just wish this first week was over already.

The whole thought of the unknown is just so unsettling. I get to the front of the line, and the cab pulls up, and I smile.

"Where to?" he asks.

"BB Backpackers in Barcelona, please?"

"Sure thing." He takes my backpack and puts it into the trunk. I get into the back seat and put my seat belt on. I wipe my clammy hands on my shorts. This is fine . . . this is totally fine.

I text my mom,

**Landed safely.
On my way in a cab.**

A text bounces back:

This is so exciting,
Call me later.

I'm glad you think so. For me this is terrifying.

I put my phone back in my bag and clasp my hands together with white-knuckle force. I stare out the window at the scenery flying past.

Twenty minutes later the cab pulls to a halt in traffic. "Ay, ay, ay, what you doing?" the driver mutters under his breath.

I look up to see a cab in front of us is stopped in the middle of the road. "What's going on?" I ask.

"I don't know."

The driver of the cab in the front jumps out of the car and opens the back door. He grabs a man by the shirt and hurls him out of the cab as he projectile vomits. The vomit hits the side of the car and sprays everywhere.

"Ew," we both say in unison.

"What the fuck are you doing?" the driver screams at the man. The driver is losing his shit and yelling and screaming at his passenger.

"Oh dear." My eyes are wide.

The driver puts his hands on his knees and bends over. He begins to throw up alongside the other man.

The first vomiting man says something to the driver, and then the driver seems to lose it and pushes him over. He falls onto the ground as he continues to vomit.

I put my hand over my mouth at the spectacle in front of us. "Jeez."

The driver begins to yell, "It smells so bad." He grabs the side of his cab to hold himself up. "Stop vomiting before I knock you out!" The driver loses control again and heaves before projectile vomiting too. It's coming out so fast it's like a fire hose.

"Fucking hell," my driver mutters. "Idiots." He pulls around the parked cab and speeds past them.

I turn and watch the vomiting duo through the back window as we drive off.

Well . . . that's something you don't see at home.

Twenty minutes later my cab pulls up at the front of a big building. "Here you go." He smiles.

"Thanks." I pay him, and he gets my things out of the trunk.

"Be careful," he warns me. "Bad people are everywhere."

"Thanks." I fake a smile. I drag my bag up the steps and into the foyer. "Hello, I'm checking in today."

"Hello." The guy smiles. "What's your name?"

"Hayden Whitmore."

"Ahh, Hayden. From America."

"Yes, that's right."

"You are staying with us for ten days?"

"Uh-huh."

"Great. Come and I'll show you around."

I follow him up the hall. He shows me the bathroom, the laundry, the bar and restaurant. "You're in the fossil room."

"The fossil room."

"Anyone over twenty-five stays in the fossil room."

"I'm just twenty-five."

He smiles as he marches off in the direction of my room. "Like I said."

I follow him, and he opens the door in a rush. "Your bunk is the one underneath here."

I stare at the unfriendly room: three sets of bunk beds and all-white linen. "Okay."

"Rest up." He smiles. "You'll meet everyone when they get back tonight. Most people sightsee all day around here."

"Okay." I force a smile. I'm missing home already. "Thanks."

He leaves me alone, and I climb into my bottom bunk. I get under the sheet, feeling the need for protection.

For ten minutes I doze. It's been a long week: lots of nervous sleepless nights and then the long flight. I really should try to take a nap. I don't want to be tired and boring when everyone gets back.

The door bursts open, and someone marches in. I can only see legs and body up to his head.

"What the fuck?" the guy mutters. He has an American accent. He tears his shirt over his head and throws it on the floor; then he rips his jeans off and kicks them to the side. "Fucking disgusting," he grumbles. "When I get ahold of that guy."

He takes his boxer shorts off and kicks them to the side.

I get a full frontal. Tanned skin, muscles, eight-pack stomach, and the hugest dick I ever saw . . . what the hell? My eyes widen. He doesn't know I'm here.

Oh fuck.

Do I say something?

He turns and bends over to get something out of a backpack. I get a full view of his naked butt . . . and then some.

The door opens, and a woman walks in.

Oh no.

"Oh," she purrs. "Somebody brought me a snack."

"Fuck off, Bernadette," he growls. "I am not in the mood. Get out!"

"When I find a snack in my bedroom, what do you expect?"

I wince. Oh hell . . . this is so bad. Nobody knows I'm here. *Please don't have sex; I will die a thousand deaths.*

66

"I am not a fucking snack," he yells. "I am a main meal. A ten-course fucking banquet, for your information."

I bite my lip to hide my smile.

He so is.

He bends and gets out something from his bag. "And now, as if the day isn't bad enough," he yells to her as he holds something up to her, "I have to shower and dry myself with this piece-of-shit fucking tiny towel."

He marches out of the bedroom, buck naked.

Bernadette hangs out the door. "You can't just walk around naked, you know," she calls.

"Watch me," he calls back.

Bernadette disappears, and the door bangs closed. I lie in bed in a state of shock.

Jeez . . . who was that . . . and who is that comfortable being naked?

Chapter 5

I lie for a moment in a state of shock, and then it dawns on me.

He'll be back for his things. If he sees me here, he will know that I was here the entire time.

Oh crap.

I jump out of bed in a rush and quickly remake my bed, and the door opens.

Oh no, he's back.

"Hey." A man smiles. He has long dreadlocks and a kind smile . . . he also smells bad.

Worst body odor ever.

It takes all my might not to screw up my face. "Hi." I smile.

"My name is Basil."

I shake his hand. "I'm Hayden."

"Nice to meet you. We're roomies." He taps the bed above mine. "I sleep above you."

"Great." I fake a smile. Oh god . . . I'll have to smell him all the time. Shit.

"Not too sure about this fossil thing, though," I add.

"Ha ha, me too. Nearly choked when he told me, but to be honest I'm glad now. There are some real dickheads in the other rooms, young and stupid. Blind drunk all the time and so, so noisy."

"Oh." Relief fills me. If he is anything to go by, that means everyone in here must be nice.

"Where are you from?" he asks.

"America, a few hours out of New York. What about you?"

"Brazil."

"Oh." I smile. "I've always wanted to go to Brazil."

"Yeah, it's awesome. You have to do it."

"You been traveling long?" I ask him.

"About a month. Hoping to meet some people and travel for another year with them."

"Oh." I smile. Me, too, but I'm holding my cards close to my chest until I know if I like the people. "Sounds great."

The door bursts open, and that guy walks back in. He's completely naked and holding a tea towel over his junk. "Hi," he says casually, as if he does this every day. He bends and begins to get clothes out of his backpack. Totally unfazed.

"Hi." I swallow the lump in my throat. His face is better than his dick . . . and trust me, the dick is good.

"I'm Hayden," I introduce myself.

He stands up, and with one hand strategically covering his junk, he holds his other hand out to shake mine. "Hi, Hayden." He gives me a breathtaking smile. "I'm Christopher."

Oh . . .

"Excuse the lack of clothes, some fuckwit just vomited all over me."

My eyes widen. "It must be the day for it. I just saw a cabdriver getting vomited on on the way here."

"Yeah." He goes back to his bag and begins to rustle around in it. "That was me, and now I have to go back to that damn cab and drive it all afternoon. I can think of nothing worse." He passes a bottle of deodorant to Basil. "Put it on," he demands.

"What did I tell you about poisoning my body," Basil huffs.

"Listen, fucker. While you are sleeping in a room with me, you will smell like a human. Put. It. On."

I suddenly feel really uncomfortable. Poor Basil, how embarrassing for him. They must be friends.

"No."

"Yes."

Who does this guy think he is? "Do you two know each other?" I ask.

"Just met." Basil rolls his eyes.

My blood boils, I feel so bad for Basil. "Firstly," I snap, "put some clothes on. Secondly, stop being so damn rude."

Hot guy's eyes flick up to me in annoyance. "Do you want to smell that every day?"

"At least he has clothes on. I would rather smell that than be forced to look at you naked," I fire back.

Not really . . . not even close.

"Is that so?" he replies. His chin lifts in defiance. "And who made you the room manager?"

"You did, when you started being insulting."

"Listen," he replies as he keeps looking through his bag. "I don't know how things work where you come from. But in my world, people don't smell like body odor. They also don't put up with it. Personal hygiene is a basic human response." He shoves the deodorant bottle back at Basil. "Put. It. On," he demands.

I narrow my eyes. I think I officially hate this guy.

"On one condition," Basil replies.

"What's that?" Rude guy pulls a pair of briefs on, and I pretend not to look.

"You teach me how to pick up women."

What?

"What?" Christopher screws up his face, also confused. He pulls a shirt on over his head.

"You heard me. I'll shower more often and wear deodorant if you teach me how to pick up women."

"Oh my god . . ." I roll my eyes. "You cannot be serious?"

"Deal." Christopher nods. "That's easy. Chicks are easy. It's like shooting fish in a barrel."

"Ugh." Okay, it's official. I *do* hate him. "Are you always so full-on yourself?" I ask him.

He smiles. "No . . . I'm usually on women but happy to be on myself too. Nobody does it better than me." He holds up his hand and gives me a playful wink.

Yuck.

"Good grief. I'm going to find someone intelligent to talk to." I walk toward the door.

"Don't forget boring," he calls after me.

I march down the hall. This is a nightmare. I'm rooming with Stinky and the Stallion.

Not to mention the horny snack lady.

This is just great.

※

It's 3:00 p.m., and I'm sitting in the lounge area of the hostel.

The staff are all rushing around. Apparently there is a full moon party on here tonight. The theme is white.

I have a white sundress that I'm going to wear, although I don't remember seeing it this morning in my bag. I hope I didn't leave it behind.

Hmm . . .

I'd better check my things.

71

I go back to my locker and take my bag out and drag it to my room. I unzip it and frown.

This isn't what I packed. Is this even my backpack? I check the label. Yep, it's mine.

I pull out the G-string black bikini, horrified. "What in the world?"

I rifle through my bag at double speed. Where is the white flowing summer dress?

Fuck . . . those bitches repacked my bags with sexy clothes. I text Monica.

Where are all my clothes!!

She texts me back.

On the farm where they belong.
You can thank me later.
Love you!

Bitch!

My eyes nearly bulge from their sockets. What am I going to wear now? There is nothing in here white except this stretchy stupid dress, and I am not wearing that slutty outfit.

God, now I have to go shopping to find something else . . . ugh.

I stomp back to my room, and Basil is in there, and although I hate to admit it . . . he now smells good. He has another man with him. "Hi, Hayden. This is Bodie." He introduces us. "He's in our room too."

"Hi." He smiles. "Do you want to come shopping? We have to find white shit for tonight, apparently."

Bodie is warm and kind looking. He instantly puts me at ease, and with that Australian accent, he sounds pretty dreamy. "Actually, I do." I smile. "Thanks."

I grab my things, and we head out the door.

)(

Barcelona is buzzing, alive with the colors and scents of an exotic country.

While the boys shop, I walk behind them, mesmerized by my surroundings.

This place is utterly, utterly beautiful.

Basil digs his phone out of his pocket. "Hey." He listens for a moment.

"Hey, man, what's up?" He turns back and smiles at me as he listens some more. "Yeah, sure thing, we're getting something now. What size?" He laughs. "Okay, bye." He hangs up the phone.

"We got to get Christo something white to wear. He'll pay me later."

I frown. "Christo?"

"Yeah, you know, the guy in our room today."

"I know who you mean. I don't understand why you like him." I widen my eyes.

He shrugs. "He's an okay guy."

"Pussy magnet." Bodie smiles. "Did you see the women surrounding him last night?"

"Uh-huh." Basil smiles. "And what about the one he went home with?"

Bodie lets out a low whistle. "Man oh man, I would have given my left nut to nail her."

Basil smiles as he holds his hands in the shape of big boobs. "She was equipped."

I screw up my face. "You guys are gross. And if you would give a testicle to bone a girl, you need to go to the hospital."

They both laugh, and I do too. Boys are ridiculous.

"When did you guys all get here?" I ask.

"Yesterday," they both reply. "And Christo too."

We keep shopping, and my mind wanders to naughty boy . . . hmm, so he slept with someone on his first night here, hey?

Figures, I guess. Why waste time when you've got a dick like that. *Asshole.*

You know what pisses me off?

The nice guys who would love a woman for forever and a day come last . . . every time. And the player cockheads who have big egos are blessed with big dicks. They never get brokenhearted, they never get left, and they are never lonely. They always come out on top.

Ugh . . .

Just doesn't seem fair.

"All right, these shirts," Bodie says. He grabs three short-sleeved button-up shirts. They're white and cotton and fit the brief.

"And these shorts?" Basil grabs three pairs of white shorts from the rack.

I exhale heavily as I look around. "Now me."

We look and look and look . . . nothing in white.

"Bernadette is wearing a white bikini," Bodie says casually as he strolls through the racks.

"What with?"

"Nothing, it's a full moon party."

"What does that mean?"

"I guess we get to see lots of moons." Bodie shrugs.

I wince. "I don't want to look at people's buttholes."

"I do." Basil smiles.

"Me too," Bodie agrees. "I would like to fuck some too."

"You idiots and your dicks." I roll my eyes. "Just find me something white."

Two hours later

"Screw this, I'll rip up my bedsheet and wear that," I huff in disgust.

"Good idea," they both agree. "We're supposed to be back there now."

"I mean, I do have a white dress."

"What?" Basil explodes. "You mean we just wasted two hours for nothing?"

"I can't wear it; it's obscenely tight. My friend snuck it in my suitcase and took out all my sensible clothes. It's so short it looks like a belt."

"I like your friend," Bodie replies. "Come on." He heads for the door.

"Where are we going?"

"Home. You're wearing your slut dress."

$$ \text{X} $$

The worst part about sharing a room is just that . . . sharing a room.

How in the hell are you supposed to get ready and privately freak out about what you're wearing?

I'm in the bathroom, in my little shower stall. Pretty boy is right. These tiny towels are fucking ridiculous. I dry myself and dry myself, and still I don't seem to get anywhere.

Laughter echoes all around, and the hostel seems packed to the rafters, but I think that's because everyone is staying in tonight for the full moon party.

I slide my bra on and then my panties and pick up the white dress. It's stretchy and seems so small. I have to stretch it out just to get it on . . , far out. I wiggle it down over my hips. It comes to above my knees. It's stretchy and tight, with a scooped-out neck.

I try to look down at myself. Damn it, I don't even have a full-length mirror here.

I suppose I should be grateful that I can't see how ridiculous I look. I brush my hair and pack up my toiletries bag and slowly open the door.

I'm dreading tonight. I do not feel comfortable at all.

I walk out to see scantily dressed girls everywhere. One smiles. "I love your dress."

"Thanks." I walk to the sink awkwardly and take my makeup out. I glance over to see a girl with a white G-string on and white body paint in the shape of hearts on her boobs, complete with hot-pink tassels on her nipples. She even has white feathers strategically pinned behind one ear. "You look great." I smile.

Damn, she does look great. I wish I had that confidence.

"Thanks. Hey, you've just checked in?"

"Yeah, I'm Hayden." I smile.

"I'm Kimberly," she says in an English accent. "Where are you from in America?" she asks.

"A few hours from New York. Where are you from?" I ask.

"Manchester."

"Oh, I would love to go there."

"New York's on my list of to-dos too," she replies as she puts on the brightest of bright hot-pink lipstick and rolls her lips.

She oozes confidence, and damn it, she looks so hot.

She looks me up and down and gives me a kind smile. "You look good." As if knowing I'm in the middle of a complete confidence crisis.

"Feel a bit . . ." I shrug. "Awkward."

"This is your first stop, isn't it?"

I nod.

"You'll get used to the crazy. Are you traveling alone?"

"Yes. Are you?"

"I had three friends with me. We've been traveling for six months. They left for home yesterday. So now, it's just me." She shrugs happily. "That's the beauty of these hostels. Everyone travels alone, so you instantly have eighty friends. I'm going to see where the wind blows me for another few months."

"Sounds great." I try to focus on my makeup.

"I'll see you outside?" she asks.

"Sure."

"Bye, Hayden." I watch in the mirror as she skips out.

"Bye."

She seems nice.

I slowly make my way back to the room and lock my things back up in my locker. Damn it, I wish I had a full-length mirror.

I can hear laughing and music coming from outside.

Oh well . . . may as well get this over with.

The bar is alive with a sea of white. There's a DJ and a dance floor.

I stand at the edge, peering in, wondering what to do. I hear a voice. "There you are."

Bernadette grabs my hand and pulls me into the crowd. "You look hot, girlfriend."

I smile bashfully. "Thanks."

"We're over here." She pulls me over to Bodie and Basil. They are talking to three beautiful blonde girls. "I'm getting us some drinks."

"Thanks."

"Wow." Basil laughs. "Look at you."

Kill me now. This is so awkward.

"Look at you." I laugh. They are both in their matching little white outfits.

"I am going to have some lipstick smeared all over this collar tonight." Basil widens his eyes. "That's right."

I giggle. "I bet you will."

"Here he is," Bodie says. We all turn to see Christo walking down the steps. His white shirt is open, revealing his chiseled abs. The shorts are tighter and shorter, revealing thick quad muscles, and even though he's wearing the same outfit as the boys, somehow, he looks completely different.

Good different.

I angrily snap my eyes away. Damn it, I hate that he's gorgeous, and more than that, I hate that he knows it.

The boys wave, and he smiles and comes over. "Hey." He laughs as he holds a bottle of Corona in his hand. "Look at us being all angelic-like." He smiles to the girls. "Girls." He raises an eyebrow at them. He glances over at me. "Grumpy." He nods in a greeting.

Grumpy.

I fake a smile. *You have no idea.*

He introduces himself to the girls. "I'm Christo. You must be models, right?"

The girls giggle, and I roll my eyes.

Please.

"I have done some modeling," one of the girls says.

OnlyFans, I bet.

"I knew it." He smiles. "Where are you from?"

"Germany," they reply. They have beautiful husky accents.

Bernadette arrives back with a drink for me and passes it over. "Thanks."

She looks Christo up and down like he's a piece of meat, which is fitting because he thinks he is. "Christo." She smiles. "Do I get a kiss hello?"

He crinkles up his nose. "Not now, Bernadette." He playfully gestures to the girls. "This is my big break with these models here."

The German girls all laugh on cue, and Bernadette does too. How does he do that? Everything he says comes out smooth.

Ugh . . .

Basil and Bodie smile goofily at each other. I think they like him more than the girls do.

"What do you do?" I hear one of the girls ask him.

"I'm a teacher," he replies.

A teacher?

"I just love kids, you know," he continues.

I call bullshit . . .

I look over to see Kimberly waving me out to the dance floor. She's dancing with a big group of people. I grab Bernadette's arm. "Come on, we're dancing."

Four hours later

I'm feeling very tipsy and having the time of my life.

Who knew that full moon parties were this fun? I've danced, I've chatted, and we won't mention how I've been watching a certain annoying person more than I would ever admit.

He has a flock—I'm not even joking—a flock of women around him at all times.

Everywhere he goes.

And he's loving every second of it, the showman and his captive audience.

Laughing and lapping up all the attention. Every now and then I see him say something to Bodie and Basil, and they listen intently. He's coaching them how to pick up and what to say.

I'm standing near the dance floor, watching everyone. I hear a soft voice from behind me. "Grumpy."

I smile into my drink. I kind of have to agree with him; he does make me grumpy. "Hello, Christopher."

"Christo," he corrects me.

"Is it?" I raise my eyebrow.

He twists his lips, amused. "It's Christopher, but don't tell anyone."

"Do you think Christo sounds hotter?"

"Don't you?"

"Definitely not."

He chuckles and takes a swig of his beer. "Are you having fun?"

"I am."

An awkward silence falls between us. He's not all flirty and playful with me like he is with everyone else.

"How was taxicabbing today?"

"Hell on a stick." He swigs his beer again.

"Didn't you just get here? Why are you working already?"

"Had my credit card stolen and my bank account wiped on my first day."

I screw up my face. "Ouch."

"Hmm. Don't talk about it."

The DJ gets on his microphone. "Women, turn directly to your left," he announces.

To the sound of giggles, all the girls turn to their left.

"Grab the man's arm closest to you," he continues. I smile. He's been doing weird games like this all night.

I grab Christopher's forearm.

"Now, after three . . . take his hands in yours and stare into his eyes."

"What?" I frown.

Christopher chuckles and puts his beer down onto the ground. Everyone is laughing and joking as they take each other's hands.

"As we wait for the full moon to come in, we are going to do two things," the DJ calls.

Christopher and I laugh. This is ridiculous.

"We are going to count down, and then you are going to look the person in the eye. Tell them how many people you have slept with, and then you are going to tongue kiss them."

The bar erupts with laughter.

What?

"Ten, nine, eight, seven, six, five, four, three, two, one."

"How many people have you slept with?" the DJ cries.

Christopher's eyes hold mine. "I don't know."

"One," I whisper.

I take his face in my hands and kiss him. My tongue slowly slides through his big lips, and he kisses me back.

Slow and tender, and his eyes flutter closed.

Oh . . .

His arm snaps around my waist, and he drags me closer. The kiss deepens.

And as I hear cheering and laughing in the background . . . we keep kissing.

Just the right pressure and a little suction.

He pulls out of the kiss and stares at me. His forehead crinkles. "What was that?" he snaps.

"I kissed you."

"One?"

Oh crap . . . that's what he's been thinking about the whole time?

Embarrassed, I nod.

"One?" He gasps.

"Uh-huh."

He stares at me for a beat, and his arm snakes around me again, and he pulls me closer. "Come here," he growls.

Shit.

"No." I pull out of his arms. "I have to go."

"Why?"

"Because you have to keep shooting those fish in barrels." I shrug. "And I have to swim upstream."

Chapter 6

CHRISTOPHER

I watch her walk off as she disappears through the crowd.

One.

One . . . how is it one? Nobody is one.

My tongue swipes over my bottom lip. It's still buzzing from that hot fucking kiss.

Hmm . . .

That was unexpected. She isn't even my type.

"Christo," I hear someone call.

I turn to see Bernadette. Her arms are wide as she rushes for me. "You didn't kiss me yet, darling." She slides her arms around my behind as she pretends to hug me. "It's the full moon."

Ugh, this woman is like a rash.

"You weren't near me." I fake a smile as I peel her hands off my behind.

Go away.

"That doesn't matter." She laughs as she leans in for a kiss . . . I lean back and glance over to see Hayden being led to the dance floor by some guy.

She's laughing, and he spins her around.

What?

"Kiss me." Bernadette smiles dreamily up at me.

For fuck's sake . . . not now, woman.

"No, no, no," I reply. "We're roommates," I tell her. "No hanky-panky."

I crane my neck to see what Hayden is doing. The guy is talking to her, and she's laughing as she listens attentively in return.

Hmm . . .

Bernadette goes up on her toes and leans in for the kiss. "Stop." I wince, annoyed. I push her off me and march toward the dance floor. I fake a smile to the guy and lean in to Hayden. "Can I have a word?"

"What about?" she says loudly, so the guy can hear.

Great.

"Bernadette, our roommate, has gone completely mad, and I need you over here for a moment to talk sense into her."

"Oh . . ." Her face falls.

"I'll wait here for you," the guy says.

"That won't be necessary," I reply. I drag her to the bar.

She begins to look around. "Well, where is she?"

"Oh, look, she's better now. Listen," I blurt in a rush. "We have other things to discuss."

She frowns.

"That kiss . . . now, that was unexpectedly hot, and we need to do it again so that I can fully gauge the situation."

"So Bernadette hasn't gone completely mad?" She frowns.

"Who gives a fuck? Listen . . . ," I continue. "About that one-lover thing . . ."

"Are you serious?" she snaps.

"Deadly." I put my arms around her and pull her close.

"Stop it." She pushes me away. "I *don't* want to kiss you."

"What?" I gasp. "Why not?"

"Ew . . . you're not my type."

"Ew?" I widen my eyes. How rude. "What are you talking about? I'm everybody's type."

"Not mine."

"You don't even know your type yet. There was only one. Here, I'll show you." I reach for her again.

"I like blond, skinny, and sensitive." She bats her eyelids to be a smart-ass.

The exact opposite of me.

I can't help myself. I retaliate. "We do have some things in common. I like blonde, skinny, and horny."

Ugh . . . stop talking, fool.

"Good for you." She holds her arms out to the crowd. "There are plenty of them here. Go get one."

What is this woman doing? Nobody has ever knocked me back before.

"Don't you think we should explore that kiss a little further, do some investigative research?" I ask her.

"No."

"Why not?"

"I didn't like it."

"What?" I gasp. "That kiss was fucking hot, Grumps. What are you talking about?"

"Not for me. It was a bit sloppy, if I'm honest."

I stare at her, horrified.

What do you mean?

"Well . . . that was all your fault," I splutter. "You threw in the number one thing right before, and I was shell shocked, that's all. I can do better." I grab for her. "I'll show you now."

"Goodbye, Christopher." She turns and walks back to that guy on the dance floor.

I stand still, outraged, my hands firmly planted on my hips.

Ha . . . what an idiot. She doesn't know what she's missing.

I walk over to the side of the dance floor and size up the guy she's talking to.

Blond and skinny . . . boring looking. I watch them for a while, and Hayden seems very interested in everything the fucker says . . . I can't even imagine what dreary shit he's talking about.

Screw this.

I march off to the bar.

"Oh, Christo." Bernadette runs after me.

Fucking hell, this woman is killing me.

I need some rat bait.

⋊⋉

An hour later I'm standing talking to a group of people, and I catch sight of the kid who works here. He's walking around and collecting glasses. I watch him for a while: so young to be in an environment like this. He seems totally unfazed and getting on with the job.

"Where are you from, Christo?" a woman asks me.

"New York, originally. I live in the UK now."

"Oh, I live in the UK. Where are you?" She smiles.

There's a group of guys to the left of the dance floor, rolling blind drunk and being obnoxious. I sip my beer as I watch them. I'm not sure where they come from, but they are speaking French. One of them steps back and bangs into the kid. He knocks the glasses out of his hands.

"*Regardez ou vous marchez, putain l'idiot!*" he yells at him. (Translation: *Watch where you're walking, you fucking idiot.*)

The kid bends down to pick up the dropped plastic glasses. He glances up, but it's obvious he doesn't understand the language.

"*M'as-tu entendu?*" the guy yells as he stands over him. (Translation: *Did you hear me?*)

I pass my beer to the girl on my left and make my way over.

"*Reponds-moi espece de putain de cochon grossier.*" (Translation: *Answer me, you fucking rude pig.*)

Adrenaline surges through me, and I stand in front of the kid. "*Recule la merde.*" (Translation: *Back the fuck up.*)

HAYDEN

The music is loud, and the laughter is endless. This is the best night of my life. I've never had so much fun. I catch sight of Christopher on the other side of the dance floor, walking over to a group of men. His stance tells me something is off.

I stop dancing and watch him. What's he doing? Without thinking, I begin to make my way over.

"*S'excuser*," I hear Christopher say. (Translation: *Apologize.*)

"*Va au diable.*" (Translation: *Go to hell.*)

I frown as I walk closer. They're speaking another language. Let me rephrase that: they're fighting in another language.

Christopher is angry, and he pushes a young boy out of the way. Who's he?

Huh?

What's going on here?

"Hayden." Someone laughs. "Got you." I'm lifted up and playfully thrown over someone's shoulder.

"Ahh, put me down."

"Make me." He laughs, thinking I'm joking. He runs me across the room, and as I'm trying to get out of his grip, I see Christopher push the guy in the chest. The guy stumbles back.

What the hell?

Next minute, all hell breaks loose.

There's an all-out brawl.

Men, all-out fighting. Everyone is stepping in, and I have no idea who's on whose side. But I see Basil and Bodie in there fighting alongside Christopher too.

What the hell?

The music stops, and the lights go on. Security guards grab the troublemakers and struggle outside with them. The guy Christopher was fighting seems super drunk, and he's yelling something. Christopher is yelling back at him in another language as they get pushed outside.

Bernadette comes and stands beside me as we watch them get ushered outside.

I glance over at her, and she's smiling goofily after them. "What?" I frown.

"He speaks French."

I roll my eyes. "You mean fights in French."

"That's even hotter."

I smirk, because she's right . . . not that I'll ever admit it.

The music starts, and she grabs my hand and pulls me to the dance floor, and we laugh as we twirl, the drama all but forgotten.

Still having the best night of my life.

I'm woken by the sound of hysterical laughter, men laughing like hyenas as they fumble and try to unlock the door.

I screw up my face. *God, no . . . go away.*

I roll over and snuggle back into my blanket in my bottom bunk. This is the first night I've actually been able to sleep all week. The three hundred drinks I had at the full moon party are responsible, no doubt.

The door busts open, and someone falls through it onto the carpet to deep belly laughter. It echoes down the quiet corridor. "Shh."

"Shh." They all giggle. "Shh, you noisy fucks."

I screw up my face as I try to open my eyes. The sun is peeking through the blinds. It's early morning.

More hysterical laughter.

What could possibly be so fucking funny at this godforsaken hour?

"Do it, do it," Bodie slurs.

It's the boys. They're back from wherever they've been.

They line up in a row and start singing words that I can't understand. "Ah, Macarena." They all jump to the left and start doing the Macarena dance.

"They all want me. They can't have me," they sing.

Oh god . . .

Christopher and Basil have no shirts on. Bodie is missing his shorts and wearing underpants with his shirt open, and Christopher has a traffic cone on his head.

"What the hell?" I moan. Oh no . . . my head. It's broken.

"Ah, Macarena." They jump to the right and keep doing the dance.

"We're fucking good at this," Christopher says as they sing. "We should be strippers."

"I know, right?" Bodie agrees.

They keep dancing to their off-tune singing, and I smile into my pillow as I keep dozing.

"Ah, Macarena," they call as they jump to the left.

"Shut up!" I throw a pillow at them. I look up to the top bunk, and Bernadette is out cold. How is she sleeping through this?

"Ah . . . my number one favorite grump waited up for me," Christopher slurs. He holds one finger up and raises his eyebrow. "Number one." He drops to his hands and knees and crawls toward me until he's millimeters away from my face. "See what I did there?"

I stare at him deadpan.

"One." He widens his eyes as if making a great joke. "Get it?"

"I get it," I snap. "And you're going to get it if you don't go to sleep immediately."

He chuckles and then flops down, his face resting on my mattress, his body on the floor beside my bed. His eyes close in exhaustion. His traffic cone digs into my pillow, and I take it off him and hurl it at the other two fools who are still doing the Macarena. "Where are your pants?" I bark at Bodie.

"They got caught on the fence."

"The fence?"

"The kebab man chased me, and I had to jump over the fence."

I sit up onto my elbows. "Why did the kebab man chase you?"

"He stole his sauce bottle." Basil hiccups. "Fucking funniest night in history."

Christopher stirs, and I push his head back down hard. "Go back to sleep, you."

"Go to sleep," I tell the two Macarenas.

With more singing and lots of grumbles, they finally undress and get into their beds, and ten minutes later the room falls silent as they drift off.

The morning light is just creeping through now, and in the filtered light I can really look at him without anyone knowing.

A secret-spy kind of mission . . .

I stare at the face beside me, his body on the floor, his face on my pillow. He has dark wavy hair and stubble that's nearly a beard. Big red lips and perfect olive skin. My eyes roam down over his shoulders and muscular back. His long dark lashes fan across his face. His forearm is strong with thick veins that course up onto the backs of his hands. They have a dusting of dark hair in all the right places. Just his close proximity swirls something in my stomach.

He's a beautiful specimen of man; there's no denying it. Large, virile, and playful.

I get what they see in him.

Even after seven hundred drinks, a traffic cone, and kebab-sauce thieving, he still smells good. How, I don't know.

90

"Hmm," he rumbles with his eyes closed. I smile as I watch him.

Pity he's such a dick.

I'm just too tired to wake him to move him back to his bed. He's harmless there and isn't hurting anyone.

I close my eyes and begin to relax.

⋈

"Oh no. Oh no . . . oh. No." A soft moan sounds through the room. "My head."

"Fuck my life," Bernadette whispers.

"Waaaatttttteeeeer," someone whispers in a husky-dry-voice kind of way. "I need water."

I smile with my eyes still closed. Hell. What a night.

Hungover doesn't come close.

"It's so hot, like an oven. Someone open a fucking window or something," Bodie whispers. "I'm being cooked alive here, man."

My heavy eyelids slowly open, and the first thing I see is Christopher propped up on his elbow, watching me from his place on the floor. He gives me a cheeky smile. "Morning, Grumps."

I frown. "What are you doing?"

"You know." He smirks. "Just admiring the view."

Who knows what I look like, but it can't be good.

"I need a swim," I whisper.

"Yep. I'm coming." He sits up and then frowns. "Why did I sleep on the floor?"

"You didn't make it to your bed."

He frowns as he looks around the room. "Why is there a traffic cone in my bed?"

"You were wearing it as a hat."

91

"Hmm." He looks around as he assesses the damage. "Good night." He stands and looks down at me. "Let's go, Grumps."

"Can you stop calling me Grumps?"

"It's a term of endearment."

I roll my eyes. "I have to get changed." He takes my hands and pulls me up to my feet.

"I'm coming," Bernadette says.

"Me too," Bodie chips in. He gets up and hits Basil. "Wake up, we're going to the beach."

"Oh fuck." Basil whimpers as he puts the back of his arm over his face. "I can't face peopling today."

"Tough. You'll feel better once you eat."

I pull my T-shirt down over my boxer shorts, suddenly feeling exposed. "I need to get my things from my locker."

"Yeah, me too. Come on."

I look down at myself. "I can't walk out into the corridor like this."

"Nobody's eyeballs can even focus today. You're safe."

"Good point."

We walk out to the corridor and down to the lockers. "How come our room doesn't have our lockers in it?"

"Fossils don't need clothes, apparently," he mutters dryly as he undoes his bag and rummages through it. "I'm buying a big towel today. I don't care if I have to throw it out tonight—I am not taking that pissant towel to the beach. I hate the fucker."

I smirk. "If you hate that damn towel so much, why did you buy it?"

"The wanker from the outdoor store said it was a must-have."

"I have one, too, although it doesn't bother me like yours does," I reply.

"Yeah, well . . ." He keeps looking through his bag. "My particulars are bigger than yours. I need more material."

I smile. *Particulars* . . . Where does he come up with this stuff?

Two guys walk down the corridor, and one turns to face me as he walks past, doing a full circle.

"Keep walking," Christopher mutters dryly.

"Be nice," I whisper. "My particulars need attention, too, you know."

He fakes a smile, and then his face drops instantly as he throws a T-shirt back in his bag. "Get dressed."

I exhale heavily and lean up against my locker. "I really don't have the energy to even get my bag out."

"Fuck's sake, woman, where's your bag?"

I point to my locker.

"Open it."

I press in my code, and he drags my backpack out and unzips it. "What are you wearing?" He begins to look through my things. "Why is this bag so messy?"

"I don't know." I bend and push him out of the way. "I'm a backpacker. It's supposed to be messy. Move."

He stands and leans his head back onto my locker. "I'm fucking dehydrated." He holds his arms out to look at his veins. They are in full glory and popping out everywhere.

"I wonder why." I roll my eyes. "Where's my swimsuit?" I keep looking.

"Seriously," he whispers angrily. "Hurry the fuck up."

"You don't have to wait for me, you know?"

"I actually do. You're wearing nana pajamas, and they are probably going to kick you out of here."

"Probably a good thing," I huff. "Seriously, I'm going to kill Monica."

"Who's Monica?"

"My best friend back home. She took some of my clothes out of my packed suitcase and snuck in ho wear." I hold up the tiny black bikini. "Seriously, what would this even cover?"

He shrugs. "Works for me."

I screw up my face. "Shut up." I push my bag back in and march past him into the bathroom, too tired to look for a decent swimming costume for one minute longer.

I put the bikini on and look down at myself.

What the fuck?

This is obscene. I can't wear this in public.

I hear Kimberly's voice as she talks to someone. I like her; we clicked last night. I open the cubicle door.

"Hey, Hazy." She smiles.

"Does this look ridiculous?" I whisper.

"What?"

I hold my arms out. "This bikini, it's . . ." I widen my eyes as I search for the right word.

"Hot." She looks me up and down. "Turn around."

I do a 360.

"Perfect, you could eat cheese off your ass."

I screw up my face. "That's not a saying."

"Yeah, it is. You know, you could eat cheese off her ass."

"I've never heard of that in my life." I frown. "You want to come to the beach?"

"You going now?"

"Yeah." I peer down at my boobs as they nearly fall out. I try to stretch the fabric to cover more.

"Okay. Give me five minutes."

"Meet by the front doors?" I ask her.

"Okay."

I walk out to see Christopher walking out of the bathrooms at the same time. He looks me up and down, and his eyebrows flick up as if he's surprised. "Hot . . . Grumps." He readjusts his dick. "You've given me a semi in that bikini."

I curl my lip in disgust. We begin to walk back to our room. "What is it with you and *semi* anyway?" I ask.

"What do you mean?" He frowns.

"Semikissed me, semidick . . . you seem to have a lot of *semi* going on."

"You couldn't handle the lot."

"I wouldn't want to." I widen my eyes.

"Good." He squares his shoulders. "Because you'll never have the chance."

"I wouldn't want it."

"Good." We walk into the room, and everyone is ready to go. "Let's go."

※

The beach is hot, and the ocean is cold.

Perfection.

We lie on our towels, the six of us. We've eaten lunch and spent nearly the entire day here. It's weird. I don't know these people, but I feel super comfortable already.

"What are everyone's travel plans?" Bernadette asks.

"Well . . ." I shrug. "My plan is to stay at a central base in each country for a month. That way, I can get a job for a few days a week and travel around for the rest of the time. If I don't work at least two shifts a week somewhere, I won't have enough money to stay for the entire twelve months that I want to."

Christopher sits up, his interest piqued. "Where do you want to go?"

"Well, I started in Spain," I tell them. "I think I'll go to Italy next. I want to do Prague. Greece. Switzerland. Germany, maybe?"

"Hmm." He thinks for a moment. "That sounds like a plan. I'm coming."

"What?" I frown.

"That actually is a good plan," Kimberly says. "I need to start working a few days a week too. Mind if I come along?"

I shrug. "I . . . no. Guess not."

"Yeah, I'm in," Basil says.

"I'm not being left out," Bernadette says.

We all look to Bodie. He shrugs. "Can we go to Portugal?"

"I guess." I shrug. "I'm not set where I go. I just need to work a few days. That's why I need a base. Totally flexible with where we go."

Christopher looks between us. "Twelve months . . . twelve countries?"

Everyone smiles as a weird kind of excitement runs between us.

"Deal."

Chapter 7

The room is silent: just what I need.

After last night's craziness, it's good to finally get some rest. The others aren't back from dinner yet. It's just Christopher and me.

Turning the page, I try to focus on my book, but I can feel eyes watching. I glance up to see him lying in his bed opposite mine, propped up on one elbow and staring at me.

"What?" I ask.

"I don't get it."

My eyes stay on the page. "Get what?"

"How have you only slept with one person?"

"Why would you still be thinking about that?" I shrug. "Drop it, please."

"After you explain it to me, I'll never mention it again."

I raise my eyebrow. "I don't believe you."

He smirks. He doesn't believe that either. "So you lied?"

"No."

"Then it's impossible."

I drop my book, annoyed. "It is completely possible. Not everyone is fucking like rabbits, you know?"

"Were you married?"

"No."

"Religious beliefs?"

"Nope."

He thinks for a moment and raises an eyebrow. "Just boring, then?"

I smile. "Maybe."

He twists the blankets underneath him as he thinks.

Ugh, he's not going to drop this until he has more information.

"Look, I was with my high school sweetheart for most of my adult life, and when we broke up . . ." I shrug.

"So you're newly single?"

"Not really."

"How long?"

"You're very nosy, you know that?"

"How long?" he repeats.

"We broke up two years ago."

"You haven't had sex for two years?" He gasps, horrified.

I feel my cheeks heat with embarrassment. Damn it, why did I say that out loud? "I've been busy."

"Masturbating?"

Nailed it.

I smirk and go back to my book.

We sit in silence for a while, and I can almost hear his brain ticking at a million miles per minute. "How long since you had sex?" I ask him.

He twists his lips as he thinks. "With myself . . . about an hour."

"You jerked off here?" I gasp. "Where?"

"In the shower. What was I supposed to do? I haven't had sex for five days; my balls were aching."

"Ew." I stare at him. "You have to wank after only five days?"

"Of course." He nods. "I *have* to ejaculate every day, more than once if possible. Morning and night is the best scenario."

I frown. "You're sick."

"All men need to come. It's genetic."

I think for a moment. I've never spoken to a man about this sort of thing before. "So who . . . do you . . . sleep with? A girlfriend or . . ."

"Girls."

"What girls?"

He exhales heavily as he thinks. "I don't know. I have a few people I see casually."

"So you have open relationships with them?"

"No. I don't have relationships with them; I have sex with them."

I frown, confused. "What happens? They come to your house and undress, and you fuck them, and then they leave?"

He nods. "Pretty much."

Yuck . . . I screw up my face.

"What?" he asks.

"I can think of nothing worse."

"I'm a very good fuck. They leave satisfied."

Gross.

I widen my eyes as I return to my book.

"What does that mean?" he asks.

"This is why I could never go out with a player like you. We come from completely different planets."

"I'm not a player. Players hurt people. The women I see know exactly where they stand. It's a mutual arrangement."

I raise my eyebrow. "And I bet every single one of them is thinking she's going to be the woman who finally tames you."

"Calm down, nobody is taming anybody." He rolls his eyes.

I smile. "Until they do."

"So?"

"So what?" I ask.

"Don't you want to know what else is out there?"

"I do." I pause as I try to articulate myself properly. "It's not that I don't want to."

"Then why?"

"To me, giving my body to someone is sacred. I just can't imagine doing it with someone I didn't know and trust."

"What you're saying is that you're waiting for marriage?"

"That's not it. I just . . . I haven't met anyone that raises any interest in me." I shrug as I think about it. "Maybe I *am* boring?"

He flops onto his back. "Maybe you've only slept with a dud, and you're not addicted to orgasms yet."

"Maybe."

"Maybe this trip is your sabbatical, and you are going to turn into the ultimate fuck-bunny hobag."

I giggle. "Maybe."

"Why did you break up?" he asks.

I think for a moment. "I don't know."

He scratches his head as he waits for my answer.

"Who was your last girlfriend?" I ask to change the subject.

He gives a subtle shake of his head.

"You don't want to talk about it?"

"I've never had a girlfriend."

I screw up my face. "What . . . never. Why?"

He shrugs. "I don't know. Never really been my thing, I guess. It's not something that I ever felt I needed."

"That's weird. How old are you?"

"Well, I am in the fossil room."

I giggle. "This is true." I think for a moment. "Maybe you need to see a therapist," I reply.

"Ask my mother; she'll tell you just how much."

We both laugh, and it feels good to talk to him like this. A silent acknowledgment runs between us. There's nothing romantic there, so no point ruining what it actually is.

He smiles up at the ceiling as if finding something amusing. "What?"

"I think Bodie has a thing for you."

I screw up my face. "No, really?"

"I think so."

"Kimberly asked me if you were available."

He twists his lips as if considering the prospect. "She's pretty hot, actually."

"I thought so." I think for a moment. "Great boobs."

He nods, thinking about it too. "Probably not a good idea if we are going to travel together. Would make for an awkward twelve months." He wrinkles his nose.

I imagine him dodging both Kimberly and Bernadette, and I giggle. "Would make for some excellent viewing for me, though."

He smiles over at me. "You're a cool chick, Grumps."

"I know."

"Need any help with your vibrator?"

"You were doing so well." I gasp as I throw a cushion at him.

He bursts out laughing, and I do too.

Maybe he's not that bad.

CHRISTOPHER

I sit at the bar of the hostel and scroll through the employment section.

I need to find a job, and stat.

My three-day shift at the taxi company is over, and we have decided that we're going to work on weekends in Barcelona and travel through the week to different destinations.

Monday, we leave for San Sebastián.

Which is a major problem because I have $300 to my name. Actually, $297 after this beer.

How the fuck do people live without money? It's so shit.

"Hey." I hear a voice and look up. It's the kid. He's arrived for his shift tonight. He walks behind the bar and puts his apron on.

"Hi." I smile.

"Thanks for the other night," he says as he fusses around and begins to clean.

"That's okay."

I watch him for a moment. He won't look at me.

"Just so you know, I kicked his ass when we got outside," I add.

He smirks as he stacks the glasses high. "Where did you learn to fight?"

I shrug. "I have three older brothers who think they are always right. Punching their faces in comes naturally."

He smiles as he continues to do his chores.

"Do you live around here?" I ask him.

He nods. "Not far." He picks up the broom and begins to sweep.

"How long have you worked here for?" I ask.

"Hmm . . . two or so years."

"You started when you were twelve?"

"Yeah." He shrugs as if it's the most natural thing in the world.

The things he must have seen.

I watch him as he works. This kid intrigues me. So capable and independent.

"Do you live with your parents?" I ask.

"My grandmother."

I wonder where his parents are.

"Got any brothers and sisters?"

"No."

"Oh . . ." We fall silent, and he keeps on working.

"I live in London," I tell him.

He nods but doesn't reply.

"Originally from New York."

His eyes shoot up. "What's it like?"

"New York?"

He nods.

"Best city in the world."

He smiles. "I'm going to go there one day." He digs his phone out of his pocket and flicks through the photos until he gets to the one he wants to show me. It's a skyline pic of New York at dusk.

I smile as I look at it. "You'll love it." I pass his phone back to him, and he goes to put it in his pocket but misses, and it falls on the floor.

He scrambles to pick it up, and his face falls. "Oh no," he cries. He throws his hands up in the air. "I broke the screen."

"What?" I frown. "Show me."

He holds it out for me to see, and the screen is smashed to smithereens.

He slams it down on the counter and puts his two hands in his hair in despair.

I stare at the phone. It's ancient, super old. It's a wonder it even works.

"It's okay," I tell him. "It's just a phone screen."

"I saved for two years for this phone," he cries. His nostrils are flared, and it looks like he's about to burst into tears.

"Oh . . ." I pick it up. "Maybe we could get the screen fixed?" I try to make him feel better.

"You can't get parts for this phone. It's too old." He slams a pot down on the counter. He's genuinely devastated.

"Eddie," a man calls from the front.

He looks up.

"Move the bottles of water from the store. I have a truck coming in with more stock."

He nods. "Okay."

"Hurry up about it," the guy calls.

I frown as I listen to the cold orders.

The kid rushes to the front to move the stock, and I sit in silence, the weight of his world sitting heavily on my chest. He works like a dog and has to save for two years for a piece-of-shit phone.

Poor fucking kid.

"I got us a job," Basil announces as he slouches onto a stool beside me.

"What? Where?"

"An Italian restaurant. They're looking for three staff members. I saw a sign on the window and went in, and he offered me it straightaway. I asked him about you and Hayden, and he said to bring you both and we can all trial."

"Great."

"We start tonight."

"Tonight?" I frown. I had plans to sort my hungry dick out tonight. I'm walking around with a constant boner.

"Uh-huh."

"Okay." I sigh. "Thanks."

Looks like it's more shower love for me. The thought is depressing.

I need my cock sucked.

※

I pick my T-shirt up and smell it as we walk along. "Did he wash this fucking T-shirt before he loaned it to me?"

"He said he washed it yesterday," Hayden replies.

"What washing powder did he use, wet dog?"

"Probably too tight for laundry powder," Basil says from up front.

I stop on the spot, horrified. "So, what . . . you don't think he didn't use powder?"

"I don't know. He loaned you a plain black shirt that you needed for our trial tonight. He did you a favor," Hayden huffs. "Stop being a princess."

"I am not being a princess," I snap. "I'm being hygienic. Does anyone around here know the fucking meaning of the word?"

Basil and Hayden roll their eyes at each other.

"I saw that," I snap as I look up the long road. "Where is this restaurant, anyway? Bangkok?"

They stay silent and keep walking in front.

I wish.

Banging my cock sounds like a job I would actually want.

"Maybe I should be a gigolo?" I tell them. "Could kill two birds with one stone."

Hayden rolls her eyes. "For someone who hates body odor as much as you, I imagine you would love all those dirty-smelling clients."

I screw up my face in disgust. "Gross."

She shrugs. "Just saying."

"Yeah, well, don't. I'm getting a bad visual right now."

"What of, a smelly girl wanting you to go down on her for an hour?" She turns and smiles sweetly at me. "Sounds perfect. You should totally look into that."

I wince. Just the thought roils my stomach.

"I would pick and choose my clients," I reply. "Obviously."

"Because hot girls pay for sex all the time," Basil replies.

We keep walking and walking and walking . . .

"Where the fuck is this restaurant?" I huff. I glance at my phone. "Aren't we supposed to be there like five minutes ago?"

"It's up here. Five minutes late won't matter."

"Won't matter?" I cry. "I hate late people," I say as we walk along. "I've given a warning letter before for being five minutes late. Get here on time or get the fuck out."

Hayden turns back to look at me, seemingly shocked. "To a schoolkid?"

"Oh . . ." Fuck, that's right. I'm a teacher. "I take no shit from my kids."

"Do you make them wear deodorant?" Basil asks.

"At all times," I reply. This isn't a lie. If I were a teacher, every fucker would be deodorized.

"I bet you hate dirty shoes too," Basil says.

"I fucking hate dirty shoes," I agree. "You can always tell how much respect somebody has for themselves by the state of their shoes."

They both roll their eyes.

"You are the weirdest person I've ever met," Hayden replies.

"I'm normal," I announce. "Why, what do you do for work?" I ask her.

"Animal husbandry," she replies as she walks in front.

I frown. "What's that?"

"I'm an IVF specialist for cows."

"Speak English. What does that mean?"

"I collect semen from bulls and impregnate cows."

Both Basil and I stop still on the spot as we stare at her, shocked to our cores.

"You wank bulls?" I gasp.

"No." She keeps walking. "I get them ready to do their business."

"How? Do they watch cow porn?" I frown, fascinated.

Hayden laughs. "No, I set them up with a hot little heifer, and then we have a fake vagina heated to sixty-three degrees Celsius and filled with K-Y Jelly, and they do their business in there. An oversize condom catches it."

My mouth falls open. "You have a bull Fleshlight?"

"I guess you could call it that." She shrugs.

"Then what?" I gasp. "What do you do with the bull jizz?"

"Bull jizz." Basil laughs. "That's fucking funny. You should get it on a T-shirt." He holds his hand up in the air and makes a rainbow shape. "Professional bull jizzer."

"I take it back to my lab, and it's frozen for when I impregnate a female."

"How do you do that?" I ask. This is the most random thing I've ever heard of.

"I have an instrument, and I inject it into the cow's uterus."

"Do you do an operation to do that?"

"No."

"Then how?"

She holds her arm up and indicates sticking it in something.

107

My eyes widen in horror. "You don't . . ."

She smiles with a nod. "I do."

"Your whole hand?"

She karate chops the top of her arm. "My whole arm."

Basil's mouth and mine both fall open in shock. There are no words for her job.

"What the fuck, man," Basil gasps.

"You think you know someone," I mutter under my breath.

"What does that mean?" she asks. "What did you think I would do?"

"Not that," I huff. "I didn't even know that was a fucking thing." We continue to walk for a while. "I pegged you for a nurse."

"A nurse?" She frowns.

"Yeah, you have that commonsense thing going on. I thought you were a nurse."

"No."

"Hmm . . ." We keep walking. "Do the bulls know that they aren't fucking the cow?"

"No, they think it's the real thing."

"Hmm . . . maybe I should buy myself a Fleshlight?" I think out loud. "I mean, if bulls like it."

"Stick to fucking cows," Hayden replies.

"Definitely had a few of them in my time," I agree.

"This is it," Basil says as we get to a restaurant. "Let's hope we get the jobs." He pushes open the door and is greeted by the server. "Hi. We are here to start work tonight?"

The girl fakes a smile and looks Hayden up and down. Hmm . . . I already don't like her. "Hi." She fakes a smile. "Just go out the back to the kitchen," she instructs us.

We walk through the huge restaurant, and I look around. There must be two hundred tables in here. This place is massive.

We go through the double doors to find the biggest kitchen I have ever seen. People are scurrying around like ants.

"What time do you call this?" a big fat dude yells. He taps his watch. "You're late!"

"Sorry," Basil stammers. "We got lost. It won't happen again."

"Do not waste my time," he barks in a strong Italian accent. He calls someone over with his hand. "Maria will show you what to do." He glares at us. "Do not mess up in my restaurant. Do you hear me?"

Who does this fucker think he is?

"Okay." Hayden nods. She hits me on the leg to remind me to speak.

"Sure," I reply. I don't like this guy already.

Maria comes over. "Hi, I'm Maria. Have you worked in hospitality before?"

"Yes," Basil and Hayden both reply.

I've eaten at a million restaurants in my life. How hard could it be? "Yes," I lie.

"Great." She smiles as she looks around. "Do any of you have bar experience?"

"I do," Basil replies.

"Okay, you're on the bar," she says to him. "And you two wait tables."

"Sure."

"Put these on, and . . ." She looks at me. "What's your name?" she asks me.

"Christo," I reply.

"What's your name?" she asks Hayden.

"Hayden."

"Okay. Put these on." She hands us both black-and-white-striped aprons.

"Cosmo, you do the front level, and Helga, you do the back corner." She turns her back to get out some notepads.

"Helga," I mouth to Hayden. She widens her eyes and tries not to laugh.

"When you hear a bell, it means order up, and you take it to the table."

"Okay." We both nod. That sounds easy enough.

"Call me if you need anything." She walks off.

"Helga," I whisper as we walk to the kitchen.

She hits me on the leg. "Shut up, Cosmo."

The bell dings. "Order up," a guy calls.

The food is laid out on a high bench with heat lamps over it to keep it warm. Staff are buzzing around everywhere.

"Hi." Hayden smiles to the chef. "I'm new, so . . ."

The chef nods, too busy to care. "This, this, and this to table forty." He slides over three plates. Hayden picks up two of them, and I go to pick up the other. "One person, three plates," he yells.

"Calm down," I mutter.

Hayden does some kind of juggling act and carries two plates with one hand and one in the other. She toddles off, out into the restaurant.

The bell dings again. "What are you ringing the bell for? I'm right here," I say.

"No talking," the chef yells.

I screw up my face. "I wasn't making conversation."

He slides over three plates. "Table forty."

I pick up two of the plates.

"Three at a time," he yells.

"I'm not an octopus," I snap. "I'll be back for the other."

"Not good enough," he calls after me.

My blood begins to simmer. *Fuckwit.*

I walk out to the restaurant and look for Hayden. She's over in the corner, delivering the plates to the table. How the hell did she know what number each table is? I walk over. The table has ten men sitting at it, who are all very tipsy. "Pasta?" I ask as I look around the table.

"What pasta is it?"

I look in the bowl. Hmm . . . I have no idea. "Spaghetti."

"What spaghetti?"

"I don't fucking know, you ordered it."

Hayden gives me a subtle shake of her head.

"What kind of pasta is it?" the guy barks.

"Whatever the one you ordered is," I bark back. "Put the wine down and concentrate."

Hayden takes the bowl from me and peers into the bowl. "Shrimp?"

"Me," someone says. She puts the bowl down, and he keeps talking.

"Thank you," I correct him.

He glances up.

"Manners are free," I say.

"Fuck off, man," he replies.

"What did you say?"

Hayden snatches the plate from me and puts it down. "This way," she whispers as she pulls me away by the elbow. "What are you doing?" she whispers as she fakes a smile.

"This job is shit."

"What are you talking about? It's a great job."

"Coming from someone who fist-fucks cows for a living, I don't believe you're qualified to call it," I whisper angrily.

She looks around the restaurant. "Just walk around and clear the tables."

"What's that?"

"You said you did this before?"

"I lied."

"Fucking hell," she whispers. "Collect the dirty plates, and take them to the kitchen."

"Okay." I nod. "That's a good plan."

I walk over to a table. A man and woman are talking, his plate neatly packed up. I pick up his plate. "I'm not finished." He snatches it off me.

"So why are your knife and fork together like that?"

"I was talking."

"Less talking, more eating. I don't have all night to wait for you, you know?" I march off.

"Excuse me," someone calls as I walk past.

I turn to see the hottest woman I've seen all week. I smile. Finally . . . something good about this restaurant. "Yes."

"Could you possibly get me an orgasm?"

"You have no idea," I reply as I imagine myself bending her over the table.

She blinks. "As in cocktail?"

"Oh . . . right?" I fake a smile. I knew that. Damn it, I need to get laid.

I march to the bar and over to Basil. "Can you make me an Orgasm, please, for Miss Salacious at two o'clock?"

He glances over at her. "I don't know how to make that."

"You said you've done this before?"

"I lied."

"Fucking hell. Google it."

"I already tried. I have no service."

"This is one colossal fuckup," I whisper angrily. "The one person I am trying to impress, and you are completely fucking this up for me."

"Go and ask her what's in an Orgasm?"

"My fucking dick, that's what. She's smoking hot." We both look over at her, sitting there in her tight black dress and her long dark hair. Another guy comes to work behind the bar. "What's in an Orgasm cocktail?" I ask him.

He shrugs like he doesn't have a care in the world. "I don't know."

"What?" I screw up my face. "How don't you know? Aren't you the barman? Isn't there a manual or some shit behind there?"

"There is, but it's written in Italian," the guy says. "Just do whatever. Nobody ever complains about bad cocktails."

"Yeah, you're right." I nod. "Just work it out between you. But make it good because I want to go back to her table at least ten times."

"Cosmo," Maria calls. "Plates."

"Yeah, yeah, I'm coming, witch," I mutter under my breath as I walk back out onto the floor. "Are you finished with these?" I ask two people.

"Yes," the man snaps.

I glare at him. Why are people being so fucking rude in this place?

It's like pig city.

I carry the plates back out into the kitchen and see Hayden waiting for food to take out. "What do I do with these?" I ask her.

"Scrape them off into the bin, then rinse them and stack them to the side for the dishy to do."

"Okay."

I scrape them off and then look at a huge thing that comes out of a large black pipe in the ceiling. It has a silver big nozzle thing on the end that looks like a drink gun. I try to read the buttons.

Is this the tap?

I look around. How is this the tap?

I hold the plate in the sink and hit the button, and a water jet capable of knocking down a war bunker hits the plate and sprays water all over me and the entire kitchen. The hot plates sizzle as the water hits them. "Ahh." I try to turn it off, and it goes harder. The hose begins to go out of control and flick around as it sprays everywhere. Everyone is screaming and ducking for cover.

"What are you doing? Turn off the tap, you fucking idiot!"

"If it were a tap, I would," I cry as I battle the wayward water. "This is a fucking fire hose. Get better equipment, fool."

Hayden runs over and tries to grab the out-of-control tap as it flies around. We are both saturated. A waiter walks into the kitchen and slips in the water, dropping his tray of plates. "Sorry," I call. "Occupational safety at its worst."

Hayden bursts out laughing, and I do too. This is ridiculous.

"Get out of my kitchen," the owner cries. "You idiots!"

I take off my apron, and Hayden's eyes widen. "We're out of here."

"What?"

I spin her away from me and undo her apron, and I grab her hand. "Let's go." We run through the restaurant, and Basil's eyes widen when he sees us. He looks around as if not sure what to do, and then he makes a run for it too. We run out onto the street and burst out laughing, completely saturated and looking like drowned rats.

"What the fuck happened to you?" Basil gasps as he looks us up and down.

"Fire hose."

His eyes widen. "He sprayed you with the fire hose?"

"Yes," I lie.

"Holy shit," he cries. "We need to report him to someone. That's just wrong, man . . . the instructions need to be in English."

I'm laughing so hard that I can hardly stand up, and Hayden is too.

"What do we do now?" Basil asks, wide eyed.

"We go out and party."

I breathe in deeply as I wake up from my dozing. Hmm . . . I have to get back to my room.

I have a naked woman under each arm, our legs entwined in the sheets. It was a good night.

I needed that.

I stir, and they both cling to me. "Where you going?" one whispers.

"Home." I sit up and climb out of bed and smile as I watch them both fall back to sleep. I bend and kiss them each on the cheek and run my hand over their naked hips.

Hot.

I make my way back to the hostel and get into the shower; the hot, steamy water runs over my head, and I soap myself up as I wash them off me.

I'm exhausted. It's been a very long day.

I sneak into my room to find Kimberly in my bed.

What?

The fuck is she doing here? This isn't her room.

Damn it, I would have stayed where I was if I'd known I didn't have a bed back here. I look around the dark room. Fuck it. I'll climb in with Grumps.

I slide in beside her and scooch under the blankets. Still asleep, she shuffles over with her back to me to make room. I roll on my side and put my arm around her from behind. I inhale the sweet scent of her hair and feel her curves under my arm.

And then, in bed with my favorite person in Spain, I feel myself finally relax.

Chapter 8

Hayden

The sound of a door slamming out in the corridor wakes me up, and I rub my eyes.

Someone is in bed with me, his body snuggled up against mine from behind, and by the heavenly smell of him, I know exactly who it is. "Why are you in my bed?" I whisper huskily.

"Shh, less talking, more sleeping," he murmurs with his eyes closed.

We doze back off as we spoon, and I must admit, the close physical contact with someone is nice. I haven't had a hug since I got here a week ago.

I hear movement. "Oh no," Bernadette gasps. "You said no hanky-panky with roommates." She looks down from her top bunk at Christopher and me.

Ugh . . .

Christopher stirs. "This is sleeping, Bernadette. No hanky-panky."

"Oh," she says as if relieved. "You could have slept with me."

"Help," he whispers as he pulls me closer into his arms, and I smirk.

"He will sleep with you tomorrow night, Bernie," I reply.

He pinches me under the cover, and I giggle.

We keep lying in each other's arms, and he snuggles in closer. His big arm is around my waist, and our bodies and bare legs are up against one another's.

"Look who's all sated and cuddly," I whisper. "I'm guessing last night went well?"

"Shh." He cuddles me closer. "You're getting annoying now."

I giggle.

His phone beeps a message, and he rolls onto his back to check it. "Hmm." He hums as he reads it. "Finally."

"What?"

He rolls me over and pulls me onto his chest. His arm is around my shoulders. "My new card is at the bank."

Hmm, I'm still half-asleep.

"Come with me to go get it?"

"No."

"Will you two shut up," Bodie snaps. "People are trying to fucking sleep here."

"I'm one of them." I bump my forehead into Christopher's, and I feel him smile above me.

He tries to sweeten the deal. "If you come with me, I'll buy you lunch."

"Hmm." I bring my hand up to his chest and notice the dark hair on it. "What are we eating on your budget, 2 Minute Noodles?"

"What's that?"

I frown as I look up at his face. "2 Minute Noodles?"

"I don't know what that is."

"Everyone knows what fucking 2 Minute Noodles are," Bodie replies from his top bunk.

"I thought you were sleeping," Christopher says to him.

"Some fucker is waking me up with dumb questions about 2 Minute Noodles."

Christopher chuckles, and he mindlessly runs his fingers up my arm. "Come on, Grumps, come with me."

"Hmm, I don't feel like it." I screw up my face. "I'm tired and hungover."

"Me too." He sits up. "Come on."

"Why can't you go alone?"

"Why would I want to go alone when I have you as a personal bodyguard?"

"Call your chickie birds from last night," I reply dryly, my eyes still closed. "They'll go."

"I'm not hanging out with them," he says as if disgusted by the suggestion. He gets out of bed. "When we get back, Basil and I are going to do our washing. Aren't we, Baz?"

"Fuck off," Basil grumbles from under his pillow. "Who thinks of this shit first thing in the morning? I've never met someone who is so horny over soap. I'm not washing clothes; I washed them last week."

"You wash everything each time it's worn."

"Who does that?" Basil scoffs.

"Men who get laid, that's who."

I can't hide my smile. How is this man so endearing? I should hate everything about him. "Speaking of soap, I need to shower."

Christopher holds his arm out toward the door. "Your five-star spa is ready and waiting."

I giggle. The shitty dorm-style bathroom is definitely not ready or waiting.

"I'll get our things from the lockers," he offers.

"Fine . . ." I sigh.

He disappears out into the corridor, and I smile goofily up at the bed above me.

"I hate how he's all perky in the morning," Bernadette says.

"That's because he got tag teamed last night by two stunners," Kimberly replies.

I get a vision of him rolling around in the sheets with those two girls, and my face falls.

Jealousy twists in my stomach. I wonder, Will he see them again? Of course he will . . . *this* is who he is.

Stop it.

It's not like that between us, I remind myself. He can do whatever he wants to whoever he wants.

The door opens back up, and he sticks his head in the door. "Just checking you're up."

"My god," I snap. "You're so annoying."

"We have to go soon."

"Why?"

"Because I need food."

"Aren't we going out for lunch?"

"Breakfast too. You're paying." The door closes, and I smirk again.

Dick.

)(

We stand at the side of the busy road. Traffic is whirling past.

Christopher looks left and then right, then left again. "Come on." He grabs my hand and pulls me across the road.

"Where is the bank?" I ask.

"Just down here." He holds his phone up and follows the map.

"How did you lose your card again?" I ask.

"Oh . . ." He rolls his eyes. "You don't want to know."

"How?"

He pulls me along by the hand. "Let's just say I had an unpleasant zoo experience on my first night here."

I frown as we walk. "What does that mean?"

"I went home with this girl, and when she undressed, she was so hairy that I thought I was with a gorilla, and I went in the bathroom to call my brother and freak out, and I left only to find out that she had stolen my card and wiped my bank account clean," he blurts out in a rush.

I blink, horrified.

"I know." He shakes his head.

"What's wrong with hair on a woman?" I ask as I'm dragged along.

"Oh my god . . ." He rolls his eyes. "Not you too."

"Well?"

He shrugs. "I don't like it . . . and it's my prerogative not to personally like it."

"What?" I shriek. "What do you mean you don't like it?"

"I mean, normal hair . . . fine. Never cut, never waxed . . . growing-a-vegetable-patch-down-your-legs-style, no fucking way."

I giggle . . . jeez, that reminds me, I need a trim. Hmm, better buy some scissors.

Maybe a home wax kit?

We get to the bank, and he walks in and over to the counter. "Take a seat." He gestures to the chair.

"I'll come." I stand beside him as he talks to the teller.

"Hello, I lost my card and ordered a new one. I got a text this morning to say it was here at this branch, ready to be collected," he says.

"Okay." She smiles. "Identification, please."

He slides it over, and she enters the information into her computer. She waits, and then her eyebrows shoot up. As if surprised by something, she looks between him and the screen. "Mr. Miles?"

He cuts her off. "Yes. Card, please."

"Just a minute." She toddles off.

"What's wrong with your account?" I whisper.

"She's mortified by the lack of money in it," he whispers back.

I giggle. "Aren't we all."

He gives me the side-eye.

"I *am* paying for breakfast, after all." I widen my eyes at him.

He smiles. "This is true, you are." He rolls his lips. "And then I'm buying you five-minute noodles for lunch."

The lady comes back and begins to type on her computer again.

"It's two," I whisper.

"Two what?"

"Two-minute noodles."

"Oh . . ." He nods. "Great marketing."

I frown. "How?"

"Well, you instantly know what it is."

"Not instantly," I whisper. "Two minutes."

He chuckles and puts his arm around my shoulders and pulls me close. The lady hands over his card. "Sign here, please." He signs, and then she gives him another thing to sign. "Sign here." She gives him a big smile. "That's it. You two lovebirds have a great day."

"Thanks." He smiles. "We will."

We walk out of the bank; his arm is still around me. And it's not weird, and it's not awkward. In fact it feels very natural to have him touch me. Which is weird in itself because I'm not regularly a touchy person.

Perhaps it's because I know it's just in friendship and nothing more.

X

We amble through the giant shopping district; my arm is linked through his. We've had the best day of all time. It's late afternoon, and somehow Christopher and I have wasted hours and hours. We had breakfast, then we went shopping, and we both bought a book.

"I'm not sure what five-minute noodles taste like, but I'm sure our lunch was better," Christopher says.

"It sure was."

"You know"—he glances down at me—"that is the first time a woman has ever bought me lunch."

"No . . ."

"True."

I frown up at him. "Don't you go to lunch dates?"

"All the time."

"And you always buy the women lunch?"

"Yes."

"Why?"

"I don't know." He shrugs. "I just do."

I roll my eyes. "God, you must date some dummies."

"Why do you say that?"

"Paying your own way is about self-respect."

He frowns as he contemplates my words.

"It doesn't matter if you are a beggar on the street or a million-aire; if a woman doesn't *ever* offer to pay her own way, then she's not with you for the right reasons."

He raises his eyebrow as we walk along, remaining silent.

"Don't you agree?" I ask him.

He offers an excuse. "But if one has more money than the other . . ."

"It doesn't matter, Christopher," I huff. I hate that these women would take advantage of him like this. "If you think that because they offer their bodies to you on a platter that you have to pay for everything . . . you are not dating them. You are paying them for sex. It's as clear as day. How don't you see it?"

He twists his lips as we walk along, still not saying anything.

I wonder, Is that how things work with him? Does he get taken advantage of because he's kind?

"Oh, I want to look in here." He pulls me into a shop. "I'll be quick."

I glance up at the sign above the door.

PHONE WORLD.

"Hello," he says to the shop attendant.

"Hi."

"Do you repair screens for . . ." He quickly looks through his photos on his phone and then holds it up to show him. "This phone?"

The guy narrows his eyes as he studies the picture. He screws up his face. "No, no, too old. Can't get parts," he says in a heavy Spanish accent.

"Oh." Christopher's face falls.

"Who has that phone?" I ask.

"Eduardo."

"Who?" I frown.

"The kid from the bar."

"Oh . . ." How does he even know that?

Christopher looks through the glass cabinet at all the new phones. "How much is this one?"

I frown. What's he doing?

"Nineteen hundred euros."

Christopher winces. "Ouch."

I tap him on the leg. He doesn't have the money for this. "What are you doing?" I whisper.

"He saved for two years for his phone," he whispers. "I broke it."

"How?"

"He dropped it when I passed it back to him."

I try to make him feel better. "Then you didn't break it."

"Yeah, but I feel like shit. I can't stop thinking about it." He points to the phone through the glass. "I'll take that one, please."

"Okay." The guy begins to bundle it up, and I look up at him in shock. He's flat broke, and here he is buying a new phone for a kid he doesn't even know.

"Chris," I whisper. "You can't afford this."

"It's okay, I'll transfer it out of my savings," he whispers. "I'll get another job this week, don't worry."

But I do worry because I know that underneath all that player bullshit is a good, kind man . . . who people take advantage of.

He and the shop attendant go through the warranty and instructions. "I'll wait outside," I say.

"Okay."

I walk out and hear someone call my name. "Hayden."

I turn to see a guy I met last night. He's staying at a backpackers' hostel down the road from ours. "Hi, Zack." We spoke for over an hour. He seems really nice.

"I've been thinking about you all day." He smiles.

"Really?" My stomach does a little flip.

"What are you doing here?" he asks.

"Waiting for my friend, my roommate. He's buying a phone."

"Oh, right." He smiles over at me.

I smile right back as the air crackles between us.

Christopher walks out the door with his phone in a shopping bag. He looks between Zack and me.

I introduce them. "Christopher, this is Zack."

"Hello," he says as they shake hands.

"So you get to share a room with her?" Zack says with a huge smile. "Lucky prick."

125

Christopher's chin tilts to the sky as if he's annoyed. "Where are you staying?" he asks in a clipped tone.

"In Rubens Backpackers." Zack turns his attention to me. "Hayden, do you want to go out tonight . . . like on a date?"

"She has plans," Christopher replies before I have a chance to even open my mouth to reply.

"Oh." Zack's eyes flick between Christopher and me.

"But you could meet us out if you wanted to?" I offer.

Zack smiles broadly. "That sounds great." He digs his phone out of his pocket. "I'll give you my number. Text me where you are."

"Okay."

I give him my number as Christopher glares at him. What *is* his problem?

"See you tonight?" I ask.

"Can't wait." Zack smiles.

"Goodbye," Christopher snaps as he grabs my hand. "We have to go, Hayden."

I frown. That's the first time I can remember that he's ever said my name.

"Who is he?" Christopher snaps as we walk away.

"I met him last night. We talked for hours."

"When?" He scoffs. "I've never seen him before in my life."

"While you were entertaining your harem." I smile. I turn my head to watch Zack walk away in the other direction. "Cute, huh?"

"I don't like him," he snaps.

"You don't even know him."

"Well, what does he do for a job?"

"I don't know."

"What do you mean you don't know? This is need-to-know information, Hayden."

"Why are you calling me Hayden all of a sudden? Are you Grumps now?"

"Shut up," he scoffs as we walk along. "Where does he come from?"

"Hawaii."

"Hawaii," he snaps. "Why would he be here? Isn't he on vacation all year round?"

"What is wrong with you?" I frown.

"Nothing." He stomps along, clearly annoyed. "You told me you weren't dating, that's all."

"I never said I wasn't dating; I said I had no interest in sharing body fluids with someone I don't know."

He rolls his eyes. "Don't be crass."

"What?" I huff. "That's the pot calling the kettle black. Every second thing you say is sexual. Your name is Christopher Crass."

"Don't try and be cute," he snaps as he walks in front of me. "Save it for Zack."

"Okay." I walk along. "I will . . . and besides—"

He cuts me off. "Don't talk to me."

I put my hands on my hips. "Are you jealous?"

"No. I'm not fucking jealous. I don't get jealous."

"Whatever." I roll my eyes.

He turns back again. "Does he know that I sleep with you and we spoon in bed?"

I frown. What the fuck is going on here? "Umm . . . for your information, lover boy, you crashed in my bed after you had an orgy with two girls. It wasn't exactly a romantic moment."

"There was no orgy," he barks as he keeps marching along. "There were only two of them."

"Oh." I throw my hands up. "Can you listen to yourself? It's okay for you to sleep with every woman in town. I'm meeting a guy in a club, and you're carrying on like a pork chop."

"I don't care what you do," he snaps.

"Good," I snap back.

We walk home in silence. How did such a wonderful day end with a childish tantrum? He's stomping along like the Hulk.

"You know, you're cute when you're angry," I tease.

"Shut up." He turns back to me like the devil himself. "Walk faster. You need to get ready for your date."

I dig out my razor from a shopping bag and hold it up. "You're right, I do." I smile as I wiggle my eyebrows.

His eyes bulge from their sockets. "You're not sleeping with him, Hayden. Get that out of your head right fucking now. You are staying at fucking one."

"What *is* your problem?" I ask.

"Nothing." He keeps walking.

"You have a harem, Christopher. Why would you care about me?"

"Don't flatter yourself," he snaps. "I don't."

"Okay, fine." We arrive at our hostel and walk up the steps.

"Fine," he says. "Go shave your pussy."

I begin to fume. Is he fucking serious?

"I will."

CHRISTOPHER

I sit at the bar of the hostel. I got ready and came straight down here. Don't want to be anywhere near that annoying woman. I lift a beer to my lips and tip my head back. I mean, if she wants to fuck around . . . then it's on her. But she can't come crying to me when her knight in shining armor turns out to be a cockhead.

I'll be busy.

I see a small person coming through the front doors, and I smile. Here he comes.

"Hey," he says happily.

"Hi."

He puts on an apron.

"How did you go getting your phone fixed?" I ask.

He shrugs as he begins to pick up the glasses and load them into the dishwasher. "I didn't go to the store yet."

"Oh . . ." I watch him for a moment. "I went into one today and asked how much it is going to cost to get it repaired."

"What did they say?"

A man comes and stands at the bar. "One minute," Eduardo says to me. He walks over to the man. "*Was wird es sein?*" (Translation: *What will it be?*)

"Pilsner."

"*Drei Euro.*" He gets a beer and opens it and passes it over.

The guy pays him and walks off. Eduardo comes back to me and begins loading the glasses again.

"How many languages do you speak?" I ask him.

He shrugs. "A few. Only what I pick up in here."

"So anyway, about your phone."

He keeps loading the cups, seemingly uninterested.

"The guy told me that it's too old to get fixed. They can't get the parts."

His eyes flick up. "I knew it." His shoulders slump in defeat.

I slide the box over. "I got you something."

He frowns. His eyes rise to meet mine. "Why?"

"I just"—I shrug—"felt bad that I distracted you and you dropped your phone."

He keeps loading glasses. "You didn't distract me."

I tap the box. "Open it."

"I'm good."

"Open it," I demand.

He exhales heavily and opens the box. A brand-spanking-new iPhone stares back at him.

His mouth falls open, and his eyes flick up.

I smile broadly. "Surprise."

His face falls, and he slams it back at me. "I'm not like that, okay?"

"Like what?" I frown.

What's he talking about?

"Stick your phone up your fucking ass."

"What?" I stand, offended.

He storms past me and out into the kitchen.

What did I do? I thought he'd be excited . . . oh. Then it dawns on me.

He thinks I want favors for it.

Sadness falls over me. This poor fucking kid. What must he see here?

I close my eyes in disgust.

He walks back out and begins slamming the glasses around.

"I don't want anything in return. This isn't a bribe. I was just being nice, that's it. I'm not like that either."

He wipes the bench down so hard that I'm surprised he doesn't break it in half. He walks around to the tables and puts out drink coasters as I watch him.

Fuck.

How can I fix this?

"Okay, if you won't accept it, you can work it off."

His ears prick up, but he still won't look at me.

"I have jobs that I need help with, and I can pay you an hourly rate."

"Like what?"

Fuck . . .

"I need a Spanish translator."

He frowns, his interest piqued.

"I have to find a job, and I need someone . . . to translate for me." I can tell he's interested. "All my roommates need help too. You could help us find jobs or something?" I shrug. I'm totally flying by the seat of my pants here.

"How many roommates?" he asks.

"There are six of us, boys and girls." I hold my two hands up in surrender. "I swear this is not what you think. We just need a translator. That's it, nothing else. We will set an hourly rate, and you can work it off. Completely professional."

He twists his lips, and I can see he's interested in the offer.

"Anyway, think about it." I slide the phone back toward me and put it away. His eyes follow it as I put it back in the bag.

I hear a low whistle from the German table, and I glance up. Hayden has just walked into the bar.

Wearing a skintight black dress that shows every last curve. Her long honey hair is out and full, and she looks fucking delicious. My cock instantly twitches in appreciation as she walks over.

"Don't look at me like that," she whispers.

"Like what?"

"Like I'm your next meal."

My eyes rise to hers. "Maybe you are."

Chapter 9

HAYDEN

We stare at each other. The air crackles between us, and I open my mouth to reply, but for the first time in my life, I'm shocked to silence.

He did not just say that.

"Hayden, meet Eduardo." He gestures to a young teenage boy that I hadn't noticed working behind the bar. I think it's the same one he had a fight over the other night.

I turn, embarrassed. "Hello." I smile.

"Eduardo is going to be our new translator."

I frown as I look between the two of them. Did I hear that right? "I beg your pardon?"

"I broke his phone, so I got a replacement one, but"—he pauses for effect—"he has to work it off," he replies sternly. "So . . . he's going to help our room members out."

I smile, the deal he's made taking shape in my mind. "Okay, that sounds like a great plan. We could really do with the help," I say as I play along.

Eduardo looks between us, seemingly excited. "I'll find you jobs," he says with a strong Spanish accent. "I know a lot of people here in Barcelona." He stammers as if trying to talk me into it.

"That is exciting." I smile. My eyes flick over to Christopher, and he gives me a subtle wink.

"But you can't have the phone until we all have jobs and you have paid it off," Christopher reminds him.

"Okay." He nods. "I'll earn it for positive."

Christopher smirks. "The word is *certain*. 'I'll earn it for certain.'"

Eduardo corrects himself. "I'll earn it for certain."

☿

The music is loud and the club is pumping. "How long . . . ," says Zack.

I screw up my face as I concentrate to hear him. "I'm sorry, what did you say?"

He leans right in close and puts his hand around my waist so that he can talk into my ear. "I said, How long have you been traveling?"

"Oh, only two weeks. Very new at it all. What about you?"

"This is my eighth month."

"Wow." I smile, then glance over to see Christopher, glaring at me from the bar . . . like he has been all night.

I thought we were friends?

Every time I turn around, I see his furious face. I'm over it.

I glare right back. Honestly, I don't have time for his childish tantrum. He slept with two women last night and then has the audacity to be pissed with me for talking to a man.

What a joke.

I will not be manipulated like this. He needs to grow the fuck up.

"I'm just going to the bathroom," Zack says.

"Okay."

He walks off, and I sip my drink.

"I'd like a word," Christopher growls.

"No."

He screws up his face. "What do you mean, no?"

"N-O." I spell it out for him.

"Listen," he spits through gritted teeth.

"No. You listen," I yell. "Do not insult my intelligence by acting jealous when we both know you have no intention of pursuing me."

His eyes nearly bulge from their sockets. "Outside. Now."

"Fine." I storm toward the door. I'm angry.

How dare he?

We burst through the front doors of the club and out onto the street.

"What is your problem? Every time I turn around, I am copping a dirty look from you."

"I don't trust him."

"You don't even know him," I spit.

"I know his type. I've been analyzing him all night."

"Ha." I explode. "And what type is that, Christopher? A man who wants women only for sex? Well, I've got news for you, mister. It takes one to spot one." I step forward and poke him hard in the chest. "If you want to analyze something, why don't you work out why it is that you have such low expectations."

"I do not have low expectations of women," he yells back. "Your expectations of men are way too high."

"Who said anything about women?" I yell. "You have low expectations of yourself."

"That's fucking ridiculous!"

"It's true." I throw my hands up in disgust. "That's why you give your body away so easily. You don't hold value in yourself."

"Fuck off."

"How can you not see it?"

"See what?"

"That deep down you think that nobody could possibly love you for you."

His face falls.

"Why is that?" I ask softly. "Because it doesn't make any sense to me."

His eyes search mine, and I know that I've hit a nerve.

"Why do you think that hard and fast is safe? When are you going to stop hiding from yourself? You're an adult. Grow up."

He screws his face up in disgust. "You have no fucking idea what you're talking about."

"I can't help you with this, Christopher. You want to fuck around, that's great. Go do it. But don't cry 'poor me' when people who care about you meet someone worthy."

"Big fucking deal. I like a good time. There is nothing wrong with me," he spits.

"Keep telling yourself that."

"You know what . . . fuck this." He turns and walks off into the darkness.

"You can't heal the wound until you find the sore, Christopher," I call after him.

"Go fuck him. I don't even care," he calls back.

I watch him walk into the darkness alone, and my shoulders slump. I take a long shaky inhale. Damn it.

How did that spiral so badly out of control?

I drag myself back inside and walk back to Zack. "Sorry," I apologize. "I had to take a call."

"That's okay. The night is young." He leans in and kisses my cheek, and I fake a smile.

I imagine Christopher walking home alone, and I feel like shit.

A real friend would have gone with him.

It's 2:00 a.m. when I get back to the room.

With Christopher weighing heavily on my mind all night, things didn't go to plan with Zach. The hostel is deserted, with everyone still out partying. I get my things out of my locker and take a long hot shower, dress in my pajamas, and walk into my room.

I flick the light on and see that Christopher is curled up in bed with his back to me. I quickly flick the light back off and climb in behind him. I snuggle up to his back and kiss his shoulder from behind.

"Don't," he murmurs.

I smile against his back.

"I'm not talking to you," he mumbles.

"Good, because I'm going to sleep."

"You showered?"

"Because I wanted a shower, not because I had sex."

He stays silent, and I hug him tighter.

"Good night," I whisper.

He doesn't answer me.

"Are you going to say good night?" I ask.

"Keep talking, and I'm kicking you out of bed."

I smile into the darkness.

With his warm body and heavenly scent surrounding me, I drift into wonderland.

Bang, crash, boom!

"Sorry." Bernadette laughs. She's tripped over someone's shoes.

Basil walks headfirst into the bunk bed and bounces onto the floor. The room is in a fit of giggles. Everyone has just arrived home, and they are rolling blind drunk.

Christopher's arm is around me from behind, our bodies spooned up against each other.

"Hey." Bernadette gasps loudly. "No hanky-panky between roommates, remember?"

"Go to bed, Bernadette," Christopher snaps impatiently.

Basil goes to climb the ladder into his bed and falls spectacularly on the floor to the sound of everyone hysterically laughing.

Bodie tries to shush everyone. "Shh."

I open my sleepy eyes to see that it's daylight. "What time is it?"

Christopher picks up his phone. "Nine a.m."

"Where have you guys been all night?" I frown.

"Beach party."

"I fucked in the ocean," Bodie slurs.

"With a sea monster," Basil adds. They all burst out laughing again.

I focus enough to realize I have something hard in my back, and I frown.

"Dick. Out. Of. Back," I grumble. "Now."

"Sorry." Christopher moves back from me. "It's morning."

We lie for a while. "I'm hungry," I say. "If we don't eat now, we will miss the free breakfast."

"Hmm." Christopher moans.

"Come on." I get out of bed and put my hair up. I walk out the door to get my clothes from my locker, and Eduardo is standing patiently in the corridor.

He smiles. "Hello."

"Hi." I frown. "What . . ." I look around. "What are you doing here?"

"I'm here to help Mr. Christo."

"Oh." I smile. My god, he's so cute. "I'll get him. Wait here."

I walk back in the room and drop to my knees on the bed. "You have a little friend waiting out there for you."

Christopher frowns. "Huh?"

"Eduardo is out there waiting to help Mr. Christo."

He screws up his face. "He is not."

"He is. Get up."

Christopher climbs out of bed and walks into the corridor. His hair is all disheveled, and he's wearing only boxer shorts. "Hey, buddy." He frowns. "What's going on?"

"I'm here to help you," Eduardo replies eagerly. "What would you like me to do today?"

I smile as I watch. Cuteness overload.

"Oh," Christopher replies as he scratches his head. "Umm . . . okay." He looks over to me as if confused what to say next.

"Why don't you give us ten minutes to get ready, and then we can talk about it?" I reply.

"All right."

"Meet you in the restaurant?" I ask him.

He nods and happily trots off.

Christopher watches him disappear. "I've got no fucking jobs for this kid to do," he whispers.

"Then you better make some up."

An hour later, we walk down the street, in search of coffee.

Just the three of us.

"So we go to San Sebastián tomorrow until Thursday," Christopher tells Eduardo. "We will be back then for four days. It would be great if you could try and find us a job for weekends. I mean, no pressure or anything."

"Okay." He listens intently as he walks along. "Can you do waiter?"

"No," I interrupt. "He's a terrible waiter."

Christopher rolls his eyes. "Admitted, I'm not a great waiter."

The boy smiles.

"And Hayden," Christopher says.

"Hayz . . ." Eduardo frowns as he tries to say it. "Hayzzz."

"Call me Hazy. Everyone does at home," I tell him.

"Lazy Hazy," Christopher replies. "Sounds about right."

"Shut up." I sigh.

"She needs a job, like . . . fishing or something," Christopher continues.

I giggle. "No fish."

The boy smiles too. "Call me Eddie."

"All right, that's easier."

We get to a café, and Christopher hands him some money. "Can you go and get two cappuccinos, please, and one hot chocolate."

Eddie nods and takes the money and walks inside. Christopher smirks as he watches him.

"Are we going to talk about last night?" I ask him.

"Nope," he replies, his eyes still fixed on Eddie.

"I mean, I had some very good points."

"That we are not discussing. Drop it."

"I didn't even kiss him."

"Don't care."

"Really . . . don't care even a little bit?"

"Shut up, Grumps."

I smile. He called me Grumps. I know that I'm forgiven.

Eduardo returns with a tray, and he passes it over. Christopher takes out the hot chocolate and passes it back to him. "For you."

Eddie's face falls, and he looks up at Christopher as if he has just given him a sports car.

My heart constricts in my chest . . . *oh*.

"But I . . . ," he stammers. "I've never . . ."

"Drink it," Christopher orders. "Be careful, it's hot."

We turn and walk back to the hostel, and I'm filled with emotion at the look on Eddie's face. He's so proud to be drinking his hot chocolate.

I can't make eye contact with Christopher, or I may just burst into tears.

I know he's a player and he's not the kind of guy that would ever fall for me or vice versa, but maybe there's more to him underneath the surface than I initially thought.

Maybe he's the kind of person that could actually help me loosen up.

No . . . he's a heartbreak waiting to happen.

Forget it.

I watch Christopher watch Eddie as he smiles proudly with his hot chocolate, and my heart somersaults in my chest.

Out of all the things that I've done on this trip, or perhaps even ever, being here for Eddie's first hot chocolate tops the list.

X

The wheels on the bus go round and round. We are en route to San Sebastián in a tour bus.

"It says here"—Christopher reads from his travel brochure—"that Basque, also known as Euskara, is one of the most fascinating languages in the world, an isolate."

"What's an isolate?" I reply as I look out the bus window. This man has an odd thirst for information; he reads everything.

"Meaning it has no relation to any other language in existence." He raises his eyebrows, impressed. "And while its origins are unknown, most scientists believe that it's the last preinvasion language in Europe." He looks over at me. "Hmm . . . fascinating, isn't it?"

"Uh-huh." I look back out the window.

He thinks out loud. "So that means it's literally spoken prehistory . . ."

I look back over at him.

"What?" he asks.

"You're odd."

"You don't find that interesting?"

"I do."

"So how am I odd?"

"'Literally spoken prehistory . . .'" I widen my eyes at him. "What does that even mean?"

He exhales heavily with a subtle shake of his head. "If you don't know, then I'm not telling you."

I go back to my dumbass scenery watching. "Can we have french fries for dinner?"

He glances over at me. "And I'm the odd one?"

"I've got a hankering." I picture my delicious meal tonight. "With a hamburger."

"Yes! Hamburgers," Basil calls from the seat behind. "I'm down."

"Did you know that it drops to five degrees Celsius in winter in San Sebastián?" Christopher replies.

More facts.

I cross my arms and snuggle down on his shoulder for a sleep. "I do now."

142

There's a reason people talk about San Sebastián in Spain.

It's vibrant, colorful, and one of *the* most beautiful places I have ever been to.

Set on the coast, it has it all. Today we browsed the township, visited the Sacred Heart giant statue of Jesus on Monte Urgull. We went swimming at the beach this afternoon, and now it's early evening. We are looking for somewhere to have dinner.

"Here?" Kimberly asks. We all peer into the packed pub.

"Looks popular." Bodie shrugs. "This will do." They all walk in, and I notice Christopher's shoulders slump.

"Can we get a table for six, please?" Kimberly asks.

"Sure." The waitress smiles. "This way." We follow her through the crowded restaurant and take a seat in the courtyard.

"What's wrong?" I whisper to Christopher as we walk along behind her.

"Nothing." He puts his arm around my waist and follows me through.

"You look like something is wrong."

"I'm just so sick of shit food," he whispers as we get to the table.

"Oh." I frown. I thought we'd been eating amazingly for our budget.

He pulls out my chair, and I sit down. We order drinks and look through the menu.

"What are you having?" I ask everyone.

They all discuss the choices and chat away, and I glance over to see Christopher staring at the menu, deflated.

"You don't like any of this?" I ask.

He forces a smile. "It's good. Don't worry." He taps me on the thigh with his big hand as if to reassure me.

He always goes with the flow. He's never once picked where we go. "What would you eat if you could eat anything in the world?" I ask him softly so that the others can't hear.

His eyes stay fixed on the menu. "I would have bluefin tuna sashimi with daikon and ginger for entrée. Beluga caviar with lobster and sage butter sauce."

I frown.

"Followed by a glass of Macallan scotch and White Truffle Bliss for dessert."

"Oh . . ." I stare at the menu. I've never had any of those meals. "That's weird food."

He gives me a sad smile. "Is it?"

"Uh-huh . . ." I keep looking through the menu. "Maybe you should put anchovies on the pizza if you want to feel exotic?"

He gives me a broad, beautiful smile and picks up my hand as it sits on the table and squeezes it in his. "Maybe." He watches me for a moment. "What kind of food do you eat at home?"

I shrug. "I never really eat out."

"Why not?"

"I live alone." I shrug again. "I don't know. I like cooking, I guess."

"What kind of things do you cook?" he asks.

"Lots of things." I smile over at him as he listens intently. "I'm pretty good, actually. When we get home, you'll have to come and visit me one day, and I'll cook for you."

His eyes hold mine. "I'd like that."

"What will it be, sir?" the waitress asks him.

"I'll have the sierra pizza with anchovies," he replies. He glances over and gives me a sexy wink.

"Mr. Exotic," I mouth.

He chuckles as he speaks to the waitress. "What scotch do you have?" he asks her.

144

"House scotch."

He winces. "Okay, I'll have a glass of red wine."

※

I laugh out loud as I am spun around. It's our last night in San Sebastián, and we are celebrating in style.

We have sunned, swum, and laughed our way through the week. Sightseeing through the day and dancing the night away until we drop into an unconscious sleep in the early hours of the morning. If this is what the next twelve months look like, then sign me up. I've never had so much fun.

The new friends I've met are hilarious, and weirdly, it feels like a little family already. We all do our own thing but always look out for each other and end up safely back in the same room at the end of each night.

Rod Stewart's song "Da Ya Think I'm Sexy" blares through the speakers, and Christopher spins me out and then pulls my body back to his as we dance. My stomach hurts from laughing.

This man . . . this beautiful man.

He's funny and smart and weirdly obsessed with factual literature. We've spent the whole week together . . . it's been perfect.

If the truth be told, I'm quite enamored of him. Not that I will ever admit it.

He isn't the kind of man I could let myself fall for. I already know how it would end.

I would lose my friend, one that I've become very attached to.

I see the women he looks at and talks to. They're the complete opposite of me. He likes thin; I'm curvy. He likes supermodel high-maintenance types. I'm simple. He likes flirty and fun, and I'm

145

quiet and shy. He likes promiscuous, and I haven't had sex in a really long time.

Too long.

Wherever he is, he's the center of attention. Everyone wants to be with him, and yet here's me, wanting to blend in with the walls.

Chalk and cheese.

We couldn't be more different.

The reality of it sucks, because we have this weird unstated connection. We're touchy with each other and always end up at the back of the pack, talking between the two of us.

He cuddles my back in bed, and I rely on him more than I should.

But I know that would all come crashing to an end if something ever happened between us. I would instantly become one of the groupies he fucks and not his treasured friend.

I couldn't hold a man like Christopher Miles—not for long, anyway.

And while I silently dream of what it would be like to be with someone like him . . . I know I can't even entertain the idea.

I'm still not over my last heartbreak, and it's been two years. If it happens again, I know I'll be a spinster for life. I came on this trip to get over heartbreak, not start a new one. But Christopher is my friend. I know I can trust him to be just that.

He spins me again, and I laugh out loud.

"Let's go swimming." He smiles.

"Now?" I gasp. "It's three o'clock in the morning."

"Uh-huh."

"What about sharks?"

"Sharks are the least of your worries," he replies as he pulls me out of the bar by the hand.

Five minutes later we are on the beach, and he takes his shirt off over his head and strips down to his boxers.

Oh crap . . .

He wades out into the darkened water and turns back toward me. "Come on, Grumps." He splashes the water up at me. "The water's beautiful."

"I don't have a swimsuit."

"So?"

I look up and down the beach. There are people everywhere.

"Stop being so uptight."

He's right. I am too uptight, and I want to change that about myself. I don't like being like this.

Oh god . . .

I wade into the water, desperately wanting to go in.

"Come on," he calls. "I want you to come swimming with me, that's all."

That's all.

Right . . . I can do this.

Fuck . . .

"Turn around," I call.

"What?" He laughs. "I've seen you in your underwear a million times."

"Just turn around."

He turns and faces out to sea, and I grab the hem of my dress and lift it over my head. I look down at myself. I have a black matching bra-and-panties set on.

Thank fucking god.

I wade into the water as I look around. "If I get eaten by a shark," I call.

"I'll save you." He swims toward me.

"You're supposed to be looking the other way," I call.

"Da na . . . da na . . . da na . . ." He begins to sing the *Jaws* music as he swims toward me.

"Stop it," I cry.

He picks me up and hurls me into the air, and I land in the water and go under deep. "Ahh," I cry as I come up. "You idiot." I look around in a panic. "You're waking up the sharks."

He picks me up again and hurls us both into the water with his arms tightly around me.

We surface, still arm in arm.

The air between us changes, and he stares down at me. Body to body, alone in the darkness.

His brow furrows as if confused as we stare at each other. In slow motion he lifts his thumb and dusts it over my bottom lip.

"Kiss me," he whispers.

I want to.

"Chris . . ."

"I just . . ." He takes my face in his hands as he stares down at me. Our bodies are so close I can feel his erection as it grows up against my stomach.

"We can't," I murmur.

"Why not?"

"Because I value what we have."

"It won't change a thing."

"It will change *everything*."

He stares at me, his chest rising and falling in the darkness. "Why?"

"Because I will end up with a broken heart, and you will end up feeling like shit about it."

He stares at me, and I know that he knows that I'm right.

"You don't want something permanent, and I don't want something casual." I smile up at him as I cup his face in my hand. "But that's okay . . ." I pull him into a hug. "I like what we have already."

"Blue balls?"

I giggle. "Go find someone else to take care of your balls."

"Or I could just drown you for knocking me back." He grabs for me, and I squeal as I try to get away from him. He picks me up and throws me high into the air again. "Come and get her, sharks," he yells. "Teach her a lesson."

I laugh out loud as I cough and splutter.

He swims to me and takes my hands in his as we stand facing each other. "Promise me something," he says.

"Okay."

"In ten years, on this day, no matter where we are in the world, no matter who we are married to, we will meet on this beach at this time and take a swim together in the dark."

My eyes well with tears, because damn it, that's romantic for a goodbye.

"I promise."

He pulls me into a hug, and we stand in the water in each other's arms.

Regretful but grateful for the honesty between us.

I smile as a thought comes to me. "My husband won't like you, though."

He laughs out loud and throws me into the air again. "That's 'cause I'm going to steal you off him."

Chapter 10

We walk up the stairs to our hostel in Barcelona. "I fucking love that place," Bodie sighs.

"Me too," everyone chimes in. San Sebastián was incredible. We had the time of our lives, but now we're back to reality. Well, not really. We are still backpacking in Spain, but what I mean is we've returned to work over the weekend before we take off again on Monday.

It's Friday night, and once again, we are heading out. The party is never ending: always somewhere to go and something to see.

We go back to our room and get ready for the night and go down to the bar to see Eduardo.

"Hey." Christopher smiles.

"Hi there," says Basil.

"Hello, Mr. Basil, Mr. Christo." Eddie smiles excitedly. "I did good."

I slide into my chair. "Hello."

"Hello, Hazen."

I smile at his inability to say my name. So freaking cute.

"I got you all jobs." He smiles proudly.

"You did?" Christopher laughs. "I knew you would."

Someone stands at the other end of the bar, and he takes off down there to serve them. We watch him drift in and out of languages as he serves different people.

"He's so intelligent," Christopher says as he watches him. "He could be an accountant for the mob or some shit."

"I don't doubt it," Basil agrees.

I get the giggles as I imagine Eduardo working as an accountant for the mob.

He finally comes back to us. "Miss Hazen, you work in a hotel." He slides me over a card with the address and time I start tomorrow. A split shift, morning and night.

"Eddie, really?" I smile as I stare at the card. "Thank you so much."

"Mr. Basil, you work on a boat."

Basil takes the card from Eddie and stares at it. "A boat?"

"Yes, yes. Very good job."

He slides a brochure over the counter to Christopher, and we all frown as we stare at it. There are pictures of slippery slides and fake mountains on it. "What's this?" Christopher asks.

"You working at the fun park," Eddie replies.

"The what?"

"The fun park, with all the children."

Christopher screws up his face in disgust. "I fucking hate kids, man . . . blah." He fakes a shiver.

I look at him deadpan. "Aren't you a teacher?"

"Yes." He rolls his lips. "Yes, I am."

Basil studies the brochure intently. "Glad I'm on the boat."

I smile as I imagine Basil on a boat in the sun all day. "So this is the time I start?" I ask Eddie as I point to a time written down on the back of the card.

"Yes." He turns to Christopher. "You have twelve-hour shift tomorrow. You start at eleven."

"Twelve hours?" Christopher gasps. "Isn't that illegal?"

"You're lazy," Eddie replies as he wipes the bar.

"I am *not* lazy . . . twelve hours is just a very long time."

Another person walks up to the bar, and Eddie serves them, once again drifting in and out of languages.

Christopher stares at the brochure in front of him. "What the hell would I be doing here for twelve hours straight?"

I shrug. "I don't know. Maybe you're in the gift shop or something?"

He nods as he thinks about it. "That would be okay, I guess. Sitting down in the air-conditioning for twelve hours, I could totally do that."

Kimberly bounces in. "Come on, Hazy."

"Where are we going?" I ask her.

"Bernadette is meeting some guy, and we're her wingmen." She pulls me out of the chair. "Catch you boys later?" she says as she pulls me from the bar.

"Bye," the boys call.

X

It's 3:00 a.m. when the girls and I are walking home. Turns out Bernadette's new friends from Sweden are funny as all hell. It was a great night.

"Hey, you," Kimberly calls to a group of guys walking in the opposite direction across the street. I glance up to see Basil and Bodie talking and laughing with a group of men I haven't seen before.

Christopher is in the middle of the group. He has a girl sitting up on his shoulders as they walk along.

She's wearing light-blue skimpy denim shorts and a tiny black bralette top. She has a baseball cap on and two long dark braids in her hair. She's gorgeous and sitting on his shoulders with her legs spread around his head like the queen of fucking Sheba. His two big hands are on her calves as he holds her tight.

My stomach twists at the sight. He's taken a visible step back from me this week since we nearly kissed in the ocean . . . and I hate it.

I've kicked myself a million times over. I wish I'd gone there.

I should have kissed him.

I wish I'd thrown caution to the wind and done it. He's backed away from me anyway now, so what was the point?

Christopher glances up and sees me. He smiles broadly and waves, without a care in the world.

I smile and wave back.

He keeps walking to wherever they are walking to. The girl on his shoulders says something, and they all break into loud laughter again. Deflation fills me.

What did she say that was so funny?

I watch them walk up and disappear around the corner. I wonder where they're going at this hour.

And that's that . . . the line in the sand, drawn in IMAX definition. Now I know for certain that he really didn't care. I was just the closest warm body at the time.

He was horny.

And while I wish we'd gone there, I'm kind of glad we didn't.

※

I lie in the darkness and stare across the room at Christopher's empty bed.

The vision of him with that girl on his shoulders runs through my mind.

I dodged a bullet. I should feel grateful. He's my friend, nothing more and nothing less, and I shouldn't be annoyed in the slightest.

Fuck knows why I am.

Tomorrow's a new day, and I'm going to make more of an effort to meet new people . . . specifically men.

My eyes roam over the empty bed, and I exhale heavily as a nervous swirl dances in my stomach. I just feel better when he's home.

I glance at my watch. Five a.m.

Where is he?

CHRISTOPHER

I wake to the sound of seagulls fighting, and I frown as I lean up onto my elbows.

Where the fuck am I?

I try to focus my eyes as I look around. The beach is full of power walkers doing their morning exercise.

What fucking time is it?

I shuffle around in my pockets and find my phone: 7:22 a.m.

Shit.

Hayden had to be at work by eight. I was going to walk her to work. I stand and look at the people sleeping on the sand around me. There must be at least ten of them.

What a crazy night.

Then I remember. Oh no . . . I have to work a twelve-hour shift in the gift shop today. I'm as seedy as fuck. What was I thinking, even going out?

One minute we were having harmless shots of tequila; next minute I'm waking up on a beach.

I begin to walk off the beach. "Where are you going?" a girl asks.

My eyes roam over her as she lies on the sand. A vague memory of her sitting on my shoulders floats through my mind. Hmm . . . *did that happen?*

"Home. Bye."

I dial Hayden's number as I begin to walk. No answer.

"Fuck."

I walk faster. I call her again.

No answer.

I hurry as fast as I can back to the hostel, and just as I approach it, she comes down the front steps.

"Grumps," I call.

Her face falls when she sees me. "Hi." She turns and begins to walk up the street, and I jog to catch up with her.

"I'll walk you to work."

"No need," she replies. "I'm fine."

"I came back to—"

She cuts me off. "I'm fine, Christopher."

"What's up your ass?" I frown.

"Nothing," she snaps as she walks faster.

I nearly have to run to catch up with her. "You really are living up to your name today."

Her eyes nearly bulge from their sockets. "Go home . . . or back under the rock you just crawled out of."

I frown. What?

She's pissed at me.

We walk in silence for a while, her rushing and me half running to keep up with her. "Did something happen?" I ask her. "Have you had a blowup with one of the girls or something?"

"Oh my god . . ." She rolls her eyes. "Please go away. I am not in the mood for your player crap today."

I stop on the spot. Huh?

Player crap . . .

The fuck is she talking about now?

A bus pulls up, and she climbs aboard. The doors shut in my face, and I watch it pull away.

Well, that was weird.

She really *is* fucking grumpy today. I turn and walk back to the hostel and into the room. Everyone is still half-asleep.

"Hey." I flop down onto my bed.

"What the hell happened to you last night?" Bernadette asks.

"Too many things." I sigh. I look over at her. "Is Hayden okay?"

"Yeah, why?"

"She's in the worst mood of all time."

"No, she isn't." She shrugs. "Why do you say that?"

"She just seemed pissed at me, that's all."

"Oh." She thinks for a moment. "Probably because of the girl you were with last night."

"I wasn't with a girl last night."

"Yes, you were. We saw you."

Horror dawns.

"I was with a girl . . . in front of Hayden?"

"Uh-huh. You walked down the street with her on your shoulders."

"Oh . . ." I think for a moment. "But Hayden doesn't like me like that."

Bernadette raises an eyebrow. "Are you sure about that?"

"I mean . . ." I frown as I contemplate the answer. "Pretty sure."

"Men are so stupid."

"What does that mean?"

"Nothing."

"You're all over her all the time, man," Basil says with his eyes still shut.

"Because we're friends," I splutter in my defense. "She's not into me like that."

Bernadette rolls her eyes and drags the pillow over her head. "This is why there's no hanky-panky with roommates, you fucking idiot."

"I'm not getting any hanky-panky," I snap.

"Spooning is hanky-panky."

I begin to hear my heartbeat in my ears, and I stand in outrage. I don't have to lie here and take this. "In what universe is spooning hanky-panky?"

"All universes," Bernadette snaps.

"Women are fucking crazy." I march out the door and then remember a very important piece of information. I put my head back around the corner. "Trust me, hanky-panky with me feels a lot better than fucking spooning." I storm into the bathroom. I can't sleep until I have a shower, so this suits me just fine.

I wash my body with vigor as I mutter to myself.

"She's the one who didn't want to kiss me . . . not the other way around. So don't cry when you see me with someone else."

Ugh, I'm infuriated.

"What does she fucking expect?" I scrub my skin until it's nearly raw. "I need sex; she doesn't. What does she want . . . me to be a fucking priest now?" I keep scrubbing. "And I didn't even sleep with that girl anyway, for fuck's sake . . . but if I did, who cares? Not me, that's for sure." I wash my hair. "I should march back to the beach and give it to that girl right there on the sand to prove a point."

I keep washing myself.

"Hayden fucking Whitmore . . . the nun. How dare she be angry with me for being fucking normal." The more I think about this, the more infuriated I get.

I get out of the shower and wrap my towel around my waist while I shave. I can't believe I have to go to a fucking fun park gift shop today for twelve hours.

I squeeze the tube of toothpaste, and it gets stuck so I squeeze harder, and it spurts out and goes everywhere.

"Fuck's sake," I bark. "I don't have time for this shit today." I grab some paper towels and wipe up the mess. I pull on my clothes and walk out of the bathroom to see Eduardo standing by my bedroom door.

His face lights up when he sees me. "Hello, Mr. Christo."

"Hello." I force a smile.

"I came to see what you need of me today."

"Nothing, buddy." I tap him on the shoulder. "Go home."

His face falls. "I was . . ." He stops himself and twists his fingers together as if nervous.

"What is it?"

"Could I please look at the phone for a minute? Just . . . quickly?"

"Oh . . ." I shrug. "Yeah, sure. Come in." I open my bedroom door, and he looks around at everyone sleeping. I go to the drawer underneath my bed and take the phone out. It's still in its box, and I pass it over to him.

He studies the box and turns it over and looks at the bottom of it.

"Sit down, buddy," I say. "Take it out of the box and play with it. I'm going to try and have a quick sleep. I don't start until eleven. That's Hazy's bed there. Sit against it if you want."

He smiles and slumps down onto the floor. He excitedly opens the box and begins to look at everything in great detail.

I lie in bed and smile to myself as I watch him. This kid is the coolest thing in Spain.

✕

A whispered voice wakes me. "Mr. Christo."

I frown as I stir.

"Mr. Christo," it whispers again. "You have to go to work, sir."

"Huh?" I wake with a jump. Eduardo is leaning over me.

"What time is it?" I sit up in a rush.

"Ten o'clock."

"Oh." I rub my eyes. "Feels like I only closed my eyes for a second." I slowly get up and look around and frown. Everyone is still asleep.

The room is spotless.

Clothes are folded into neat piles, everyone's shoes are lined up, and Hayden's bed is made. The water bottles are all filled and placed in a neat row by the sink. The phone is back in its box and set carefully on the end of my bed.

"Did you do this?" I ask him as I look around.

He smiles proudly, and I smile too.

"Good job, buddy."

A little voice from deep inside says, *He probably stole shit* . . . No, I won't think like that. Just because he has less than me doesn't mean he is less than me.

I'm trusting my gut with him. It tells me he's a good kid.

"I have to get ready." I walk out to my locker, and he follows me. I take my backpack out and begin to go through it. "What will I wear?" I ask him.

"Clothes."

"No shit, Sherlock," I mutter. "What are you doing now?" I ask him.

"I'll hang around until I start at four."

I glance up at him. "You won't go home in between?"

"No."

"What does your grandma say about you being out so much?"

He shrugs. "She's busy."

160

"Hmm, okay."

Poor fucking kid . . .

"I can do your washing if you want while you work?" he offers.

I smile. He's trying to get his phone as quickly as he can. "Okay, that would be great." I take out the plastic bag with my dirty clothes from San Sebastián in it and pass it over to him. "Thank you."

"Miss Hazen have washing? I'll do hers too."

I consider it and then wince. "Women have weird stuff in their dirty washing . . . best to ask her for permission to do that."

He nods.

I throw on my clothes and brush my hair. "Wish me luck." I smile.

"Good luck."

"Thanks for getting me this job." I mess up his hair, and he swats my hand away.

"Don't get fired," he says casually.

"Ha . . . me, get fired? They'll love me."

※

Half an hour later I walk into the reception area of the fun park. "Hello, I'm starting work here today. I was told to be here at eleven."

The bored guy on the front desk looks me up and down. "Just a minute." He gets on the radio and then says something in Spanish. Someone says something back to him, and he laughs and hangs up. "Have a seat. Someone will be right out."

I sit down in the lounge area and look around. This looks all right, actually.

A lady comes walking out. She's older and tough looking. A take-no-shit kind of woman. "Hello. You must be Christo?"

"Yes." I smile and stand. I hold my hand out to shake hers, and she frowns at it.

Oh . . . I tuck it away. "I'm Christo."

"Hello, Christo," she says in a sarcastic voice. "This way." She walks off and through a double set of doors.

I roll my lips. I don't like her already. I follow her out into the park. The sounds of kids' screams as they come down the waterslides are deafening. There are rides and roller coasters and animals and a million fucking people. Balloons and food stalls. Flashing lights and bells sounding.

Everything is magnified in IMAX.

Ugh . . . this place is my worst nightmare. I hope the gift shop is soundproof.

We walk into a building and down a series of corridors until we get to a locker room.

"Okay, you're Binky Bear." She slides a coat hanger along a wire rope that hangs from the ceiling. A huge bear costume is dangling from it.

"Excuse me?" I frown. "I don't understand."

"You put it on."

"What do you mean?" I frown.

She widens her eyes and taps the huge bear head. "You're Binky Bear. Put the costume on and get out there."

"And do what? Shit in the woods?" I gasp. "I have no idea what fucking bears do."

"Walk around and play with the kids."

"I am not qualified to do this," I scoff.

"You want the job or not?" she snaps.

No . . . no, I don't.

"Put the damn suit on and walk around the park."

"And then what?"

"Then you have a break, and then you get dressed into this." She pulls another coat hanger along the ceiling. A huge disgusting costume comes into view.

"You wear the brown tights and the brown stocking over your head, with the costume as a dress."

"I am not dressing up like a piece of vomit," I snap.

"It's pizza," she corrects me.

"And I draw the line at a stocking over my head. It's not happening. No way in hell. I'm not a fucking cat burglar."

She exhales heavily. "All right, princess."

I narrow my eyes at this tyrant. "I am *not* a princess."

"That's right," she replies as she shoves the giant bear head into my arms. "You are Binky Bear and Pete Pizza." She walks toward the door. "Hurry up. Get out there." She leaves, and the door bangs behind her.

I look at the stupid huge head, and I drop-kick it hard against the wall. "I hate this prick of a job." I call Eduardo.

"Hello?" he answers.

"Eddie, I am not in the gift shop. I have to dress up like a motherfucking bear."

"Oh . . ." He falls silent. "Um . . . what will I do?"

What am I doing . . . this isn't his fault.

"Nothing," I snap. "I just want you to know how messed up this shit is, but it will be fine. Goodbye." I hang up in a rush.

I scratch my head and sit for a while as I stare at the suit. Damn it . . . what do I do now?

Eddie got me this job. I can't fuck it up.

I unzip the suit and peer in. "Ew, has this ever been washed?" I inhale and wince. "Oh no . . . it smells like ass." I feel the blood begin to drain out of my face.

I can't do this.

The doors burst open, and the tyrant comes marching back in. "That a boy."

I glare at her. "What are you doing?"

"I've come to help you get into the costume."

"This isn't sanitary," I mutter as I step into the bottom. "I need a rabies shot."

She exhales heavily and turns me away from her and zips up the bottom.

The suit is huge, and I slip my arms into the big goofy paws. "This bear is fucking ugly," I grunt.

"I know."

"If I was a child, this would traumatize me."

"Yep." She pulls it up over my shoulders and zips up the top.

"In fact, I'm traumatized as an adult," I continue.

She lifts the huge head and puts it on. My vision is suddenly a tunnel, and I feel like I can't breathe. "It's fucking hot in here," I yell as the walls begin to close in on me.

"You'll get used to it," she says calmly.

"Get used to it?" I gasp. "Nobody could get used to this."

She grabs my hand and leads me out. "You'll have someone with you for a while until you acclimatize to the suit." The feet are huge, and I feel like I am walking in huge skis or Moon Boots or something.

"It fucking stinks in here," I yell.

"I know."

"If you know, why don't you wash the fucking thing?" I call. "Stop being so lazy."

"Listen," she growls. "Just walk around the park, and keep your dramatics to a minimum."

"My dramatics are well warranted," I yell.

I walk out into the blazing sun, and I begin to sweat.

Oh no . . .

It's hot . . . hotter than hot. Butter-melting-on-a-hot-plate hot.

She introduces someone, although I can hardly see him. "This is Diego." I think it's a teenage boy.

He takes my big goofy paw. "This way." He leads me along.

Kids start to scream. I can hardly see what's going on out there. I stumble and fall and land on my hands and knees. "What the hell are you doing, Diego?" I yell.

"Oops, sorry," he says as he helps me up.

Kids are screaming and yelling and clamoring around me. Where are the parents?

I hear a phone ring, and Diego drops my hand. "Just a minute," he says.

"What do you mean, just a minute?" Kids bunch around me, yelling and trying to hug my legs. I subtly push them off me. "Don't," I tell them. "Calm down."

Through my tunnel vision, I see Diego talking on the phone, totally distracted.

"Get off the phone," I snap.

He rolls his eyes and turns his back to me.

Fucker.

I feel a swift kick to my shin, and I look down to see a boy. He's about six. "Watch it," I warn him.

He kicks me again, and I gently push him away.

A million kids swarm around me, and I've come to the conclusion that this suit is hotter than Satan's asshole.

I'm dripping with perspiration. There's no air in this thing. I can't breathe.

Help.

I look back over to Diego. What is that fucker doing?

I feel something being wedged up my ass. "Ahh." I turn around to see that same kid who was kicking me before. "Fuck off, kid," I yell. I push him hard, and he goes flying back.

He stands, infuriated. Then he charges me. I push him back. "Diego," I yell.

Diego is still facing the other way, and he holds his hand up in a *coming* signal.

The kid pushes me again, and I stumble back but catch myself. He comes at me again and kicks me up the ass, and I snap. I grab him around the throat with my paws. "Leave me alone," I growl. "Diego," I cry. "We have a situation."

Another kid jumps on my back and starts punching the bear head, and then another one and another one, and I stagger around with ten kids on each leg. "Get off me, you fuckers," I cry with my hands around the first kid's neck. He escapes and punches me right in the balls, and I snap.

I rip the bear head off. "Diego. Get off the fucking phone," I yell.

The kids all scream and run for cover.

"You!" I scream to the devil child. "Where is your mother?"

I hear a voice. "You're fired." I turn to see the tyrant, hands on hips, looking furious.

"You can't fire me, because I quit," I yell. I drop-kick the bear head into the crowd, and the kids all scream. "And I pissed in your suit," I yell.

Not really . . . but in hindsight I should have.

I storm over to Diego and snatch his phone. "Get me out of this suit before I strangle you!"

HAYDEN

"You did great today, Hayden." Maria, my new boss, smiles. "See you tomorrow?"

"Thanks." I smile. "I had a great first day." And I did too. This job is a dream.

I walk out the front doors and into the street, and I see a man standing on the sidewalk in the shadows, and my step falters. It's midnight, not the time when people are just standing around.

I hear a familiar voice. "It's me, Grumps."

"Christopher." I frown. "What are you doing here?" I ask.

"I came to walk you home."

"That wasn't necessary."

He holds something out for me.

"What's this?"

"I brought your cardigan. It's cool."

Oh.

Chapter 11

"I mean"—he pauses as if feeling stupid—"I just thought . . . I thought you might be cold on the walk home."

I stare at the cardigan in his outstretched hand.

So thoughtful. Damn it, I've been hating him all day, and now he goes and does something sweet. "Thanks." I take it from him and put it on. "You didn't need to come and collect me."

"It's sketchy here," he replies as he walks along beside me. We fall silent, and there's an awkwardness between us that isn't usually there. Christopher and I are a lot of things; uncomfortable with each other has never been one of them.

"Do you want to go and get a drink or perhaps some dinner?" he asks.

I *am* hungry. "Sure."

We walk along until we find a little bar and restaurant. "Table for two, please?" he asks the waiter.

The waiter looks around. "We only have the bench seat by the window."

I glance over to the bifold windows he gestures to. There is a high counter that faces out onto the street. Christopher looks over to me for approval.

I nod. "That sounds great." We take a seat. "Thanks."

"Can I get you anything to drink?"

I quickly pick up the drink menu. Damn it. If I'm going to lie to someone's face, I at least need a good drink to do it to. "I'll have a margarita, please."

"Do you have Patrón tequila?" Christopher asks.

"Yes."

"Then make that two."

"It is cool tonight." I wrap my cardigan around me. "Thanks for bringing my cardigan."

He smiles. "That's okay."

"How did your job go?" I ask.

"Oh, that . . ." He rolls his eyes. "I wouldn't call it a job. More like a torture chamber."

"Why? What happened?"

"Well." He twists his lips as if trying to find the right words. "I had to put on a suit that smelled so bad it was inhumane, not to mention hotter than Satan's asshole, and then I got punched in the junk so hard that one of my balls is still lodged in my esophagus."

My eyes widen. "Are you for real?"

"Deadly." He shrugs. "Being Binky Bear was definitely not one of my greatest moments."

I burst out laughing. "You were Binky Bear?"

"The best they ever had."

"I don't understand. Who punched you?"

"Some prick of a kid. Don't worry, I took care of him . . . and then . . . got fired for it."

"I can't imagine why." I get the giggles as I imagine him being accosted by a four-year-old. "You got fired?"

"Uh-huh."

"You needed the money, and what about poor Eddie? He got you that job."

"I feel like shit, in hindsight."

"You should have stuck it out . . . for him."

His shoulders slump. "I know."

"When you have no money, any job will do."

"I know." He exhales. "I'll stick it out next time, but seriously, it wasn't a job, it was an assault."

I giggle as I imagine it. "I wish I was there to see it."

He smirks. His pointer is steepled up along his temple as he stares at me, and the way he is looking at me, it's crystal clear that he has an agenda.

"What?" I ask.

"Are we going to talk about this morning?"

I act casual. "What about it?"

"You were angry with me."

"Your drinks." The waiter puts our two drinks in front of us.

"Thank you," we reply.

Play it cool.

"No, I wasn't," I lie.

He frowns.

"I was just tired and grumpy."

"You don't get grumpy with me."

"Then why do you call me Grumps?"

His eyebrows flick up as if he's unimpressed.

"Just saying."

He takes a sip of his margarita. "Not bad." He rolls his lips to taste the salt, and we fall silent. "I didn't sleep with her."

Fuck . . . he knows.

I widen my eyes. "Don't care if you did."

"Really?" His sexy eyes hold mine.

"What are you doing?" I snap.

"What do you mean?"

"It's like you're goading me for something . . . what do you want?"

"Answers."

"Answers to what?"

"What's going on here," he says.

I act dumb. "I don't know what you mean."

"Bernadette told me that you like me."

Fucking Bernadette.

"I don't know where she got that from," I lie.

"So you don't like me . . . ?" His face rests on his hand, so sexually casual, as if he has this conversation every day.

"I do like you, Christopher, but you are not the kind of man I would want to be with, if that's what you're referring to."

"Why not?"

I stare at him while I think for a moment. "You're not my type."

"I'm everyone's type."

I smile. "And there it is."

"What does that mean?"

"I'm not looking for everyone's type."

"That came out wrong." He rolls his lips as if annoyed with himself. "Poor choice of words. I mean, how am I not your type? Explain it to me."

"Look . . ." I pause as I try to get my wording right. "You are Mr. Fun, Mr. Make Everyone Relaxed, and Mr. Looking for a Good Time. Mr. Into Appearances and Being Popular, and although we get on exceptionally well—"

He cuts me off. "Get to the point."

"You just don't . . ." I shrug.

"Don't what?"

"You just don't have the emotional intelligence I'm looking for."

He stares at me as if dumbfounded. *Keep going . . .* , I coach myself.

"What the fuck is that supposed to mean?" he snaps, annoyed.

I put it back on him. "Why are you asking me this? Are you declaring that you like me, or are you just trying to fish me out to see what's in my head?"

He stays silent.

"Because an emotionally intelligent man would tell me how he feels, not find out what I'm thinking to weigh up his options."

He sits back, affronted.

"I am not the kind of girl you normally go for, Christopher. Admit it."

"I'll admit it freely. You're not."

"And you are not ready to stop having sex with other people. Maybe you never will be. Maybe monogamy isn't in your future."

He twists his lips, and I know that I'm right.

Damn it, I hate that I am.

His eyes hold mine. "I could try."

I frown. "Try what?"

"Not to sleep with anyone else . . ." He shrugs. "We could see how it goes."

Not exactly a romantic declaration of love. I smile sadly. "Wow."

"What?"

"Having a man tell me that he can try not to sleep around to see how it goes . . . is not enough to ruin a friendship for me."

His eyes hold mine. "You want the fairy tale?"

"I deserve the fairy tale."

His eyes drop to his drink, and he nods. "You're right, you do."

We fall silent as we both get lost in our own thoughts.

"One day you're going to meet a woman, and you will know for certain that she is the one you want to be with."

His haunted eyes rise to meet mine. "What if I don't? What if I'm so fucked up that I miss all the signs?"

"Then you will live happily in bachelor land. Probably have a couple of kids to a few different women and then grow old with the children you see every second weekend."

He frowns as if shocked by my prediction.

"I don't want that," he whispers.

I take his hand over the table. "I can't help you with this, baby."

"But we get on so well," he whispers.

"We do." I squeeze his hand in mine. "And I will be your friend to the very end, but I want to wait for Prince Charming." I smile hopefully. "He's coming for me, I know it."

He stares at me. "How will you know? How will you know when you've met him?"

I already know.

"Because he won't have to try to not sleep with anyone else . . . he will love me so much that the thought of sleeping with another would turn his stomach. Because that's what love is. Putting another person above all else. Giving yourself over to them completely. Trusting your heart with the woman you love."

I see the confusion rolling around in his eyes. He can't even comprehend what I'm explaining.

"I have faith it will happen for you one day." I sip my drink with a smile.

He exhales heavily. "I wish I shared the same optimism."

"And for the record, for future attempts, telling a woman that you can *try* not to sleep around is probably the most unromantic thing I have ever heard."

He gives me a beautiful broad smile, and I know it's going to be okay between us. "I thought it was pretty good, actually."

I laugh. "You idiot."

"I can't believe you're knocking me back, Grumps." He frowns. "I'm a catch, you know?"

"I know. Crazy, huh?"

"So where do we go from here?" he asks.

"We keep being friends, and you practice how to fall in love with someone."

A trace of a frown crosses his face. "How do I do that?"

"You let your guard down."

"I don't—"

I cut him off. "I know. It isn't an easy thing to do."

He sits with his head resting on his hand, his elbow on the table. "Why did you break up with your boyfriend?"

"He tried not to sleep with someone else . . . and failed."

His eyes hold mine.

"Broke my fucking heart in the process."

"It wasn't about you," he says softly.

"I know." I sip my drink as the memory of how hard my heart broke sinks back into my bones.

We fall silent again, and a thought comes to my mind. "Why did you come on this trip?"

He shrugs. "Lots of reasons."

"What was the main one?"

"To try and find out who I was."

"And what have you discovered?"

Holding the stem of his glass, he spins it where it sits on the table, his eyes focused on it. "I don't always like who I am."

"Like when?"

"Like now."

My heart sinks. He knows . . . he knows what I want, and he knows he can't give it to me.

My affection *is* one sided, just like I thought it was.

Ouch . . .

I pushed for a definite answer to where we stand, and I got it. Move on.

"I'm tired." I fake a smile. "Let's get going."

CHRISTOPHER

The walk back to the hostel is made in silence. Hayden's arm is linked through mine, and we are walking along like we always do . . . except I'm not in comfortable silence like normal with her. There are a million questions running through my head at the speed of light.

You just don't have the emotional intelligence that I'm looking for.

Everyone keeps telling me that I don't have emotional intelligence, but why?

What is the point that I'm clearly missing?

What the fuck does an emotionally intelligent man do? Because I literally have no idea what I'm doing wrong here.

We get to the hostel, and as she goes to walk up the stairs, I pull her back and turn her toward me. "Hayden . . . wait."

"What?"

I swallow a nervous lump in my throat. "I know I'm not the romantic kind of guy you want."

Her eyes hold mine.

"But can you do something for me?"

"What?"

"Kiss me goodbye."

"Chris . . ."

"Just once."

I need to know.

"That's all I'm asking, and then we'll just be friends, and everything will return to normal."

She goes to say something, and I cut her off as I kiss her softly. She tastes sweet and . . .

Delicious.

I slide my arms around her and kiss her properly this time, my tongue sliding between her parted lips. She kisses me back, and unexpected goose bumps scatter up my arms.

My cock begins to thump.

Oh . . .

Her body fits perfectly up against mine, and we kiss again. She's measured, slow, and seductive . . . not at all what I was expecting. My eyes flutter closed.

What the fuck is this?

She jerks out of the kiss and steps back from me. Her eyes hold mine. "Goodbye, Christopher."

She turns and bounces up the stairs and disappears into the building. I watch her, shocked, aroused, and confused.

Hmm . . . interesting.

I look down at the erection tenting my pants. "What are you fucking looking at?" I whisper angrily at him. I drag my hands through my hair in disgust. "Forget it. You can't have her."

✕

I lie propped on my elbow and stare over at the seductress in her pure little pink pajamas, and under the covers she looks comfortable and relaxed.

Completely fuckable.

Hayden Whitmore.

Has there ever been a more annoying, infuriating temptation in the history of life?

I don't think so.

It's been a week since she casually kissed me, a week of imagining bending her over, a week of wanking in the shower until I nearly draw blood. And a very long week of following her around like a fucking puppy.

Not that she'd notice. She's completely self-absorbed and most definitely not into me.

I think if I was on fire, she wouldn't even notice, which is ironic because it feels like my dick actually is.

Everyone is out at the beach, and we are alone in our room. She glances over. "How's the book going?"

I curl my lip in disdain. I glance at the title:

EMOTIONAL INTELLIGENCE

"It's okay, I guess."

This book is a load of fucking baloney. The person who wrote this is not emotionally intelligent; they're just plain fucking stupid.

"What made you buy that book?" she asks.

I fake a smile. *I wonder.*

She smirks knowingly and goes back to her book. "I like that you're reading that."

Shut. Up.

"I'm going to go out tonight," I say to her.

"Okay." She turns the page in her book, her eyes glued to the text.

"You going to come?" I ask.

"Hmm." She scrunches up her nose. "Probably not."

I frown. "Why? What are you doing?"

"I met some people downstairs last night. They've asked me to go to dinner with them."

I narrow my eyes. "What people?"

I'm on high alert. Some romantic fucker is going to swoop in and steal her off me with pretty words and promises . . . wedding rings.

Not that I have her . . . but still.

"Some guys," she mutters, uninterested.

"What guys?"

"The ones from Holland."

Blond fuckers . . . ugh, my blood boils. She likes blonds.

"Suit yourself," I snap.

She nods as she keeps reading, totally unaffected.

"Why don't you come over here? I'll cuddle your back while you read."

"I'm good." She rolls over and puts her back to me.

I know you're fucking good. Good at being a prick-teasing asshole.

With no shame at all, I get up and climb into her bed. I'm allowed to spoon in bed with her; it's something we've always done.

Only now I know how it ends.

I lie with her in my arms and imagine a million ways I could fuck her; I get turned on; she keeps reading her book—god only knows what's so interesting in it—then I go to the shower and pull my dick alone.

I put my arm around her from behind and pull her close. I inhale her scent and smile into her hair as the world disappears.

She has this calming effect on me. As soon as she's in my arms, all is well in the world.

She keeps reading . . . and reading . . . and reading.

Does she even know I'm here?

"What could possibly be so interesting in that stupid book?" I huff.

"Everything," she murmurs, distracted. "I'm just getting to the good bit."

"I don't . . ."

"Shh."

"Did you just shush me?"

"I did, baby. Go to sleep."

"You're infuriating, you know that?"

"Shh."

"I mean . . ."

"Christopher," she snaps. "I'm reading. If you are not going to sleep, go back to your own bed."

"A lot of women would die to have me in their bed, you know?" I huff.

"Why don't you go and see where they are, then?" she mutters as she turns the page.

"I'm going out," I warn.

"Okay."

Fucking woman has me bent over a barrel, and she knows it.

"I'm going out to meet women," I warn again.

"Okay." She kisses my arm. "Have fun."

Screw this . . . I am going out to meet women, and I *am* having sex tonight.

No more Hayden Whitmore puppy patrol.

I sit up.

"If you are going to the locker, can you get my white dress out?" she says.

I narrow my eyes. I know that white dress . . . the one that makes me hard as a rock on sight.

"No, you're not wearing that out without me."

"Why not?"

"Because we don't know those fuckers?"

"What fuckers?"

"The ones from Holland," I snap. "Who knows what kind of perverts they might be."

"Oh . . ." She keeps reading.

I climb out of bed. "Is Bernadette or Kimberly going with you?"

"I haven't asked them."

"Why not?"

"I don't need a bodyguard, Christopher."

"In that dress, I disagree."

She turns her head. "Are you going to cuddle my back and go to sleep or keep mouthing off?"

"I'll give you mouthing off." I pull her into my arms aggressively from behind. "Why don't we fuck?" I suggest.

"Be still, my heart," she whispers as she reads. "If you're horny, just go and find a girl to play with. You're getting annoying."

"You would rather read a book than . . ." I press my lips together because words fail me right now.

"Yes," she snaps. "I would, actually."

"I have needs, Grumps."

"Then go and meet them. We are not fucking, Christopher. Not now, not ever. Stop suggesting it. You're beginning to piss me off."

Right. That's it. I don't need to stay here and cop this abuse. I get out of bed in a huff. "I *am* going out."

"Okay."

"Don't come looking for me."

"I won't."

I stare at her as I begin to fume.

She really doesn't want me.

How?

I march outside and go to my locker in a huff. I get my things out to wear tonight.

Screw this.

I'm not coming on to her again . . . ever again!

I'm done being her puppy.

I go through her bag and retrieve her white dress, and I stuff it into the bottom of my bag. She'll never find it here. This dress is for my eyes only.

I'm done with Hayden Whitmore.

HAYDEN

"Happy birthday, baby," Christopher's soft voice whispers.

I drag my eyes open to see a white box with a red ribbon sitting in prime position on my pillow. "Huh?" I frown. "You bought me a present?"

He kisses my cheek from behind me. "Of course I bought you a present. It's your birthday."

"But we have no money." I frown as I sit up in bed.

"I would sell my left nut for you."

"I wouldn't do that if I were you." I giggle as I pick up the precious gift and shake it at my ear. "You might need that one day."

He chuckles too. "Open it."

I slowly unwrap the present as he watches. It's a necklace. A fine chain and a silver disk. I smile. "It's perfect."

He turns it over in the box. "It's engraved."

I read the words:

GHW

ALWAYS

C

My eyes flick up to him. "GHW? What's that?"

"Grumpy Hayden Whitmore." He pulls me closer into his body and hugs me tight.

I giggle. "Or Gorgeous Hayden Whitmore."

"Goofy Hayden Whitmore." He pokes me in the ribs.

I laugh as I pull it out of the box. "I love it." I hold it out. "Can you put it on me?" We sit up, and he carefully pulls my hair around my neck and puts it on me. I hold it as it sits on my chest. "Christopher, this is so special." It is truly special. I know he can't afford it.

He gives me a beautiful broad smile. "Only the best for my girl."

His girl.

We stare at each other as the air swirls between us.

"You shouldn't have spent your money on me." I smile.

"It's okay." He shrugs. "I didn't need that nut." He hugs me tighter. "I have a full day planned for us, starting with birthday cake for breakfast. Then we are going swimming and having a picnic, followed by dancing our way around town tonight."

I smile, excited. We always have so much fun together. "I can't wait."

My phone rings on the side table, and the name lights up the screen.

Regi

What?

My ex-boyfriend. What the hell is he calling me on my birthday for?

"You going to get that?" Christopher asks.

I think for a moment. Why would I want to talk to him when I have everything that makes me happy right here? I don't feel inadequate or insecure or any of the things that Regi makes me feel.

I stare at Christopher as a new realization sets in.

I'm over Regi. *I'm finally over him.*

When did that happen?

"No." I smile over at my beautiful, reliable friend, the man who's never lied to me. The man who cares for me, day in and day out.

"No, I'm not." I sit up in a rush. "Let's go eat that birthday cake."

He spins me out, and to the sound of his laughter, I twirl, and then he slams me back up against his body.

Dancing with Christopher Miles will never get old. We're dancing our way around the world.

Christopher *loves* dancing, and I, I am his forever-faithful dance partner.

He spins me again and then pulls me back to him with force, and when I'm in his arms like this and listening to him sing to me, nothing else seems to matter.

"I have a request," the DJ calls from his podium as everyone falls silent to listen.

"This song is for a Grumpy Whitmore," he calls.

Christopher's mouth falls open as he fakes shocked horror, and I goofily smile up at him.

The DJ holds a card out as he reads the written message. "It says here that the song is from the sexiest man alive."

I laugh out loud.

Christopher holds his hands out as if on a stage and takes a bow, and everyone laughs, realizing it's him.

The song comes on, "Halo," by Beyoncé, and I smile up at my heavenly dance partner as he takes me into his arms. "This is your song, Grumps."

"How is it my song?"

"Because you have a halo." He kisses my temple as he holds me close. "My angel."

"It's you that has the halo, my darling," I whisper.

"You're right, I do. We should totally fuck to this song." He spins me hard, and I laugh out loud.

"You're ruining it."

He smiles down at me as we dance, and a strange feeling comes over me . . . warmth and belonging and, for the first time in my life, safety. We stare at each other as the words roll over us.

Maybe we really should fuck to this song.

Six weeks later

I glance at my watch. An hour until I get to see him.

Weekends go so slow.

How can you miss someone so much when you saw them just this morning? It doesn't make any sense, not even to me.

Christopher, Basil, and I return to Barcelona every weekend so that we can work.

We all have great jobs here and get nearly a full-time wage for just two twelve-hour days. It's well worth the trip back, plus there's the fact that Christopher secretly wants to stay near Eddie. He can't bear to leave him just yet. The rest of the gang are in Portugal, and we'll meet up with them again on Monday.

We've been all over: Germany, Italy, Switzerland, and now Portugal. The world is a beautiful place . . . even more beautiful with him by my side.

Christopher and I have a weird thing going on. When he first tried to kiss me in the ocean and I rejected him, he pulled back. A week later, we had it out, and he told me he was incapable of the kind of relationship I wanted.

Then we kissed, and I knew in that instant that I wanted more.

He tried to pursue it for not even a week and then gave up, just like I knew he would.

We fell back into the friend zone for a couple of months . . . but then he came back to me.

And something changed.

I can't put my finger on exactly what that is or what it means, because technically we're still just friends and nothing has ever happened between us.

But it's different.

All I know is that when I'm with him, nothing else matters.

Which makes life pretty good at the moment, because we're together all the time.

I finish my shift and clean up until finally it's knockoff time. "Bye. Have a great week, everyone," I call as I head off.

I walk to the corner, and there in the shadows I see him, standing silently in the dark as he waits for me.

My cardigan in his hand.

My heart constricts because in his mind he doesn't know how to be romantic.

If only he knew . . .

Saw in himself what I see in him.

It's all there, deep inside . . . just waiting to be let out.

"Hi." I smile.

His big eyes hold mine. "Hey, baby," he whispers as he pulls me in for a hug.

We stand in each other's arms as if we haven't seen each other for a month. I want to blurt out that I missed him today . . . but I won't.

Because that's not the game we're playing.

"How was your day?" he asks as we begin to walk. He takes my hand in his and kisses my fingertips.

"Long . . . hellish." I sigh.

"How's your tummy? I was worried when you were ill this morning."

I poke him in the ribs. "Did you ever think you would ever be worried about period pain?" I tease.

He chuckles. "Definitely not."

"Are the pharmacies still open?" I hold my aching tummy. "I need to find a heat pack somewhere."

"Is it still hurting?" He frowns.

"I've just had some paracetamol. It will be fine in a little while."

We go to a few pharmacies, and they're all closed.

"I'll be fine. The pills are working already. Let's just go home."

"You sure?" he asks.

I smile. Who knew that my player friend would be so caring? Underneath all that popular bullshit, he's an absolute sweetheart.

We get back to the hostel and into our room. Basil is working tonight and won't be home until late.

"You heading out?" I ask.

"No." He frowns. "Unless . . . do you want to go out?"

"No, I'm going to take a shower and go to bed."

"Sounds good to me."

We head into the bathroom and take showers. I get dressed in my pajamas and head into the room.

Christopher is already in my bed, and my stomach does a little flip.

We've been sleeping together lately, tangled together beneath the sheets. Our bodies snug up against each other.

And I feel so close to him that . . . I can't explain it. It's a weird situation.

I climb in beside him, and he rolls onto his side. "I found a heat pack."

"Did you? Where?"

He puts his large hand over my lower stomach. "How's this?" he whispers.

We stare at each other in the darkness, electricity crackling between us.

"Better," I breathe.

This is the first time we've been alone in our room. Usually there are four other people with us, all chatting and laughing.

Tonight, it's different.

There's something in the air . . . something more.

His face is millimeters from my face, his big warm hand protective over my stomach, and a sense of belonging pours over me.

"What are you doing here with me?" I whisper. "You should be out chasing girls."

"You're my only girl," he whispers.

We stare at each other.

And I desperately want to believe him . . . but I don't know if I'm brave enough to let myself go there. But I want to . . .

"Chris . . ."

He leans down and kisses me. Softly . . . tenderly.

Perfectly.

Chapter 12

He pulls back, and his eyes search mine as if waiting for approval. His lips take mine again, only this time I can't help myself. I kiss him back. My tongue gently curling around his, my hand sliding up over his strong shoulders.

We kiss again and again, and he rolls me onto my back and wraps my leg around his waist. His body leans half over mine, and I can feel the large erection in his boxers as it grows against my thigh.

Oh . . .

He's so muscular and big and . . . frigging hell, I've never been with a man like this.

Our kisses get deeper and more heated, inferno hot, and we lose control.

He pulls my leg up aggressively; my knee is now near his chest as his lips drop to my neck.

He bites me and trails his lips over my skin, his erection rubbing on my panties. Holy fucking hell . . .

His teeth gently tug at my bottom lip, and I feel it deep in my sex.

Yes.

He rolls over so that he's on top of me, his body cradled between my legs, and he begins to slowly slide up and down over my sweet spot as we kiss.

My legs wrap around his waist, an unstoppable force building between us. An atomic bomb, waiting to explode. I need this.

Fuck, I need this.

I grab the waistband of his boxers and slide them down. His large cock springs free, and then I remember.

Oh no.

It's that time of the month . . . what the hell? This is the worst timing ever!

"Shit," I mutter.

"It's all right," he murmurs against my lips as he kisses me. He hasn't forgotten at all.

Why did I take his boxers off if I can't do anything?

You idiot.

He pulls my pajama top off over my head and smiles as he looks down at my breasts. He bends and takes my nipple into his mouth. His eyes flutter closed in ecstasy. "Yes," he whispers. His hands roam up and down my body as if he doesn't know where to touch me first, his hips gently pumping by themselves.

My heart is in my throat as I watch. Seeing him like this is a new level of excitement. He's so lost in the moment, so aroused that I swear I could come just by watching him. Let alone how good he feels.

He grabs the waistband of my pajamas and goes to pull them down.

"Chris," I whisper. "We're not."

"Relax, baby. We're just playing around," he murmurs against my lips. He continues to slide my boxers down and takes them off.

Okay . . . what the hell?

We're both naked. This is a dangerous kind of playing around.

Don't go there.

We kiss, and he rubs his fingertips through my pubic hair. "Hmm." He whispers softly, "You have no fucking idea how badly

I've wanted to touch you like this." As we kiss, he circles his fingers over my clitoris in a way that sends shivers down my spine.

Oh no.

"Making you come is all I've thought about for months," he whispers. "You have no idea how much your body turns me on."

Arousal instantly builds deep inside me.

His fingers are just the right pressure, and my mouth falls open.

Oh . . . oh . . . how does he know the exact spot? It's like he has a map. My head plunges back. He does that too well.

Damn him and all his womanizing experience. I don't stand a chance to play it cool.

His breath on my neck, his fingertips gently circling, his erection up against me.

Keeping my legs closed is a near-impossible task.

I shudder, and he chuckles against my neck, knowing full well that he's hardly even touched me and I'm about to blow.

No.

I'm so embarrassing.

I need to deflect. I go to pull out of his grip, and he pushes me back down. "Don't move," he demands as he holds me still.

The dominance of him is next level, and my arousal hits fever pitch.

I'm coming tonight . . . whether I like it or not.

I reach down and take his hard length in my hand, and what the hell?

Big.

I can hardly get my hand around him. I swallow the nervous lump in my throat.

He pushes my legs back, my thighs up against my chest, and rolls over onto me.

"Christopher," I warn.

"Playing," he snaps.

This doesn't feel like playing. This feels like he's about to nail me to the bed. "But . . ."

"Shut up, Grumps," he whispers.

I giggle. That's not something I ever expected to hear in the heat of the moment.

He adjusts his dick so that without being inside of me, he rubs himself through the lips of my sex. He slowly drives forward and right over my clitoris.

That feels . . . good.

Oh fuck . . .

His dark eyes hold mine, and he turns his head and licks up my calf muscle. His tongue is thick and strong. I see stars, and I shudder hard, unable to hold it.

Oh, the horror.

I'm a two-pump chump.

"You're going to be so much fun to break in, Grumps," he murmurs. He takes my face in his two hands and kisses me deeply. "Suck. My. Cock."

My eyes widen . . . jeez.

He talks dirty.

I'm suddenly unsure of myself. I feel like a little girl, inexperienced and immature.

Way too come-y.

He kisses me deeply and grabs a handful of my hair and guides me down his body.

Well . . . here I go. I've given head before, but never to a master.

I lick his tip, fluttering my tongue over his end. He lies back, and with his eyes locked on mine, he inhales deeply.

He likes that.

His reaction spurs me on, and I slowly take him into my mouth. His breath quivers, and I know he's close too. I take him in my hand and stroke while I suck. Our eyes are locked, and he spreads his legs wider.

Inviting me in.

I take him rougher and suck harder, and his eyes flutter as he moans. "That's it."

I want to be more for him. I want to say something unexpected . . . dirty.

"Fuck my mouth," I whisper around him.

His eyes darken, and he grabs two handfuls of my hair and slides deep down my throat.

Oh no . . . too far.

I gag at his size, and he pushes the hair back from my face and smiles down at me. "You probably shouldn't tell me to do that, Grumps."

Bastard.

Determined to do it better, I take him in my mouth again. I get into a rhythm, and he moans and tips his head back, and damn it, I wish I was riding him home.

Tonight, I'd be the jockey of all jockeys.

His grip on my hair tightens, and he shudders, and I brace myself.

"I'm going to come." He moans, "Grumps." He's giving me an out if I don't want to swallow.

To hell with the rules. I'm in bed with a sex god. Where the rules are, there are no rules.

"Do it," I dare him.

Fire flares in his eyes, and he spreads his legs wider and holds himself deep. He comes in a rush down my throat.

Oh . . . god . . . I forgot this part . . . aah.

Ugh . . .

Stop it.

I let myself go and drink him down, taking my time. I lick him up. With my eyes locked on his, I lick my own fingers that still have him on them.

He stares at me. His brow is creased, and as his chest rises and falls as he struggles for air, I'm not sure if he's impressed or horrified.

Maybe a little of both.

I kiss his dick and crawl up his body and snuggle up into his chest.

He lies still, so still that I look up at him. "What?"

He puffs air into his cheeks as if surprised. "That was . . . fucking good."

I kiss his chest beneath me.

It was.

I smile sleepily in his arms, cradled in his warmth, and the key sounds in the door.

Oh crap, it's Basil.

"Fuck," Christopher whispers. "What's he doing home so early?"

I sit up and grab both of our pajamas from the floor and get back under the covers just as the door opens.

"Hey," Basil says casually as he walks in. He doesn't even look down at us.

"Hi," we both reply. My heart is still racing.

"You wouldn't believe what happened today." He begins to chat away, and we lie and listen, but with every word he says, I can feel Christopher pull away, although I'm not sure if it's Basil or me that he's trying to escape.

"I'm having a shower," Basil eventually says.

The minute the door closes, Christopher dives out of bed and pulls his boxer shorts on. "Get dressed," he whispers as he throws my pajamas at me. "Quick. He can't know."

I frown. Huh?

Why can't he know?

"I'm going to take a quick shower." He rushes out of the room, and I stare at the back of the door, dumbfounded.

We've been dancing around this for months. Why can't Basil know? I would have thought that this was something worth screaming out to the world.

Maybe not.

I get dressed and go to the bathroom, and with every minute that passes, a sense of dread creeps in. Does he regret it? He's not acting like I thought he would.

This could be one big disaster.

I come back to the room to find Christopher back in my bed. He gives me a soft smile and flicks back the covers.

Relief fills me.

Okay, everything is fine. I'm imagining things that aren't there.

I crawl in, and he wraps his arm around me, and I put my head onto his chest. He kisses my temple as he holds me close. "Good night, my sexy Grumps."

I trail my fingers through the scattering of his dark chest hair. It feels so good to finally be able to touch him like this. "Good night."

He puts his mouth to my ear and whispers, "You give great head."

I smile into the darkness. Crisis averted. The closeness between us is back.

Basil comes back into the room and begins to talk. He goes on and on and on and tells us every little detail of his day, like he does every night.

We lie in silence and listen. "Has anyone ever told you that you have verbal diarrhea?" Christopher asks him.

I poke Christopher in the ribs.

"No, why? What's that?" Basil replies without a clue.

I poke Christopher again. "Don't," I whisper.

"Just a bug that's going around," Christopher lies.

"I hope I don't catch it," Basil replies. "It doesn't sound good at all."

"I guarantee that if you keep your mouth shut, you won't," Christopher mutters dryly.

"Good idea," Basil replies as he climbs into bed.

I giggle. "Good night, Baz."

X

"Grumps," a voice whispers.

I drag my eyes open to see Christopher fully dressed and leaning over my bed. "What's wrong?" I frown.

"I have to go."

"Where?"

"Home."

My eyes fly open. "What?"

"I have to sign some paperwork with my brothers."

What the hell?

I sit up and rub my eyes. "What do you mean?"

"There's paperwork concerning my parents' estate, and I need to sign along with my brothers on the same day."

I blink.

He didn't mention this at all yesterday.

"When will you be back?" I frown.

"A few days."

"Do you want me to come?"

"No," he replies, way too fast. He kisses me quickly on the lips. "You have fun here. Go to Portugal with the others."

I think for a second. "Actually, I'll stay here and work for the week. Maria is off sick, and they offered me her shifts." I glance over, and his full backpack is packed by the door. "Just leave your backpack here with me."

196

"It's fine."

My eyes search his. *He's not coming back.*

"I'm fine," he snaps.

But I didn't ask him anything . . . he's not fine. He's freaking out.

"Okay?" He smiles. "We good?" He nods as if trying to convince himself. "Okay? Everything's all right." He's tripping over his words and stands in a rush.

I get out of bed and watch him. He's fussing around and looking everywhere but at me.

"Christopher."

He keeps putting things in his bag and fiddling with the zipper.

"Christopher," I say, sterner. "Look at me."

His eyes rise to mine.

"It's okay."

"Yep, it's sweet." He nods as if convincing himself. "I know. Totally sweet."

Sweet is not a word I've heard him use. *He's never lied to me before.*

"Bye." He kisses me quickly and picks up his backpack and without looking back rushes out the door.

I stare at the back of it, shocked to silence.

What the hell just happened?

"You slept together, didn't you?" Basil says dryly.

I exhale heavily.

"Hayden, have you learned nothing?" He sighs. "No hanky-panky with roommates."

My eyes well with tears. If I'd thought we were only roommates, I wouldn't have.

I thought we were more.

CHRISTOPHER

I throw my bag into the trunk and get into the back of the cab. "Airport, please."

"Okay." The driver calmly pulls out and into the traffic.

My heart is hammering hard in my chest, and I turn and look at the hostel through the back window.

I drag my hand down my face. Fuck.

Fuck. Fuck. *Fuck*.

I take out my phone and call Eddie. He answers on the first ring. "Hello, Mr. Christo."

"Hi, buddy. Listen, I have to go out of town for a while. Can you look after Miss Hazen for me please?"

"Where are you going?"

"I have to sign some papers at home." I'm not lying. I do have to sign some papers, but I wasn't due to do it until next week, but I know the boys are all in New York this week. I need to go home.

"Are you coming back?" he asks softly.

I can hear the disappointment in his voice, and I close my eyes. Damn it. "Of course I am."

"When?"

"A couple of days."

"What day?"

"I don't know yet," I snap. "Can you watch over her for me or not?"

"Fine."

"Good. She's too trusting, and I just—"

He cuts me off. "I'm on it."

"Thank you."

He hangs up before I can say anything else, and I exhale heavily. It's a weird world where the person I trust most is a fourteen-year-old kid who works nights in a bar.

Perspiration dusts my skin, and I wipe my brow. Damn it, sleeping with that woman—or nearly sleeping with that woman—has me on the verge of a complete fucking meltdown. I've never felt so unstable.

I take a deep steadying breath as I stare out the window. I shouldn't be going.

But I can't stay.

The walls are closing in around me, and I didn't sleep the entire night.

I pursued this . . . I wanted this.

And now?

Fuck . . . what have I done?

I just need some time with my brothers.

I rub my fingers over my stubble as I stare out the window. *Go back.*

Don't fuck this up. She's the best thing that's ever happened to you.

Go back.

"Can you just . . ."

The driver's eyes flick up to meet mine in the rearview mirror.

"Never mind." I correct myself. "Drop me off at the international terminal, please."

X

I walk out of JFK Airport just at 7:00 p.m. The black limo is waiting by the curb for me.

Brandon, my driver, smiles warmly with a nod. "Good evening, Mr. Miles."

I smile and shake his hand. "Hello, Brandon. It's good to see you."

He pops the trunk, and I put my backpack in and get into the back seat.

He pulls out into the traffic, and I look around my hometown in awe. It's like I'm seeing it for the first time.

So busy.

Yellow cabs are everywhere, and I smile as I feel my equilibrium return.

"Are we picking anyone up, sir?" Brandon asks.

I frown. Do we normally pick people up? I guess we do.

"No, not tonight."

I sit quietly in the back as we drive through New York. I glance at the time on my phone. It would be 1:00 a.m. in Spain.

I should call Hayden and tell her that I landed safely . . . and then say what?

I imagine how the conversation would go, and I exhale heavily.

I'm not in the mood for the third degree. I stuff my phone back in my pocket.

Fifteen minutes later we pull up in front of my building. "Home sweet home." Brandon smiles.

"Yes." I smile. "I've missed this place."

"I'll carry your bag up for you, sir," he offers.

"No. I've got it, thanks." I sling the huge backpack over my shoulder.

"What time will you be heading out, Mr. Miles?"

I frown. That's right . . . I do go out every night when I'm here.

"I'm staying in tonight. Go home. Have the night off."

Brandon's eyebrows flick up as if he's surprised.

"Thanks for coming to get me."

He frowns.

I smile and make my way into the foyer.

The concierge staff all run when they see me with my heavy bag. "Mr. Miles, it's good to see you, sir. Let us take that."

"I'm fine," I reply. Why are they all running?

I look around. Everything is marble and over-the-top luxurious. Huge bouquets of fresh flowers are everywhere, and the staff are all in black suits. The floor is so highly polished it looks like a mirror.

I frown. Was it always this luxurious? Did I just never notice it before?

Hmm . . .

I get into the elevator, and Harold, its operator, is standing quietly. "Hello, Mr. Miles." He smiles.

"Hello, Harold." I turn to face the front. "Have you had a good day?" I ask him.

"I have, sir." He smiles. "Have you?"

I shrug. "It was okay," I lie. I had the shittiest day of all time.

We continue to ride up to my penthouse, and a thought crosses my mind. Does he just stand in the elevator all night, waiting to take people up to their floors?

"How long have you worked in the elevator, Harold?"

"Seventeen years, sir."

I stare at him.

He smiles broadly. "And tonight was the first time you have ever called me by my name."

I blink. *What?*

The doors ping as we get to my floor. They open, and I stare at him, horrified.

"Have a wonderful night, sir."

"You too," I reply softly, taken aback. Surely that can't be right, although deep down I know that it is.

I'm an asshole.

I walk out of the elevator and into my private foyer. I scan my fingerprint, and the double doors unlock. I push them open to walk in to floor-to-ceiling windows, stunning views over New York.

With a heavy heart, I drop my backpack and walk over to a window and stare out over the city. New York is buzzing down below, a sight that I have seen for all of my life—taken for granted, even.

Tonight, it feels foreign.

So foreign.

I turn and look around my grand apartment. It's huge and spans two floors. Slouchy leather couches, polished concrete flooring, and bright abstract paintings hang on the walls.

I walk into the kitchen and look around. It's as if I'm seeing every detail for the first time. Stylish appliances and expansive marble countertops. I open a door and stare in. Strip lighting illuminates a staircase leading down to the refrigerated room that's bigger than most people's living rooms. My wine cellar, where I house hundreds of thousands of dollars of exotic wine.

I frown, perplexed.

I close the door and walk up the grand double stairs beside the internal elevator.

I amble up the hall, and sensor lighting on the floor lights up as I walk along.

Hmm, why do I even need this? Since when has turning on a switch been so hard?

I arrive at my bedroom and stand at the door and look in at the oversize king bed.

A million visions run through my mind of the women I've had here, the parties, the orgies . . . the orgasms, both given and taken.

Deflated, I walk into my bathroom and turn the shower on. I stare up at the ceiling. It's a triple shower with ornate brass fittings. Even though I used to see it every day, I never noticed it before. It's something that I took for granted. Why do I even have a triple shower?

You know why . . .

There are usually three people in it.

I look around with fresh eyes. The marble is white, and the fittings are brass. There is a marble seat along one wall and a sunken spa bath in the floor. Fluffy navy-blue towels are folded perfectly on the shelving, along with four navy robes hanging perfectly on brass hooks on the wall.

Four robes.

This apartment has the best of the best of everything in it, packed to the hilt with luxury . . . but somehow, it's empty.

So empty.

Deflated, I get into the shower and stand under the hot water. My heart is racing, and for the tenth time today, I feel the walls closing in on me. I swear to god, I'm fucking losing it.

I don't feel like I'm home, and this all feels foreign . . . which is fucked up, because I *am* home.

New York has always been the one place I do belong.

If this doesn't feel like home, then where is?

London.

If I was at my penthouse in London, then it would feel different, I'm sure.

Yes, that's it . . . London.

I inhale deeply as I try to calm myself. Of course I'm rattled and feeling off. I didn't sleep a wink last night and am exhausted. Jet lagged, even. I'm not going to call my brothers to meet tonight. I'm feeling way too off kilter.

I get out of the shower and dry off, and too tired to eat any dinner, I crawl into bed.

In the dark silence, I stare up at the ceiling.

The bed is huge, the sheets are crisp, and everything feels so clean and sterile.

Lonely.

My life is a mess.

Chapter 13

Top floor, Miles High Building. The elevator doors open, and I stride out.

"Good morning, Sammia." I smile. It's good to see a familiar face.

"Christopher." She gasps. "My god." She stands, and I lean over the desk and kiss her cheek. "Miss me?" I ask.

"Definitely not." She smirks.

Sammia and I have a strong friendship. Been play flirting for years. "Still married?"

"Yes, Christopher." She rolls her eyes.

"Such a shame," I reply as I walk past her. "One of these days," I call as I walk away.

I hear her giggle, and I head down the corridor to Jameson's. I walk in, and he's on the phone. He glances up and stops midsentence. "I'll call you back." He hangs up without waiting for a reply and stands immediately.

I chuckle and hold out my arms, and he rushes me and pulls me into a hug. Emotion overwhelms me. I didn't realize just how much I missed him up until this very moment. "I thought you weren't coming until Friday?" he says as he regains his composure and steps back from me.

"Change of plans."

He circles me as he looks me up and down. "Fuck . . . look at you."

"What about me?" I smile.

"Tanned."

I put my hands on my hips proudly.

"You've put on weight."

"Fuck off, I have."

He sits back at his desk, his eyes not leaving me for a minute, and he picks up his office phone. "Get in here. I have a surprise for you."

I knew the three of my brothers were all in New York. There's a board meeting at nine o'clock, and attendance by all is compulsory.

I walk to the bar and eye the assortment of all the alcohol I haven't been able to afford. "Is it too early?" I ask.

"It's five o'clock somewhere," he replies casually.

I pour myself a scotch and hold up the bottle. He smirks with a subtle shake of his head. "I'll wait till it's five here."

"Still boring, I see." I sip my drink and smile as it burns all the way down. "Ahh." I hold the glass up and stare at the amber liquid. "That's the stuff."

The door bursts open, and Tristan and Elliot come into view. They both laugh out loud and rush me with a hug. Elliot holds me a little longer than he should. "Let go of me, you creepy fucker." I smile as I pull out of his arms.

He punches me hard. "Thank god that's over."

"Miss me?" I ask.

"No. Just sick of doing all your work."

His eyes linger affectionately on my face, and I pull him into another hug. "I missed you."

"London fucking sucks without you there."

"Tell me everything," Tristan says as he pours three glasses of scotch.

Jameson winces. "It's eight thirty in the morning."

"Stop being fucking boring," Tristan huffs as he passes their glasses out. He holds his in the air to propose a toast, and we all raise ours too. "Together."

My eyes well with tears. Fuck. *I really missed them.*

This is where I belong, with my brothers, running our company.

"Together," we all repeat.

"So . . ." Tristan smiles. "Tell us everything. What's been happening with gorillas in the mist?"

I burst out laughing. "Fucking hell, that was the night from hell, and to top it off, the witch stole my credit card."

They all chuckle.

"The taxi driver." Jameson smirks. "You. A taxi driver. That will do me . . . that's the best fucking story I ever heard in my life. And when that dude vomited in the car, and then you vomited in sympathy."

"Oh no." They all groan.

"Don't remind me." I wince.

"When you were a bear and got punched in the nuts."

The three of them burst out laughing as they imagine it.

"Yeah, yeah. Laugh all you want." I roll my eyes. "I can still taste blood."

They laugh harder, and I drain my glass. "We've got to get moving. Meeting in ten minutes. Can we sign the trust documents tomorrow? What are we buying now?"

"A skyscraper on Fifth. I'll call the lawyer and make an appointment. You all around tomorrow?"

"Yes, yeah, sounds good," they all reply.

"Dinner and drinks tonight?" I ask.

"You're on." Tristan slaps me on the back, Elliot messes up my hair, and Jameson gives me a knowing smile. "I'm glad you're home. No more cockamamie ideas."

"I know." I smile. "Good to be home." We begin to walk to the boardroom.

Only it wasn't cockamamie; it was great. Probably the greatest time of my life.

I was shown a different way of living, one where it was okay to be whoever I am.

No expectations, no deadlines . . . just me . . . and her.

Sadness twinges, and my face falls. Elliot catches it and frowns. "What's wrong?" he whispers as we walk.

"Nothing."

His eyes hold mine.

"Drop it." I brush past him.

I'm not in the mood for his psychobabble bullshit.

Hayden

"You slept with him?" Bernadette shrieks.

"No." I brush past her into the shower. The girls are back from Portugal unexpectedly. Their backpackers' hostel got closed down because there was an electrical fault and it had no power. They couldn't get in anywhere so came back here.

"Then why did he leave?" She follows me.

"He had to sign something at home," I reply.

"Did you kiss him?"

I hesitate.

"You did." She gasps. "I knew it."

"He's not coming back. You know that, don't you," Kimberly says as she turns on the shower in her stall.

"He'll be back," I snap as I put my head under the water.

"What makes you so sure?" Bernadette calls.

"Because . . . I know him."

"Did you know he was going to leave before you kissed him?"

"I knew he was going to freak out, if that's what you mean."

"Then why did you kiss him?" she demands. She's angry that we kissed. She adores Christopher. In her mind, I've pushed him away.

"Because there is no way around it. He has to get over this and come back of his own free will."

"What if he doesn't?"

"He will."

"I'm not so sure."

"You don't know him like I do."

"Don't be a fool. He left and took all his things. Can you hear yourself right now?"

"I know this sounds stupid, but I know we have something. And it's real . . . and I'm trusting it," I call.

"You're right, that does sound stupid. A man doesn't run when he sleeps with a woman unless he doesn't want to see her again. He got what he wanted, and now he's out of here."

Am I being stupid?

No.

I'm trusting him. I trust in us.

"We didn't sleep together, and he has some shit to work through, that's all."

"Has he called you?"

"No."

Why hasn't he called me?

"What if he sleeps with someone else while he's gone?" Bernadette asks.

My heart sinks because I know that's a real possibility. Scared people do dumb things. "Then it's over between us." I sigh. The thought makes me sick to my stomach. "He will tell me if he did. Christopher is a lot of things. A liar isn't one of them. He will know if he's fucked up, and he'll tell me. He's not a sleazebag."

"That's if you ever see him again."

"I know he'll be back."

"What makes you so sure?"

"Eddie is here."

"So?"

"He would never leave him without saying goodbye."

"But . . . he *would* leave you . . ."

"Just leave it, Bernadette," I snap as I lose the last of my patience. "I'm not discussing this anymore."

"Broken heart coming right up," Kimberly mutters.

"Right," Bernadette agrees.

I exhale heavily. I hope they're wrong.

God, I hope they're wrong.

※

I walk out of the bedroom to shower. "Good morning, Miss Hazen."

I turn to see Eduardo patiently waiting by my door. "Good morning, Eddie." I smile. Damn, this kid is the cutest human of all time. "What are you up to?" I ask as we walk to my locker.

"I'm here to help you today."

"That's not necessary, honey. Go and relax. I don't need any help."

His face falls as if he's disappointed, and he twists his fingers nervously in front of him.

I correct myself. "That's if you have something else to do. I am going to the market. You could come and keep me company if you like?"

His face lights up. "Okay, I can do that."

"Give me ten minutes to shower and we will go."

"Where will I wait for you?" he asks excitedly.

"Wherever you want."

He gives me a big beautiful smile, and my heart skips a beat. I know why Christopher is so smitten with this boy. I'm pretty smitten myself.

I shower and dress and walk out to find Eddie sitting on the floor by my door. "You don't have to sit on the floor, honey," I say. "You could have waited in the lounge area."

He shrugs as he climbs to his feet. "I don't mind the floor."

He's telling the truth. He doesn't mind anything and never complains. He is the most hardworking, intelligent little boy I have ever met. His grandmother must be so proud.

Well, he's not so little, but you know what I mean.

211

We walk out of the hostel and down the street. The sun is shining, and the weather is warm and balmy. "Nice day, isn't it?"

"Uh-huh." He smiles as he looks around.

We walk in silence for a while. "I want to buy some fresh fruit today and some tomatoes and lettuce."

"I can carry those," he suggests.

"Okay," I reply. "That would be great." I smile hard on the inside; every minute I spend with him, he pulls me more under his spell.

"You probably should get some apples and bananas too," he says.

"I think I will." I smile.

His phone rings, and he digs it out of his pocket. "It's Mr. Christo," he says.

"I'm not here," I stammer. "Pretend you're not with me."

"I can't lie."

"Yes, you can," I snap. "Do it."

"Hello," he answers. He listens and then smiles broadly.

I stand and watch him on his new fancy iPhone.

"Yes, I'm good." Eddie smiles. We begin to walk again while I'm listening like a hawk.

"Miss Hazen?" Eddie's eyes flick to me. "She's good." He listens again. "No, she didn't go to Portugal. The others are back here now too. Their hostel closed."

Eddie listens again and he frowns. "Last night? I don't know what she did last night."

"I went out," I mouth.

"She went out," he lies for me. His eyes flick to me again. "Who with?" he repeats Christopher's question.

"Men," I mouth.

Eddie frowns as he holds his hand up. "What men?" he mouths back.

212

"All of them," I mouth.

Eddie nods, finally understanding the game. "A big bunch of guys. Good-looking dudes too."

I smile goofily as I listen.

He cares.

"What did she wear?" Eddie frowns as he repeats the question. His eyes meet mine, and he scrunches up his face.

"White dress," I mouth.

Eddie lies for me again. "I don't know, a white dress." Eddie listens and then rolls his eyes. "I'm not cutting up her dress."

I put my hand over my mouth to stop myself from laughing.

"I'm not sure," Eddie replies. He listens a bit. "Okay, I'll try."

"What?" I mouth.

He waves his hand in a *don't worry* sign.

"I'm good." He smiles. "No, it's sunny." He listens again. "I start at three. I'm going to the market with Miss Hazen this morning to buy fruit." He frowns, and his eyes meet mine. "Don't tell her you called? Why not?"

My heart sinks as I wait for the reply.

"Oh . . . I see." He listens, and then eventually, he smiles. "Okay, bye." He hangs up.

"What did he say?" I blurt out.

"Not to tell you he called."

"Why not?"

"I don't know . . . I forget," he lies.

"You're covering for him?" I gasp.

"He'll call you, don't worry."

"When?"

"I don't know."

"Well, is he calling you back?" I ask him.

"He said he'll call me tomorrow."

"Oh . . ." I go over the conversation they had, desperately trying to work out what it all means, and we walk in silence for a while.

"He likes you," he says.

My eyes flick up. "Did he tell you that?"

"He didn't have to."

"Well then, how do you know?"

"Men know these things . . . and besides, how could he not?"

I smile. This adorable young man is everything and more. I link my arm through his, grateful for his friendship. "Let's get an ice cream on the way home too."

Eddie smiles broadly. "Okay."

CHRISTOPHER

The restaurant is busy and bustling, loud music is playing, and in typical New York style, everyone is out on a Monday night.

The city that never sleeps.

My brothers laugh and chat, and with every moment that I spend with them, I feel a little more myself.

Jameson holds his hand and makes a fist. I've seen him do it a few times today.

"What's up with your hand?" I ask.

"Fuck knows." He opens his hand and makes a fist again. "My two middle fingers are sore, like, aching."

I sip my scotch. "Did you injure them?"

"No." He opens his hand again. "It's in the knuckle and up into my fingers and down into the palm of my hand."

Elliot winces. "That can't be good."

"RFI," Tristan replies casually into his glass.

"What's RFI?" I ask.

"Repetitive fingering injury."

I snort my drink up my nose. "What?" I cough.

"No shit," Tristan says in all seriousness. "It's hard work keeping these women satisfied."

"Right," Jameson agrees. He opens his fist and closes it again.

Tristan holds out his two middle fingers and curls them up, simulating his fingering action. "Does this hurt?"

Jameson does it, and he winces. "Yes. It does." His eyes flick around the table. "I *do* fucking have it," he snaps, horrified.

"It's all downhill from here," Elliot says. "You'll never get laid again if there is a kink in the warm-up chain."

"Fucking hell," Jameson mutters under his breath. "The warm-up chain is already well and truly fucked up by the three cockblockers who live in my house rent-free."

"You mean . . . your children?" Elliot mutters dryly.

Jameson narrows his eyes as he crunches a piece of ice.

I smirk, amused.

"I'm hearing you, man. I got a huge-ass lock . . . so now instead of barging in, they just stand out there banging, scream-ing, 'Open the door!'" Tristan curls his lip in disgust. "And now, with the RFI kink in the warm-up chain . . . I'm basically fucked."

"And not in the right way." Elliot smiles.

Jameson rolls his eyes and drains his glass. "This wasn't in the brochure."

The table erupts into laughter, and I look around the table at my three happily married brothers. "What *was* in the bro-chure?" I ask them.

"What do you mean?" Tristan asks.

"How did you know you'd met the . . ." I pause.

"The one?" Elliot asks.

"Yeah." I shrug. "For interest's sake."

"Hmm." Jameson runs his fingers over his stubble as he thinks back. "I didn't really know at the time. Like, there wasn't a lightning-bolt moment when I knew, as such."

"Yeah, me too," Tristan agrees. "But there was something different about her."

"Like what?" I ask, my interest piqued.

"I guess . . ." Tristan pauses. "She was like this really cool friend who was way cooler than me that I desperately wanted to fuck."

216

I chuckle.

"For me it was different. I didn't . . ." Jameson purses his lips as he thinks. "I just wanted to be near her all the time. Like, I was obsessed with her, but different obsessed."

I frown. "What do you mean?"

"I hated going home with her not there and would avoid it at all costs."

I listen intently. This is all news to me. I thought they'd had this primal urge to marry their women the day that they'd met them.

"I felt more at home in her tiny apartment than I did in my penthouse," Jameson adds.

What?

"Me too," Tristan agrees. "I missed her. When I wasn't with her, I missed her. I found myself rushing to get home and cook her dinner and watch television on her couch . . . and suddenly, somehow, it wasn't about sex anymore."

"Which is helpful now that you have RFI and a useless lock on the door." Elliot holds his glass up toward Tristan.

Tristan chuckles. "Facts."

"So what you're saying is your sex life is shit." I frown.

"Not at all," he replies. "The sex is ridiculously good, but more than that, I wanted to talk to her because she was the first person who actually listened. My life became better because she was in it."

My heart begins to hammer.

Sounds familiar.

"I guess my biggest thing for me was"—Elliot chips in—"I didn't want to sleep with anyone else. I lost all attraction to other women overnight."

I feel the blood drain from my face. I haven't had sex in two months.

It's like the urge has completely left my body. I would rather lie on my bed and watch Hayden read than have sex with another woman. I end most days jerking off in the shower and then happily cuddling her back.

Fuck.

"What's wrong? You look like you saw a ghost," Tristan says.

"All good." I fake a smile.

The conversation changes subject, and I sit still as their words of wisdom roll around in my head.

My life became better because she was in it.

I glance over to see Elliot's gaze fixed firmly on me. He raises an eyebrow, and I snap my eyes away.

Don't even.

"Christopher?" I hear a female voice call. I glance over to see Heidi as she approaches our table. Nicki is with her too.

My two favorite girls.

My eyebrows rise in surprise and I stand. "Heidi." I kiss her cheek and turn and kiss Nicki. "Hello."

"You're back? Why haven't you called us?" Heidi smiles sexily and looks me up and down.

The girls and I have a thing going, a very good thing. *Had,* I correct myself.

"I just got in." I glance down at my brothers, who are all goofily smiling up at them. Yeah, yeah. I get it: they're gorgeous. "These are my brothers, Jameson, Elliot, and Tristan."

Heidi gives a sexy little wave with a playful sashay. "Gentlemen, I've heard a lot about you."

"Hello." They all smile up at her as if she's Aphrodite herself.

"What are you doing after?" she asks. "Let's catch up?"

218

"Ah . . ." I frown as she puts me on the spot. "I can't tonight." I gesture to my brothers. "I'll call you?"

"You promise?" She smiles as she leans in and pecks me on the lips.

I step back from her. "Sure."

They turn and walk off through the crowd, and we all stare after them. Heidi in her hot-pink tight dress and figure to die for: nothing is left to the imagination. And Nicki is just a walking wet dream, every man's fantasy.

I drop back into my seat, deflated.

"What the hell are you doing?" Tristan whispers. "Go and bend them over the bar, right now."

"Totally," Jameson agrees.

I scratch my head, flustered. I pick up my drink and drain the entire glass.

They did look good . . .

Fuck.

I glance over, and Elliot raises his eyebrow again.

"What?" I snap angrily.

He holds his two hands up in surrender. "Nothing."

"I'm not in the mood, okay?"

He widens his eyes, realizing he's hit a sore point.

Tristan's phone rings on the table, and he answers. "Hey, dude. Yeah, I'm ready." He glances at his watch. "Pick me up on your way through." He listens. "Okay, see you then." He hangs up. "Harrison just finished work. He's picking me up on the way home."

"Yeah, I've got to get going too," Jameson says as he puts his hand up for the bill.

"Let's have another one," Elliot says.

I nod, feeling more unstable than ever. "Get the whole fucking bottle."

Jameson's eyes rise to meet mine, and he frowns. "What's wrong with you? You're acting weird."

"Yeah," Tristan says. "I was just thinking the same thing."

"Nothing," I snap.

Elliot leans back in his chair. His knowing eyes hold mine, and he signals to the waiter. She comes over. "We'll have two more scotches, please."

Hayden would have had a margarita.

"Actually"—I cut him off—"I'll have a margarita . . . make it two."

"Margaritas." Elliot winces. "The fuck *is* wrong with you?"

"Four," I say to the waiter.

"No scotch?" she asks Elliot.

"No," I reply for him.

Jameson chuckles and slaps Elliot on the back as he stands. "Good luck with that one. Christopher left his taste buds in Spain."

Tristan stands too. "Thank fuck I'm not staying. I can't handle that shit." He pulls his jacket on. "What time we signing contracts tomorrow?"

"Nine," Jameson replies.

"See you then." I fake a smile. They amble off through the restaurant, and my eyes come back to Elliot. He's now leaning on his hand, his finger steepled up along his temple, his gaze fixed firmly on me.

"Who is she?"

"Nobody," I lie.

"Cut the shit. Who the fuck is she?"

"Just drop it."

"I can't help you if you won't talk to me."

I stay silent.

"Listen, dickhead . . . don't lie to me. I know there is something going on with you, and I want to know what it is."

"Four margaritas." The waiter puts them down on the table in front of us.

"Thanks." Elliot picks his up and takes a sip. He winces. "The first one is always so rough." He licks the salt from his lips. "Christ almighty," he mutters under his breath. "Tastes like fucking shit."

I exhale heavily. "Her name is Hayden Whitmore."

"Nice name." He smirks as he takes another sip. "Sounds like a character from a Jane Austen book."

I smirk and take a sip too. "She is."

He watches me and waits for me to elaborate.

"Kind, loving, innocent, and . . ." I pause. "Different to the women I know. Curvy and sweet, intelligent and witty. She's fucking perfect."

"So what's the problem?"

"I don't know."

He frowns. "What do you mean, you don't know?"

"I literally don't know." I tip my head back and drain my margarita glass until it's empty.

He takes another sip and holds his drink up and studies it. "It's tasting better now. Those first few mouthfuls were . . ." He fakes a shiver.

"It is."

"How do you know her?"

"She's one of my roommates in the hostel. We've been traveling together for three months."

He nods. "And how long have you been sleeping with her?" he asks.

"I haven't slept with her."

He screws his face up in confusion. "What?"

I shrug and drain my other glass. "I know."

"So . . . let me get this straight. You haven't even slept with this woman?"

I shake my head.

"So you're not even with her?"

"Well . . . technically, no."

"How is there a *technically* in that sentence?"

"Because I *am* with her. I spend every minute of every day with this girl and follow her around like a puppy, and she doesn't sleep around and hasn't been interested in me at all, and then we kissed and fooled around, and I freaked out and came home."

He stares at me. "Define *fool around*."

I puff air into my cheeks. "There was a head job involved."

His eyes widen in horror. "You made her go down on you and then flew the coop?"

"No," I stammer. "It wasn't a good time for her, and . . ." I pinch the bridge of my nose. "Yes."

He stares at me.

"We're friends, like, best friends, and she's all I can think about, and then I've gone and fucked it up," I blurt out.

"Why have you fucked it?"

"Because I'm . . ." I try to search for the right terminology. "Me."

He drains his glass, too, and puts his hand up to signal for more drinks. "I need more tequila for this conversation."

We sit in silence for a while.

"So . . . you don't want her?"

"That's the problem. I do."

He screws up his face. "So why aren't you pursuing this?"

"Because I already know I'm going to fuck it up, and she's the one person I can't hurt."

"Why do you say that?" He frowns.

"I'm not good enough for her."

"That's fucking ridiculous," he scoffs.

"Is it?" I reply. "I've thought long and hard about this, and the reality is, Elliot—and you and I both know this is true—I can't hold a relationship for even a week. I get bored. I have a wandering eye. I've never been able to take something to the next level." I try to articulate myself better. "I'm just not built to be with one woman. I don't want anyone depending on me."

"Because you've never been in love before," he snaps.

What?

My face falls.

"You're scared."

"I am *not* fucking scared," I fire back.

"Bullshit. You've fallen in love with this girl, and you're fucking shit scared."

"I am not in love with her," I fume. "I couldn't be. We don't even sleep together."

I drain my other margarita.

"And yet . . ." He holds his hand out toward me. "Look at you."

I drag my hand down my face in disgust.

"Look, I know that you have always said to me that when it's time to get married, you will pick someone and just do it. But let me tell you a secret, little brother . . . it doesn't happen like that. It isn't a conscious decision that you make. One day a woman will weave her way so deep under your skin that you will have no choice but to follow your heart."

I stare at him, my mind a clusterfuck of confusion. "I can't be divorced, Elliot."

His face falls. "Why would you even say that?"

"Because I can't." Anxiety tightens in my chest. "I would rather be dead than be divorced. A failed marriage is something that I couldn't forgive myself for. If I can't do it right, I don't want to do it at all."

"That's ridiculous." He screws up his face. "What the fuck are you talking about?"

The waiter puts another four margaritas down in front of us.

"Thanks." Elliot nods. We fall silent, both lost in our own thoughts.

"What do you think is going to happen?" he asks. "If you pursue this, what do you think is going to happen?"

"I *know* what's going to happen."

"What?"

"I'll fuck up . . . and she'll leave me. I'll be brokenhearted and see my kids every second weekend. They were her words, not mine."

"But . . ."

"I don't want to talk about this anymore," I snap. "I'm not going there with Hayden. She was the dream that I can't have. I'm coming back to London. My backpacking days are over. Trust me, she's better off without me."

"You're a fucking idiot," he snaps.

I drain another glass and slam it on the table. I feel myself get fuzzy. "Less talking." I hold my hand up for another round. "More drinking."

Four hours later Elliot and I stumble out of the bar and roll into the back of our waiting car.

"I'm margarooted," Elliot slurs to our driver.

I laugh hard. "That's true, he is." We carry on laughing in the back seat, and finally the car pulls to a halt outside Elliot's apartment.

He opens the door, and I put my foot on his behind and kick him out of the car. He stumbles onto the sidewalk, and I laugh. "Drive," I tell the driver.

We drive off, and ten minutes later we pull up in front of my building. I get out and stumble inside, and as I walk through the foyer, the concierge smiles. "Good evening, Mr. Miles."

"Hello." I smile.

"Your guests are waiting in the bar, sir."

"Huh?"

He gestures to the private lounge area, and I walk in to see Heidi and Nicki waiting. Their eyes light up when they see me, and I stop on the spot.

They both rush me and slide in and put their arms around me. Heidi leans up onto her toes and kisses my neck. "We've missed you, darling."

I look between the two beautiful women, and my cock tingles.

It's been a long time.

"Shall we take this upstairs?" She smiles darkly.

My eyes drop to her lips. "Yes, we shall."

Chapter 14

We walk through the foyer and get into the elevator as the staff pretend not to notice us. I turn to face the doors and push the button to my floor.

"God, it's been so boring without you in London." The girls are models and, like me, live in London but frequent New York.

I smile, amused. I must say I've missed their playful nature too; they live completely in the moment, and it is so fucking refreshing. "I'm sure you've found some poor unsuspecting bastards to keep you company."

Heidi runs her hand down over my behind and gives it a squeeze. "None like you, though, boss."

"You're in a league all of your own." Nicki smiles. She stretches up onto her toes and comes in for a kiss, and I turn my head. "Ease up," I warn her. "Wait until we're in my apartment."

She pouts her bottom lip as she fake sulks.

"Don't pull that face, or I'll wash your mouth out." I raise my eyebrow. "And you know what with."

She licks her lips as her dark eyes hold mine.

Fuck yeah.

My cock hardens, a dull ache forming between my legs.

I've missed my bad girls.

We get to the top floor, and I scan my fingerprint. Without missing a beat, Nicki bends and takes her dress off over her head and throws it to the side as she walks in front of me. My eyes drop down her hell-hot body and the black G-string she's strutting.

"No bra?" I ask her.

"Thought I'd save you the time." She bends and takes her G-string off with straight legs, like a stripper.

She slingshots it at me, and I smirk as I catch it. "Very thoughtful of you."

Heidi follows suit. She unbuttons her shirt and slowly slides it off. My eyes roam over her large breasts in her black lace bra.

Hmm . . .

I begin to hear my heartbeat in my ears.

It's the weirdest thing. Nicki's body has always appealed to me the most . . . but tonight, it's Heidi's curves that are doing it for me. Why do I like curves all of a sudden?

Hayden.

Startled by my realization, I clear my throat. "I'll get us a drink." I stumble into my bar; another drink is the very last thing I need. I fill a glass and drain it down. I glance into the other room to see the two girls are now completely naked.

Heidi is on all fours on my couch, waving her ass around in the air.

Fuck.

I fill the glass so fast my drink sloshes over the sides, and I tip my head back and drain the glass again.

Keep it together, man.

I fill three glasses, and with a deep steeling breath, I walk back into the room to find Heidi on her back with her legs spread and Nicki lying beside her. Nicki's fingers are parting the lips of Heidi's sex for me, pink and wet. Ready and waiting.

"Come and get it, boss." She smiles darkly.

Fuck.

My stomach roils, and I frown.

Huh?

I stare at them both for a beat, and if I do this, I know that it will mean the end of Hayden and me.

"What are you waiting for, boss?"

"Stop calling me that."

"What?"

Fuck this.

I can't believe I'm doing this. "You need to leave," I reply.

"What?" Heidi sits up onto her elbows, seemingly shocked.

"Don't be ridiculous." Nicki smiles as she begins to crawl toward me on her knees. She leans up and undoes my fly. She leans forward and breathes hot air onto my hardened cock through my boxers.

Warmth heats my blood . . . fuck.

Hayden.

I step back from her. "Now." I zip up my fly and march to the front door and open it in a rush.

"What the hell is wrong with you?" Heidi snaps.

"Everything," I bark. "And I don't appreciate the temptation. Don't come back here."

"Temptation?" Heidi's face falls. "You're with someone?"

Who the hell knows? Not me, that's for sure.

I roll my lips, choosing to remain silent, because any answer I give would be a lie.

"So what? Big deal," Nicki whispers as she sashays over to me. "I don't give a fuck if you got married, as long as I get to have you. I won't tell if you don't," she whispers sexily as she undoes my tie. "We can keep a secret . . . can't we, Heids?"

I stare at her. It would be so fucking easy to have her . . . them, and she's right: nobody would ever know.

Hayden.

I pull out of her grip and bundle up her clothes and throw them at her. "Get dressed."

"What?" they shriek.

I march back into the other room and pour the drinks down the sink. "Leave. Now," I call.

"Why did you bother bringing us up here if you didn't want to see us?" Nicki calls.

"Brain snap," I call back. *Dick snap, more like.*

Nicki tries again. "I can make you feel better."

"For fuck's sake, Nicki," I yell as I lose my patience, "enough." I point to the door. "Get out. Right now." I grab Heidi's dress and throw it at her and pick up the G-string and stuff it in her hand. "Please, I'm sorry." I'm flustered and tripping over my words. This is the first time I've ever done anything like this. "Just . . . you really need to go."

Nicki storms out the door, and Heidi hangs back. "You all right?" she asks softly.

My nostrils flare as I stare at her.

Do I look all right?

"Goodbye, Heidi."

Her eyes hold mine for a moment longer than they should, and I know she actually cares.

Hayden.

I turn and walk to the window and stare out at the city below. I hear the door quietly click closed, and regret swims deep in my stomach. I close my eyes, ashamed of myself. What the hell is wrong with me?

I'm fucking losing it.

I walk into the office at eight thirty sharp, and Jameson and Elliot are standing in reception. "Morning."

Jameson cringes when he sees me. "You look like shit."

"Margarooted." I march past them. "I hold you responsible," I say to Elliot.

Elliot chuckles. I walk down the corridor and into my office. I slump into my seat.

Fuck, I feel bad.

Headachy, nauseous . . . embarrassed.

Heartsick.

What must Heidi and Nicki think of my literal prick teasing last night?

Knock, knock sounds on the door.

"Come in," I call.

The door opens, and my mother appears. "Hello, darling."

And there she is, the most glamorous woman in New York. Dressed to the nines in a camel-colored designer dress and heels, hair done to perfection, with a ramrod-straight back. I smile. "Hi, Mom." I stand and kiss her cheek. "You look lovely."

She smiles up at me. "I've come to take you to breakfast." *Fucking Elliot.*

"I'm too busy today, Mom."

"Nonsense." She smiles. "I have only seen you for two hours since you got back. I need more time, sweetheart."

"I already ate."

"Come." She walks out of my office, ignoring everything I just said to her. "I'm stealing Christopher," I hear her announce to my brothers.

I trudge down the hall to see Elliot and Jameson still hanging around reception, chatting, and I narrow my eyes at Elliot. "You're fucked," I mouth as I walk past him.

230

He smiles and waves with his fingertips. "Have fun," he mouths back.

It's blatantly obvious Elliot has tattletaled on me, and I am not in the mood for this today.

We get into the elevator, and she links her arm through mine. "Tell me about your trip."

"It was great."

"Was?" She frowns up at me. "Does that mean you aren't going back?"

"No."

"Hmm." The elevator doors open, and she keeps her arm linked through mine as we walk through reception.

"Where do you want to have breakfast?" I ask her.

"I've got a table booked at Lamberts."

"That's too far. Let's just eat across the road in the café."

"Good lord, no. Have you tasted the coffee in that place?" Her driver opens the back door of her black Mercedes, and she climbs in. "Thank you, Roger." She smiles.

I exhale heavily and climb in after her. The thing is . . . you can't argue with my mother. She is the boss of everything. She says *jump*, and we all ask, *How high?*

⋇

Twenty minutes later, we are sitting in her favorite breakfast restaurant, and I smile over at her drinking her coffee out of a pink-and-gold fine-china cup and saucer.

Her eyes hold mine, and she smiles knowingly. "So . . . darling."

I roll my eyes. Here we go. "Spit it out."

"I don't spit. I'm not a camel, Christopher."

I smile broadly, and there it is, her obnoxious wit. I think we boys are all more like her than we are like Dad.

"Elliot told me you are having a few issues."

"Nope," I lie. "He got it wrong."

"Now, darling." She stares at me, unrelenting. "We are not leaving this restaurant until we discuss this."

"There's nothing to discuss, Mother."

"You don't want to talk about the little gold digger you met."

"She is *not* a gold digger," I snap. "She thinks I don't have a cent to my name."

"And there it is." She smiles sweetly. "I knew that would make you spit it out. Tell me all about it."

I narrow my eyes. Damn this calculating woman.

"So . . . she thinks you're broke?"

"Yes."

"And from what I hear she's not that attractive."

"What?" I scoff. "She's fucking beautiful."

"Language," she reminds me with a knowing smile.

We stay silent for a moment as we both sip our coffee.

"You know"—she puts her fancy pink cup down in its matching saucer—"she's not the girl for you."

I feel my hackles rise. "What makes you say that?"

"She's backpacking in filthy hostels and taking you for granted. She's obviously hurt you in some way if you've had to come scurrying home. Probably sleeping around on you, and I bet she won't commit to a relationship either."

"It's the other way around, Mom," I snap. My face falls. "Wait . . . you know I'm backpacking?" I ask.

"Do you really think I was born yesterday?" she replies as she watches me. "The stories about your fake course in Paris are fascinating, though. Definitely give your father and me a chuckle."

"Fucking hell." I drag my hands through my hair. She's just said that entire thing to catch me out.

"Talk to me, sweetheart," she urges.

My eyes hold hers, and I roll my lips, the closest to tears I've been in my adult life.

"I fucked it up, Mom."

"What happened?"

I shrug. "I don't know."

"Why did you leave?"

"I don't know." I stare across the restaurant as I go over the last few months. "We're friends, and she's just . . . so beautiful and sweet and everything I'm not, and then we kissed, and . . ." I shrug.

She smiles softly as she watches me.

"Anyway." I straighten in my chair. "It's over now."

Her eyes hold mine. "Is it?"

"I want it to be over."

"Some things you cannot choose. They choose you."

I sip my coffee. I have nothing more to say.

"Do you remember the time I pulled you out of school and you stayed home with Dad and me for the year and went to the speech therapist Miss Theresa on Tuesdays?"

"Vaguely."

"Do you remember what you used to talk about with her?"

"Not really."

"She used to talk about your problems and fears with you."

I frown. "Miss Theresa was a shrink?"

She pulls out a book from her bag. "Would you like to read it?"

I take it from her and look it over. It's a notebook, and typed-out letters are all glued inside. I check the date on the front page. I would have been ten when this was written.

It is my belief that Christopher is experiencing traits of perfectionism.

The next part is scribbled down in my mother's writing, as if she has researched the word *perfectionism*.

Perfectionism in psychology is a broad personality style characterized by a person's concern with striving for flawlessness and perfection and is accompanied by critical self-evaluations and concerns regarding others' evaluations.

Traits that Christopher readily displays:

All-or-nothing attitude.

Being highly critical of himself and others.

Feeling pushed by fear.

Having unrealistic standards.

Focusing only on results.

Feeling depressed or terrified by unmet goals.

Fear of failure.

Procrastination.

Defensiveness.

*Although he does not display the usual low self-esteem,
he does rely heavily on his brothers, which may indicate
a codependent relationship. Christopher feels that to be
accepted he needs to excel in all areas of his life.*

Failure isn't an option.

What?

I frown and read on. The next paragraph is from the therapist.

> **Moving forward, I would suggest that
> Christopher continue his therapy, as if he
> is left untreated, I would expect that these
> traits may worsen when he approaches adult-
> hood and enters into personal relationships.**

I close the book and pass it back to her, annoyed. "I was ten."

Mom's knowing eyes hold mine.

"All ten-year-olds are weird." I shuffle around in my chair, feeling uncomfortable. "I'm not a perfectionist."

She stays silent.

"I don't care what that stupid book says. I'm not a fucking perfectionist."

She sips her coffee.

"What made you take me to a damn shrink when I was ten, anyway?" I snap.

"You wouldn't do anything new."

"What do you mean?"

"If you didn't think you were going to be good at something, you point-blank refused to even attempt it."

"Like what?"

"It started in class. You refused to do algebra."

I frown. I don't remember any of this.

"You and your teacher came to blows. You dug your heels in and simply refused. She called me. It was at that time that we started to take notice of things that we had always seen as your little quirks."

I stare at her.

"Sweetheart." She takes my hand over the table. "It isn't easy being the youngest Miles brother, growing up like you did with so much pressure on you to be perfect."

"I don't feel pressured, Mom."

"Not within our family . . . but it has affected your personal relationships with women. You are thirty-one and never had a girlfriend. Don't you ever wonder why?"

I stare at her, horrified.

"You can do this, Christopher." She squeezes my hand in hers. "I know you can, but you need to know that it's okay if you fail."

No. It's not.

I get a lump in my throat.

"Loving someone is frightening; I know that," she whispers. "But one day, you *will* have to give control over to someone. The only decision you have to make now is . . . Is this particular girl going to be the one you trust with your heart, or is she going to be the one who got away?"

Hayden.

My eyes well with tears.

My mother passes me the book. "Take this home, sweetheart, and read it. Study it. Better still, go and see a therapist. I don't want to see you break your own heart."

"It's too late." I sigh sadly. "She's gone."

HAYDEN

I sit on the bench seat outside our hostel. I glance at my watch. Where is he? I start work in an hour. He's usually here by now.

I wait for another ten minutes, and then finally I look up the street and catch sight of him and wave. Big beautiful brown eyes smile back at me. "Hello, Miss Hazen."

"Hi, Eddie." I hold my breath. "Did he call?"

Eddie's face falls, and he shakes his head. "No."

My heart sinks.

It's been eight days since Christopher left, and damn it.

I got it wrong.

He's not coming back.

He stopped calling Eddie four days ago, and now Eddie is just as sad as me.

Which is sad, really sad.

The others all left for Germany on Monday. I couldn't bring myself to go with them. What if he comes back and I'm not here? Even if it is only to say goodbye.

I hope he's okay.

The thing is, I know that he cares. I get a lot of things wrong, but I haven't imagined the feelings between us. All along, I knew he was fucked up. I guess I didn't realize how badly.

I've overanalyzed this until I've nearly driven myself insane.

And I've come to the only conclusion there is. Maybe my body just wasn't enough for him. I've seen the girls he hooks up with, and I'm not even in their stratosphere. Maybe he got a taste of what I'm not and decided to run for the hills.

The thought is depressing, reality is depressing, and here I am on the other side of the world, and all I want is a hug from my mom.

Eddie walks me to the bus stop, and we wait silently, both lost in our own thoughts.

"What time do you finish work tonight?" he asks me.

"Eight."

"I can't pick you up at that time. I'm still working."

"That's okay." I smile and put my arm around my sweet little bouncer. He's taken Christopher's place as my personal bodyguard, coming to collect me when I'm working late. "It's hardly even dark then. I'll be fine."

The bus pulls up, and I kiss his cheek. "Thanks for walking me to the bus stop." I smile. "Have fun at work."

"I won't." He rolls his eyes. "You too."

"I most definitely won't either." I climb on the bus and take a seat and wave as we drive away.

I love Eddie.

Four hours later

I clear up table nine and wipe it down. I collect all the dishes and put them onto the tray, and I turn to go back to the kitchen, and I stop on the spot.

Christopher is standing at the front of the restaurant; his big eyes search mine.

I smile softly, and so does he. He walks toward me, and I put the tray of plates down and walk toward him.

"Hi," he whispers as he takes me into his arms.

Emotion overwhelms me. "Took your sweet time," I whisper.

"Trust me, it was anything but sweet." He kisses me softly, and his lips linger over mine.

"What have you got to say for yourself?"

He gives me a big beautiful smile. "Let's fucking do this."

Chapter 15

He takes my face in his hands and kisses me, a mix of relief and happiness with a perfect swipe of the tongue. We smile against each other's lips, and we kiss again and again. "Are you okay?" I whisper.

"I am now." He kisses me again.

"That was your first and last chance," I murmur.

"Fair call." His kiss deepens, and we forget where we are.

"Hey," my boss calls. "She's working."

"I've got to go." I smile as I try to step back.

Christopher holds my face to his as if unable to let me go. "Not yet." He kisses me again, and I feel it to my bones. "What time do you finish?"

"Eight."

"I'll pick you up?"

"Okay." I step back from him.

"We'll go on a date?" he asks hopefully.

I smile. "Okay."

"Okay," he repeats as he stares at me. "Okay . . ." He nods as if reassuring himself.

"You said that already."

"Okay." He frowns. "I did, didn't I?" He steps backward into the cutlery stand. "Sorry," he says to it before realizing it isn't a person. He chuckles, embarrassed. "Eight?"

He's nervous.

"Okay." I laugh.

"That's lots of *okay*s," he replies.

"Will you two knock it off?" my boss calls.

Christopher's eyes hold mine, and I smile an over-the-top smile. "See you tonight."

He turns and nearly skips out of the restaurant, and I proudly spin toward the kitchen.

He came back.

CHRISTOPHER

I walk at a quick pace down the street and glance at my watch. Four p.m.

Fuck.

I only have four hours.

"Where the fuck do you take a girl on a date to?" I think for a moment and then dial the only romantic person I know, Elliot.

"How'd you do?" he answers.

"She was surprisingly . . . forgiving."

He laughs. "Good news."

"I told her we'd go on a date tonight."

"Good idea."

"Was it?" I frown. "Because right now, romance is the last thing on my fucking mind."

"Hmm. You need to get through the date part to get to the good part."

"No shit, Sherlock," I snap. "I've got four hours to prepare so I can blow her socks off. What the fuck do I do?"

"Okay . . . um." He thinks for a moment. "What do you want to do?"

"Not spend our first night in a shitty shared room, that's for sure."

"Book a hotel room."

"She thinks I'm broke."

"Tell her . . ." He thinks for a moment. "Tell her that your grandfather knows the owner and has some free-night coupons that he will never get to use, so he gave them to you."

"Actually"—I nod as his plan rolls around in my head—"that's not bad."

"Then take her out for dinner."

"Uh-huh."

"But don't drink too much, or else you will fuck up while having sex."

I frown. "Define *fuck up*?"

"Be too rough."

"That's a fucking thing?" I gasp, horrified.

"Yes. That's a thing. Nice girls who haven't had sex in forever don't fuck like you do. You need to train her up. Gentle and easy the first few rounds."

"What?" I shriek. I'm so distracted that I bump into an old lady walking past. "I'm so sorry," I call as I watch her hobble away.

"What are you doing?" he asks.

"Knocking over grannies. What do you fucking mean, gentle and easy? How do you fuck gentle and easy, and more importantly, why would anyone want to?" I begin to sweat. "I'm going to screw this up for sure."

"It's fine."

I begin to freak out. "I don't . . . this is a bad idea . . . I don't know why. What the fuck was I thinking?" I cry.

"Calm down."

"Calm down." My eyes nearly pop from my head. "Calm down? You calm the fuck down," I cry. "This is a disaster."

"I'll book a hotel for you."

"Okay." I stop on the spot and begin to pace. I inhale deeply as I try to calm myself. "Something nice . . . with a spa."

"All right, I'll text you the address."

I imagine being naked in a spa bath with Hayden, and nerves simmer in my stomach.

Fuck.

I stop on the spot, the importance of this night suddenly now more evident than ever.

As if sensing my impending meltdown, Elliot says calmly, "It's okay, buddy. You've got this. Just stay out of your head, and you'll be fine."

I nod.

"Don't even think about it. I'll text you the address of the hotel. Pack an overnight bag and go and pick her up from work like normal, and you'll be fine."

"Okay." I nod. He's right.

"Maybe swing past a pharmacy and pick up some lube."

I pinch the bridge of my nose.

"Are you listening?"

"Yes," I spit. "I'm not having this conversation with you." I hang up in a rush.

I march up the stairs of the hostel and walk straight to my locker. I get out the gift I bought for Eddie. I've missed that little fucker.

I walk out to the bar area. He's serving up the other end and doesn't notice me. I slink onto a stool. He drifts in and out of languages like a pro, and I watch in awe. He turns and notices me, and his face lights up, and my stomach does a flip.

I frown. *What was that?*

"Hey." He smiles.

"My man." I laugh.

"Where the hell did you go?"

"I had some shit to do at home." I pass him his gift. "I got you something."

He stares at the baseball cap with wide eyes. It's navy blue with the white letters *NY* on the front. "That stands for New York," I tell him.

His mouth falls open, and it's as if I have bestowed him with a sacred family jewel. "Oh my god," he whispers. "This is incredible." He passes it back to me. "But I can't accept it. It's too much."

"I want you to have it."

"You've already given me so much."

"Put it on," I demand.

He puts it on and bends down to look at his reflection in the shiny refrigerator doors. He smiles proudly. "How do I look?"

"Great." I smile. His happiness is infectious.

Fuck, I love this kid.

"Thank you so much." He puts his hand over mine on the bar, and I just want to hug him. But I won't, because I'll come off creepy, and he's just a kid behind the bar that I shouldn't want to hug.

"Miss Hazen." He gasps.

"Yes, I'll see her tonight."

"She's been waiting for you to come back."

Thank god.

"I'm taking her somewhere special tonight." My phone beeps with a text. Elliot.

Bella Donna
Two nights.

Shit, two nights. That's a bit presumptuous, isn't it? Who the hell can be gentle for two nights in a row?

Ugh, this is all . . .

I guess I'll play it by ear. I could be in dumpsville tomorrow anyway. The spa bath will come in handy to drown myself.

245

There are people waiting for Eddie to serve them. "You want a beer?" he asks.

"Um." I frown, and Elliot's words come back to me. "No, I'm good. I'll catch you later, buddy."

He smiles. "Thanks for my hat. I'll never take it off."

HAYDEN

I fly around the restaurant at lightning speed. Cleaning up has never been more urgent.

I glance at my watch. He'll be here any minute. I wipe my palms on my apron, wet and clammy. Shit . . . I'm nervous. And I shouldn't be. It's just Christopher, but seeing him be nervous—someone who has absolutely zero to be nervous about—has now made me nervous. I *should* be nervous.

I haven't slept with a thousand people and am totally inexperienced, I don't have a figure to die for, and damn it, last time we made out, he ran for the hills.

I peer out the front window and see him walking up the street toward our meeting spot. I narrow my eyes to study him further. He's dressed in a nice shirt and jeans and has an overnight bag with him.

Huh?

Are we going somewhere?

Oh no . . . I need to shower, and I need to shave my legs, and damn it, he can't just surprise me with a night away on our first date. Another thought comes to my mind. Oh crap, he would have gone through my backpack to get my clothes, and I have dirty washing in there, and . . . ugh.

Without his drill sergeant ways of washing every day for us, I haven't been doing it at all. The very last thing on my mind when I have a broken heart is housework.

I bet he's done all my washing. *Shit.*

Why is he so damn neat?

I bet he's made my bed and cleaned the room, and what happened to the stereotypical woman nagging the man? What if I wanted that job? I mean, I don't . . . but still.

"Good night, Hayden," my boss calls. "Thanks for today."

"Okay." My stomach flips. "See you next weekend."

I go out into the kitchen and wash my hands and go to the bathroom. I try to fix my hair in the mirror and wipe the mascara from under my eyes.

Right . . . I drop my shoulders.

It's fine.

I grab my bag and make my way out and up the street. Every step closer I get to him, I get a little more nervous. He stands waiting patiently, an overnight bag in his hand.

"Hi." I smile.

"Hi." He bends and kisses me softly, his lips lingering over mine.

I've missed him.

"What's with the bag?" I ask.

"I . . . thought that . . . if it's okay"—he's tripping over his words—"I booked a hotel for the night."

"Oh . . ."

"But that doesn't mean I'm a sure thing," he adds. "Don't get any ideas."

"Right." I giggle. He takes my hand, and we begin to walk up the road. "Are you a sure thing, though?" I ask.

"Absolutely." He gives me a sexy smile with a wink.

"We don't need to stay in a hotel. That's way too expensive, and the others aren't even here."

"I didn't know that when I booked it." He pauses. "Well . . . my brother booked it with some coupons he had."

"Which brother?"

"Elliot."

248

I smile as I listen.

"So if the hotel is shit, we have him to blame."

"Good, I will." I smile. We walk in silence for a little way. "Did you pack me some things?"

"Yes."

"Did you do my washing?"

"Maybe . . ." His eyes flick over to meet mine. "I did *our* washing."

"You just got here today," I reply.

"I had things to wash."

"Did you make my bed?"

He raises his eyebrow. "Possibly."

I roll my lips.

"In my defense, I had a wank in your bed to your scent on the sheets. I made the bed out of gratitude in a postorgasmic glow."

I burst out laughing, and he laughs too. Our eyes linger on each other's, and my heart melts. He leans over and kisses me. "I missed you, Grumps."

"Not as much as I missed you."

He drops the bag and takes me into his arms, and we kiss, slow and tender, right here in the street in the middle of everyone.

"You're very kissy today." I smile up at him.

"I am, aren't I?" He frowns. "I'll have to work on that."

He takes my hand again, and we begin to walk. "Where are we staying?" I ask.

"I don't know, some hotel."

"Please tell me it has a bath."

"You like baths?"

"I love baths and haven't had one for three months. It's the one thing I hate about the hostels."

He winces. "But would you really want to get into a bath at the hostel with all the depraved dirty fuckers who stay there?"

"Well, my roommate wanks in my bed while I'm at work, so . . ." I shrug, and he laughs out loud.

Oh, this feels so good . . . and normal, laughing and being ourselves. I was worried that it was going to change between us. I'm so relieved that so far it hasn't.

"We're going out for dinner tonight." He smiles. "To celebrate."

"Okay."

Excitement bubbles in my stomach.

"What did you do when you were away?" I ask.

"Stuff."

I glance over. "Stuff?"

"Boring stuff. What do you want to eat tonight?"

He's changing the subject. "Something spicy."

"Spicy?" He frowns. "I wouldn't advise that."

"Why not?"

"We *are* sharing a bathroom."

I giggle. "Good point."

He glances down at the maps on his phone. "Actually, the hotel is too far from here. We'll catch an Uber."

"Okay." He punches in our coordinates. "We'll wait here." He pulls me onto the curb and pushes me up against the wall.

"What are you doing?" I whisper. People are beginning to look at us.

"Kissing my girl on the street. What does it look like?" His lips take mine.

His girl.

I smile against his lips; the night is already a raging success.

✕

Twenty minutes later the Uber pulls up in front of the fanciest hotel I've ever seen, and I peer out the window. "Are you sure this is it?"

"Uh-huh." He climbs out of the cab and helps me out.

"It looks too fancy," I whisper as doormen come running to help us.

"It'll do." He shrugs.

I smile as we walk into the reception. The doormen all run to hold the door open.

"Good evening, Mr. Miles." One nods.

Huh.

"How does he know your name?" I whisper.

"You know what these fancy places are like."

"No, I don't, actually."

He gestures to an elegant-looking sitting area. "Sit here while I check us in."

"No, I'll come."

He pushes me into the couch. "Sit."

Jeez. "Fine."

He goes to the front desk, and I look around at the concierge and all the staff, all wearing black suits and looking more distinguished than anyone I've seen so far in Spain.

Five minutes later we are riding in the elevator to our room. "What did you pack me?" I ask.

"Guess." He smirks.

"My white dress."

"Bingo."

"Aren't you sick of the sight of that old white dress?"

"Never. You can get married in it if you like." His eyebrows shoot up, horrified by what's just come out of his mouth. "That's fucking weird that I said that . . . ignore me." He begins to trip over his words again. "I mean, I don't . . . fucking hell."

"Relax, I know what you meant. You like the dress, I get it." I roll my lips to stop my smile. He's hilarious.

We get to our floor and walk up the corridor, and he opens the door. We walk in, and the air leaves my lungs. "What the hell?" I gasp. "That must be some coupon."

It's a full apartment, with beautiful art and luxurious furnishings. We walk through to the bedroom, and there's a four-poster bed and huge spa bath sitting in the middle of the room. "Wow," I gasp, wide eyed. "This is . . ."

Christopher narrows his eyes as he looks around. "Subtle, Elliot," he murmurs.

"What does that mean?" I ask as I walk over to the window.

"Nothing. My brother is a fucking idiot, that's all," he snaps.

He's still flustered about the wedding-dress comment.

"I want to shower; can you give me half an hour to get ready?" I ask him.

His eyes hold mine.

"Why don't you go to the bar downstairs and book us a restaurant and have a drink while you wait for me? I'll come down and meet you there."

"Okay, a drink sounds good." He pecks me on the lips and practically runs from the apartment. Poor bastard thinks he just proposed to me or something.

Right.

Operation hot chick.

I unzip my handbag and pull out the dress I bought today. It's rolled into a tiny ball. Thank god it's stretchy and doesn't need ironing. After Christopher came into work today, I rushed out on my lunch break and bought a date dress. Even grabbed some sexy underwear. It wasn't in my budget, but screw it—it is a special occasion.

I go through the bag of things he brought me and find my toiletries case. I quickly look through it, relieved to find a razor.

"Thank god."

I glance at my watch in a panic . . . "Okay, let's do this. I have twenty-eight minutes to make myself utterly irresistible."

Thirty-two minutes later

I stare at the reflection in the mirror. Not bad. My hair is up, not by choice. Unfortunately someone didn't pack my straightener, but that's okay. My makeup is minimal, and I have an excited glow oozing out of me. I turn and look at my behind. Again, not bad. How I found a dress this nice in three minutes I'll never know. It's fitted and ruched with spaghetti straps and in the most beautiful mauve color. It's not something I would have normally bought, but with one store to choose from and seven minutes to decide, it made the cut. I smile proudly. I kind of like it.

I take a deep steeling breath. This is it, the night I've been waiting for, and damn it, I just really want it to go well. I honestly believe we have something.

I put on a bright lipstick and cringe. Ew, I look like a stripper. I grab a tissue and wipe it off and put on another. "Gross." I wipe that off, too, and finally decide on a natural gloss. "This will have to do." I slide on my shoes: not the ones I would wear with this dress, but anyway . . . it is what it is. Christopher seems to like these shoes. He constantly gets them out for me to wear.

"Okay." I close my eyes. "Please let this go well."

I make my way down to the hotel restaurant and look around, and I spot him sitting at the bar. He turns at precisely the moment I see him and gives me the most beautiful broad smile as his eyes roam up and down my body.

I nervously make my way over to him. "Hi."

"Hi," he purrs as he slides his hand around my behind and pulls me close to him. "You look fucking hot, Grumps." He kisses me softly.

"Thanks." I shrug, embarrassed. "Didn't feel like wearing my wedding dress tonight."

He chuckles. "Thank god." He kisses me again as the air swirls between us. Screw the date—let's just go back upstairs right now. "I got you a drink."

I look down to see two margaritas on the bar. "My favorite," I reply as I slide onto the stool beside him.

His eyes hold mine, his chin leaning on his hand as he smiles dreamily over at me. "You're *my* favorite."

I nervously sip my drink, not sure how to reply. "What are we eating?"

"I know what I'm eating." His dark eyes hold mine.

Fuck.

"I mean food."

He raises an eyebrow as if unimpressed and sips his drink. "I don't know, we'll just go for a walk, I guess. I didn't even know the names of any restaurants around here."

"Okay." I pick up my drink and take a sip. "Hmm, heaven in a cup." I smile.

"I had a particularly large margarita night when I went home in your honor."

"You did?"

"Elliot and I got margarooted."

I giggle. "Margarooted?"

"Uh-huh."

"Tell me about Elliot." I smile. "You two seem to be close."

"Hmm, actually"—he thinks for a moment—"he's a lot like you."

"How so?"

"He's a tragic romantic, grumpy. Reliable and loyal."

I smile. "He is?"

"Uh-huh."

"And you have three brothers?"

"I do. Jameson is the oldest, Tristan is next, and Elliot, and then me."

"You're the youngest child?"

He nods.

"Are you all alike?"

"No." He shakes his head. "Opposites. Jameson is driven and grouchy. Tristan and I are very much alike. We even look alike. I guess Elliot is a good mix of the three of us combined."

I smile. I love hearing about his family.

"What about you?" he asks.

"I'm an only child."

His face falls. "An only child?"

"My mom hemorrhaged during childbirth with me and, to save her life, ended up having a complete hysterectomy. There were no other children after me."

"Oh." He listens intently. "How was that, growing up without siblings?" He frowns. "I can't imagine it."

"I don't know any different." I shrug. "So."

He nods as he listens intently.

We fall silent and sip our drinks. There's an elephant in the room that we are both avoiding talking about.

I don't want to be the one who brings it up. He needs to.

"Germany this week, huh?" I smile.

"Yeah." He nods. "Or we could stay here for a while longer. There's a bartending course I wouldn't mind doing. I already inquired about it, and there's a vacant position next week."

"Really?" I frown, surprised. "You want to be a bartender?"

"Well . . ." He shrugs. "I've been thinking about what I could do for the next nine months, and there are only really two things I'm interested in."

"What are they?"

255

"Being your PA and making cocktails."

"My PA?" I frown.

"Pussy attendant."

I giggle. "Oh, I do like the sound of that."

"Do you pay bonuses?" he asks.

"I pay in orgasms."

He chuckles and taps his glass with mine. "My favorite currency."

"Okay." I shrug. "Do the bartending course and then we'll go, I guess."

"Deal." He smiles. He runs his hand up my thigh under the table, and I sip my drink. Is he going to bring up anything at all about why he left?

We fall silent again.

"What else did you do while you were home?" I ask. "You said you had to sign something."

"Yeah, I did." He shrugs. "That and had a near mental breakdown."

"About what?"

"You."

My eyes search his. "Why did you leave?"

"I panicked."

"About what?" I whisper as I put my hand over his on my thigh. "Why? It's just me."

"Just you is . . . a lot."

My face falls. "What does that mean?"

"Nothing." He sips his drink as if trying to think of the right thing to say. "I've never . . ." He exhales heavily, lost for words.

"Christopher," I prompt him, "you can talk to me. We are friends before anything else."

His eyes search mine. "You're the first girl I've ever wanted more with."

I lean in and kiss him softly.

"You're the first girl that I've ever been loyal to."

"We only just got together."

"I haven't been with anyone for a few months."

What?

My heart flips . . . he's doing it without me asking.

It's all falling into place.

He shrugs. "I couldn't . . . and I . . . I don't want to screw this up."

I smile over at my beautiful man. "You won't." I kiss him again.

"How do you know?" he asks.

"Because as long as we're communicating openly, you can't screw things up."

He stares at me.

"Running away is how you screw things up."

"I'm sorry, I was just so . . . and . . ." His eyes hold mine; he's lost for words.

"I'll make a deal with you," I say.

"What's that?"

"If things get too heavy and you feel yourself freaking out or being uncomfortable, just say to me, 'I'm going to need a minute.'"

He frowns.

"And then I'll know what's going on, and I'll step back for a while to let you adjust."

"I don't want you to have to tiptoe around me," he replies.

"I won't be. Asking for some space is completely healthy in a relationship. You need to learn to trust us."

He nods, seemingly deep in thought.

"You're lucky that I know what a big baby you are," I reply as I sip my drink.

His mouth falls open in fake horror, and I want to lighten the mood.

"And maybe you just need a good punishing. I'll smack you tonight."

"What does that mean?"

"There's a few things you don't know about me too," I reply as I try to keep a straight face.

"Such as."

"Christopher." I take his hand in mine, acting serious. "I'm a dominant, and I want to tie you up and whip you with a belt and fuck you up the ass with a strap-on dildo."

He snorts margarita up his nose and chokes. "What the fuck?" He coughs.

"And . . . I want you to wear anal beads," I continue. "I bought you some. I know they're big, but this is the size I want you to be stretched to."

His horrified eyes hold mine.

"I have them in my handbag. I'll put them in," I reply seriously as I keep playing along. "We can go into the bathroom and do it now if you want. You just have to bend over and touch your toes. I've got some lube, and it will only be uncomfortable for a moment, but you will learn to love it . . . for me."

"Absolutely fucking not." He slams his drink down onto the counter in an outrage. "That is *not* happening. Hayden, get that shit out of your head right fucking now," he demands.

I burst out laughing, unable to continue the ruse any longer. His eyes widen as he realizes I was pulling his leg. "Are you serious?" he gasps. "I just had a fucking heart attack."

I giggle.

"Don't," he cries. "I thought I was dating Jack the fucking Ripper or some shit."

I laugh hard and so does he. Relieved, he grabs the back of my head and drags me in and kisses me. "The only person who is getting fucked up the ass around here is you," he murmurs against my lips.

"Aah . . . that's a no." I pull out of the kiss. "That is not my thing. I've never even done that before."

His eyes widen in amazement. "So . . . it's all *mine*?" he whispers in awe.

"No," I reply. "It's mine, actually."

His eyes blaze with fire, and damn it, why did I even joke around about that subject with a sexual deviant? This is going to come back and bite me on the ass . . . literally.

The bartender comes over. "You two after anything?"

Christopher's eyes flick to me. "You want to get going to somewhere else?"

"No." I smile. "I'm happy with what I have right here."

※

We burst through the hotel room door. Our lips are locked.

Desire between us has hit fever pitch.

The apartment is darkened, lit only by lamps.

The mood in here is sexual, but maybe that's the company I'm with.

Christopher Miles is sexual.

It's late. We didn't even leave the hotel. We drank and ate and laughed right downstairs, and it's already the best night of my life.

Christopher bends and lifts my dress over my head, and the room falls silent.

His dark eyes drop down my body. He licks his lips as he drinks me in.

I stand before him in nothing but lace underwear and high heels.

"Do you have any idea how badly I've wanted to touch you like this?" he murmurs as his lips take mine. His tongue swipes tenderly through my lips, and my eyes close.

Oh . . .

"How many times I've jerked off imagining it was you?"

I smile against his lips as we kiss.

He undoes my bra and slowly takes it off. His eyes drop to my full breasts, and he inhales sharply. He cups them in his hands. His thumbs dust back and forth over my hardened nipples as he kisses me.

He drops to the floor and undoes my stilettos. With his eyes locked on mine, he licks up my thigh, and I hold his shoulders for support as I watch.

He kisses me there . . .

I can't breathe.

Thump, thump, thump, goes my heart.

Oh god, can we just get on with this? I'm so nervous that I'm about to pass out.

He pulls my panties to the side and licks me with his thick strong tongue, and I shudder.

It's been a long time.

"Hmm," he moans into me. He stands as if spurred on and takes my hand and leads me into the bedroom. The room is lit only by the lamp. The ambience in here is perfect.

He lays me down on the bed, and then he slides my panties down and spreads my legs.

"That's it," he whispers. His voice is deep, husky. Different from how it normally sounds.

He runs his hand down my face, over my breasts, and down between my legs. Without hesitation, he slides his finger deep inside of me and inhales sharply. "Fucking hell, you feel good," he breathes.

I clench around him, and arousal blazes in his eyes. "Do that again."

I do it again, and his jaw tics. He stands with urgency and kicks off his shoes. Then, with his eyes locked on mine, he undoes the buttons on his shirt, and his beautiful body comes into view: broad tanned chest, stomach rippled with muscle, and a trail of dark hair that disappears into the top of his jeans.

I hold my breath as he slides down the zipper on his jeans and then slides his jeans and boxers down and takes them off, and my eyes widen in horror.

What.

The.

Fuck.

His dick is huge and angry looking . . . not like any dick I ever saw before. I open my mouth to say something, but no words come out.

He smiles, reading my mind, and puts his hands proudly on his hips. "Well?"

"Umm . . ." My saucer-size eyes are going cross-eyed. "I'm going to need a minute."

"You don't have one." He smiles as he crawls over the top of me.

"Seriously . . ." I begin to freak out. "That's . . ."

"Yours."

My heart somersaults in my chest, and I smile up at him.

Mine.

"Kiss me," he breathes.

In those two words, my fear disappears, and I lean up and kiss him. We take our time, kissing slowly, enjoying being here and in the moment with each other. So many nights we've lain together, and now we're here, doing this, naked and aroused.

It's surreal.

He goes to move down my body, and I stop him.

"No."

His brow furrows. "What?"

"Can you just . . . kiss me through this. I feel better when you kiss me."

I'm too nervous for him to go down on me the first time.

"Okay." He smiles against my lips. "I can do that, baby."

The thing is, I know he's a player and has probably slept with more people than I even know . . . but this feels special.

He watches as his fingers work my body, the perfect pressure, the perfect depth.

I'm writhing beneath him, begging for more. "Now," I whimper. "I need more, now."

He holds himself at the base and rubs his tip through my lips. "Condom," I whisper.

"Really?" He frowns.

"I'm not on the pill, unless you want a baby?"

"Fuck no." He bounces out of bed in one minute flat and shuffles through the overnight bag. He comes back and kneels on the bed. I watch as he rolls one on, and then he crawls over me and lies between my legs. Our kisses turn desperate, and my hands roam up and down over his muscular back.

Damn it, he's perfect.

He pushes forward and is met with resistance.

Ow.

He kisses me deeper and pushes forward again. The stretch burns.

"Ahhhh," I whimper.

"It's okay, babe," he murmurs against my neck. "I'm here." He bites my neck. "Relax. Let me in."

I nod. I'm trying, I really am, but fucking hell . . . what kind of dick is this?

A big one.

His kiss turns frantic, and I know that he's grappling with control. His breathing is labored as he tries to hold himself back.

I lift my legs to wrap around his waist, and he drives me into the mattress. Searing pain racks me, and I whimper.

"Shh, shh," he whispers in my ear. "I'm in." I feel him smile against my neck. "I'm in, baby." He kisses me. "Do you have any idea how fucking hot this is, Grumps?"

I giggle. "What . . . that I'm tight?"

"You're tighter than tight." He smiles darkly. "Fucking perfect." He lifts my leg up to his chest and turns his head and kisses my ankle with an open mouth.

"Careful," I warn him.

His eyes flicker with fire, and goose bumps scatter up my spine. He slowly circles one way and then the other to try to loosen me up. "I need you to relax for me," he whispers. I thrash beneath him, the burn so good. "Hayden," he says, bringing me back to the moment. "Look at me."

I drag my eyes to his.

"Relax or I'm going to hurt you. Do you understand?"

I nod.

"You need to tell me if I'm too rough."

"I'm okay."

With our eyes locked, he pulls out and slides back in. I stretch wide.

Oh god . . . so, so good.

I've never been fucked like this.

He slides back in, and I get a rush of moisture and loosen up a little. "That's it," he coaches me. "Good girl, just like that."

His husky voice does things to me, and I open my legs to the mattress, granting him full access. His eyes roll back in his head as his strong arms hold his body up off mine. He spreads his knees so he can ride me better, and I rise to the challenge. We go slow for a while. Measured and gentle pumps, and each time he pulls out, I get a little braver.

My body begins to lift off the bed to meet him, and he moans as his eyes flutter closed. "Fuck . . . so good." He pants as we get rougher and rougher.

Soon we are hard at it. The bed is hitting the wall, and I can see nothing but stars.

I can hardly breathe, it's so good.

"Hayden," he moans. "Oh . . . I'm going to come." He moans. "So fucking hard."

Hearing his husky, aroused voice does things to me, and my body contracts as I spiral out of control, headfirst into a killer orgasm. "Ahhh," I cry out.

"Fuck." He moans as he slams into me, hard and piston fast, and then he holds himself deep. I feel the telling jerk as he comes deep inside my body.

We kiss as we move together, completely emptying our bodies, and he drops his head to my chest. Our skin is wet with perspiration as we pant. I feel him smile.

So close, so perfect.

I stare up at the ceiling, horrified.

I'm going to need a moment.

Chapter 16

I drag my eyes open to see big brown eyes. Christopher is lying on his side and leaning up onto his elbow, watching me.

I frown. "What are you doing?"

"Admiring the view." He smiles and leans over and kisses me. "Good morning."

"Hmm, morning," I grumble with my eyes closed. Why is he so perky this early?

I begin to doze again, and I can feel he's still watching me, and I open one eye. Yep . . . sure enough, still staring. "Go back to sleep."

"I'm hungry."

It's too early for this shit. I roll over and put my back to him. "Raid the minibar."

"No."

I ignore him.

"Let's go out to breakfast." He taps me on the shoulder with his finger.

I shrug him off. "Don't."

He does it again and again until he's doing it continually.

"Why are you so annoying?"

"I'm fucking starving over here."

"You are not starving, Christopher. We ate last night."

"I didn't eat much."

"Well, that's your stupid fault." I try to continue sleeping.

"No, it's your fault," he replies.

"How is it my fault?"

"I didn't eat much all day yesterday because I was nervous."

I smile into my pillow. He leans over me and pulls me back into his arms, his lips on my temple. "Feed me."

"Let me sleep for half an hour."

"No." He rolls me over onto my back and pulls my top leg over his body, and he gently runs his fingertips over the lips of my sex. "How *are* your particulars this morning?"

I smirk. "Particulars?"

"At my service"—he taps my sex—"and ready for duty?"

"Absolutely not." I close my legs. "My particulars are annihilated and in no shape for war."

He chuckles. "Wimp." He bends and kisses me there. "What if I kiss it better?"

I smile. "No."

"Okay, I'll settle for second prize."

"What's second prize?"

"A breakfast date."

"Hmm." My eyes are still closed. "Why don't you go and practice your wanking in the shower like a good boy?"

"No more wanking." He bends and bites me on the behind. "I have my very own sex doll now." He bites me again. "And she fucks like a demon."

"You're about to see how demonic she can be," I reply dryly.

He rolls me over onto my back and holds my arms over my head and looks down at me. "After we eat, we can do whatever you want for the rest of the day."

His dark hair hangs over his face. His big brown eyes are playful and full of fun.

I smile up at him. "I had a wonderful night last night."

He kisses me softly, and I feel him harden up against me. "Me too."

"Does that thing ever go down?"

"Occasionally." He smiles as he kisses me again.

I can't have sex. I'm seriously sore.

"Aren't we going out for breakfast?" I ask.

"Yes, but now I'm hungry for something else." He licks my lips, and I feel it all the way down there.

"How often do you like to have sex?" I ask.

"In this situation"—he pumps me with his hips—"I imagine twice a day."

"You're a sex maniac." I smirk. "What *is* this situation?"

"Like . . . my very own fuck doll."

I smile goofily. Who would have ever thought I would like to be called his fuck doll? Three months ago, I would have died at the mere thought. Now I see it as a term of endearment.

"You mean girlfriend?"

He chuckles. "*Girlfriend* is so last year. I prefer the term *fuck doll*. Much more diverse."

I giggle. "And what are the terms and conditions that come with your fuck doll?"

He frowns as if contemplating his answer. "Well . . . I'll keep her well fed . . . with cock, of course." He pumps me with his hips.

"Didn't see that answer coming." I smile.

He chuckles. "And I'll wash her clothes."

"Wank on her bed?" I act serious.

"Of course."

"Lecture her about being messy?" I ask.

"On the hour."

I giggle. "Looks like nothing is changing, then."

He kisses me softly, his lips lingering over mine, and I begin to feel a rush of arousal building.

"And what about other fuck dolls?" I ask.

"What about them?" His eyes hold mine.

"You tell me."

"There'll be no other fuck dolls, if that's what you're asking."

I smile up at my man.

"Unless . . . we could have a threesome sometime. That's okay if you're there, though, right?"

My eyes widen in horror.

He pokes me in the ribs. "Got you," he teases.

"That's not remotely funny," I snap.

"Although, we are going to the sex shop today," he says as he pulls me by the hand out of bed.

"What for?"

"I need to buy you a vibrator."

"What?" I gasp. "You have more than enough dick for the both of us."

He chuckles as he pulls me into the bathroom. "That's the problem. I need a warm-up toolbox."

I stare at him as he turns on the shower.

"What's a warm-up toolbox?" I ask.

"Toys for us to play with to stretch you out when I'm not lost in the moment." He pulls me in under the water and soaps up his hands and begins to wash my back.

What the hell?

"What's wrong with being lost in the moment?" I ask as he massages my shoulders from behind.

He kisses my ear. "See how sore you are today?"

"Yes."

"I was using about five percent of the tank."

My eyes widen. *That* was 5 percent . . . what the actual fuck?

He chuckles and pulls me back toward his body. I feel his hard cock up against my back. "Can't wait to give you one hundred percent, baby," he breathes into my ear. Goose bumps scatter up my arms.

His fingers slide down, and he runs them over my back entrance, gently probing me where he shouldn't. "All barrels, both tanks." He pushes the tip of his pinkie finger in, and I jump forward and grab onto the tiled wall as my senses go into overdrive. "It's going to be so fucking hot, Grumps," he whispers darkly as he massages me there. "I can't fucking wait."

Jeez.

I swallow the nervous lump in my throat as I grip the tiles for dear life.

Fuck . . . I'm a real-life sex doll for a perverted deviant.

Let the training begin.

⋈

I watch him sip his coffee casually as he reads the morning paper . . . as if he hasn't just had the world completely rocked to its core.

Or maybe that's just me . . .

The café we are having breakfast in is busy and bustling. Christopher had an omelet, and I had pancakes. And while he's completely calm and sated, on the other side of the table is a completely different story. I'm flushed, heated, sated, shocked that I like his depravity, and damn it . . . even a little embarrassed.

We didn't have sex this morning. We didn't need to.

He came listening to me moan while he showed me what I've been missing in the shower.

I came while being horrified that I liked it.

He sips his coffee, and his dark eyes rise to mine, and I feel myself flush in the face.

He raises an eyebrow in question. "What?"

"Nothing." I smile bashfully.

He smiles knowingly and goes back to his paper, totally unfazed and utterly gorgeous.

I glance around at the people sitting at the tables in the restaurant. Can they tell what we've been doing?

I feel like a teenager again, experiencing everything for the first time.

Sex with Christopher Miles isn't just sex . . . it's an apocalyptic event in history.

A revelation for womankind.

Who knew . . .

"What are we doing today, Grumps?" he asks casually.

I smile goofily. *More of that . . . please.* "I don't know. We have another night in heaven, so I will need to collect some clothes from the hostel, and then"—I shrug—"what do you want to do?"

"Maybe a swim at the beach." He twists his lips. "I need a new book to read, and I want to find a sex shop."

"Shh," I whisper as I look around guiltily. "Keep your voice down."

He smirks at my embarrassment. "Sex shop," he mouths.

"What book do you want to get?" I ask to change the subject.

"Don't know yet. I'll see what grabs me." His phone buzzes on the table, and the name *Elliot* lights up the screen. He answers it. "Hi." He chuckles and traces his finger in a circle on the table as he listens. "Perfect."

I listen intently.

"No, it was good." He smiles. "Thanks for organizing it."

They're talking about the hotel room.

"Hayden"—his eyes rise to meet mine—"she was fucking incredible." He gives me the best come-fuck-me look in all of history.

I feel myself blush.

Jeez. Does he have to tell his brother everything?

"Uh-huh," he answers, and then he laughs out loud once more. What's so damn funny?

The waitress comes over to collect our plates. She leans over Christopher, and her eyes linger on him a little too long. She wipes the table down and smiles playfully as she waits for him to notice.

Huh?

I'm sitting right here, bitch.

He continues to chat, completely unaware of her.

The thing is, I know how much female attention Christopher receives, and I get it—he's utterly gorgeous. It annoyed me before how brazen these women who flirt with him are, but now that I am actually sleeping with him, it's downright infuriating.

She lingers and lingers, waiting for him to make eye contact with her.

What the hell?

She leans over him again, and he glances up. She gives him a sexy smile, and his brow furrows. He's noticed it too.

Right, that's it.

"Are you taking your time on purpose so you can ogle my boyfriend?" I ask her.

She turns to me, startled.

Christopher smirks and nods behind her back.

"I just . . ."

"Our table is clean," I reply, unimpressed.

"Of course." She scurries back to the kitchen. "Sorry."

Sorry she did it or sorry she got busted?

Stupid idiot.

"Go, Grumps." Christopher smiles. He listens to Elliot, who must be asking what's happening. "Hayden's going all caveman over here and waving girls along," he tells his brother before he laughs again.

"What the hell?" I whisper angrily. "Don't tell him that."

"I've got to go," he says. "I'm about to get dragged back to the room by my balls." He laughs. "I can only hope." He hangs up.

"Don't tell your brother I'm waving girls along. He's going to think I'm a psychopath."

"Were you waving her along?" he asks.

"That's not the point," I snap. "And why did you tell your brother I'm dragging you home by the balls?"

"Because I'm hoping you are, right before you suck on them and slap them up against your ass cheeks." He gives me a playful wink.

"Will you be serious for one minute?" I whisper angrily. "There will be no ball sucking . . . or slapping, for that matter."

He exhales heavily as if he has the weight of the world on his shoulders. "I guess you want to go and buy a book instead?"

I smirk, feeling embarrassed by my little jealous and antifun outburst. "No," I announce. "I thought you were taking me to the sex shop?"

His eyes light up, and he rubs his hands together in glee. "Now we're talking."

Five hours later we walk out of our hotel lobby hand in hand. We're on our way to the hostel to pick up some more clothes for tonight.

And . . . just as Christopher predicted, we went to the sex shop, came back to our room, and spent the last two hours in bed. I can confirm there was both sucking and slapping. I can also confirm that the man is an animal. I'm feeling pretty animalistic myself, actually.

272

I feel flushed, excited, and utterly well fucked.

"Good afternoon," Christopher says to the doormen.

"Good afternoon, sir," they all reply.

He looks around. "You want to walk, Grumps?"

"It's a bit far, isn't it?"

"It is a nice day." He twists his lips. "Uber then?"

"I guess."

"We do have bicycles, sir," one of the doormen replies.

"You do?"

"Yes, sir. At the other entrance on the side street, we have bicycles you can use."

Christopher's eyes meet mine. "Want to ride a bike?"

I smirk. I have been riding all day.

"Sure."

"Great, thanks." We walk around to the other door, and the bikes are all lined up.

They are bright yellow and vintage-style with the big loopy handlebars.

"Can we have two bikes, please?" he asks the attendant.

"Sure thing." The attendant unhooks two bikes, and we put on our helmets and climb on.

I wobble around as I push off. "I haven't ridden a bike in years." I laugh.

"Same," Christopher replies as he concentrates. "Woo." He gets the wobbles and crashes into the curb. He has to dive off before he falls.

I laugh so hard I jackknife the handlebars, and I fall off too. I lie on the side street, giggling as he and the attendants help me up.

"Our date tonight might be in the hospital," Christopher says as he pulls me up by the hand.

"I know." I giggle. Oh, this is so fun.

The attendant looks worried. "May I call you a cab, sir?"

"No, it's okay," Christopher replies happily. "You all right, Grumps?"

"Uh-huh." I push off again, this time concentrating on keeping the handlebars straight. I stand as I pedal, and he does too. We both laugh out loud like little kids riding bikes for the first time. We get to the intersection and look both ways. To the right is full-on traffic chaos, and to the left it's deserted.

We glance at each other. "Left," we say together. We push off, and with huge goofy smiles on our faces, we ride off into the sunset . . . only there is no sunset.

※

The backpackers' hostel is packed to the rafters with new travelers. The sound of laughter is echoing down the halls, and the distinct smell of body odor lingers in the air.

I'm in my room collecting a few things, and Christopher is holding the door open as he waits for me. "This place is a fucking hole," he murmurs as he looks down the corridor.

A guy walks down the hall toward the bathroom and looks Christopher up and down. "What's your fucking problem?" Christopher says.

The guy grunts and keeps walking past.

"Rude prick," Christopher huffs.

I smile and quickly make my bed.

"Seriously, our days of backpacking are nearly over," he says to me.

"Yeah, well . . ." I pull the sheet up. "Where else can we afford?"

He rolls his lips, unimpressed. "Somewhere better than this, I'm fucking sure of it."

The sound of drunk men screaming laughter from the bar echoes down the hall, and Christopher shakes his head, disgusted. "I hate that Eddie has to work here."

"Eddie loves his job," I reply, distracted.

"But does he? He's fourteen and being forced to work to support his grandmother; that's not a childhood."

"Also . . . not for you to judge."

"Hmm." He glances at his watch. "He starts in two hours. Hopefully those drunk fuckers are gone by then."

"If not, we can hang around until they leave," I reply, knowing he'll be worried all night if we don't.

"Okay." He nods.

"Why don't you call him and ask him to come to the beach with us?" I say.

"Yeah?" He smiles, surprised. "You wouldn't mind?"

"Why would I mind? I love Eddie too."

"Okay." He walks out into the corridor to call him, and I look around the shitty room. Christopher is right. I think it is nearly time for a change in scenery.

We wait on the curb, sitting on our bikes. "Here he comes." Christopher waves excitedly.

Eddie laughs and walks down to meet us, his NY cap firmly in place. "The fuck you doing, man?"

"Language," Christopher says. He takes off his helmet and passes it to Eddie. "Get on."

"Huh?" Eddie hangs on to the helmet as he looks the bike over. "What do you mean?"

"Get on my handlebars. I'm driving us to the beach."

Eddie's eyes flick to meet mine. "Can he drive this thing?"

"Not really. I suggest the helmet."

Eddie chuckles and puts the helmet on over the top of his cap. He sits on top of Christopher's handlebars. His skinny legs are bunched up.

Christopher pushes off and wobbles at the extra weight, and Eddie laughs. "Faster," he cries.

"I'm not a fucking donkey," Christopher calls.

"I beg to differ," I call.

Christopher's eyes flick over to me at the double meaning.

"You're a weak donkey," Eddie cries into the wind. "Faster. Go faster."

"I'll give you a weak donkey." Christopher stands and starts to power pedal. Eddie laughs out loud, and I pedal hard and try to keep up.

This is the most fun I've had in forever.

We stagger down the street arm in arm. It's past midnight, and we are on our way to our hotel. We've had the best day. We went to the beach with Eddie this afternoon, and Christopher threw us around in the sea for hours.

We went back to our hotel and then went out to dinner and had another night of drinking fancy drinks in exotic bars.

"Oh my god, we have spent so much money," I say as we walk.

"Who cares," Christopher replies. "Stop worrying about fucking money."

"You'll be worrying about money in the morning," I remind him.

"I'm doing this bar course, and then I'm going to get a great job, and then we can afford somewhere better to stay." He frowns and then mouths the word *we*.

I hold him in my arm just that little bit tighter. He's done so well since he came back.

Not one freak-out. He's ready for this . . . for us.

It's obvious.

We turn the corner, and there's a bunch of buskers on the street. There's a band with drums and a saxophone. Such a cool vibe. People are gathering around, and as we walk up, Christopher takes me into his arms and begins to dance. He twirls me around, and I hold my arm up in a dramatic fashion. He tips his head back and laughs out loud.

The band gets excited that we are dancing and begins to play louder dance music, and a few other couples begin to dance. Christopher is throwing me around, and we are laughing and having the best time. He pushes me out and pulls me back to him with a thud. He spins me and spins me and then holds me close. I look up at his beautiful face, so handsome and carefree.

"Today was the best day I've ever had," he says softly.

My eyes search his, and I kiss his big perfect lips. I want to blurt out that it was my best day, and that every day in his arms is like a dream come true.

That . . . I love him.

But I won't, because then . . . he *will* freak out.

"Can we go home now?" I whisper. I want to show him what he means to me, even if I can't say it out loud.

"And miss out on this amazing dance floor?" He gasps as he tips me back. I laugh as I see the upside-down road come dangerously close to my face. "No way." He keeps dancing, having the time of his life.

"No way?" I laugh.

"Grumps, this is the only entertainment we can actually afford. Tomorrow it's back to stale bread and water. We have to live it up while we can." He spins me out and snaps me back.

I smile goofily up at my man. "I love being broke with you."

He laughs out loud. "Don't get used to it."

Chapter 17

"Okay, thank you," I hear Christopher say. He dances into the bathroom and puts his hands on his naked hips. "Guess who got us a late checkout?"

"You did."

"I'm the man." He points to his chest. "Move over."

I scooch over in the deep bubbles, and as he sits down, the hot bath sloshes over the sides, flooding the floor. He slides into the water up to his neck as we lie top and tail.

It's ten in the morning, and we're taking advantage of every last minute in heaven.

A bath is a luxury we haven't got access to in the hostel.

"I don't want to leave this place," I groan.

He closes his eyes in peaceful bliss. "You think I do?"

"What days is your course on?"

"Friday and Saturday."

"Okay." I think for a moment. "I guess we'll head on to Germany on Sunday to meet the others?"

He nods.

"I think I'm going to quit my weekend job at the restaurant."

"Why?"

"It's holding us back."

"No, it's not."

"We've been traveling for over three months and somehow are still stuck in Barcelona, where we started."

He tries to justify it. "Not all the time. We come and go as we please. We're only back weekends."

"It costs money to come back here every weekend."

"Not that much."

I know there's no easy way around this topic. "Eddie will be okay, Christopher."

His eyes meet mine.

"He has his grandmother and his job, and this is his life. He's happy here, and just because this isn't your normal, you can't forget that this is his."

"I know."

"You being his private bouncer at the hostel isn't achieving your goals. You took twelve months out of your life because you wanted to travel the world and see everything. Returning to Barcelona every weekend is not achieving that for either of us."

He exhales heavily and begins to soap up my feet as they rest on his chest.

"Just think about it, that's all I'm saying."

"Well, what will you do if I decide I want to keep coming back here?"

"I don't know." I shrug. "I won't be coming back with you every weekend, only sometimes, I guess."

His eyes hold mine. "So we would spend weekends apart?"

"Babe." I sigh sadly. "I don't want to have regrets when I get home. In a year's time this will all be over, and I'll kick myself I didn't see more when I had the chance."

He nods.

"And the thing is, you also need to think of yourself. If you are this attached to Eddie in three months, where will that leave you in another nine months? I'm not saying cut all contact; I just mean that you can be a friend to him from wherever you are in the world. Call him; send him letters; visit him once or twice a year. Friendship is more than protecting someone at the bar. And besides, we both know Eddie is way tougher than you."

He smiles sadly as he listens. "True."

"What is the fascination that you have with him, anyway?" I ask. "Apart from the obvious of him being amazing, of course."

"I admire him."

I smile.

"He's one of the most interesting people I've ever met." He smiles wistfully. "I just like being around him. He's intelligent and strong." He shrugs. "I can't explain it, really."

"Okay," I concede.

He falls silent for a while. "But . . . you're right."

"Meaning?"

"I'll do this course, and then we'll leave Barcelona for good on Sunday."

I smile sadly, already dreading saying goodbye to Eddie. "Is it wrong of me to say this?" I ask him.

"No, you're right. I need to get on with it."

His phone beeps with a text in the other room, and he frowns. "Jameson."

"What?"

"That's a text from Jameson. My oldest brother."

"How do you know?"

"I have a different ringtone for all my brothers." He gets out of the bath and goes to retrieve his phone and walks back into the bathroom reading the text, and then he smiles broadly. "Fuck yeah."

"What?"

He passes the phone to me, and I read the message.

I booked you another four nights at the hotel.
Happy Birthday.
Jay, x

My mouth falls open. "It's your birthday?"
He chuckles. "I guess it is."

Four days, four heavenly nights.

This has been the best week of my life.

Sun, laughter, luxury hotel, and Christopher Miles. As if the universe knew we needed this time alone, it delivered.

With every day, every hour . . . every minute, I've slipped more and more under his spell. With every breath, fallen just that little bit harder.

With no distractions and being left utterly alone, we've bonded in a way I didn't even know was possible. Sexually, mentally . . . intimately.

So, so close.

It's our last night in our ritzy hotel room. Christopher starts his bar course tomorrow, and in three days, we leave Spain forever for Germany. I'm excited for what's to come for us, because so far, our story is incredible.

The television is on softly in the background, and we are lying in bed. My bedside lamp is on, and the rest of the room is in filtered darkness. I have my book in my hand, and Christopher is lying the other way, his head near my feet, perched up on his elbow, staring at me. His finger is trailing up and down my leg as he lies seemingly deep in thought.

"A penny for your thoughts?" I ask.

He smiles softly, his eyes fixed on his fingers as they roam over my skin. "I'm just wondering how it is that the more I have you . . . the more I want you."

We stare at each other in the darkness.

"Is it always like this?" He frowns. "Is this"—he gestures to the air between us—"normal?"

"No," I reply without hesitation. "This is not normal. This is . . . special."

He falls silent again, and I can see his brain ticking a million miles per minute. He has questions. This relationship stuff is all so new for him. "And?" I prompt him. "Ask me anything."

"Your boyfriend . . ."

"You're my boyfriend," I correct him.

"Ex-boyfriend . . ."

"It wasn't like this," I reply, reading his mind.

His brow furrows. "How was it different?"

"Well . . ." I pause as I try to navigate just how honest I'm going to be with him. "Looking back, and now that I've met you, I don't think I even really loved him . . . or him me, for that matter."

"Why?"

"We were kids when we met. We were each other's first."

He listens intently.

I smile as I remember. "There was a lot of fumbling around in the dark, and sweetness. We cared for each other for sure, but it wasn't that raging love that would conquer the world in a war."

"What is this?" he whispers.

Love.

"You know what it is."

You love me.

His eyes search mine.

"We could win the war *and* blow up the world."

He smiles softly and leans down and kisses my foot before licking it.

Sex between us has hit a new high.

It's changed.

We don't always fuck now; sometimes we make love, and I have to say Christopher Miles is the master.

Tender.

Intimate and personal . . . the kissing, the care he takes of me, the way he worships my body . . . he takes me to a higher place than I ever knew existed.

He kisses my foot with an open mouth, his eyes locked on mine. "How long?" he whispers.

We've been waiting for my pill to kick in. "We're good to go."

His eyes flicker with arousal, and he inhales sharply.

I smile and spread my legs as an invitation. "You got something you want to give to me, baby?"

"Fuck yeah." He stands and rushes into the bathroom and returns with some towels and a bottle of oil.

He lays the two towels out on the bed and then pulls me up onto my knees as he stands beside it. He lifts my nightdress over my head as he kisses me. He pours a little of the oil on his rock-hard erection, and with his hand over mine, he strokes himself.

I smile against his lips. Dirty bastard.

We kiss as our grip on him gets harder, the jerks almost violent, and I know he's running on instinct. The primal urge to come inside of me has taken him over, and he is no longer in control.

He turns me away from him and bends me over onto my knees. I feel his stubble on my behind as he licks me.

God . . .

I drop to my elbows to open myself more for him.

He really begins to eat me, and I scrunch the sheets in my hands beneath me.

I need him. I need all of him inside me. I wiggle my behind in a silent invitation. "Fuck me," I whisper.

I'm not scared anymore. I can ride his dick like a pro now.

He pours oil all over my behind. It drizzles down over my sex, and he rubs it into my swollen lips. "Fuck . . . you look good," he murmurs. He slides his finger in and then another and then another, with a delicious twist at the end as he warms me up.

"Tell me how hard you're going to blow," I breathe.

He chuckles and slaps me hard on the cheek. I jump with a yelp. My skin stings, and I drop my head and smile. This is what he does so well. I'm never quite sure what the hell is happening. There is always an edge of pain with the pleasure he delivers.

So good with a side of ouch.

He holds himself at the base and bounces his hardened dick on my sex and then, without warning, slides home in one sharp movement.

The air leaves my lungs, and he stills to let me accommodate his size. My body ripples around his.

He moans, and I smile darkly. That's it . . . the perfect sound.

Christopher Miles aroused is next level . . .

He takes my two hip bones in his hand and drives me into the mattress, hard and fast.

The oil slapping between our skin.

I close my eyes to try to deal with him. The strength that oozes from his large muscular body is taking mine over.

Powerful, piston-fast pumps.

Deep and wet, the sound of my body sucking him is loud in the room.

The bed is hitting the wall, the sound of our skin slapping is deafening, and good god . . .

I see stars . . . all the stars, maybe even the moon.

How can anyone be this good at sex? He's an Oxford scholar on the subject, a professor, master of the universe.

I'm positive that if he ever did porn, he would break the internet.

With the sound of his moans and the feel of his thick, hard cock deep inside me, I lose control. My body contracts around his, and I come hard.

He slaps me on the behind and follows as he holds himself deep. I feel the telling jerk of his cock thrusting deep, and I smile into the mattress.

He tips his head back as he pants, gasping for air, and perspiration dusts his skin.

His hands tenderly rub my behind and up over my back: such a contrast to the beating his body just gave mine. "That was fucking good," he replies in his husky aroused voice.

"Where we at?" I pant.

He chuckles and pulls out. "Getting there." He rubs his fingers through the lips of my sex to feel himself there. "Eighty percent." He keeps rubbing me there, and he inhales sharply, transfixed with what he's staring at. "You have no idea how fucking hot this looks, Grumps. Me . . . inside you." He lifts his hand to show me. Semen drips off his fingers. "Fucking hot," he mouths before sucking his fingers clean.

Jeez . . .

What the hell?

The man's a bona fide deviant.

CHRISTOPHER

We walk up the corridor of the hostel. It's early morning. I have my bartending course today, and I wanted to check Grumps back into the hostel before I go.

We didn't check out before we went to the hotel, so we still have the same room.

I open the door and am instantly hit with the stench of alcohol.

Fuck.

There are other people now staying in our room.

Strangers.

I look around at the four people in the beds, all men in only their underpants.

Still half-drunk.

One of them is naked, his soft dick on display as he sleeps.

Fuck.

"Close the door," one of them grumbles.

I turn to Hayden; her eyes are wide as she looks around at the naked bodies. Up until now we've been blessed with good, respectful roommates.

"Screw this." I pull her out of the room by the hand. "You're not staying in there."

"We have to," she replies as I drag her down toward the office. I glance at my watch. Fuck it, I don't have time for this shit this morning. "It will be fine."

"It is not fucking fine," I snap. I march into the office to see Howard, the manager. "Hi, Howard."

"Hey, Christo."

"Listen, we've got a problem. I need a private room for Hayden and me for three nights, please."

He looks between us. "Finally got the balls to make a move, did you?"

"Fuck off. Listen. There are a bunch of drunk idiots in our room, and I'm not leaving Hayden with them. I have a bartending course on all weekend, and she has nowhere else to go. They're all naked and drunk in there. What's she supposed to do?"

"I'll just go to the beach and read my book," she says.

"It's raining," I snap.

"I'm fine," she replies, indignant. "I'm not a damsel in distress, Christopher. I can look after myself, you know."

"No private rooms left," Howard replies.

"Fine. We'll go back to the hotel." I begin to drag Hayden from the office.

"We are not going back to the hotel. We're not wasting that money." She digs her heels in. "We're staying here," she demands. "I'm not a princess."

"No." I begin to see red. "Howard, we have stayed here every weekend for three months. Surely we get some preferential treatment, for fuck's sake."

He stares at me.

"How many fights have I broken up for you in that bar?"

"You caused half of them."

"I mean it," I splutter. I'm going to be late for my course.

"Fine, you can have a room on one condition."

"What's that?"

"You said you were doing a bar course?"

"Yeah, so?"

"You have to work behind the bar for me tonight."

"I don't even know what I'm doing yet."

287

"It would be good practice." Hayden smiles hopefully.

Damn it, I can't leave her here with nowhere to hang today. "Fine. But I want the room keys now."

"Deal."

He holds up the keys, and I snatch them out of his hand. "And you're paying me for tonight."

"You can keep the tips." We go to walk out of the office. "Oh, and Christo."

"What?"

"It's a full moon party tonight."

"Are you fucking serious?" I bark. "Every man and his fucking dog will be here."

"Thus the need for more bar staff." He fakes a smile.

Great.

I drag Hayden down the hall quickly to the room, and I open the door. A tiny double bed sits in the middle of the room. "This place is a fucking shithole," I snap.

"You're just used to the hotel. It's not so bad." Hayden shrugs. "Looks like the perfect reading spot to me."

"I am done with hostels." I kiss her quickly. "See you tonight."

"No, you won't. You're working," she teases.

"Don't remind me."

)(

I sit in class and stare at the blackboard. The teacher goes on and on and on.

This is the most boring and pointless course I've ever done in my life. I glance at my watch: 11:00 a.m.

Fuck.

My god . . . has time completely stopped?

I can't sit here for another seven hours. I will literally die a long and painful death.

I exhale and flick my pen against my forehead as I try to focus.

I wonder what Grumps is doing. I slide my phone out of my pocket onto my lap, and I text her under the table.

Hi Babe,
What's doing?

I wait for her reply . . .

The teacher goes on and on some more, and I keep glancing at my phone.

Why isn't she answering?

I text her again.

Are you okay?

I wait for her reply . . .

I shuffle around in my chair. Why isn't she answering?

An hour passes. Still nothing.

I get a vision of all the drunk assholes in the hostel, and I begin to sweat.

What if something has happened?

I text her again.

Grumps,
I'm getting worried.
Text me!

I stare at my phone under the table as I will it to ring.

Hayden . . . call me, fuck it.

"Mr. Miles," the teacher calls.

I glance up.

"Distracting you, am I?"

Yes, you are, actually.

"Phone away. Now."

I fake a smile. "Sorry." I slide my phone back into my pocket, and I stare at the blackboard.

This course is pointless. Who cares about rules of alcohol consumption?

Not me, that's for sure.

⋈

Finally, it's lunch break, and I rush from the classroom and dig out my phone.

No missed calls.

No texts.

I march to the cafeteria as I dial Hayden's number.

It rings out.

"Where the hell is she?"

I dial her number again . . . still no answer. I hang up and call her again.

No answer.

That's it—I text her.

Call me RIGHT NOW!

I grab a sandwich and sit at the table and eat alone. I'm beginning to sweat.

What if something has happened to her?

I go over all the possible scenarios in my head.

She could be asleep . . . she could be getting harassed by idiots. She could be getting attacked as she walks to the shops. Maybe she's getting drugged and raped right now.

Fuck.

I call her again . . . no answer.

I've got better things to do than worry about a missing girlfriend all fucking day.

Oh my god . . . *she's missing.*

I call her again.

𝕏

Five o'clock, and I dive out of the cab as it pulls up in front of the hostel.

I'm frantic.

I've had the worst day of my life. Hayden is missing, probably dead in a ditch.

I pay the driver and run inside and take the stairs two at a time. The place is packed with people in white.

Stupid fucking full moon party.

I run down the corridor and burst into our room. It's empty.

My chest tightens . . . fuck, where is she?

I run down to the bar and look around in a panic. I see Eddie. "Where's Hayden?" I stammer.

He looks around and points over to the corner. Hayden is sitting with a group of people, laughing and having the time of her life. She's relaxed and having fun.

In her white dress . . . the sky turns red.

We make eye contact, and I turn and march back to the room, furious.

I storm into the shower, and I'm so angry that I can't even see straight.

I shower and go back to the room to find Hayden lying on the bed. "Hi, babe." She smiles happily. "How was it?"

"Why haven't you answered your fucking phone?" I yell at the top of my voice.

Her face falls. "What?"

"I've been calling you. All day, worried sick."

"What do you mean?" She picks up her phone and frowns as she reads the screen. "Forty-two missed calls?" She looks up at me. "What's wrong?"

"I thought you were dead in a ditch," I cry.

Her eyebrows rise. She's surprised by my tone. "Don't yell at me, Christopher."

"Don't yell at you!" I explode. "I've been worried sick all day. Do you know how fucking irresponsible you are?"

"What?"

"You heard me."

"My phone was on silent while I read, and then I went to the bar and must have left it in the room. I wasn't expecting a dog squad tracking my every move."

"Dog squad!" I yell. "I'll give you fucking dog squad."

"I'm sorry you were worried, but I wasn't expecting you to call me." She rolls her eyes.

"That's unacceptable," I fire back. "Don't fucking patronize me."

She rolls her eyes. "You're being a drama queen. I'm going back to the bar."

"Are you serious?" I yell.

"Yes. And you are supposed to be out there working right now . . . remember?"

I point to the door. "Get out!"

She smiles goofily, totally unfazed by my anger. "Okay." She pecks me on the lips and leaves. My eyes nearly pop from my head. She did *not* just walk out midargument . . . I'm infuriated.

My blood pressure is through the roof.

I head out to my locker and pull out my backpack, and a drunk couple comes ambling down the corridor. They start making out, and as the girl walks backward, she falls on top of me.

"Watch what you're fucking doing," the guy growls to me.

I raise my eyebrows, my temper simmering dangerously close to the surface. I help the girl up. "I'm sorry you didn't see me."

She's laughing and falling all over the place. "Hey, I'm glad I did," she flirts.

The guy narrows his eyes at me, and I clench my jaw as I glare at him.

Come on, fucker . . . try me . . . I'm in the mood to sort you right out.

"Are you coming to the party?" The girl smiles sexily.

I roll my eyes and return to my backpack. *Don't go there.*

I look through my backpack for something. I have to wear stupid white.

Shit, I discover that I only have a white sleeveless T-shirt and shorts. Not ideal to work behind the bar in, but it will have to do.

I get dressed and look in the mirror. Fuck, I look like a poser. My arms are too big for sleeveless. It will have to do; I have no alternative. I make my way out to the bar.

"Hey." Eddie smiles excitedly. "I get to work with you tonight."

"Great." I nod. "Where do you want me?" My gaze wanders around the room as I search for Hayden.

"Oh . . . you're hot." A girl swoons. "I'll have an Orgasm." She smiles.

"Make that two." Her friend laughs.

"A multiple. Bet you've given a few of those in your day," the first girl adds, and they both burst out laughing. "And we're next."

Great . . . horny drunk girls . . . just what I need.

I turn my back to them. "Where's the cocktail book?" I ask Eddie.

He passes it to me and goes back to serving. The people are standing ten deep, waiting to be served.

What the hell does a full moon have to do with people getting wasted? is what I'd like to know.

I read the directions for the Orgasms. I make them the best I can and hand them over. They're guaranteed to taste like shit. "There you go."

"What are you doing later?" the girl murmurs darkly. "We'd love to repay the favor and do a multiple for real."

I fake a smile. "I'm busy."

My eyes scan the crowd, *busy* trying to locate my wayward fucking girlfriend. Where the hell is she now?

"I'll have a Corona," a guy says.

"Sure." I turn to get the Corona and glance over to see Hayden dancing with a group of girls.

There she is.

I serve a few more people, my eyes constantly flicking over to linger on Hayden.

She's dancing and having the time of her life, totally unfazed. In her hot white dress.

I hate that she looks so edible.

A guy approaches her, and I stop what I'm doing. He puts his arm around her, and she steps back.

I keep watching.

"I'll have two Guinnesses," someone yells.

I turn to get the beers, my eyes fixed on my girl. The guy keeps talking to her and talking.

She takes a step back, and he takes a step forward.

He leans to say something in her ear.

Something snaps. The next thing I know I'm on the dance floor with my hand around the guy's throat. "Back the fuck off."

HAYDEN

My eyes widen in horror. "Christopher," I yell. "What are you doing?"

Christopher glares at the guy he has in a choke hold. "You do not fucking touch her. Do you understand me!" he yells in his face.

The guy pushes him off. "Fuck off, pretty boy." He then grabs me aggressively around the waist and slams my body into his. "I'll do whatever I want with her."

Oh no.

Christopher snaps. He pulls me from the idiot's grip and pushes me out of the way and then punches the guy full in the face.

"Ahh," I cry as the hit connects.

The guy returns a hit, and Christopher staggers back. He runs forward and tackles the guy to the ground as they fight. They wrestle around, arms and punches flying everywhere.

"Oh my god, stop it," I cry. I try to run in to break it up, and someone holds me back. People are shuffling in, trying to see. A few people step in to help Christopher, and then some stick up for the other guy.

It gets broken up, and the two men are held back from each other.

Christopher's eyes find me across the crowd, and I throw up my arms. "What the hell are you doing?"

His nostrils flare. He turns and marches out of the hostel.

What the hell is wrong with him?

He practically runs down the corridor and pushes out the large front doors and down the stairs. He begins to walk off into the darkness up the road as I follow.

"Christopher," I call.

He ignores me and keeps walking.

"Christopher," I yell. "Don't you dare ignore me!"

He stops, his back still to me.

"What the hell are you doing?"

"Getting the fuck out of here," he says, his back still turned.

I catch up and walk around to see his face, and my heart drops. He's upset.

"What are you doing?" I ask softly.

His eyes hold mine.

"What's going on?" I ask.

"I don't fucking know," he cries. His eyes are wild, his hair is tousled, and his chest rises and falls as if he's gasping for air. The adrenaline in his system must be through the roof.

I frown, taken aback. Something's going on with him. He's in the middle of another major freak-out.

"It's okay . . . ," I say softly.

"Nothing about this is okay, Hayden," he cries. "I'm going fucking crazy."

I stare at him, unsure what to say.

"I've been frantic all fucking day over you, and now . . ." He throws his arms up in surrender. "I saw him touch you, and . . ." He drags his hands through his hair.

"You got jealous," I say softly.

"I do *not* get jealous," he yells, infuriated.

He's having some kind of episode here, and I don't want to throw fuel on the fire.

I need to try to calm him down.

"I'm sorry I didn't answer my phone today. I didn't mean to worry you," I say.

"That's the point. I don't worry. I don't get jealous, Hayden. I don't know if I'm up or down or just going fucking crazy," he cries. "What the hell is wrong with me?"

I stare at him. He really has no idea . . .

"You're in love with me," I say softly.

His face falls.

"But that's okay." I smile hopefully. "Because I love you too."

His eyes search mine.

"And now you've gone and ruined a very special moment between us." I put my hands on my hips.

He stares at me, shocked to silence.

"Get your shit together and go back inside and finish your shift," I demand.

Perspiration beads on his brow. His eyes are crazy, and I'm unsure if he's about to run. I just need him to calm down and go back and work. If he runs now, it's all over between us. I'm not going through that shit again.

"This is unacceptable behavior, Christopher. You can't beat up every man who tries to talk to me. It's not okay." I shrug, frustrated. "I'm not a possession. You don't have the right to act like that."

"He was asking for it."

"So be the bigger person and walk away. This isn't who you are. You're a lover, not a fighter."

His eyes hold mine.

"Go and finish your shift. I'm going to bed."

"You're not coming back to the party?"

"No. My dickhead boyfriend spoiled my mood."

He exhales heavily, disappointed in himself.

"Just go." I point inside, and he turns and trudges back up the stairs.

"You're really going to bed?" he asks me again.

"Yes," I snap. I march past him down the corridor to our room as he follows me.

I open the door to our room, and I glance up at him.

"I'll see you when I finish?" he asks hopefully.

"If you carry on like an idiot and get in one more fight tonight . . . so help me god."

"I won't."

"Good." I march into the room, and he stands tentatively by the door. "And you're sleeping on the floor tonight," I add.

He nods and then lingers as if waiting for something.

"And I'm not telling you I love you . . . because you're just an idiot." I turn down the blankets in a huff.

"I'm not telling you either," he says.

I smirk, trying to hide my smile, and I know it's going to be okay. "Good, don't then." I climb into bed. "Get out."

His eyes twinkle with a certain something. "I think you have anger issues," he says.

"So help me god, Christopher." I throw a cushion at him. "Get out." It hits the wall beside his head, and he smiles his first genuine smile.

"Good night, Grumpy."

"There is nothing good about this night," I lie.

The door quietly closes, and I smile into the darkness.

We fought, and he stayed . . . *progress.*

It's just at 3:00 a.m. when I hear the door open. Christopher tiptoes in to the flashlight on his phone, undresses, and climbs into bed behind me and snuggles up to my back. He smells of soap, freshly showered, and I smile with my eyes closed.

He's home.

It's been a long night without him. Even when fighting, he was still missed.

"What time is it?" I mumble.

"Three." He kisses my temple. "Go back to sleep, baby." He kisses my shoulder from behind, and goose bumps scatter up my spine. He pulls my hair back and gently kisses my neck. "I'm sorry about tonight," he murmurs against my skin; his fingers trail up and down my skin as he thinks. "I just can't stand the thought of someone taking you from me," he murmurs sadly. "It makes me fucking crazy."

I can feel his erection as it grows behind me. Christopher Miles is a sexual being. This is his way of making up. He's scared; I want to make him feel better.

I stretch my neck out, granting him access and taking the cue. His hand roams over my skin up to my breast, his thumb dusting over my nipple as he takes my earlobe between his teeth.

His erection digs into my hip, and even in darkness I can see it so clearly.

I roll over and straddle his large body. He stares up at me.

The air crackles between us.

I lift myself onto my knees and slide down onto his large erection. I rock from side to side to loosen myself up and grant him entry.

His length is thick and hungry. My body slowly sinks deep down onto his. He holds my hip bones as he stares up at me in awe.

"I'm not going anywhere, baby," I whisper. "I'm all yours."

He sits up in a rush, his lips crashing against mine as he kisses me and holds me close. Emotional overload. Too intense to try to contain. An intimacy that I never knew I needed.

We rock together in the darkness, feeding our bodies, surrendering to the feelings between us.

I've made a lot of bad decisions in my life, done things that I regret. But there is one thing in life that I do know for certain . . . I am utterly and irrevocably in love with the beautiful Christopher Miles.

We were meant to meet.

He's the one.

Chapter 18

I wake to the feel of the bed dipping, and I frown as I drag open my eyes. Christopher is sitting on the side of the bed, elbows on knees. He's wringing his hands in front of him as if the world is about to end. Waging a war against himself.

Ugh . . . so not in the mood for his dramatics today.

I put my foot on his behind and gently push him. "Can you go get me a coffee, please?"

He frowns over at me. "You want coffee?"

"Yes, please." I need to keep him busy and out of his own head.

He stands. "Okay. I can do that."

"We need some fruit too."

He begins to dress. "On it."

"Oh, wait, you have your course on today, don't you?"

"It doesn't start until ten."

"Okay." I close my eyes. I have so much to say about his behavior last night, but now is not the time. He's still processing. I'm giving him some space to get his head around it.

He gets dressed. "Do you want to come?"

"Not really."

He lingers, long enough that I look up.

"I'd like you to come."

I exhale heavily and flick the blankets back. "Fine." I get out of bed and pull some clothes on as he watches.

"How are you so even tempered all the time?" he asks.

"I'm not even tempered. I'm being the adult in our relationship." He frowns.

"Your turn is next week, when I'm being ridiculous."

He gives me a stifled smile. "Is that what you do . . . take turns?"

"Uh-huh." I stand on my tippy-toes and kiss his big beautiful lips. "As long as we take it in turns to be the adult . . . everything will be fine."

"And if we be dickheads at the same time?" he asks.

"Then the outcome isn't good." I kiss him softly again.

He nods and stares at me as if I have taught him a sacred secret . . . how doesn't he know this stuff? For a worldly man, he's so inexperienced about all things relationship.

"Buying coffee and fruit is pretty adult." He smirks as he takes my hand in his.

I smile. "I guess it's your turn today, then."

Ten hours later

We stand on the sidewalk with our backpacks on the cement. Christopher glances at his watch. "Where is he? The cab is going to be here soon."

"He'll come."

I look up the street. To be honest, I'm getting a little worried he won't. Eddie is meant to be here to say goodbye to us, but he hasn't shown.

It's so unlike him.

302

Our flight to Germany leaves in a few hours, and we can't wait much longer. "Call him again."

Christopher calls his number, and it rings out. He stares up the street in search of his little friend. "If I knew his address, I would go there." He begins to pace. "Damn it, why didn't I get his address?"

He calls him again. "What if something's happened to him?" He's beginning to get frantic.

"Don't worry . . . he'll come."

Eddie

I stand in the alleyway, and from my spying spot I watch as Mr. Christo and Miss Hazen wait for me across the road in front of the hostel.

They're here to say goodbye . . . and I want to go over.

But . . . *I can't.*

I watch as Christo dials a number on his phone, and my phone vibrates again, the name lighting up on my screen.

Christo

My heart sinks, and I put it back into my pocket.

I watch as Christo paces and rants and raves as Hazen talks calmly to him.

With every moment that they wait, it gets worse. I want to run across the road and beg them not to leave.

But I know they will anyway . . . so what's the point?

A cab pulls up, and Christo stares up the street to where I usually come from, and I get a lump in my throat. Through tears I watch him put their backpacks into the trunk.

Don't go.

With one last look up the road, he finally gets into the cab, and it pulls out and drives away.

I drop my head . . . they're gone.

Hayden

Sightseeing by day, partying at work by night.

I'd always heard about Amsterdam. Everyone said it is the one place that you have to experience at least once in your lifetime. I imagined drug cafés and sex workers, high-as-a-kite people walking around being idiots in the streets.

What I didn't expect was that it would be a culturally diverse, beautiful city.

Long canals that have these beautiful little bridges over them, twinkle lights that line the streets at night, beautiful restaurants, and the eclectic sound of laughter in the distance.

Christopher and I do love a chocolate brownie with magical ingredients and many a night get the giggles on our way home. This is such a fun place, and not one bit frightening like I imagined.

And the bicycles . . . I never expected to see so many.

People don't drive in Amsterdam; they ride their bikes everywhere. So in front of every restaurant and club and shopping district are rows and rows of beautiful old-fashioned bikes, chained up in stands, the ones with little cane baskets attached to the front.

It's so cool, and when you walk down the street, you don't hear cars; you hear bicycle bells as people warn you they are coming fast.

It's the little things about traveling, the idiosyncrasies that make each place different.

Never in a million years did I imagine that I would associate cute old-fashioned bikes with Amsterdam, but I know that I always will.

I walk around the tables and collect glasses with Basil. "This is the worst fucking job we ever had." He rolls his eyes.

I giggle. "Will you look at us?"

Who would have ever thought that I would work in a place like this? Christopher has changed my outlook on life. Nothing is off limits anymore.

I feel liberated and sexually confident like never before.

We're working in a nightclub in Amsterdam. There are live sex shows on stage for ten minutes every hour, and we're scantily dressed. I'm in a short French maid outfit complete with suspender stockings and a long dark wig, and Basil is wearing black suit pants and a bow tie.

This place is hilarious, and the things we've seen would curl your hair.

Basil and I are the official glass collectors. Kimberly and Bernadette are in the kitchen, and Bodie and Christopher are behind the bar.

"Will you look at those two fucking wankers." Basil curls his lip in disgust as he looks over to the bar.

Christopher is wearing black suit pants and a black bow tie, completely shirtless and a ball of rippled muscle. His dark hair is a little longer, with a curl to it, and he looks utterly gorgeous.

I smile as I watch him. He's working the bar like a pro. Laughing and joking with the customers, shaking his cocktail shaker in the air as he and Bodie joke around.

He's having the time of his life in this job.

A song that he loves starts, "Edamame," by bbno$, and he starts to dance as he works; the female customers are lined up at the bar, enjoying the show . . . and I don't mean on the stage.

I giggle as I watch them play off each other. "Hot wankers, though."

"I'm so doing a bar course." Basil sighs.

"You should."

I keep collecting glasses and walk over past the bar. "Hayden," Christopher yells across the crowd. I glance up, and he waves me over. He introduces me to a man sitting at the bar. "This is Mr. Escott."

"Hello." I smile.

"He's offered a job on a luxury yacht in the Greek islands." He keeps serving people.

"Oh." My eyes widen. "Great."

"All of us." Christopher smiles excitedly.

My eyes flick to Mr. Escott. "The six of us?" I confirm.

"Yes, I need this energy on my fleet." He gestures to Christopher, who is laughing out loud. He shakes a cocktail shaker for three women. His arm and stomach muscles are flexing as he shakes it. The women are all smiling goofily as they watch.

"That's a whole lot of energy right there," I agree.

"If you're all like him, it's going to be amazing."

I laugh. "There is nobody like him, Mr. Escott. He's in a league of his own."

I smile as I watch my beautiful man. I'm not even joking—he really is. Every night I watch him work the crowd and fall a little bit more in love with him. I don't feel one ounce of jealousy over the way he is.

He is who he is.

He isn't sleazy or flirty; he's playful and fun, and he makes me feel like I'm the only woman in the world.

And to him, I am.

Christopher comes back over. "Can you go and ask the others if they're in?"

"Okay." I smile.

"I'll wait here for you," Mr. Escott says.

"When would you want us to start?" I call over the loud music.

"Monday."

"Oh." I frown. "That soon?"

"Yes, we have had an entire crew for a charter trip come down with the chicken pox. It's next week, or unfortunately I won't be able to offer all of you a position."

"Okay. I'll go find out." I take off through the crowd to find our friends.

Ten minutes later I return. "We're in." I smile to Mr. Escott.

"Great." He hands me a business card. "Call me when you get to Mykonos."

"Okay." I put his card in my pocket.

"Ten minutes till break, Grumps?" Christopher yells over the music.

I glance at my watch. "Yeah, okay."

We always take our tea breaks together.

"Nice to meet you, Mr. Escott. See you next week."

"I look forward to it."

I take off through the crowd. I have a lot to do.

Twelve minutes later, I walk out into the back area and down the corridor. As I walk past a storeroom door, I'm yanked inside and pushed up against the wall as the door is slammed shut. Christopher's lips drop to my neck as his hands lift my French maid skirt. "I know what I want for tea."

This man and what he does to me . . . the deviant of all deviants.

Loving him has changed my life. He's shown me a better version of myself.

A spontaneous, sexy version, and I like her a lot.

I giggle as I lift my leg and put it on a shelf. His hand slides over my suspender belt and up my thigh.

"The barmen at this establishment are always so helpful." I smile against his lips.

"Happy to be of service." He pushes my panties to the side and slides his fingers through the lips of my sex as he kisses me deeply. "My bad girl is ready." He spins me around and bends me over. I hear his zipper right before he slides in deep.

My eyes flutter closed as we both moan in pleasure. He pulls out and slams back in. "I love this fucking job."

CHRISTOPHER

We stand on the dock at the Mykonos marina as we wait. The luxury yachts are lined up.

"What the fuck do we know about boating?" Basil sighs as we watch all the crews on the yachts. "There seems to be a lot of shit to do."

"I hope our uniforms are cute." Kimberly smiles as she looks out.

"Can't be worse than our last fucking uniform." Basil frowns. "I should have just worked with a piece of meat strapped to my chest."

"Those women did love you, Baz." Hayden laughs.

Baz curls his lip in disgust.

A guy walks toward us. He's very serious looking and wearing white shorts and a white short-sleeve button-up shirt. It has gold buttons and navy-blue straps over the shoulders. He's got a formal captain hat on. "He looks like a pilot," Bernadette whispers.

"Please be on our boat," Kimberly says softly as her eyes linger on him.

"Yacht," I correct her. "It isn't a boat."

"Please be on our yacht . . . and in my room," she continues.

We all chuckle, and he reaches us. "Hello, I'm Captain Mark, the skipper. I'm assuming one of you is Hayden?"

"Yes, that's me." She smiles as she shakes his hand. Hayden always seems to be the point of contact for our jobs. She introduces us. "These are the others, Christo, Basil, Bodie, Kimberly, and Bernadette."

"Hi." He smiles. "Welcome." He turns and walks down the dock, and we all follow. "You come with a very high recommendation," he continues.

We all exchange glances. Nobody except me has even been on a yacht before.

Not that I can even admit to it.

"We're very excited." Hayden smiles as she tries to be friendly.

"Thank you so much for stepping up and helping. My entire crew has fallen ill and can't work for another two weeks. We had charters booked all week, so you've saved the day."

We all exchange looks again, and Hayden rolls her lips to hide her smile. This could be a real fucking disaster.

"There she is." Captain Mark smiles. "Isn't she beautiful?"

We all look up and stop still as the blood drains from our faces.

"Yes." Everyone fakes a smile.

Oh no.

This isn't a yacht; it's a superyacht. Four stories high and at least 160 feet long. It's black and sleek and . . . *fuck.*

How in the hell are we supposed to man this vessel? We have no fucking idea what we're doing.

Oh . . . shit. I feel myself get hot under the collar.

OBSIDIAN.

That name . . . I frown. It's familiar.

Obsidian . . . how do I know this yacht? I troll my mind for a memory of some sort.

"Is it always moored here?" I ask as I act casual.

311

"No, it's usually in Monte Carlo."

"Right." I watch the Grand Prix from our yacht in Monte Carlo every year. Let's hope it's just from there.

Hayden's scared eyes flick over to meet mine. "What the hell?" she whispers.

"It's fine," I mouth.

This is anything but fine. This is a living nightmare.

We walk across the bridge and onto the yacht, and over-the-top luxury hits us in the face.

A huge deck with a spa and plunge pool, an outdoor lounge area, bar—everything is the most beautiful wood and finished to perfection. I look around. Hmm . . . not bad.

We glance through the double doors into the inside. A huge luxurious living area with plush furnishings. An elevator and stairs going up and down are to the right, as well as a large corridor.

"Wow," everyone whispers in awe as they look around.

"Come, and I'll show you to the servants' quarters belowdecks. We need to get ready. The owner is boarding tonight with a group of his friends."

"Who owns this vessel?" I ask.

"Julian Masters," he replies.

Fuck.

"Where's he from?" I ask as I act dumb.

"The United Kingdom. Loaded, as you can tell. Old family money . . . but he's a judge. He has his extended family from Australia over here for a bachelor party."

The blood drains from my face. I know them. I know them all.

Julian Masters is one of my brother Jameson's best friends. They went to boarding school together.

I'm totally fucked.

Chapter 19

"Put your bags down, and I'll show you around," Captain Mark says. He's holding a clipboard under his arm. We do as he asks and follow him around the yacht. "On this level, you have the living area and formal dining, cinema, and two bathrooms." Three huge white couches are around an apricot marble coffee table. The floors are all herringbone dark timber with big cream exotic rugs. Stunning art hangs on the walls.

It *is* beautiful . . . I'll give it that.

"Wow." Everyone gushes in awe.

I trail behind while desperately trying to devise an escape plan.

Man overboard is sounding very fucking appealing.

"Upstairs." He takes the stairs, and we follow him up. "Another large living area, casual dining, and cocktail bar. There are four guest bedrooms on this floor."

"Oh my god." Hayden's eyes are the size of saucers, and she grabs my hand. "Can you believe this place, babe?" she whispers in awe. "I've never seen anything like it."

Meh . . . I raise my eyebrow as I look around . . . *my yacht is better.*

"Top floor, master suite." We walk up another level, which is all bedroom, with 360-degree views. A huge bathroom with a sunken spa bath and walk-in his-and-hers wardrobes.

Now *this* is nice.

"Through here"—he slides open a hidden door—"is the nursery. Mr. Masters likes his children close." We peer in to see two cots and two single beds. Toys and books are all displayed. The room is all pastels and decorated prettily.

"Is there a nanny on board when they're here?" Hayden asks.

"No. They don't have a nanny; they do all the parenting themselves."

Hayden smiles over at me and squeezes my hand. "I like them already," she whispers. "I would never have a nanny."

I frown. What? No nanny . . . at all . . . like, ever?

When do you get to fuck your wife if you don't have a nanny? Are you supposed to get sex for five minutes only at night or something? Ugh . . . that won't be happening in my household.

I'll have four nannies on rotation.

Actually . . . I smile as I remember something.

Masters's wife *was* his nanny. She's fucking hot too.

I bite my lip to hide my smile. Dirty bastard. Wonder how that went down?

"Let's go down to belowdecks, where you'll be staying," Captain Mark continues. We follow him down three levels. "This is the kitchen."

He shows us around. "Helga, the cook, will be here this afternoon. You will all rotate being her assistant. She runs a tight ship." He frowns and pauses as if choosing his words carefully. "She's an interesting character."

Great, that's code for *she's a bitch.*

"Here's the staff living quarters. Three bedrooms. One is for Helga; she rooms alone. A double with two single beds, and the other has four sets of bunk beds."

"Hayden and I have the double," I announce before anyone else has the chance to.

"Yeah, yeah," they all mutter.

"So." Captain Mark smiles. "That's our lady. I hope you'll be very comfortable and happy here. Take the morning to settle in and make yourself at home. This afternoon we'll do some training, and then our guests will be joining us around six p.m."

"How long will they be on board for?" I ask.

"Two days."

"So . . . what happens then?" Basil asks.

"This vessel is chartered whenever Mr. Masters isn't using it. We pick up another group on Wednesday."

"Ah, okay," Basil replies. "We keep working even when the owner isn't here."

"Exactly."

"Have you got a guest list?" I ask. "I'll look over it and begin to get everything sorted out."

"Yes, here it is." He passes over the clipboard. "I'll see you all in a few hours." He disappears up the stairs, and everyone begins to walk around and do their thing. I fold back the piece of paper and read the list.

Julian Masters

Spencer Jones

Sebastian Garcia

Fuck.

I put the folder down immediately. No need to read the rest of the guests.

The first three are the biggest pranksters on earth. I will not last one hour with them, let alone forty-eight.

This is a living nightmare.

They're going to blow my cover and tell Hayden, and fuck it, she doesn't love me enough yet. She'll leave me for lying to her.

Who could blame her?

For weeks, I've been trying to work out how to tell her who I am, but we're having so much fun that we haven't even had the discussion about what's happening when this is all over. I don't want her to find out that I've been lying to her like this. I need to be the one to tell her.

Fuck.

It's weird that she hasn't told me she loved me since that night of our first fight over six weeks ago—although we often say the words *I don't love you*, which to me are code for *I do . . .* but what if to her they're not?

What if it's just something she says?

I drag my hand through my hair, sick to my stomach.

I want Hayden in my life. The thought of losing her because of a lie . . . tightens my chest.

I follow her down the stairs with our backpacks and walk into our room. It's little and doesn't have a window. We do have privacy, though, which is the main thing.

There's a wardrobe and a desk in the corner. Hayden begins to unpack her things into the drawers. I sit down on the bed as I watch her.

I have to tell her.

"Beautiful yacht, huh?" I say.

"Incredible." She folds her shirt. "This is going to be the job of a lifetime."

My heart is hammering in my chest. "Can you imagine yourself ever owning a yacht like this?"

"Me?" She laughs. "No way."

"You wouldn't want to have money?" I ask. "Like this-yacht type of money?"

"God no, I hate rich people."

My eyebrows shoot up in surprise. "Do you know any?"

"Not really." She keeps folding her clothes.

"That's a tad discriminatory, don't you think?"

She looks over at me and stops what she's doing and then comes and sits on my lap. I wrap my arms around her as she kisses my lips softly. "I love the life we have, Christopher."

I stare up at her, and she brushes the hair back from my face as she looks down at me. "You don't need to worry that you don't have money."

Huh?

"There is so much to love about us." She kisses the tip of my nose. "I love the fact that you're my best friend." She kisses me with a smile. "I love that you give so much to everything you do. I love that you're kind and loving. I love that you look after me. You're perfect just as you are."

My eyes search hers. I'm speechless.

There is not a single word in my head. For all my life I have wanted to hear those words, that someone wanted me for me.

I love this woman.

She smiles softly as she hugs me tight.

"I need to tell you something," I murmur.

She takes her shirt off over her head. "And . . . I need to show you something." She stands and unlatches her bra; her full breasts fall free, and unable to stop myself, I reach up and cup one in my hand. Instantly my cock begins to thump. "Go on, baby, you were saying," she murmurs as she bends and kisses me. My hand slides up her thigh and underneath her panties.

Concentrate.

Hot, soft, wet lips in her panties steal my thoughts. Fuck . . . *she feels good.*

"You were saying?"

"I'm not a teacher," I murmur against her lips.

She frowns as she pulls back from me. "What are you?"

My eyes search hers. *Yours.*

Her face falls. "You lied to me?"

My stomach twists at her disappointed tone. *Don't fuck this up, you idiot.*

We have eight more months together before we *have* to have this conversation.

If I can just get through this weekend and make Masters keep his big fucking mouth shut. I mean, it's not like I'm pretending to be rich. I'm pretending to be poor. Surely she can't hate me for an upgrade?

I stare at her as I tuck a piece of her hair. Damn it. This is the happiest I've ever been in my life. I'm not ready for the dynamics to change between us.

I need more time.

"Well?" she asks me. "What do you do if you're not a teacher?"

"I'm a janitor in a school," I blurt out. "I was embarrassed to tell you."

Her mouth falls open. "Sweetheart," she whispers softly, "that hurts my heart."

Of all the things to say . . . fuck! Why that? Is there a brain in my head at all?

"You're a cleaner?" she repeats.

"Yes." I nod, feeling like a lying piece of shit.

"Baby," she whispers as she pulls me in for a hug, "I don't care what you do. What matters to me is if you're a good person. And you're better than good; you're the best."

I wrap her in my arms and hold her tight. I close my eyes as I nestle into her neck.

This woman . . .

This beautiful woman loves me thinking I clean toilets for a living.

I don't deserve her.

"This isn't just fooling around for me, Hayden," I say. "I want a future with you."

"I want that too." She smiles. We lie down on the bed and kiss. There is one more question I need an answer to.

"Where do you see yourself living?" I ask. "When this is all over . . ."

"As long as I'm with you, I don't care."

There it is.

My heart explodes with an unfamiliar feeling: a sense of belonging. This is happening. She *will* move for me . . . this *is* real.

She slides down my body and pulls my hardened dick free and takes it in her mouth. I stare down at her as her dark eyes hold mine. She licks up my length and then sucks me hard, and my toes curl. I lean back onto my elbows to enjoy the view.

She flickers her tongue over the tip of my cock, and I inhale sharply as I push the hair back from her forehead.

"You're mine," I whisper.

"All yours." She smiles around me. She licks her lips. "Now . . . fuck my mouth."

X

The sound of Hayden's gentle breathing lets me know she's drifted off to sleep.

This matchbox bedroom has the best orgasm voodoo of all time. We just had the best sex of my life.

I quietly throw some clothes on and sneak out of the bedroom. Everything is silent. We went out last night for a supposed quiet drink and ended up getting three hours' sleep. Everyone is supposed to be unpacking, but my guess is they're exhausted and catching up on some much-needed sleep before the shitstorm tonight.

And when I say shitstorm, I mean shitstorm.

I sneak up the stairs and out onto the deck. I look around. Where's Captain Mark?

I walk to the front of the yacht and catch sight of him up in the captain's chair. I practically run to the back of the yacht, and I scroll through the numbers on my phone.

Masters

I dial his number, and it rings.

"Miles." He laughs as he answers. "What do you want?" he jokes.

"Listen, I've got a situation," I whisper as my heart beats hard in my chest.

"What? Speak louder. Where are you?" He's in a bar or something. I can hear people laughing out loud.

"I'm undercover."

"What?"

"I took a year off, and under an alias I have been backpacking around the world."

"What?" he explodes before bursting out laughing. "You . . . backpacking?" He laughs out loud again. "That's fucking hilarious."

"I'm traveling with a group of people who don't know who I am, and we got a job on a yacht, and I just found out it's your fucking yacht," I blurt out in a rush.

"Bullshit," he snaps.

"You can't tell anyone who I am when you get here later."

He laughs hard. "That *is* a situation."

"Stop it," I whisper angrily.

320

"Christopher Miles is being an undercover bellboy on my fucking yacht," he tells someone.

"Get fucked." I hear someone laugh.

I narrow my eyes. Spencer Jones. I'd know that voice anywhere.

Captain Mark begins to walk down the side of the yacht. He waves happily.

Fuck.

"I've got to go," I stammer. "Not a fucking word. You don't know me."

"Wish I didn't." He's laughing, and I hear him telling someone else about me.

I have no choice but to hang up on him.

Fuck.

"Enjoying the view?" Captain Mark smiles.

"Yes." I fake a smile as I stuff my phone back in my pocket. I'm hot and flustered and damn it . . . stressed the fuck out.

"Did you get unpacked?" he asks.

"Yes, just had to make a quick phone call."

"We'll meet on the deck in an hour. I'll hand out uniforms, and we can start the training."

"Sounds great." I fake a smile. Not really . . . sounds like a literal hell.

"See you then." He walks back up the front of the yacht, and I turn and look out at the marina. I snap a photo and send it to Eddie.

Mykonos.

I wonder how my little buddy from Barcelona is doing. I'll call him on Wednesday when this shit is all over . . . if I haven't jumped overboard by then.

I go back down to my room and snuggle up to Hayden's back as she sleeps.

My mind is in overdrive.

If this doesn't go to plan . . .

I run through the million scenarios that might happen, how badly this could backfire, and although I know I'm doing the wrong thing, one thing *is* undeniable.

My life at home is something that only a strong love can withstand.

The people, the places . . . the pressure from the paparazzi.

I need to prepare her better. We need more time.

※

"These are your uniforms," Captain Mark says as he hands out zipped-up suit bags. "We ordered the sizes you requested, and if something doesn't fit, we do have a few extras downstairs in the storeroom."

Captain Mark begins talking about the yacht and telling us every boring little detail, and I glance over at Basil. He's unzipped his suit bag and is frowning at something inside. His eyes rise to meet mine.

"What?" I mouth.

He holds up a red glitter bow tie. "What the fuck?" he mouths.

Huh.

As Captain Mark keeps talking, I slowly undo my suit bag. There are three uniforms and then a black pair of suit pants and a red glitter bow tie on a hanger.

"Captain Mark, what is this?" I hold up the bow tie.

He glances over. "That's your uniform for tonight."

"My what?"

"Mr. Escott wanted a diverse crew so he could hold themed parties. You each have a party uniform like the one you were wearing in the club he met you at." He smiles proudly. "He was very impressed with you all."

I imagine the boys' faces when they see me in this uniform.

Dear god, no.

This can't be happening.

Hayden unzips her bag and pulls out a tiny French maid uniform, complete with suspender belts. "I'm not wearing this," she says adamantly.

"But . . ."

"I wore that outfit when I was in a private club where people had sex on stage. Nobody was even looking at me, and I blended in. Wearing that here in this environment is just damn sleazy. I'm not a stripper for rich men to ogle."

"I agree," Kimberly says.

"Same," Bernadette chimes in.

Captain Mark frowns as he looks between them. "Fine, the girls can wear something else. But the uniform sticks with the men. The theme for tonight is cabaret. You girls will have to come up with something in that theme. I want over-the-top fun. There are costumes and decorations in the storeroom belowdecks."

He looks at me. "Mr. Escott said you dance, Christo. Do you have your music with you?"

"I don't fucking dance," I scoff, horrified.

Hayden gets the giggles.

"This isn't funny," I spit.

"He sent me a video of you dancing while you make cocktails."

"That was goofing off, not professional fucking dance routines."

"Just do that, then." He glances at his watch. "We have a DJ boarding in half an hour."

"A DJ?" Basil frowns. "How many people are coming?"

"Around thirty, but most of them aren't staying on the yacht. We will drop them back at the mainland once the party has finished."

"What time will that be?" I ask.

"Whenever they want."

We all exchange glances. Great. We will be up all night with these fuckers.

"Helga and Agnes will be here soon."

"Agnes?" Hayden asks. "What does she do?"

"We haven't had her on board before, but she's an MC, and with so many on board tonight, we thought we could use a master of ceremonies who will run the timetable for tonight."

"Timetable?" I frown. *That's a bit over the top, isn't it?*

I glance over at the boys, and they shrug.

"Fucking hell," Basil mouths.

Captain Mark takes off in the direction of the stairs. "Let's continue the training."

⋈

"You look great." Hayden smiles up at me as she straightens my bow tie.

I'm wearing black pants and a red glitter bow tie and am shirtless.

This is the bottom of the fucking barrel. I already know that I will never live this down.

"Everybody on deck," a voice calls over the speaker system. The woman's voice is husky and deep, with a Nordic accent.

"Who's that?" I frown.

"Must be Agnes." Hayden smiles as she kisses me quickly. "Do I look okay?"

I step back. "Twirl."

She twirls, and I smile at her getup. She and the girls are wearing fruit suits.

She has green stockings on and a big puffy red strawberry dress and a headband that has strawberry leaves coming out of it. Big red love hearts are drawn on her cheeks.

"Cutest strawberry I ever saw." I bump her with my hips. "May have to eat you later." I bump her with my hips again. "Make some strawberry jam."

She giggles and holds up her phone. "Selfie."

I stand behind her and put my face to hers, and we smile up at the camera. "This is so fun." She laughs.

"It totally is."

Is it really, though? Because I'm not feeling it.

She does a little dance on the spot, and I smile. Her excitement is contagious.

"Hurry up," the voice demands through the speaker.

Hayden widens her eyes with a giggle.

I frown. "Calm down, Agnes."

We open our bedroom door and hear the others all arguing in their cramped quarters. "I just don't see why I couldn't be the orange," Bernadette whines.

"Because I look better in orange," Kimberly snaps.

"You look good in everything," Bernadette fires back. "I don't want to be the grape. I hate grapes." She fiddles with her headband. "This thing is fucking itchy."

"I like grapes," Basil says as he combs his hair in the mirror. "I like oranges too. Why isn't it a bachelorette party tonight? I'm horny as." He fiddles with his hair some more. "Wish we got a job on one of those Studs Afloat boats where the waiters fuck all the girls . . . now *that* would be a good job."

"Where is she?" Bodie snaps as he holds his phone to his ear. "She's not answering my fucking calls. This is the tenth time I've called today."

"She's met someone else, and you're being creepy," Kimberly replies casually as she pushes Basil out of the way of the mirror. Bodie met a girl on shore last night. He's obsessed.

"Hurry up," the voice nearly yells through the speaker.

I smile down at my hot little strawberry and take my phone out and snap a photo. She pretends to blow me a kiss, and unable to help it, I take her into my arms and kiss her.

"Ugh, don't you two ever get sick of each other?" Kimberly rolls her eyes.

"Nope," I reply. I kiss Hayden again. "How could anybody ever get sick of this strawberry?"

A voice sounds. "What are you doing? We are running late, people." We turn to see a very angry short woman barreling down the hall. She has two braids in her hair that are pinned across her head. "Upstairs. Right now," she demands.

"Sorry." Hayden winces as she scurries up the stairs, and we all rush after her. We get to the main living area and look around at our handiwork. There are balloons and streamers everywhere. Very cabaret, if I do say so myself.

"Line up," Agnes demands.

We all frown at each other. *What?*

"Line up," she repeats. "Tell me who you are."

We all introduce ourselves as we stand in a line, and she walks along. She looks us up and down. "Now . . . I run a tight ship," she says, serious. "You will be professional at all times and"—she holds her fingers up to air quote—"on tonight."

"On?" I frown.

"Performing." She smiles calmly. "I want cabaret. I want over the top. This has to be the most fun time that these guests have ever had in their life."

I stare at her as she walks up and down the line. *Calm the fuck down.*

"I am on trial here tonight, and I want this job . . . so please don't mess it up for me."

"Yes, Agnes," we all reply.

She goes behind us and rifles through a box. "Come here, Christo," she tells me.

Huh?

I step forward, and she sprays a can of something all over my bare torso. "What is this?"

"Body glitter."

What?

I look down at myself. She's sprayed me with oil and gold glitter.

No . . .

Hayden sees my face and gets the giggles. She drops her head as she tries to hide from Agnes.

"Step forward," Agnes tells Bodie and Basil. They do as they're told and are covered in gold glitter oil as well.

Basil's eyes meet mine, and I wince. What the ever-loving fuck is going on here?

"Now, I'm going downstairs to check on the menu. The guests will be here in ten minutes. Remember, their wish is your command."

She disappears downstairs, and we all stare at each other. "Are you all feeling *on*?" Kimberly asks.

"Just get through tonight. She's gone tomorrow," Hayden whispers.

Ugh, not in the mood for this shit.

The DJ starts the music on the balcony above us. It's loud dance music, and disco lights begin to flash. I walk to the bar and duck down behind it. I take a swig of tequila out of the bottle.

I text Masters, just to be sure.

Don't fuck this up.
YOU DON'T KNOW ME.

Ten minutes later

We all line up at the entry onto the yacht to greet our guests. I see the large group walking down the boardwalk. I glance down at myself: black pants, red bow tie, and gold glitter oil over my body.

Kill me now.

I can hear Masters's deep voice as he gets closer, and I clench my jaw. This is humiliating. There are about twenty men and a few women . . .

Women? I thought this was a bachelor party. They must be strippers.

They walk across the bridge, and Masters, Jones, and Garcia all stop on the spot as they see me. Wide eyed, they burst out laughing.

Fuck my life.

They begin to circle me as Garcia lets out a low whistle. "We have a situation." Masters smiles darkly. He reaches up and tweaks my nipple. "I like these."

I clench my jaw as Hayden's eyes widen.

Garcia walks behind me and slaps my ass. "Aren't you just a fucking delight?" They keep walking around me like I'm a hunted animal.

"My very own play toy." Spencer smiles darkly.

My friends' horrified eyes are wide as they watch.

"Welcome aboard, sir." I nod.

They throw their heads back and laugh out loud.

This is un-fucking-believable.

"Welcome aboard, gentlemen. May I introduce your crew for the night?" Agnes smiles. "We're here to give you the best night of your life."

"Mission accomplished." Masters's mischievous eyes hold mine. "It already is."

The other men all come on board and begin to dance through the yacht. They are already well and truly intoxicated. Loud and laughing.

Everyone takes off to their working positions for the night.

I go behind the bar; the three boys come and sit in front of me. "What will it be?" I ask dryly as I wipe the bar.

"Mimosas."

I pour a shot of tequila.

I look left, and I look right. I drink it down and lean in real close. "Listen here . . . if you fuck this up for me, I'm going to kill you with a smile on my face," I whisper.

They laugh like this is the funniest thing they've ever seen . . . it probably is.

"You'd do all this for a girl?" Masters smirks.

"She's not a girl," I spit. "She's *the* girl."

Chapter 20

HAYDEN

I pick up a tray of appetizers in the kitchen, fancy-looking sushi. "Take those around and then come back," Helga, the cook, says.

"Okay." I walk up the stairs, and Kimberly is coming down. "Bloody hell, they're already tipsy," she says.

"It's going to be a long night." I get to the lower level and decide to go up to the dance floor first.

Men are standing around and chatting. A few are dancing with the four girls.

Basil's working behind the bar. His eyes are planted firmly on the scantily dressed women as he watches them dance. I hold my tray out to a guest. "Can I tempt you to eat something, sir?"

"Thank you." They all begin to take the sushi, and the tray empties in no time at all. I go back down to the lower deck and make my way to the kitchen.

"They loved it," I tell Helga. "It was a hit."

"Good news." She smiles as she pushes another tray over. I go back upstairs and head out onto the deck. There are three men sitting at the bar talking to Christopher and Kimberly.

Gorgeous men.

A little older, maybe mid- to late thirties . . . next-level hot.

My eyes linger on them as I do the rounds. I don't know what they're talking about, but whatever it is must be hilarious. They haven't stopped laughing.

Kimberly leaves them and weaves through the crowd over to me. "Who are those men at the bar?" I ask.

She looks over. "I just met them. The one in the middle is Mr. Masters. He owns this yacht. He must be fucking loaded," she whispers.

"And the other two?"

"The blond one is Spencer Jones." Her eyes linger on him. "Fucking gorgeous. Have you seen his smile?"

"I have."

"The other one is a politician, apparently."

"Oh." I widen my eyes. "Jeez."

They laugh out loud again.

"Christo must have told them he's dating one of us."

"Why do you say that?"

"They just asked me which one of us is his girlfriend because they want to meet her."

"Oh." I screw up my face. "Great." I plaster on my fake smile and head on out to the deck.

"Come over here." Masters holds his arm out for me as he waves me over.

I walk over and awkwardly hold my tray out with a smile. "Sushi, gentlemen?"

"Put that down and talk to us," the man with the black hair says as he pulls up a stool beside him.

"Hayden is very busy," Christopher replies. "Get back to work, Hayden."

What?

"No, no, no. Never too busy for us," Spencer replies as he taps the chair. "Sit down."

"Hello." I smile.

"Julian Masters." He holds his hand out to shake mine. "How do you do?"

"Hello. I'm Hayden."

"Hayden who?" He raises an eyebrow in question.

"Funeral Home," Christopher cuts in before I can answer.

Huh? My eyes flick to Christopher in surprise. "I beg your pardon?"

"That's the cocktail I'm making." He fakes a smile. "To the funeral home we go."

They roar with laughter.

"I'm Spencer." The blond man smiles as he holds out his hand. "You can call me Spence."

Christopher shakes his cocktail shaker hard and at lightning speed above his shoulder as he glares at Spencer.

I frown over at him. He's acting very weird tonight.

"I'm Sebastian Garcia," the dark-haired man purrs in a deep, sexy voice. He takes my hand in his and kisses the back of it.

A tea towel flicks at high speed past my face and whips Mr. Garcia in the face. "Damn flies," Christopher snaps.

Huh?

"There are no flies at night," I say.

"Sand flies."

The men laugh out loud again, so hard that they can hardly stay seated on their stools.

What the hell is so funny?

Christopher fills the three cocktail glasses in front of him. "Here you go. Three trips to the funeral home."

Masters picks his up and takes a sip. "That'll do it." He winces.

Spencer takes a sip and scrunches his face up. "Fuck, that's bad."

"Are you having fun?" I ask them.

"Sure am," Sebastian replies. "There's only one thing that will make this night better."

"What's that?" I smile.

"A foot massage from Mr. Christo here."

What?

Christopher glares at him.

Mr. Masters tips his head back and laughs hard. Spencer nearly slides off the chair in hysterics.

Okay, I'm lost . . . they must be on something.

High as a kite.

Nothing being said here is even remotely funny. I raise my eyebrows in disgust. "I'll leave you to it." I walk off and begin to offer the tray of sushi around again.

"Can I offer you some sushi, sir?" I ask.

"Sure." The man smiles. I glance over to see Sebastian sitting down on a deck chair. He's kicking his shoes off.

What the hell?

Christopher isn't really going to massage his feet, is he?

My god, rich people are the worst.

Christopher kneels in front of him and picks up one of his feet.

"This is the best night of my fucking life." Mr. Masters smiles. He holds the phone up as if filming it.

I keep offering the platter, and I glance over to see Christopher twisting Sebastian's big toe so hard that he nearly breaks it off.

"Ahh," he cries.

What the hell is he doing?

Christopher twists it again, the whole foot this time, as if he is trying to dislocate it or something.

"Ahh," Sebastian screams.

The two other men are hysterical. Tears are running down their faces.

I march over. "Christopher. Can I speak to you for a moment, please?"

"Sure." He stands. "I'll just make you more comfortable, sir," he tells him. He pulls the lever on the chair and tips it backward with force. Sebastian goes flying onto the floor.

I grab Christopher's arm and drag him around the corner. "What the hell are you doing?" I whisper angrily. "You're going to get us all fired."

"I don't care."

"There are five others who do."

"Man overboard," we hear Captain Mark call over the speaker. "All hands on deck."

Bodie comes running up the side of the yacht with a ring and throws it into the sea.

A naked man jumps into the water to the cheers of his friends.

Why the hell would anyone have a bachelor party on a yacht? This is just ridiculous and completely out of control.

"We've got a problem," Kimberly snaps from behind us.

"What now?" I whisper.

"Basil has gone missing."

"What?" I frown.

"I can't find Basil. He's supposed to be on the bar upstairs, and he's not there."

"Well, where is he?" Christopher asks.

"I don't know," she stammers. "I've looked everywhere."

"Did he fall overboard?" I gasp in horror.

"Who fucking knows. This is a disaster." She storms off through the people.

334

Christopher and I walk out onto the deck to watch the dramatics as the two men are pulled from the sea. Their friends are all hanging over the rail and calling out and heckling them.

"Umm . . . I found Basil," Christopher says.

"Where?"

He points up. I look up the three levels to the master suite to see a woman with two hands on the glass being fucked from behind . . . by Basil.

"What the hell?"

"Attaboy." Christopher laughs. "Go guard the stairs."

"I am not guarding the fucking stairs while Basil fucks a stripper."

"Do you want me to?" He raises his eyebrow playfully.

"No," I snap. "I'll go. Stop breaking people's toes."

1:00 a.m.

We wave as the men amble up the boardwalk back at the dock. They ended up all leaving in search of a club. They're singing arm in arm and making a hell of a racket as they disappear into the darkness.

"It was a pleasure to meet you, Hayden," Mr. Masters says.

"Likewise." I smile.

His eyes twinkle with mischief. "Maybe we'll meet again one day."

"You never know." I smile.

I will never see this man again in my life.

Christopher shakes his hand and says something under his breath, and they chuckle.

I don't know what it is with these two. They seem to have a lot of private jokes for having just met.

He steps onto the dock and follows the others up the boardwalk.

Thank god. I don't know how much more I could take.

We all fall to sit down, utterly exhausted. "Fucking hell, that was hectic," Bodie sighs.

"Best night of my life," Basil says.

"She loved it, Baz." Christopher slaps him on the back.

Basil smiles proudly, clearly feeling ten feet tall.

We sit in silence for a while, too tired to even speak. "Will you look at this place?"

We look around at the trashed luxury yacht.

"That was a raging success." Captain Mark smiles as he comes down the stairs. "Well done, guys." He claps his hands as if he has all the energy in the world. "A quick cleanup, and we can all retire to bed." He disappears up the stairs in the best mood ever.

Christopher's shoulders slump. He looks like he just ran a marathon or something. "Thank fucking god that's over," he mutters under his breath.

There will be nothing quick about this cleanup. It's a disaster.

June
Croatia

The sound of the ocean gently laps on the sand as Christopher and I walk hand in hand through the edge of the water. It's midnight, and while the others are all still at the club partying, we've come for a walk to be alone.

It's happening a lot lately: preferring to stay in or go out to dinner than to party with everyone else.

We've been in Croatia for a week now, and I cannot believe just how beautiful this big wide world of ours is.

"Do you know what tomorrow is?" Christopher asks me.

"Wednesday?"

He takes me into his arms. "Tomorrow we've been together for three months."

My eyes widen. "It's our anniversary?"

"Monthaversary . . ." He shrugs. "Is that a thing?"

I smile up at my beautiful man. "It is now."

"The happiest three months of my life, Grumps." His lips take mine, and as the moonlight bounces off the water, I know I'm in heaven.

"Mine too."

His eyes search mine. "I love you."

My heart stops.

"I've wanted so badly to hear those three words from you," I whisper.

He smiles softly as he takes my face in his hands. It means so much more to me that he's waited to say those words, because I know he truly means them.

"I love you too." We kiss, and it's soft and tender, filled with so much love.

My crazy party boy has manned up and tamed down. Faced his demons and won.

For me.

"I can't imagine a life without you in it," he murmurs against my lips.

"You'll never have to."

We kiss in the moonlight . . . and on the perfect night, two become one.

He loves me.

September
Copenhagen, Denmark

Who knew that this place existed?

The scenery, the nightlife, the sexy man in front of me.

The dance floor is crowded with bodies writhing to the techno beat. It's 4:00 a.m., and with Christopher's large hands on my hip bones, he grinds up behind me as he dances. His erection is hot and hard against my back, and his lips drop to my ear.

"I need you," he whispers darkly as he bites my ear.

We keep dirty dancing, oblivious to the people around us. Our friends are in the club, but as usual, we're in our own little world.

Where the rules are, there are no rules. We love sweet, and we fuck hard.

He slides his hand up my leg and between my legs on the crowded dance floor and slips his fingers in, and I smile against his neck.

He's so naughty.

He feels how wet I am and inhales sharply and grabs my hand and drags me through the club.

Next thing I know I'm up against a wall in a service hallway with my legs around his waist, and he's pulling my panties to the side as he slides in deep.

We stare at each other. The feeling of his thick cock deep inside me makes me moan, and he bites my bottom lip and fucks deep, hard, and fast.

Right here in the club without a care in the world.

He owns me.

November
Historic town of Gamla Stan, Sweden

Snowflakes fall on the cobblestone streets, and the colorful buildings blend into the night. This place is straight out of a fairy tale.

The room is cozy and warm, and I lie in bed and doze. I'm under the weather and not feeling the best.

I hear the key in the door, and Christopher appears with a shopping bag. "Hi, babe."

"Hi." I smile up at him.

"Got the supplies. Paracetamol." He unpacks the grocery bag. "Strawberries." He holds them up. "Tampax." He holds up the box. "And chocolate?" He holds up a huge block of my favorite chocolate. He digs through the shopping bag and pulls out a small bar of chocolate. "This one's for me . . . because we both know you're not sharing yours."

"You know it." I smile.

He fusses about and showers and then comes and climbs into bed behind me. He puts his big warm hand tenderly over my sore stomach and kisses my temple. "You okay, baby?" he whispers.

"I am now that you're home."

He looks after me so well. Treats my body as if it's his body too. In a way, it is. It's something we share.

My protector, my lover, and my very best friend.

"Sleep now, angel. I'm here."

December
Thailand

We sit around the outdoor table under the trees on the water's edge.

The view over the beach is picture perfect.

It's Christmas Day, and to splurge we rented a house in Ko Samui for two weeks.

The boys are cooking on the outdoor grill, and we're all wearing our colorful hats from our Christmas cracker bonbons.

These are the best five people I could ever have hoped to have met.

The best of friends, we've been through so much together as we've traveled the world.

Christopher pops a cork on a bottle of champagne and fills all our glasses and then holds his glass in the air. "A toast."

We all smile and hold our glasses up as we wait for his wise words.

"May all our Christmases be as happy as this one." He lifts his glass up higher. "To happiness."

His eyes find mine across the table, and they twinkle with a certain something. I feel it to my toes.

"To happiness."

We all sip our champagne, and our faces screw up as we wince in silence.

"What *is* this? Tastes like fucking shit," Christopher cries in disgust. "I paid twenty-two dollars for this fucking horse piss."

Everyone bursts out laughing as they choke on what is possibly the worst champagne in the world.

"To dying in Thailand from poison," Basil says as he holds his glass up for another toast.

We all laugh hysterically as we toast again. "To poison."

March
Germany

We stand on the curb outside the hostel. The bus is coming to collect the others for the airport.

Our trip of a lifetime is over.

It's time to go home.

Christopher and I are flying out of a different airport. Our cab is coming in half an hour to collect us.

We are going to see his parents, then mine, and then we are going to visit Elliot in London . . . and then I guess we will see where we end up.

Christopher's been quiet all week, and I know it's because our trip is over.

He's dreading going back to cleaning.

But I know it will be okay. Maybe he can do a course or go back to school or something. I don't want him to do a job that he's ashamed of. It hurts my heart.

I stand back and watch Christopher hug everyone goodbye. We're all in tears.

Because no matter how much we say we're going to keep in touch, we won't.

We live in completely different parts of the world, and soon these people will be nothing more than memories. They'll be nothing more than people in photos, ones I went on a trip with once.

Their car is waiting.

It's my turn to hug everyone, and with tears running down my face, I say my goodbyes.

Christopher helps load their bags into the bus, and they sadly climb on.

I can hardly see the bus as it drives away.

The end of an era.

Christopher puts his arm around me as we watch it disappear into the distance.

"That's it," he says softly.

I nod.

"The trip's over."

"Yep." I nod as I wipe my eyes. "Time to go back to reality."

He rolls his lips. "There's something I need to tell you."

"You want to stay longer?" I smile hopefully.

"I wish we could."

I smile sadly. If only.

His eyes search mine. "Hayden . . . I'm not who you think I am."

I frown.

"I'm not a cleaner."

"What do you mean?"

He grabs my two hands and leads me over to a bench seat and sits me down. "Sweetheart." His voice is soft, cajoling, as if delivering a fatal blow. "Have you ever heard of Miles Media?"

"No."

"It's a media company in New York."

"Yeah, so?"

"I'm Christopher Miles."

I frown. "What are you talking about?"

"Babe." He widens his eyes, hoping I will get a clue. "As in Miles Media Miles."

"I don't understand." I frown.

A black limousine pulls up, and the driver in full uniform gets out and pops the trunk.

"Our car is here."

I look to the fancy car, horrified . . . that's *our* car?

What the fuck?

Chapter 21

My eyes search his.

Time seemingly stands still . . . I don't understand. I look back at the pristine limousine and then back to him.

What do you mean . . . that's our *car?*

"Babe, we have to go. We have a plane to catch. Let's just . . ." He gestures to the limousine and the driver waiting by the open trunk. "We can talk about it on the way."

I stare at him, shocked to my core.

"Grumps." He kisses my lips quickly. "It changes nothing. Relax." He carries my backpack down to the car. "Hello," he says to the driver before passing the backpack and coming back for his. "Get into the car, sweetheart."

How can he say this changes nothing? This changes every single thing.

"Babe." He points to the car as if reminding me. "Get in."

It's then that I realize what's going on here. I'm being railroaded. He's purposely withheld this information until two minutes before the car turned up so that I wouldn't have time to get upset.

He opens the car door and smiles warmly. "Come on," he mouths.

My eyes flick to the driver, and he smiles warmly. Feeling stupid and not wanting to cause a scene, I get into the back of the limousine.

Christopher slides in beside me and pulls my face to his and kisses me softly. "Off we go." He smiles happily as he takes my hand in his lap.

The car pulls out from the curb and drives down the street, and I stare out the window as people watch us drive by.

I have no words.

To break the awkward silence between us, Christopher chats away to the driver, like, he's overly chatty, and I know what he's doing. He doesn't want to talk about this with me until we're safely on the plane.

He picks up my hand and kisses the back of it. "I love you," he mouths. "What a great trip. That was the best time of my life. I'm going to miss those guys." He happily chats away. "We should try and catch up with everyone at least once a year."

Distracted, I nod and fake a smile as my attention turns back out the window.

Why would he lie to me?

$$\text{\Large)\kern-0.6em(}$$

An hour later we drive through a boom gate and out onto the tarmac, and I frown. Where are we going?

If I was talking to Christopher, I would ask. However, I'm choosing to remain silent.

Because if I open my mouth, I'm not quite sure what's going to come out. I need to process this before I blurt out something nasty that I'll regret.

Because believe me, there's a whole lot of fucking nasty going on in my mind right now.

The car pulls up beside a plane, and I peer out. It looks all swanky, like a Learjet or something. The driver gets out and opens the trunk, and I glance over to Christopher. "What's this?" I ask.

344

"Our plane."

"You have a plane?"

"Yes." He nods. His brow furrows as if he's stopping himself from saying something.

He has a fucking plane?

I blink in surprise as I look out at it. "Is it safe?"

"Yes, of course." He smiles and puts his arm around me and kisses my temple. "I would never risk you."

But you would *lie to me.*

The driver opens my car door, and I smile up at him. He's kind looking. "Thank you."

Christopher gets out and smiles. "Thank you." He holds out his hand and discreetly passes him some notes as a tip.

I blink again. This is like *The Twilight Zone.*

Christopher takes my hand and leads me up the stairs. Two stewardesses and a captain in full uniform stand inside the door. "Good evening, Mr. Miles." The captain nods.

"Thomas." Christopher laughs. "Good to see you, my old friend." He shakes his hand excitedly.

"It's been a long time, sir."

"It has, it has." Christopher looks around. "Where are the normal crew?"

"This is Angela and Michelle. Our other girls are both on maternity leave."

"Babies, ha! Great." Christopher smiles. He shakes the two women's hands. "Nice to meet you. This is Hayden." He presents me proudly.

"Hello." I smile as I shake their hands.

"Lovely to meet you, Hayden."

They seem nice.

"This way, babe." Christopher holds his arm up, and I look around. White leather seats, plush carpet, and the most exotic-looking cabin of a plane that I've ever seen. It looks like something out of a movie, only I haven't seen it in a movie because it's too swanky. He takes my hand and leads me up the cabin. "Where do you want to sit?" he asks.

Don't insult my intelligence and pretend that I have any control of this situation . . . it's quite obvious I don't.

I shrug. "Anywhere will do."

He gestures to a double seat at the back, and I fall in beside the window. The engine starts, and I stare out at the limo as it drives off across the tarmac.

I glance down at myself in embarrassment. I'm wearing shorts and a T-shirt, feeling completely underdressed and inappropriate. I drag my hand through my messy ponytail. God . . . what must I look like? I did wonder why he was dressed up today in jeans and a button-up shirt.

Now I know.

Christopher fusses around and then sits down beside me. He leans over and does up my seat belt. "You okay, sweetheart?" He smiles as he kisses me.

The stewardesses are hovering around.

I nod with another fake smile. I don't want a scene with anyone in earshot, and I'm still trying to calm myself down enough to think straight.

This is a lot.

The plane pulls out and drives around for a while. Christopher chatters on and makes small talk, overcompensating for my silence.

He knows.

We take off into the air, and he slides his hand onto my thigh. "You all right, babe? You're very quiet," he whispers.

I smile and nod. I'm not. It's a lie.

"Can I get you anything?" the hostess asks me.

"Um . . ." I think for a moment. "Can I have a lemonade, please?"

346

"Of course." She smiles and then turns to Christopher. "What would you like, Mr. Miles?"

He rolls his lips as he thinks for a moment. "I'll have a Blue Label scotch and beluga caviar, please." His eyes flick over to me. "Do you want something to eat, darling?"

I stare at him for a moment as I process his order.

Blue Label scotch and beluga caviar.

Since when has he liked those things? I shake my head. "No, thank you."

The stewardess smiles warmly. "Yes, sir."

She disappears out to the kitchen, and I watch as Christopher puts his head back against the seat as if starting to relax.

I don't know him at all.

✗

Nine hours later

The plane pulls to a stop on the tarmac, and I read the sign out the window.

WELCOME TO NEW YORK

Christopher bounces his leg as he sits beside me, impatient to get off the plane. He knows I'm off. I pretended to sleep the entire nine-hour trip so that I wouldn't have to talk to him. Mainly . . . because I don't know what the fuck to say.

He had a few glasses of scotch, ate caviar, and then watched a few movies, all with his hand protectively on my leg.

"You may disembark, Mr. Miles," the captain says over the speaker.

Christopher stands and gets my handbag out from the overhead and fusses around. He takes my hand and leads me out.

"Thank you." He shakes everyone's hands as they line up by the door.

"Have a nice night." The captain smiles. "Goodbye, Hayden. Lovely to meet you."

"See you next time."

I smile, detached from the situation. I feel like I'm having an out-of-body experience right now. Like I'm physically here . . . but I'm so shocked that I'm not.

He lied to me. For twelve months I have been falling in love with a man who doesn't even exist.

I don't know if I've ever felt so betrayed.

We walk out to the stairs, and I look down to see another limousine waiting on the tarmac. The driver is in a black suit and standing beside the car. He looks up and waves, and Christopher laughs and waves excitedly back. He nearly runs us down the stairs to get to him. "Hello, Hans." He laughs as he pulls the driver in for a hug.

"Hello, Mr. Miles." The man laughs, seemingly just as excited to see him too.

Christopher puts his arm around me. "This is my Hayden." He smiles proudly.

"Hello," Hans says as he shakes my hand.

"Hello." I smile. Oh, he's a nice old man, I can tell.

They throw our things in the trunk, and we get into the back seat. Christopher leans over and kisses my temple as he puts his arm around me. "Do you know how much I love you?" he asks.

I stare straight ahead as I hold my tongue.

Not really.

CHRISTOPHER

Hans gets behind the wheel, and we pull out of the airport and onto the main road. "There's a bit of traffic tonight, I'm afraid, sir," Hans says. "Bumper to bumper when I was driving in."

"That's okay." I smile as I hold Hayden's hand firmly in my lap. "Can't be helped."

Hayden's gaze is fixed firmly out the window. This is the quietest I've ever seen her, and I have no idea what's going through her head.

I'm unsure if she's shocked or furious . . . I'm hoping for shocked but beginning to expect furious.

I should have told her earlier, but I just . . . didn't know how.

Hans sighs as the traffic comes to a complete standstill. "Looks like there has been an accident now to top it off." I look up to see lights flashing from a traffic-control van.

I exhale heavily. Great. This is just what I need.

My phone lights up.

Eddie

Shit, now is not the time. I can't even pretend to be in a good mood. He's calling to check we landed okay. I'll call him back tomorrow.

I turn my phone on silent.

"Would you like a glass of wine or champagne?" I ask Hayden as I open the minibar fridge.

Her eyes flick over to me, and I feel the venom behind them.

Hmm . . . I've never seen that look before . . . which is a good thing, because I don't fucking like it.

"No, thank you," she replies curtly.

I roll my lips. Well, I would. I pour myself a glass of champagne, and unable to help myself, I hold my glass up in a sarcastic cheers sign. "I'll drink alone, then."

Her eyes hold mine, and silent animosity swims between us. *Would she rather I be fucking broke?*

I take a large gulp of my champagne. It's smooth, cold, and delicious.

Unlike her in this moment.

※

The longer we sit in the back of the limo, the more I feel Hayden's anger festering like a volcano that's ready to blow.

The more I feel it, the more pissed I get.

Seriously?

She would actually rather I clean fucking toilets for a living?

That's not loving someone . . . that's enabling . . . to what, I don't know, but I'm sure there's some form of emotional abuse in there somewhere.

The more I think about this, the more I know I'm right. If I was broke and I told her I had money, then I would understand.

But this?

I will not be judged for having money . . . my parents have worked fucking hard to build the Miles empire. What . . . does she think she's above it? I clench my jaw as I watch her and swish the champagne around my mouth as I silently fume.

How dare she?

I don't judge her for fist-fucking cows for a living. And I could. Trust me, I could.

350

I drain my glass and then immediately pour myself another one without even asking her if she wants one. I put the bottle back into the fridge.

That's enough.

The night is already spiraling out of control. Alcohol is only going to pour kerosene on the fire.

The car has been at a standstill for over forty minutes now. What the hell is going on up there?

I glance at my watch. Fuck it. This night is a disaster. I made a booking at my favorite restaurant, thinking tonight was going to be epically romantic.

Guess not.

I sip my wine as I stare at her staring out the window . . . my anger gently simmering on the stove.

"Are you cold?" I ask her.

"Nope."

"What's with the attitude?" I mutter under my breath.

She throws me a dirty look. Her eyes dart to Hans as if to remind me that he's here.

Really?

I stare at her as I hear my heartbeat in my ears.

I've done nothing wrong. If she didn't care that I had no money . . . why would she care that I do? Why has she gotten pissed off without so much as a discussion?

I treat her like a queen, and for her to sit beside me for ten fucking hours without one word is infuriating.

Hans's eyes meet with mine in the rearview mirror. "I'm sorry for the delay, Mr. Miles. I should have checked the radar before I came this route."

I exhale, annoyed. *Yes, you should have.* "That's fine, Hans."

Hayden tsks beside me, and my eyes sweep across to her. I raise my eyebrow in question.

She raises her eyebrow right back.

Don't fucking piss me off.

I snap my eyes away. Don't tell me our first-ever fight is going to be in the back of my limo while stuck in traffic.

I. Am. Not. In. The. Mood.

One and a half silent hours later

The car pulls into my building, and Hans fusses around nervously. Even he can tell she's pissed. Who am I kidding? The space station on Mars can tell she's pissed.

"I'm so sorry about the delay, Hayden," Hans stammers.

Hayden smiles calmly. "Please, don't be sorry. It's not your fault."

"Thank you for understanding."

She gives him a huge smile as she opens her door before the doormen get a chance to. They all come running to help her out of the car.

Her being nice to Hans infuriates me even more. So she's not pissed in general.

Just with me.

I climb out of the car behind her. "Mr. Miles," they all say excitedly. "Welcome home, sir."

"It's good to be here," I reply. They go to take our bags, and I stop them. "I've got it. Thank you."

We walk into the foyer. "Good evening, Mr. Miles." The staff all smile. "Welcome home, sir."

"It's great to be here." I smile back. It is genuinely good to be back.

"This way." I gesture to the elevator, and we get in and turn to face the front. I push the button to the penthouse.

Hayden's eyes flick over to me. "You live here?" she says, unimpressed.

"*We* live here." I glare at her.

She fakes a smile, and I see red.

Game on.

The doors open to my foyer, and I step out and scan my fingerprint. The double doors unlock, and we are met with a floor-to-ceiling magical view over New York, the city lights twinkling as far as the eye can see.

Hayden stops on the spot, shocked to silence.

How you hating that money thing now?

I walk in and put the bags down, and she tentatively follows as she looks around.

I try to imagine what it must be like to see it for the first time. It's industrial trendy, with the best of everything over two floors.

She walks over to the window and peers down at the road way below. "How high are we?"

"Sixty floors."

She frowns and steps back from the window as if frightened.

"I'll give you the tour," I say. "Living area." I gesture to the room we're standing in. I walk down to the other end of the penthouse. "This is the kitchen." I open the invisible door. "Wine cellar downstairs."

Her eyes are wide as she looks around.

"Down this end are four bedrooms, each with their own bathroom, and the laundry room. Gymnasium." I walk her down the large hallway, and she peers in at all the rooms. I gesture up the stairs. "This way." I take the stairs, and she follows me in silence as she looks around.

"Up here we have another living area, bedrooms, and another living area or theater room." She looks around, still choosing to remain silent.

"The master bedroom is down here." I open the double doors to my bedroom. The floor-to-ceiling glass walls have 180-degree views over New York.

Hayden's mouth falls open, and she makes an audible gasp.

I smile proudly.

This is the most impressive bedroom of all time, if I do say so myself.

Hope fills me.

"Look." I open the walk-in wardrobe doors in a rush. "This will be your wardrobe here." She peers in at the huge empty room. "We can fit it out however you like."

"And look at this, babe." I lead her into the bathroom. "Look at the bathtub." I smile. "It's a spa. We can spend hours in there. You love baths," I remind her.

She nods and steps back, still processing.

I open my wardrobe door. "This is my wardrobe."

She peers in, and then a frown crosses her face, and she walks past me into the wardrobe. I hold my breath as I watch her look over my three bays of expensive suits. Her hand runs over the shoes neatly lined up. Her eyes rise to the floor-to-ceiling tie rack I have for my ties. She goes to the set of drawers that is freestanding in the middle.

Don't open the . . .

Too late. She opens the top drawer and peers in at my designer watch collection, displayed in a glass cabinet.

She swiftly closes the drawer and walks past me out of the wardrobe.

Huh?

What the hell does that mean?

I wait for a moment and walk out to find her staring out the window over the city.

"Are you going to say something?" I ask.

354

"It's beautiful." She forces a smile.

She has more to say.

"And?"

"What . . ." She pauses as if searching for the right words. I wait.

"What do you do at Miles Media?"

"I'm the head of marketing."

She frowns as she stares at me. I can see her mind running a million miles per minute. "Where is your office?"

I roll my lips. Here we go . . . "London."

Her eyebrows shoot up. "You live in London?"

"Yes."

"London." She gasps. "You live in fucking London?"

"I do."

"And when were you going to tell me this?" She gasps, affronted.

"I'm telling you now."

She stares at me, horrified.

"You're going to love it there, Hays."

"I am *not* moving to London, Christopher."

"What does that mean?" I snap.

"Exactly what I said. I'm not moving there."

"You said you would live anywhere as long as we're together," I splutter.

"When did I ever say that?"

"Oh, you said it, all right; I clear-as-day remember. But what you really meant was that you would move anywhere for a pauper, but you won't fucking move for me?" I bark.

"Would *you* move for me?" she fires back.

"If it meant we were together, then yes."

"Okay, great. That settles it." She dusts her hands together. "We'll live in the country."

I see red.

"Don't give me your smart-ass fucking attitude, Hayden," I yell. "I have responsibilities with Miles Media."

"And what about your responsibilities to me?" she yells. "My work is in the country."

"I run a multibillion-dollar company, Hayden. I need to live between London and New York. I can't live in Bumfuck, Nowhere, while you play with cows."

"Play with cows!" Her eyes bulge from their sockets.

"My job *is* important."

"Obviously." She throws her hands up in the air and then marches from the room.

"Get back here!" I yell.

"Go fuck yourself."

Chapter 22

I march after her, infuriated. "Where are you going?" I demand.

"To bed."

"Your bedroom is back here!"

"That isn't a bedroom, Christopher; that's a Tinder auditorium. I can hear the moans that are ingrained into the paint."

"What the fuck does that mean?" I explode.

"It means I don't want to sleep in there!" she cries. "I'll sleep in the fucking laundry room before I get into that bed." She marches down the stairs at high speed and up the hall into one of the spare rooms.

"What the hell are you talking about?" I lose all control. "Don't you *fucking* dare throw my past in my face. Just because you chose to be a nun before we met, don't dare judge me for having fun," I scream as I follow her.

"And now I see the whole picture of just how much fun you've had."

"What the hell are you talking about right now?"

She keeps marching.

"You are judging me based on your assumptions of what you think wealthy men live like. Do you have any idea how childish that is?"

She turns like the devil herself. "Am I wrong?" she demands. "Please, tell me . . . am I wrong? I want you to correct me if I am. That is a show-pony bedroom if ever I've seen one . . . do they all gush and goo when they see your apartment, Christopher?"

I screw up my face. *What?*

"Why are you being such a raving bitch?" I yell. "I don't know who the hell you are or what malfunction has happened in that brain of yours today . . . but bring *my* sweet Hayden back to me right now."

"Whatever."

"Don't fucking push me, Hayden," I yell, infuriated. I've never been so angry.

"Or what?"

"Or you'll find yourself fucking single, that's what. I am not putting up with your fucking tantrums that have nothing to do with the subject we are even arguing about."

Slam!

She slams the door in my face, and I lose control and punch it hard. It shudders as it nearly comes off the hinges.

"Hayden. You get out here right now!" I demand.

"Go away," she yells, and I can hear in her voice that she's crying.

My heart drops . . . *she's upset.*

Adrenaline is pumping through my veins, and I drag my hands through my hair as I try to calm myself down. I begin to pace up and down the hallway.

What the fuck just happened?

6:00 a.m.

I'm beat. Didn't sleep a wink all night, and I still haven't seen Hayden.

God knows what the hell she's doing in there.

I write on a piece of paper and put the note on the table near the front door.

Gone for a run,

Back soon.

Xo

I tiptoe out the door and close it behind me as quietly as I can. I get in the elevator and press the ground-floor button.

I need to see my brothers.

※

Twenty minutes later, the car pulls up to the curb, and I get out and walk. I pass a newsstand on the street and see that they have postcards. I pick two New York ones up. "I'll take these, please," I say to the salesman.

"Sure thing." He bags them up and hands them over, and I put them into my inside pocket. I'll send these to Eddie later. I've been sending him postcards from all over the world. He collects them.

Eddie would fucking love my apartment.

Speaking of which, I'll call him now. I dial his number as I walk up the street. "Hi, Mr. Christo," he answers.

"Hey, little buddy." I smile. "What's poppin'?"

"Nothing, on my way to work. Running late."

I can hear that he's walking fast.

"How was the flight?"

Infuriating.

"Good, good," I lie. "What time you working until tonight?"

"Close."

I roll my eyes. Why the fuck do they put a kid on the closing shift? I'll never know. I glance at my watch to do a time check. "I'll let you get to it. I'll call you tomorrow?"

"Okay, sounds good."

"It's good to hear your voice, man." I smile.

"You too."

I hang up and cross the street and walk into the café to see Jameson and Tristan sitting at the back, and they both laugh and stand. I smile and almost run to them.

Thank god.

"Hey." They laugh as they both pull me into a hug. "If it isn't Romeo himself," they tease.

I drop into the chair. There are three coffees sitting on the table. They must have been here for a while.

"How was it?" Jameson asks.

"Great, amazing. Incredible."

Tristan frowns. "So what's the emergency?"

I called them both early this morning. I needed to talk to someone. I pinch the bridge of my nose and exhale in exasperation. "I told Hayden who I was yesterday."

"And?"

"She went fucking batshit crazy!"

They frown. "What do you mean?"

"I mean . . ." I shrug, lost for words. "This girl—and I'm not exaggerating—is the calmest, most stable, and sweetest human I've ever met. I've never seen her get ruffled over anything, I mean fucking anything. There is just no temper there . . . or so I thought."

They listen intently.

"I told her who I was just before the car came to collect us."

"Why did you leave it so late?" Jameson frowns. "I thought the plan was that you were telling her last week."

"I was going to . . ." My voice trails off. "In hindsight I should've."

"So then what happened?" Tristan asks.

"I told her who I was, and she went silent. Didn't speak to me all the way home for twelve fucking hours, and then when we got to my apartment, she went off on a tangent, bringing up bullshit."

"Like what?" Jameson asks.

"Said she didn't want to sleep in my bedroom because it was a Tinder auditorium and the women's moans were sunk into the paint on the walls."

"She does have a point." Tristan raises his eyebrows as if considering the statement. "Your entire apartment smells like sex," he teases.

"I like her already." Jameson chuckles.

"This isn't funny," I snap.

"Sorry." Jameson tries to straighten his face. "Go on. What happened then?"

I exhale heavily. "She started bringing up my past and chucked the tantrum of all tantrums, marched downstairs, and slept in the spare room."

They both frown as they stare at me. "When she calmed down, what did she say?"

"Nothing."

"You didn't try and talk to her?"

"No. Why would I?" I snap. "I did nothing wrong."

"You lied to her . . . for twelve fucking months," Tristan scoffs. "What did you expect?"

"Not this, that's for sure. And I didn't lie to her; I just left some minor details out."

I fall silent, not sure what to say next.

"Well . . . I guess you did it," Jameson says dryly as he sips his coffee. "Mission accomplished."

"Did what?" I sigh.

"You wanted to find a girl who loved you for you." He shrugs. "If this doesn't count as sufficient evidence, I don't know what will."

I roll my eyes.

"She feels betrayed," Tristan says.

"I haven't looked at another woman," I scoff. "How the hell could she feel betrayed?"

"She feels like she doesn't know you."

"She knows me better than anyone," I whisper angrily. "Probably better than I know myself." I roll my eyes. "I did not fall in love to have someone turn on me at the drop of a hat."

"Christopher"—Jameson pats me on the back—"women are complex creatures. This is the first fight of many. You're just beginning to feel the tip of the cock before you get bent over and completely fucked up the ass."

Tristan chuckles. "Truth. What else did she say when you were fighting?"

"She told me she's not moving to London and then asked me if I would move for her."

"What did you say?"

"I said I'm not living in Bumfuck, Nowhere, for her to play with fucking cows."

"There you go." Jameson throws his head back and laughs out loud as if it's the funniest thing he's ever heard. "You are *so* fucking stupid."

I exhale heavily, and we sit in silence for a while.

"It's a control thing," Jameson says.

"She's not a controlling person," I say. "Not in the least."

"Not wanting control and not having control are two different things."

"She said she'd live anywhere as long as we're together," I reply.

"That was before."

"Before what?"

"Before she knew that where you live is out of your hands."

"London is beautiful," I scoff. "I don't get it. It's not like we won't ever come back. We can buy a house in Bumfuck, Nowhere, as well." I shrug as I look between them. "What's the fucking problem?"

"She has no commitment to that."

"She wants a commitment, I'll marry her tomorrow," I whisper angrily. "In my mind, I'm already married anyway."

They both look at me, horrified.

"It's *that* serious?"

"Yes!" I look between them. "Are you two dumb fucks listening to me at all? This is her. This is *the* one."

Jameson widens his eyes. "Out of all the women in the world, you fall for one that hates money." He laughs again. "Oh . . . the irony."

"You think?" I scoff. "I didn't sleep all night, petrified that she was going to leave me."

"Give her time. She'll calm down. It took Claire a while to come around to my life," Tristan says.

"Same here."

I can only hope that's true.

"And for Christ's sake," Jameson sighs, "keep your big mouth shut."

"That's it?" I screw up my face. "That's the brotherly advice you're giving me? To keep my big mouth shut?"

My phone beeps with a text.

> **Can't wait to see you today and**
> **finally meet Hayden.**
> **See you at 1.**
> **Mom, xo**

"Oh no." I drag my hand down my face.

"What?"

"I've got lunch with Mom and Dad today to introduce them to Hayden." I roll my eyes. "I completely forgot that I arranged it last week."

"Tip of the day: keep her well away from Mother. That will be the final nail in your coffin." Tristan widens his eyes.

"Yeah, good thinking." I text back.

> **Sorry mom,**
> **Super jet lagged.**
> **Can we take a rain check?**
> **I'll call you tomorrow.**

My phone instantly rings, and the boys both laugh, knowing exactly who is on the other end.

"Fuck it." I answer the call. "Hi, Mom." I fake a smile as I act happy.

"Darling, what's happening?"

"Nothing, we're just super tired, and I want Hayden to settle in a little. Can we reschedule lunch for in a few days' time?"

She stays silent and calculating. "Is everything all right?"

"Yeah," I sigh. "Hayden just found out who I am, and it's . . . a lot."

"She's overwhelmed?"

"Yes."

"I hope you're being patient with her."

I stay silent.

"I can't imagine how upsetting it would have been if I found out your father had lied to me for twelve months."

"I didn't lie, Mom."

"Yes, you did, Christopher. Blatantly."

Ugh, not in the mood for a lecture. "I'm going."

"Call me later."

"Okay." I widen my eyes. "Fine." Last thing I need is another woman busting my balls. I hang up in a rush.

"What are you going to do now?" Tristan asks.

"I don't know . . ." I shrug.

Jameson smiles into his coffee. "I suggest groveling."

HAYDEN

I lie in bed and stare at the wall. I feel terrible. Heartbroken and sad.

I've cried all night.

The man that I'm desperately in love with doesn't exist, and I don't even know what's real anymore.

Twelve months of deceit.

If he lied about who he is, what else has he lied about?

I keep going over and over our fight last night and how badly it got out of control. How furious I was and the horrible things that I said. I have no idea why his bedroom triggered me . . . all I know is that it did.

And maybe that's my insecurities, which are my problem and not his. Maybe he's right. Maybe I am discriminatory against wealthy people? Maybe I really do have preconceived ideas about how they are? I mean . . . I don't know any, so I have no idea why I'm so angry about it.

I just need some time alone to think about things and what it means for my future.

Knock, knock sounds softly on the door before it opens a smidge. "Hayz?" Christopher asks. "Can I come in?"

"Yeah."

He comes into view, and his face falls when he sees me. "Baby," he says softly, "look at your eyes." He sits on the bed beside me and brushes the hair back from my face as he looks down at me. "I'm so sorry. I hate that I've upset you."

Unexpected tears fill my eyes again, and I blink to try to stop them coming.

Stop crying.

"I should have been the adult last night," he says as his eyes search mine. "And I should have told you sooner."

"Why did you lie?" I whisper.

He stares at me for a moment before answering and then exhales heavily. "This won't make any sense to you, and it doesn't excuse my behavior at all. But . . . everyone in my life knows me as the billionaire Miles Media heir."

"You're a billionaire?" I frown.

"You like how I just snuck that in there?"

"Not really."

Jeez.

"I wanted to experience a life where nobody knew who I was. I wanted to make friends who I knew for certain liked me for me and not my bank balance or my social status."

I frown as I listen.

"And then I met you." He smiles softly as he looks down at me. "And you were so different to anyone I had ever met. Kind and sweet. Beautiful." He frowns. "With a well-hidden temper."

I smile, embarrassed.

"And I fell madly in love."

I get a lump in my throat as I listen.

"And it was selfish, I know. But I wanted all the time alone with you that I could get, every single minute, where our life was simple. Because I knew that the moment you found out about my money that it would change your perception of me."

My eyes well with tears.

It did.

"Hayden . . . my life is complicated. And busy and super stressful. The one pure, joyful, and real thing in it . . . is you." He lifts my hand and kisses my fingertips. "You have taught me so much about love and what I want from life."

367

I smile through tears.

"The man you met on the trip is the real me. I haven't lied about my feelings about you at all. I can promise you that what we have is one hundred percent real."

"I have no idea how to live this life, Christopher," I whisper.

"I know."

"It terrifies me."

"I know, baby." He bends and kisses me. "Just give me three months."

I frown.

"I have to go to London for three months. Elliot has been looking after everything, and he has a two-month vacation booked. I have to be there to manage while he's away. I can't go without you. Don't ask me to."

I stare at him.

"If you just . . . try it for three months, and then we can . . ."

"Can what?"

"Reevaluate where you want to live."

"What if I hate London?"

He stares at me. "Then we have to reevaluate the situation."

"What does that mean?"

"I don't know." He shrugs. "I would be lying if I said I did." He frowns as if getting his wording right. "With my role at Miles Media comes a great deal of responsibility. I don't have the freedom that a cleaner would have to live where he pleases."

He kisses me softly as he cups my face in his hand. "Give me three months. That's all I'm asking."

I stare at him.

"Hayden . . . I love you. We need to work this out, because now that I know how perfect a life with you is, I can't go back. And I know this isn't the life you planned . . . but as long as we're together, do the semantics really matter?" His eyes search mine, and he looks so lost and sad, and my heart constricts.

This fight is stupid.

I'm upset, and this lie is unforgivable, but on some level, I do understand. I can't imagine living this life and never knowing what is real.

"You're right." I lean up and kiss him tenderly. "As long as we're together." My lips linger over his, and his arms snap around me, and we hold each other close, cheek to cheek, raw emotion running between us.

"I'm sorry I was a bitch last night."

I feel him smile above me. "You really were."

I smirk. There he is. The smart-ass is back. "Be careful today, Christopher. You are skating on very thin ice."

He laughs and holds his two hands up in surrender. "Okay, okay." He kisses me again and then rolls me onto my back and spreads my legs with his knee. I feel his erection grow up against my leg.

"Don't even think about it," I mutter dryly.

"What?"

"Sex is the very last thing on my mind today."

His face falls. "What happened to the awesome makeup sex I hear all about?"

I sit up and climb out of bed. "I don't know, but it's not happening now."

He exhales heavily and flops back on the bed, disheartened.

I turn the shower on in the en suite.

"Well, what do you want to do today?"

"I don't know." I shrug. "I guess you can show me around this museum of an apartment, and then I have to go shopping to buy some new clothes." I take my pajamas off and throw them on the floor as I step into the shower.

"Why do you need new clothes?" he asks.

"Because I've been living in the same six outfits for twelve months, and you're stupid rich, and I look like a beggar."

He smiles as he leans onto his elbow as he lies on the bed. "Beg me for sex, why don't you, and I'll see what I can do."

I roll my eyes. "Not happening."

Half an hour later I sit at the fancy marble counter as Christopher makes us an omelet. I look around at the kitchen, and it's straight out of a magazine. He's got bacon and mushrooms and orange juice, croissants and all the yummy trimmings.

"How come you have food to cook? We didn't go to the grocery store yet."

"My housekeeper does the shopping."

I frown. "You have a housekeeper?"

"We." He gestures to the air between us. "We have a housekeeper." He flips the omelet. "Do whatever you want to the apartment. Make it how you want it. Hire an interior designer if you like."

What?

"I'm not touching a thing. It's not my apartment."

"It is your apartment. You live here, so it's yours too."

"We're not even married." I roll my eyes.

"We will be." He gives me a slow, sexy smile and widens his eyes. "Give me time."

I roll my lips to hide my smile as my stomach flutters. That's the first time he's ever said anything like that.

I like it.

I look around some more. I feel like a little kid in some kind of fancy store. I don't want to touch anything in case I break it.

He puts my plate down in front of me with a quick kiss. "Eat your breakfast, and then I'm taking you shopping."

"Where do you even buy clothes in a place like this?"

"Madison Avenue."

"Is there a budget department store there? Because my funds are low."

"I think I can cover it."

"No."

He widens his eyes in jest as he points to my plate. "Eat your breakfast before I march you into the bedroom to be fucked."

I smirk as I take a bite of my toast.

His phone vibrates on the counter in front of us.

Mom

He keeps eating.

"Are you going to answer that?"

"No. She's calling to hassle me."

"About what?"

"She wants to meet you." He rolls his eyes. "They *all* want to meet you."

I stare at him. You learn a lot about a person from their family. And I have so, so much that I want to learn. This will give me a true insight into his life and who he really is.

"Call her back. Organize a dinner for tonight with everyone. I want to meet them too."

"Are you sure? My family is full on."

"I mean"—I shrug—"how bad can it be?"

He chuckles. "Pretty fucking bad."

Chapter 23

I grip Christopher's hand with white-knuckle force as we walk down the street. I peer around like a child seeing the world for the first time. A million cars, beautiful people, and I can hardly see the sky for skyscrapers. The shops look like luxury stores, nothing at all like where I would normally buy my clothes. Even the mannequins in the windows are hot.

And tiny.

Does anyone sell anything in normal sizes?

Madison Avenue . . . code for teeny tiny.

I look around at all the women who are buzzing around in a hurry, stylish and gorgeous, groomed to perfection. I catch sight of Christopher and me in a shop window, and I inwardly cringe. He's looking all suave, in black jeans and shirt, and I'm wearing a casual T-shirt and shorts that I've practically lived in for over a year.

They're worn and faded. My hair is all over the place, and I have no makeup on. I look like a complete wreck, and last night's crying puffy eyes and face don't help my cause.

I sure am missing our relaxed backpacking life right now.

We walk past a huge fancy boutique, and the mannequin is wearing a black dress and nice shoes. "In here," Christopher says.

"It looks expensive," I whisper.

He widens his eyes.

"Fine."

He pulls me in by the hand. "Hello." He smiles.

"Hi." The shop assistants smile as they look him up and down and then to me with a subtle frown.

Great, I must look like his fix-up-the-hooker project or something.

"Can I help you with anything?"

Christopher goes to open his mouth, and I throw him a look and cut him off. "Just looking, thanks."

He raises an eyebrow.

"Don't even," I whisper.

He rolls his lips to keep his mouth closed and loiters behind me as I look around.

I see a nice black dress, and I look at the tag.

$4300.00

"What the . . . ," I whisper as I drop it like a hot potato and keep walking.

He takes it off the rack and throws it over his arm.

"Don't bother," I whisper. "That's daylight robbery, Christopher. I'm never paying that for a dress. Does it have gold fucking stitching or something?"

"Shh . . . no talking," he whispers as he fakes a smile at the salesgirl.

I widen my eyes, annoyed.

He gestures to a rack of dresses. "What else do you like?"

"Nothing here," I whisper. "These prices are ludicrous."

He puts his hand around my waist and pulls me in and kisses me softly as he lowers his voice. "When we get to Bumfuck, Nowhere, you can go shopping wherever you want. But tonight, we have a dinner date for you to meet my family, and we need to buy you a dress and shoes. So humor me and try some things on, or this is going to be an all-day fucking ordeal."

I stare at him.

"*Comprender?*"

"Fine." I flick through the rack. I get to a nice gray dress, and I turn the price tag over, and he snatches it out of my hand before I get a chance to see the price.

I roll my eyes and keep walking.

"Do you have these dresses in her size, please?" Christopher asks the shop assistant.

"I'll check, sir." She smiles before walking out the back.

"How does she know what size I am?" I mutter under my breath.

"Because it's her job," he mutters back. "You get what you pay for in New York."

"So there's a car hiding in that dress, is there?"

He chuckles as he keeps looking. "Maybe." He takes a few more things off the rack and throws them over his arm.

"Well, where are we going for dinner tonight, anyway?" I ask him. "Do I really need to wear a dress? Couldn't I just wear jeans?"

He smiles softly and leans in and kisses me. "I love you?"

"Is that a no?" I frown.

"That's a"—he stops while he chooses his words—"that's a . . . you wear whatever you want, sweetheart, and I will love you in it."

I roll my eyes. He thinks I should wear a dress. "Fine."

The shop assistant comes back over. "I have the dresses waiting in the changing room, ma'am."

"Hayden," Christopher corrects her. "Her name is Hayden."

"Hello, Hayden." She smiles. "I'm Camelia."

"Hello, Camelia," he says in his sexy, deep voice.

"And your name, sir?"

"Christopher Miles."

Her eyes widen, and she glances to the other girls. "Mr. Miles."
She knows who he is.

Fuck.

"That's right." He smiles. "Hayden has a"—he pauses—"a special occasion tonight, and she's from out of town. Can you help her find what she's after, please?"

"Of course, sir." She smiles knowingly.

Oh crap.

I totally do look like his fix-up-a-hooker project. I exhale heavily as I look around. This is so embarrassing. He walks over to the counter and slides his credit card across to the girl. "Hayden has no clothes with her at all."

"Yes, sir."

He comes back and kisses my lips. "I'm going to get a coffee next door, sweetheart. I'll leave you in the capable hands of Camelia."

You're leaving me here?

"I'll be just next door," he replies as if reading my mind.

"Fine." I scratch my head in embarrassment and watch as he walks out the front door.

"Hayden." The assistant smiles, bringing my attention back to her. "Let's make you absolutely stunning for tonight."

"Not sure that's possible." I exhale, feeling defeated.

"Where are you going, darling?"

"I'm meeting his parents."

"Oh." Her eyes widen. "We need to bring out the big guns." She walks around me as she looks me up and down. "Stephanie," she calls to the other assistant.

"Yes."

"Can you ring the salon and make an urgent hair appointment for Hayden, please? She needs a blowout."

"What's wrong with my hair?" I frown.

Camelia raises an eyebrow. "Everything, darling, everything."

※

I glide the lipstick smoothly over and roll my lips to my reflection in the mirror.

"Seriously, though," Christopher murmurs into my neck as he nibbles down to my collarbone.

"Stop." I shrug him off and look down at myself. I'm wearing a fitted black wrap dress with sheer sleeves and nude strappy stilettos, and my girls are up high in the boostiest bra of all time. I'm even wearing a sexy G-string. My hair is so amazing I could swear it's a wig, and my makeup is natural and glowy.

I hate to admit it, but Camelia knows her stuff. I look a million bucks.

Christopher's hands glide up and down my body. He's impressed, never having seen me like this before. "Kiss me," he whispers darkly.

"I just put lipstick on."

"Kiss me." His teeth nip my earlobe.

"You do not want to kiss me." I roll my eyes. "You want to bend me over the bathroom cabinet and fuck me from behind."

"Hmm." He smiles as if imagining it. "You're right, I do. Let's do that instead. Much better plan." He lifts one of my legs to sit on the cabinet.

"Listen, after your little-rich-boy act"—I correct myself as I pull my leg down—"poor-boy act, you owe me a montage of multiple orgasms."

"Ready, willing, and able." He grabs my hip bones and pumps me with his pelvis.

"Not. Now." I pull out of his grip and turn to look at my behind. "Do I look okay?"

He grabs my hand and puts it over the large erection in his pants. "What do *you* think?"

"I think you're a sex maniac, that's what I think."

"You could be onto something," he murmurs against my neck as his teeth graze my skin. "Punish me for it."

"Stop," I snap, annoyed. "I'm not going to meet your family for the first time smelling like sex."

"Hand brake."

I try to keep a straight face and fail miserably. "Let's go."

$\bigwedge$

Half an hour later, the car pulls up to the curb on a busy, congested street, and Christopher opens the door and climbs out. "Thanks."

"Have a good night." Hans smiles.

"Thank you." I smile. Christopher holds his hand out to take mine and helps me from the car, and we begin to walk up the street toward the restaurant. I'm as nervous as all hell. "Any tips?" I ask.

"For what?"

"To meet your family."

He puts his arm around me and kisses my temple as we walk. "They're going to love you, Grumps."

"How do you know?"

"Because I love you."

I smile up at him, and he stops and kisses me softly. "Thank you."

"For what?"

"For . . ." He shrugs. "Putting up with me."

I smile, feeling a lot better about us, and we kiss again. Our lips linger over each other's. "You ready to do this?" he asks.

"Ready as I'll ever be."

He takes my hand and leads me into the restaurant. It's trendy, and every table is full.

"Good evening, Mr. Miles." The waiter smiles.

"Hello," Christopher replies.

"This way." The waiter turns and walks off, and we follow him. I notice a few people turn their heads to watch Christopher walk past.

Does everyone in this godforsaken town know who he is?

We walk through a large archway into a semiprivate area. Still a part of the main restaurant but a little separated. People are sitting around a huge round table, and they see us and all stand. "Hi, everyone." Christopher smiles. "This is Hayden."

"Hi," I squeak as I look around nervously.

"Hey," they all cheer, excited.

"This is my brother Jameson and his wife, Emily."

"Hello." I feel faint. He didn't tell me his brother is ridiculously hot.

They both kiss me on the cheek. "Hello." His wife is pregnant.

"And this is my mother and father, Elizabeth and George."

"Hello."

His father kisses my cheek, and his mother pulls me in for a hug. "Hello, darling, it's so good to finally meet you." She holds my two hands in hers as she studies me.

She's so well put together that she looks like a queen or something, super attractive for her age.

"Okay, Mom, you're being creepy now." Christopher widens his eyes at her as he pulls out my chair. I fall into it beside his brother's wife, wishing this night was over already.

Emily fills my glass. "Drink," she whispers.

I giggle. I like her already. "Good idea."

"Where are the Anderson Mileses?" Christopher asks.

"Oh, they'll be late as usual, darling," his mother says as she picks up her wineglass. "Hayden." She smiles over at me. "Christopher didn't tell me you were so beautiful."

"Oh." I frown, embarrassed.

"She is, isn't she?" Christopher smiles proudly as he reaches over and takes my hand in my lap.

Emily watches us and then hunches her shoulders in excitement. She looks around the table at the others, and I feel like an amusement in a freak show.

"So . . ." His mother smiles as she looks between us. "Tell us how you two met."

"Come on, Mom." Christopher sighs. "We just got here. Can we leave the fifty questions until Hayden is drunk, please?"

Everyone chuckles, and I sip my wine. Not a drill. *For real.*

A boy comes running through the restaurant. "Grandma," he yells as he grabs her in a headlock from behind.

She laughs out loud. "Hello, my sweet Patrick."

He dives to sit beside her, and she wipes the hair back from his forehead as they talk between themselves. I would say he's around ten years of age.

"Hello, Patrick." Everyone smiles.

"This is Patrick, my brother Tristan's son," Christopher says. He gestures to me. "This is Hayden."

Patrick looks over at me in surprise and then back to Christopher. "Where have you been?"

"I went on a trip."

"Why so long?"

Everyone chuckles.

"Sorry we're late," a woman says as she takes off her coat. She's pretty, with dark hair, and heavily pregnant. "I'm Claire." She smiles as she shakes my hand. Christopher stands and laughs and takes her into his arms. It's obvious the two of them are close.

"What have you done with my brother?" he teases.

"He's coming." She rolls her eyes.

I turn to see a large boy, a teenager, walking toward us, and behind him is a man who is Christopher's double. My mouth nearly falls open. The resemblance is uncanny.

"Hi," he says. "Sorry we're late." He smiles and comes straight over to me. "You must be Hayden?"

"Yes."

He pulls me out of the chair and into his arms for a hug. He's tall and good looking like the other two brothers. Talk about a gene pool.

Oh . . . *he smells good.*

"I'm Tristan."

"Hello."

"This is my son, Harry." He introduces me to the large boy. God . . . he must have had this kid when he was ten.

"Hello." The boy smiles as he shakes my hand.

Tristan pulls the chair out, directing Harry where to sit. "What do you want to drink, babe?"

Claire exhales, clearly sick of being pregnant. "You know what I want to drink."

He raises a cheeky eyebrow. "Lemonade?"

"Can't wait," she mutters dryly.

Claire smiles over at me. "How long have you got to go?" I ask.

"I'm eight months. Hopefully a few weeks."

Tristan reaches over and puts his hand protectively on her pregnant stomach. "You stay in there and behave yourself," he says casually. He turns back to talking to Jameson.

Claire rolls her eyes. "Tristan is obsessed with babies. This is our third in four years."

Emily and I laugh.

"He'll annoy the poor thing to death." Claire rolls her eyes again.

I look to the older boys sitting at the table in confusion.

"These are my sons," she explains. "Tristan's now too. He adopted them when we got married. Their biological father died."

"Oh." I smile as I connect the dots. "I see."

I look to Tristan with love hearts in my eyes. He took on her children: not at all what I would expect. *He's a good guy.*

Harry is watching something on his phone with the volume turned up so loud that everyone can hear it. Tristan gestures to his neck as if saying, *Cut it out.*

Harry rolls his eyes, and Tristan looks at him deadpan. Harry exhales and turns it down, and I bite my lip to hide my smile.

Patrick is chatting away to his grandmother, and she is laughing and talking to him like she has all the time in the world as he fiddles with her hair. He's telling her some in-depth story about what happened at baseball practice as she listens to his story intently.

I like her.

I turn my attention to Emily. She has dark hair and is pretty. "How far along are you?"

"Five months."

Oh, I would have thought further along than that.

"I'm huge." She exhales. "Baby number four. My stomach is stretched to the shit. It's like a fucking tent in there."

Claire hushes her. "It will bounce back."

Jeez.

Jameson stretches out and puts his arm across the back of Emily's chair as he talks to the boys. His finger traces a circle on her shoulder.

"Everyone's babies are so close." I smile.

"Too close." Emily rolls her eyes. "Jameson wants the diaper stage over as quick as possible."

"Makes sense."

"How do you like New York?" Claire smiles warmly.

"It's . . ." I shrug.

"It's a lot to take on," she whispers.

Emily reaches over and takes my hand in hers. "We were the same."

They know.

"Tell me this gets easier."

They exchange looks and laughs. "Oh, sweetie," Claire says. "It doesn't, but you do get used to it."

I force a smile.

"Dad," Patrick says across the table.

Tristan keeps talking to Jameson and Christopher.

"Dad."

He still doesn't hear him.

"Dad."

Tristan keeps talking.

"Dad."

"Dad's talking, Patrick," Claire says. "Use your manners, please."

"Excuse me, Dad!" he screams.

The whole table stops talking, and Tristan looks across the table, startled. "Yes, Patrick, what is it?"

"I want fries tonight."

Tristan looks at him deadpan and sips his beer. "That's great, buddy. You do that."

Jameson chuckles, and I try not to smile. It's obvious the boys are pretty full on.

We chat, and we laugh, and this isn't what I expected at all.

Harry reaches over and knocks his drink over. It spills all over the table, and Tristan reaches over and mops it up with a napkin as he talks, totally unfazed.

Dinner comes, and we eat as we talk. It's delicious.

They all make me feel so welcome, and the conversation isn't forced at all.

Patrick reaches over and knocks his drink over too. Tristan rolls his eyes. "Fuck me dead," he mouths to Jameson, who is chuckling again.

"Jay." Emily rubs her chest. "I'm getting angina."

"That makes two of us," Tristan mutters dryly as he mops up the mess. "You keep that baby inside of you, Anderson. I've got enough on my plate out here."

"Table," Jameson corrects him.

I giggle as I watch. Everyone is laughing and talking through the messy chaos, and nobody is batting an eyelid.

I glance across the table to Christopher; his eyes hold mine, and he gives me the best come-fuck-me look of all time.

The air crackles between us as we stare at each other.

Him, his family, these kids . . . the night went well.

⋊⋉

Christopher opens the front door and pulls me into the apartment. "Do you want a drink or anything?"

"No thanks."

He leads me in by the hand and hesitates as he looks up the stairs. "That's right, we're burning that bed in the Tinder auditorium, aren't we?"

I smile, grateful that he can find the joke in it.

He pulls me up the hall downstairs. "Although for future reference, I want it noted that I have never been on Tinder." He

383

pushes me into a spare bedroom. "We'll need to burn this bed tomorrow too." He kisses me roughly as he walks me backward into the room. "It's your moans that will be ingrained into the paint."

With his eyes locked onto the task in front of him, he undoes the tie and slowly slides my dress off over my shoulders and throws it onto the floor.

I stand before him in my sexy black lace underwear, and his dark eyes hold mine as he drops to his knee in front of me.

He kisses my hip bones and then my lower stomach, and I feel like I can't breathe as I watch.

Everything is intensified between us. It's like we've hit a higher level of consciousness.

Things are different now that I know who he really is. He could have any woman in the world, and yet he loves me.

A simple country girl.

He kisses me tenderly through my panties, and his eyes close in ecstasy.

I love this man.

He drops lower and licks up my inner thigh as his dark eyes hold mine. He turns his head and gently bites my thigh again.

Thump, thump, thump, sounds my heartbeat in my ears, and I try to calm my breathing.

He nips my sex through my panties and inhales sharply as his hand goes to his cock. He rearranges it in his pants as if it's painfully crumpled.

He slides my panties down my legs and takes them off, and I stand before him in stilettos and a black lacy bra.

He hasn't tried to take my shoes off, so I'm assuming he wants them left on.

He's so naughty.

With his eyes locked on mine, he runs his fingertips through the lips of my sex. His fingers glisten with the evidence of my arousal, and then he puts them in his mouth and sucks them.

Fuck.

My arousal hits fever pitch.

He stands and walks around me. His eyes are hungry as they drink in every little detail of my naked skin, a hunter sizing up his prey.

He's different . . . darker.

More in tune with himself, but maybe he's just being his true self now.

I had the backpacker version . . . now I'm getting the billionaire in all his dirty glory.

He walks behind me and unlatches my bra and slowly takes it off. His hands come around, and his thumbs swipe over my hardened nipples. His teeth graze my earlobe, and goose bumps scatter over my skin.

"Bend over," he says. His voice is deep and husky.

I frown, not understanding. "What?"

"Bend. Over."

I bend over, and he inhales sharply as he stares at my sex.

"Good girl," he coaches me.

Bang, bang, bang, goes my heart in my chest as I lean over. My hands are on my knees.

"Straighten your legs." He taps my feet and spreads them apart. He touches the fronts of my knees, insinuating he wants me to straighten.

Jeez . . . I'd better start stretching up. I'm not a contortionist, you know.

He stands behind me and runs his hand up my spine. I look through my legs to see the huge bulge in his pants, and I smile.

Dirty bastard.

Without warning, he grabs a handful of my hair and tears my head back. He slides three fingers deep into my sex. My knees go weak.

Crack.

He slaps me across the behind. "Keep your fucking legs straight."

Jeez.

I try to focus on keeping my legs straight. In high heels it isn't an easy task.

His fingers plunge deep into my sex as he fucks me with them. The grip he has on my hair is painful, and I screw up my face.

I don't know what kind of fucking this is . . . but holy hell, it's good.

My arousal hits a new level. The sound of my wet body sucking him echoes throughout the room. He's fucking me so deep with his fingers that I can hardly breathe.

I shudder.

"Don't you dare fucking come," he moans.

"What?"

"You wait for me. You understand?" His voice is deep and husky, deeply aroused.

My eyes roll back in my head at the sound of his voice.

Okay . . . Billionaire Miles is *fucking hot*.

He fucks me again with his fingers, and I shudder hard.

Crack.

He slaps my behind, and I let out an unexpected giggle. The fact that I'm loving this is fucked up.

He walks around the front of me, and I stare at his immaculate expensive black shoes. His breath is quivering, and I know he's hanging on to control by a thread.

He runs his hand down my spine and walks behind me again. He rubs his hand over my skin in a circle, as if slowing himself down. Trying to regain control.

I hear his pants unzip.

I close my eyes and wait. Yes.

Fuck me.

He grabs a handful of my hair and winds it around his hand, giving him full control over my body.

I peer through my legs to see his thick, hard cock hanging heavily between his legs.

Pulsating and angry, engorged with veins, dripping with preejaculate.

Dear lord.

He swipes it through my wet lips, and he chuckles darkly.

I smile. I love that sound.

Then he slams in hard, so hard that the air is knocked from my lungs.

My body begins to spiral out of control.

The painful grip on my hair, the stretch of his large cock. The piston pace of his hard pumps.

My body is at his disposal. The master and his domain.

Slam.

Slam.

Slam.

Oh . . . *fuck.*

I see stars, and I fall hard into a subspace I've never been before. I cry out as I come hard, shuddering out of control.

He pulls out and throws me on the bed onto my back and spreads my legs open.

I lie there quivering like a puppet, and his dark eyes hold mine as he takes his shirt off over his head. His broad shoulders come into view, his thick chest with a scattering of dark hair. The ripples in his stomach, the perfect V of muscle that leads to his perfect package.

He kicks his jeans off, and I hold my breath.

What's he doing now?

He drops between my legs, and with his fingers he spreads me open and licks me.

His dark eyes hold mine as he takes his time. His arousal hits another level, and he's all in, whiskers, face. Rough as hell in my most intimate area.

His thick tongue taking no prisoners as it cleans me up. I've only just come for him, but I can feel it building again.

Fuck.

How is this man so hot?

He smiles darkly. His lips glisten with my arousal, and my heart free-falls from my chest.

I think we might be hitting 100 percent tonight.

Chapter 24

CHRISTOPHER

I lie on my side and watch Hayden sleep; her chest rises and falls, and her lashes flutter as she breathes.

I've never seen such a beautiful creature, so peaceful and serene.

I smile softly. It's like I'm in the presence of greatness, constantly awed by perfection.

I am *so* in love with this woman.

Last night when I was watching her with my family, I had this defining moment where suddenly, I knew.

I can't imagine a life without her, nor would I want to.

And it all became crystal clear: I want to marry Hayden Whitmore . . .

I'm going to look for an engagement ring once we get to London, and I want to try to plan the perfect proposal.

I want to really wow her.

How?

Maybe I could . . . my mind begins to wander over the possibilities. Where would we get married? I imagine her walking down the aisle toward me in her white wedding dress, and excitement fills me.

Who even am I?

Her eyes flutter open, and she sees me watching her and smiles softly. "Good morning, Miss Whitmore." I pull her into a hug and feel her smile against my chest. She kisses my skin as I hold her close.

We lie in comfortable silence for a while. "Why are you awake?" she asks in her husky, sleepy voice.

"Just planning our day."

"Hmm . . . what are we doing?"

"Well . . ." I kiss her temple. "I thought we could go to your parents' a couple of days earlier than planned."

She pulls back to look at me. "Really?"

"Uh-huh. We could go today so that you can have more time with them before we go to London."

"But what about your family?" She frowns.

"Meh." I shrug. "I'll see them through work all the time. They'll live without me. We'll leave after breakfast if you like."

"Oh my god." She smiles in excitement. "Okay." She jumps up and runs for the bathroom and then runs back and kisses me. "I love you."

I smile broadly as I watch her run into the bathroom once more.

An hour later

We walk through the underground parking lot as Hayden looks around at the surroundings. I hit the button, and my garage doors begin to slowly rise. "This is it."

She frowns as she looks in. "*This* is your car?"

390

"Uh-huh." I smile proudly. She's low and black and purrs like a kitten.

"What kind of car is that?"

"A McLaren."

She twists her lips, unimpressed. "Do you have anything less wankerish?"

"This car is not wankerish." I gasp, horrified. Actually, she may have a point. "I do need to wank after driving her because it makes me fucking hard."

"Christopher." She frowns as she stares at it. "We can't take this to the farm to meet my parents."

"Why not?"

"Because it's ridiculous."

"It is not ridiculous, Hayden." I put my hands on my hips in exasperation. "It's a work of fucking art."

She rolls her eyes. "We are not taking this to the farm."

"Why not?"

"I just told you, my father will laugh in your face."

"Not a car man?"

"Not a wanker man."

"News flash. All men wank, Hayden." I roll my eyes. "Okay, what about we take the Porsche." I gesture to the car beside it.

"No."

I wince. "The Aston Martin?"

"Haven't you got something less—"

I cut her off. "Magnificent?"

"Showy."

"No," I snap, annoyed. "I don't, and why would I want to?" I square my shoulders. "Eddie would love these cars," I mutter dryly.

"Eddie's not here." She turns and walks toward the elevator.

"Where are you going?" I call.

"To call a rental-car company," she calls back.

"What for?"

"Because my father will eat you alive if you turn up in that poser car."

I march after her. *"Poser car?"*

)(

We bounce up and down as we drive along. "Can't complain about the suspension in this piece of shit." My eyes flick over to her. "There is none."

The Toyota utility she made me hire is just that, a piece of fucking shit, and to top it off the only color available was red.

A red utility. Kill me now.

I'd rather be dead than be seen in this hunk of junk.

Hayden smiles as she rides along. She rubs the dash. "I love this car."

"This?" I scoff.

"Uh-huh." She smiles broadly. "She's so sexy."

I look at her deadpan. "Nothing about this car makes me want to fuck something."

"Well . . ." She giggles with a shrug. "I like it."

I roll my lips. "Thankfully you have better taste in men."

"This is it." She gestures to a road. "Turn right." I turn in to the road, and we drive up and over rolling green hills with huge big trees. It's gorgeous.

Wow.

"Beautiful country," I say as I look around.

"God's country."

I smile, impressed.

"Just don't say anything about anything," she says.

"Huh?"

"I haven't told them anything about you yet. I have to find the right time."

My eyes flick over to her. "What does that mean?"

"It means . . ." She widens her eyes as she articulates herself. "It means just don't let on anything until I talk to them. I haven't even told them I'm not coming home to live yet."

My eyes widen. "You haven't?"

"No."

"When do you plan on doing that?"

"Today."

My eyes flick between her and the road. "What time today?"

"Christopher," she snaps, "I'll tell them when I tell them. Just keep your big mouth shut until I do."

"Fucking hell, Hayden," I mutter. "I thought you sorted this shit all out."

"I'm not facing the firing squad alone."

"Firing squad?" I frown. "What does that mean?"

"This is it." We get to the top of the hill and a large clearing. There is a main farmhouse and a scattering of small cottages around it. It looks homey and nice, straight out of a family movie. "Park in there." She gestures to a clearing where a collection of utilities is lined up.

Hmm . . . maybe the McLaren wouldn't have fit in among these hunks of junk.

I park the car, and I hear a screen door slam. "Hayden?" a woman yells.

"It's me, Momma. I'm home."

"Ah." The elderly woman cries as she and Hayden run to each other. They hug, and the woman cries tears of joy. Hayden cries too.

Jeez . . . I try not to roll my eyes.

Dramatic.

They hug and hug and hug, and I stand to the side like an idiot.

Hello . . . I'm right here, remember?

"Momma"—Hayden smiles—"this is Christopher."

Her mom looks me up and down and smiles. "Well . . . aren't you just the handsomest man I ever did see?"

"Hello." I smile. I hold out my hand. She ignores it and hugs me tight, so tight that she nearly breaks a rib.

Strong.

"Hello, Christopher." Hayden's mom smiles. "I'm Valerie."

"Hello, Valerie."

She puts her arms around the both of us and begins to lead us into the house. "Thank god you're home, baby girl. We missed you so much."

Hayden smiles broadly and kisses her mom's temple.

"I love you, Mom. It's so good to see your face." Hayden smiles. "Where's Dad?"

"He's working. He'll be back for lunch soon."

Hayden smiles over at me. She's so happy and in her element. "I can't wait to see him."

Hmm . . . the firing squad comment is getting some real context here.

Fuck.

We walk past three large dogs, who look dead as they sleep, and up the stairs, onto the veranda, and into the house. "Oh, you look lovely, Hazy. So much color and so relaxed."

"Oh, Mom, it was so amazing. You and Dad have to travel."

Hayden and her mom chat and laugh, and I look around at the house. It's eclectic, as if everything has been salvaged from a thrift store. Four couches, none that match. The dining table is antique looking, but the chairs are all different. The artwork on the walls varies from tapestries to paintings to crayon drawings.

Huge rugs in unmatching colors are everywhere, and there's a huge fireplace. A collection of antique-looking saucers are displayed on the walls as if they are national treasures. It smells like warm cake and has a very serene Hayden feel.

I smile. This is not what I was expecting, but it all makes sense. Another piece of the Hayden puzzle falls into place.

"Have some cake." Valerie smiles as she lifts a tea towel to reveal a cake.

"Straight out of the oven." Hayden smiles as she cuts it up. Steam rises as the knife slices through it.

"You baked it yourself?" I ask, surprised.

"Of course." Valerie frowns as if that's a stupid question.

"Mom is the best cook in all of Finger Lakes." Hayden smiles proudly.

"Great." I smile. I have no idea what to do with that information, but anyway.

The door bangs open, and we all turn and see a huge burly man taking his boots off at the door.

He looks like John Wayne . . . only tougher and more weathered by the sun. His work clothes are dirty and old, and he has a no-nonsense kind of vibe.

"Is that my girl home?" he calls.

"It's me, Dad." Hayden runs to him, and they hug.

"About time you showed your face around here," he says in his deep voice.

Hayden laughs in pure joy.

He's big, scary looking. I stand, unsure whether to shake his hand or run.

"Who's this?" he says.

"Dad." Hayden holds her arm out toward me. "This is Christopher. Christopher . . . this is my dad, Harvey."

"Hello, Mr. Whitmore." I smile. I shake his hand.

His hand is so rough that it doesn't actually feel like a hand . . . could be a piece of sandpaper or a chunk of wood. Who could tell?

He looks me up and down. "Christopher, hey?"

I fake a smile, and Hayden takes my hand. "He's important, Dad."

It's like she's warning him to be nice.

Great, just what I need.

He points to the chair. "Sit down, boy."

Boy.

The hairs on the back of my neck rise.

Don't say anything, don't say anything. Don't fucking say anything.

Unimpressed, I drop to my seat.

His assessing eyes hold mine across the table, and I fake a smile back.

Bring it, old man.

"Where do you live?" he asks me.

"Dad," Hayden splutters, "let Christopher settle in before you give him the tenth degree."

Or maybe don't do it at all.

"Oh my god," Hayden cries. "Who is this?"

We all look to see an entirely black cat. He's long and skinny. More of a rat than a cat, really.

"That's Milly's baby." Valerie smiles.

"Milly had a baby?"

"She had eight."

"He's like a jaguar." Hayden swoons.

Only much less impressive.

"Good cat, that one," Harvey says sternly. "Good judge of character. His name is Bryan."

Harvey is a cat man?

Good fucking grief, we have literally nothing in common. Hayden smiles over at me, and I'm reminded why I'm here.

Focus.

I try to make conversation. "Beautiful place you have here."

"Thank you." Valerie smiles. "We've lived here . . ." She keeps talking, but I can't concentrate. The cat is now rubbing up against my leg. I subtly move my leg out of its way, and it flops across my feet.

"The farm two properties over . . . ," Harvey continues.

Bryan begins to chew my shoelaces, and I edge my foot away.

Fuck off, cat.

"Where do you come from, Christopher?" Harvey asks.

Bryan grabs my legs between his two claws and bites my shin. "Ahh." I jump and look under the table. "Bryan's getting a little vicious down there." I frown as I watch the sneaky fucker. "Little-jaguar-for-real kind of thing."

"New York," Hayden replies for me. She sips her coffee casually.

Sharp, vicious teeth sink into my anklebone through my socks, and I inwardly wince, pretending that nothing is wrong.

Ahh.

The fuck is going on down there?

Harvey carries on the conversation. "Busy damn town, that place."

"Yes, yes, it is." I peer under the table to see Bryan winding up to attack me again. His tail is whipping side to side as he leans back, ready to launch, and I begin to sweat.

A little help over here, Hayden?

"Where do you live?" Harvey asks.

Do you catch rabies from cats? Sharp pain shoots through me as Bryan attacks for real. "Ahh," I cry.

"What's happening?" Hayden frowns.

"Don't he like you?" Harvey asks dryly.

"Oh, he likes me." I smile as razor-sharp teeth sink straight to the bone. "Maybe a little too much. My mother is allergic."

"You don't like cats?"

"Love them," I lie with a smile. "Looking forward to snuggling with little Bryan later tonight."

Not an actual lie. I am a pussy whisperer from way back. Small inferior jaguars with attitude problems, maybe not so much.

Harvey's cold eyes hold mine.

"Let's go unpack into our room." Hayden stands, breaking the moment. "It's so good to be home, Dad."

Harvey pulls his daughter in for a hug.

"Dinner at six." Valerie smiles.

I follow Hayden out the front door and over to the car. We grab our bags, and I go to go back into the house.

"This way," she says.

"Where?"

"I have my own house on the property."

"You do?"

Thank fuck for that.

"Great."

We walk about 150 yards up the road and come to a pretty little cottage. Hayden opens the door, and I smile.

Now this . . . is more like it.

It's decorated in pastels and homey, comfortable furniture, and instantly I can feel Hayden's calming presence. "This is beautiful, babe." I smile as I look around.

"I like it." She looks around as if seeing it for the first time. "My bedroom is upstairs." She leads me up the stairs, and the entire top floor is her bedroom. It's feminine and sweet and romantic . . . just like her.

And unlike my bedroom, where she can hear the moans, all I can feel in here is the love she had with her ex.

I look at the bed as I imagine another man in it. Did he have her in there? Of course he did. I snap my eyes away angrily.

I fucking hate that he had her.

"It's a new bed," she says as if reading my mind.

I nod, grateful. "Good news." I take her into my arms and kiss her softly. "Your father hates me."

She giggles. "My father hates everyone."

We kiss again, her tongue curling around mine, and I walk her backward. "We need to christen this bed." I smile.

She looks up at me, all gorgeous and fuckable. "How did I know you were going to say that?"

I throw her onto the bed. "Lucky guess."

※

I pull the razor down my face as Hayden gets dressed in the bedroom behind me.

"So you know the plan?" she asks.

"Yes."

"What is it?"

"Let you do all the talking." I roll my eyes as I wash the razor out.

Hayden is freaking out, and I have to admit it's catching. I'm sure dear old Harvey has a shotgun or two around here.

And then there's that feral cat who wants to eat me alive under the table. Let's just hope that fucker is out hunting what cats hunt at night.

"And whatever my mother dishes up, you eat it."

I look up from shaving. "Huh?" I stare at her as my brain misfires. "What do you mean?"

"My mom is real country. Just . . . if you want to stay on the good side of my father, eat whatever she plates up."

"Like what, what would she cook?"

"I don't know." She rolls her deodorant on. "She likes to cook with offal."

"Offal?" I frown.

"You know, like brains and kidneys and stuff."

"You're joking, right?"

She shakes her head. "Nope."

I stare at her as I begin to sweat. I imagine organs all laid out on a table, and I feel faint.

"Just. Eat. It." She widens her eyes.

"Of course I'll eat it. What kind of wimp do you think I am?"

Fuck me dead.

"Move out of the way while I do my hair," she says.

I leave her to it and walk downstairs. I text Elliot.

**Just about to have dinner with her family.
Her father hates me.
Her mother cooks organs and the cat wants to
rip my nuts off under the table.
Send this to the police if you never hear from me
again.**

Chapter 25

"Hi." Hayden smiles as we walk into the kitchen.

"Hello." Valerie smiles as she stirs something on the hot plate. "Dinner in ten."

"Hmm, something smells delicious," I say. I'm not even joking; it really does smell delicious in here.

"Only the best for my loves," Valerie replies. "Your father is in the living room."

Hayden disappears into the living room, and I hang back, and I watch Valerie for a moment. She's the epitome of country loving. I know where Hayden gets her warm and happy disposition from.

Valerie has it in spades. It oozes out of her, and I felt it the moment we met, and I feel like I know her already.

The exact opposite of her prickly husband. I'm dreading that Harvey and I are not going to get along and it's going to screw everything up.

Hayden worships the ground her parents walk on. If I fuck it with them, I fuck it with her.

I hang in the kitchen for a bit. "How was your day?" I ask Valerie.

"It was good, love." She smiles warmly as her knowing eyes hold mine. "He's not as scary as he looks, darling."

"Good to know."

I loiter a little longer. "Any advice?" I ask.

"To deal with Harvey?"

I nod.

"Be yourself."

I frown.

"More than anything, Harvey respects honesty."

"Me too."

"You do." She rubs my arm. "I know."

"You know?"

"Darling, I speak to Hayden every day. I feel like you and I are already close friends."

I smile, feeling a little better. "Well . . . your daughter is a credit to you, Mrs. Whitmore. She's the most beautiful person I've ever met."

Tears fill her eyes as she gets emotional. "I know."

"What are you guys doing in here?" Hayden comes around the corner.

"Just talking." Valerie smiles.

"This is the best night." Hayden slides her arms around my waist to hug me. "My favorite people all in the one house."

I kiss her temple.

"Come see Dad." She grabs my hand and pulls me into the living room to see Harvey sitting in his recliner chair in the corner of the living room.

"Hello, Mr. Whitmore." I smile.

His eyes hold mine, and he gestures to the couch. "Take a seat."

"Thanks." I sit on the couch.

"You two chat between yourselves. I'm going to help Mom," Hayden says.

Don't leave me here with him.

402

"Okay," I reply.

Harvey keeps watching television with the remote in his hand.

I twist my lips. I look between him and the television. I should make conversation or something.

"It's good to be back on American soil," I say.

He nods and keeps watching television as if uninterested. I wait for him to say something . . . he doesn't.

Rude prick.

"A farm this big must be a lot of work," I say.

"We have Hayden home to help us now," he says as his eyes stay fixed on the television.

I pinch the bridge of my nose. *Walked straight into that one.*

I stay silent, unsure what to say next. He's going to hit the roof when he finds out she's coming to London with me.

I roll my fingers on the armrest of the couch as I troll my brain for an attack plan.

"Dinner's ready," Hayden calls.

Harvey gets up and walks past me out of the room, and I glare after him.

Seriously?

Could he be any less hospitable?

Thank fuck Hayden takes after her mother and not this rude prick.

I walk in to find a spread on the dining table, plate after plate of delicious food.

Jeez . . . has she been cooking for a week? I don't know if my mother has cooked this much food in my entire life.

"Are there others coming?" I ask.

"No." Hayden smiles as she gestures to my chair. "Just us."

"Wow." I sit down. "Looks delicious."

Hayden sits down beside me and takes my hand in hers and smiles over at me.

It's fine. This is for her.

We dish out our plates in silence. "What do you do for a living, boy?" Harvey asks.

"Christopher," I correct him. "Don't call me *boy*."

Hayden steps on my foot under the table.

Behave.

His eyes hold mine, and I take a mouthful of food off my fork.

Oh shit, I forgot to check . . . is this offal? I study my plate as I chew. I can't see anything out of the ordinary.

"I asked you a question."

"I'm in advertising," I reply curtly.

Hayden reaches over and puts her hand on my thigh to remind me to shut up.

I need to change the subject. "Where's that jaguar?" I ask.

"Oh, Bryan?" Valerie smiles. "He'll be home for dinner soon."

"Where does he go throughout the day?"

"Who knows," Harvey replies. "Mousing, probably."

Right, just keep the conversation off me. "How long have you owned the farm?" I ask.

"We're third generation on this land," Harvey says. "Soon to be fourth." He winks at Hayden.

Hayden smiles over at her father, and my stomach twists.

Fuck.

It's like a cult.

"Where do you live, Christopher?" Harvey asks.

He called me Christopher. I chalk up a small victory. "I live . . ." I pause. Oh shit, how do I answer this? "I live between New York and London."

404

Harvey frowns. His eyes flick to meet Valerie's.

"Christopher's family is very successful," Hayden says.

"Like how?" Harvey replies dryly.

"You know the big company Miles Media?" she replies.

"Nope."

"The one that makes the newspapers?"

"What about it?" he replies.

"That's Christopher's family business."

His eyes meet mine. "So . . . you're a pen pusher?"

I begin to hear my heartbeat in my ears.

Don't piss me off, old man.

"I work in advertising for a successful company, and I don't appreciate your lack of respect, Mr. Whitmore."

A trace of a smile crosses his face as his eyes hold mine.

"I use a computer, not a pen. Wrong decade," I mutter as I take a bite of food off my fork.

Harvey chuckles, clearly amused with himself at my expense.

Fucker.

Hayden taps my thigh under the table in a subtle *calm down* signal.

"So . . . how do you think this"—he gestures to the air between us—"will last with you two living in different countries?"

I stay silent and glance over to Hayden. I raise my eyebrow.

Tell him. Tell him now.

"Well . . . I have some news." Hayden pauses. "I'm moving to London to live with Christopher."

The clang of knives and forks hitting the plates sounds through the room.

Valerie gasps.

I begin to perspire. Fuck me dead.

Harvey's cold eyes hold mine, and he chews the food in his mouth as he processes the information.

"It will be a . . . new adventure," Hayden says as she looks between them nervously.

"Where do you live in London?" Harvey directs the conversation at me.

"I have an apartment in the city."

"An apartment?" He frowns. "You really expect Hayden to live in a box with no fresh air in the middle of the city?"

"Dad," Hayden whispers.

He holds his hand up to her in a *stop* sign. "Now, baby girl, you need to think about this long and good. There are no cows in the middle of London, Hayden."

Hayden stays silent.

"I don't like this. I don't like it one bit," Harvey says.

"It's a trial."

"A trial?" Harvey explodes.

"For Hayden," I correct myself. "If she doesn't like city living . . . then . . ." I shrug.

"Then what?" he snaps.

"I don't know, but please know, Mr. Whitmore, I love Hayden," I announce. "I would never trade her happiness for mine."

Hayden takes my hand as it sits on my lap.

"And I *am* going to marry her one day. With or without your permission."

He narrows his eyes as he glares at me.

"If Hayden doesn't like living in London, I would never keep her there against her will."

"And if she wants to live here?"

"Then I will." I shrug.

"What's the fucking shrug mean?" he barks. "A shrug isn't enough to bank my daughter's entire future on."

"It means . . . I will understand," I snap.

"As long as I'm with you, I'll be happy." Hayden smiles over at me.

I lean over and kiss her. "Me too, baby."

"Give me a break," Harvey snaps. He throws his napkin on the table in disgust and storms from the room.

"You not going to eat this?" Valerie asks him.

"I just lost my appetite," he calls. We hear him march up the hall, and the bedroom door slams.

Hayden exhales, and her mother sits still, seemingly in shock.

"I love him, Mom," she whispers.

"I know." Valerie smiles sadly.

"I just have to—"

Valerie cuts her off. "I know."

The cat walks in and lies on the floor, all cute-like, as if purposely trying to distract us, and I roll my eyes.

Where were you ten minutes ago, stupid cat?

You're fucking late, Bryan.

⋈

Two hours later we lie in bed watching television. Hayden is quiet and has hardly said two words since her dad stormed off.

My hand is on her hip as she lies on her side facing away from me.

"He'll come around," I say. "Once he gets to know me, I'm sure—"

She cuts me off. "I know."

But in all honesty, I really don't know if he will.

We couldn't be more different.

Hayden switches off her bedside lamp. "Good night," she says.

"Do I get a good-night kiss?" I ask.

She sits up and kisses me. "I love you."

"I love you too." I smile. She lies down and puts her back to me again.

Hmm . . . I guess it's no country loving for me, then.

"Did I eat an organ tonight?" I ask.

Hayden giggles. "I was pulling your leg, you idiot."

"Oh." I smile. "Thank the lord." I completely fell for it.

I turn the television and my side lamp off, and we lie in the darkness.

"Mooooo" sounds in the distance. "Mooo."

I listen to the symphony of cows for over half an hour.

"Why is that cow doing that?" I ask. "Doesn't it get a sore throat?"

"We have a few calves coming. I would say someone's in labor."

"Oh." I frown. How odd. "How do you know when they're pregnant?"

She giggles. "You're an idiot."

"But . . ."

"Oh my god, Christopher." She laughs. "You're hysterical."

Hysterical?

I lie in the dark, pondering why I'm a hysterical idiot for not knowing the answer to a legitimate question.

But seriously . . . how do they fucking know?

I wake to the sound of a large engine roaring, and I frown.

What the hell is that?

Hayden isn't in bed with me.

It's dawn, early. The sun is just coming up, and I get up and walk to the window and narrow my eyes . . . huh?

Am I seeing this right?

Mist is rolling around on the ground, and Hayden is driving a huge-ass tractor across a paddock and into the distance. There's a dog sitting on her lap.

What the fuck?

She drives a tractor? And . . . dogs ride on tractors?

Fucking hell, what next?

I go downstairs and make myself a cup of coffee and take a shower. The sun is fully up now, and Hayden still isn't back.

I open the front door, and another huge dog is lying across the front of the doorway.

"You're a log of a dog," I mutter as I step over it. "What's wrong with you, too fat to climb on the tractor?" I walk out into the paddock and look around; the sun is shining, and the birds are chirping. Even I have to admit it is pretty beautiful out here. I walk in the direction that Hayden drove to. I wonder where she is.

※

Fifteen minutes later I come over the top of the hill to see the tractor stopped and Hayden and a bit of a fuss going on.

What are they doing up there?

I narrow my eyes to try to focus. I think that's Harvey too . . . hmm, I can't turn around now. They've seen me already.

Oh well. If he hates me, he hates me.

I walk closer and closer, and I have no idea what's going on up here.

A cow is lying on its side, leg up in the air, and all the cows in the paddock are crying out as they watch.

This is so strange . . . I keep walking, and as I get closer, I see Hayden is down on her knee beside the cow.

What's she doing?

Oh . . .

My eyes widen in horror.

Hayden has her arm up a cow's ass to the armpit . . . or is it a vagina . . . or is it . . .

I feel the blood drain out of my face as my knees go woozy.

I don't feel so . . .

HAYDEN

Thump . . .

"For fuck's sake," Dad moans.

I glance up to see Christopher hit the ground hard as he faints.

I get the giggles as I try to turn the calf. "Go help him."

"No, Hayden," he replies dryly.

"Dad, I'm kind of busy here."

"I don't have time for his pretty boy bullshit," he mutters as he walks toward Christopher, who is still out cold.

"Whoa, girl," I whisper as I get the calf in position. "This will help you."

I watch as Dad bends to Christopher, and I smile as I watch him gently slap his face.

I'm going to hang back and see what happens.

Christopher comes to and sits up. "You okay, babe?" I call.

He nods, embarrassed.

"He's fine," Dad calls. He grabs Christopher's head and looks in his hair and says something that I can't hear.

Christopher shrugs him off. "Don't fucking touch me," he scoffs.

I roll my lips to hide my smile.

"This damn fool needs stitches in his head," Dad calls.

"Oh no." I stand.

"You stay there," Dad calls as he helps Christopher to his feet. "I'll take him into town."

I stare at them for a moment as I do an internal risk assessment. Okay . . . I need to let them do this. If they fight it out, they fight it out. I have faith that they will come to appreciate each other.

411

"Is that all right?" I call. "I can't leave her."

Christopher nods, and I jog over to him. He has a trickle of blood dripping down onto his shirt from the back of his head. "Are you hurt?"

"Only my pride." He shrugs.

My dad throws his head back and laughs out loud, and I try not to laugh, I really do, but I fail miserably.

"I'm glad you two think this is so funny," Christopher snaps. "I have internal bleeding. Perhaps an aneurysm is coming on."

"Dad will look after you." I smile.

"Will he, though?" Christopher widens his eyes.

"Come back in the house, boy. I'll stitch you up," Dad teases. "Got a needle and thread in the first aid box."

I bite my lip to stop myself laughing out loud.

"There is no way in hell you are touching my fucking head, you maniac. I need a specialist plastic surgeon. And don't call me *boy*!" Christopher yells.

Dad laughs harder as he holds Christopher up by the arm. He's still woozy and maybe a little concussed. "You're a bigger fucking idiot than I thought."

I go back to the cow and kneel down beside her. Everything should progress with her as planned now that the calf has been turned.

I could take Christopher to the hospital myself . . . but I won't.

They need this.

X

It's 11:00 a.m., and I am freshly showered. I've done a load of washing and am waiting for Christopher to get back from the hospital. Dad called me while he was getting his stitches put in. He's fine, and they should be home soon.

I have one week to make Dad see in Christopher what I do. I'm just not sure exactly how to do that. It took me living with Christopher for three months to finally see his true colors.

And what beautiful colors they are.

Knock, knock sounds on the door.

Why is he knocking? "It's open," I call. I pull the clothes out of the dryer and into the basket and walk out into the living area and stop in my tracks.

Regi is standing there.

The air leaves my lungs. This is the first time I've seen him since he broke my heart three years ago.

He's older, broader . . .

"Hello, Haze." He smiles hopefully.

I frown, too shocked to speak.

He steps toward me. "You look . . ." He swallows a lump in his throat. "Beautiful."

"What are you doing here?" I frown.

"I wanted to see you."

"Why?"

"I think about you all the time."

I hear my angry heartbeat in my ears. "Don't."

"Do you ever think of me?"

"No," I spit.

I mean, I did . . . every damn day, until I met Christopher.

Not anymore.

"I miss you . . . ," he whispers.

"What?" I screw up my face.

"I was young, Haze." He shrugs. "I didn't know what I had."

The door bangs, and Christopher walks in. My heart does stop this time.

Fuck.

He looks between Regi and me. "Hello."

413

"Hi, babe." I smile. "This is Regi. Regi, this is Christopher, my fiancé."

A frown flashes across Christopher's face before he catches it. "Who are you?" he asks Regi.

Regi tilts his chin, angered by my introduction. "I'm Hayden's childhood sweetheart. Her first love."

Oh no.

Christopher raises an eyebrow. "You've got a fucking hide, coming here."

"What does that mean?" Regi frowns.

"I think you owe Hayden an apology."

"For what?"

Christopher glares at him and steps forward. "You want me to kick your ass to remind you, you gutless prick?"

Regi steps back.

My heart swells with love for Christopher, my knight in shining armor.

"I've got nothing to apologize for," Regi spits.

"One," Christopher says calmly.

My eyes widen . . . what the hell? He's counting him down?

"Two . . ."

"Christopher," I stammer, "just leave it."

"He owes you an apology, Hayden," he snaps. "I want to fucking hear it."

"I'm not apologizing for being young," Regi snaps. "It's none of your business."

"Hayden is my *only* business." Christopher grabs him by the shirt and hurls him out the door. He throws him down the five steps. "You had your fucking chance, and you blew it," he yells. "Don't try and ruin mine. You stay the fuck away from her, or you'll have me to deal with."

Regi looks up at the house in shock. His chest is rising and falling as he struggles for air.

"Do you fucking hear me?" Christopher warns him.

Regi nods, and with one last look, he marches off toward his car as he acts tough.

I walk out the front, shocked, and I turn to see my father standing beside the door. He's heard the entire thing.

My eyes are wide. I'm shocked to my core. "Dad . . ."

A trace of a smile crosses Dad's face, and he winks. Without a word he turns and walks off toward the house. "Dinner is at six," he calls.

I look to my man, all pumped up and angry, and I smile down at him. "You are going to get *so* lucky tonight."

"About time," he huffs as he marches past me into the house. "I fucking hate that guy."

The screen door bangs hard, and I smile proudly.

That's my man.

A week later

We sit in the boarding lounge of the airport. We had the best week, and although my parents aren't happy with me moving, I think they understand what I see in Christopher.

His smart-ass mouth had my dad smirking a lot more than he would like to admit.

And my mom . . . well, she's practically half in love with him too.

Christopher's reading a book, and we're catching a commercial plane; his family planes are already in use.

"I'm going to buy a magazine," I say.

"Okay, babe."

I go to the newsstand and look through the choices, and I stop still as I see a headline on a paper.

What the hell?

Is that *my* Christopher? I pick up the paper. "I'll take this one, please." I pay the cashier and sit down and flick through the paper until I get to the story.

My eyes widen. There's a half-page photo of me and him. It's the morning after we arrived in New York, when I'd been crying all night.

We're holding hands as we cross the street on Madison Avenue. I'm wearing scruffy clothes, and the way the light shines on me, my leg looks like it's all cellulite right to my ankle.

My face is puffy from crying. I look utterly hideous.

I read the story.

Christopher Miles has returned from a sabbatical with Miss Average.

Chapter 26

CHRISTOPHER

I watch Hayden disappear into the store to buy her magazine with a smile.

"What you thinking about?" Harvey asks from his seat beside me.

"Just how lucky I am."

"That you are," he replies.

"We just got her back." Valerie wrings her hands in her lap, and I know this can't be easy for her.

"I'm going to look after her, Mrs. Whitmore. You have my word."

She nods, her eyes filling with tears, and as if sensing an impending meltdown, she stands. "I'm going to the bathroom," she says before rushing off.

I watch Valerie walk away while wiping her tears away, and despair fills me.

"Christopher . . . ," Harvey says as he stares at me.

"Yes."

"Now . . . if you know Hayden like I think you do, you understand that she's special."

I nod. "I do."

"Hayden isn't like other people. She's different. She's kind and trusting and hates drama. You'll never hear her complain."

"It's those qualities in her that I love, Mr. Whitmore."

"Her empathy for those around her is her biggest strength and yet her greatest weakness," he continues. "We had hoped that she would toughen up on that trip around the world, but she's come back so madly in love with you that she can't even see straight."

My eyes search his.

"What I'm trying to say is that it is up to you to make sure that she's happy."

I frown.

"She will put *your* needs and *your* happiness before her own because when Hayden loves, it's forever."

I get a lump in my throat.

"Hayden doesn't say much, but I'm trusting you to read between the lines and guarantee me that you will protect her at all costs . . . even if that means hurting yourself."

I imagine if Hayden ever left me . . . and the devastation it would cause.

I would never recover.

His silhouette blurs as my eyes fill with tears. "You have my word." I shake his hand, and his eyes fill with tears too.

Fuck me dead.

I wipe my eyes, embarrassed. "Stop." I laugh.

He pulls me into a hug. "I'm trusting you with the most important thing in the world. Promise me to keep her safe."

"I promise." He slaps me on the back, and I know that this is it.

From here on in, I have to adult. There is no room for mistakes in my life anymore. If I want to love someone like Hayden, I need to step up and be the man that she deserves.

"I don't believe it," Hayden's voice says from beside us. "You two hugging it out now?"

We step back from each other in a rush. "I was just telling him how much I hate him," Harvey says in his stern voice.

I chuckle, because now I know. This man is a big softy. "Sure, you were."

"Where's Mom?" Hayden looks around.

"Crying in the bathroom, I suspect," Harvey replies.

"Oh." Her face falls. "I'm going to check on her." She hands me a paper and raises her eyebrow. "Got you some interesting reading material."

I frown at her undertone and glance down at the *Ferrara News* and see the headline.

Fuck.

Harvey and I sit back down, and as he continues talking, I casually flick through the paper until I get to the story.

Christopher Miles has returned from a sabbatical with Miss Average.

I inhale sharply as the sky turns red.

How dare they.

How. Fucking. Dare. They.

Do not *mess with Hayden.*

Screw me over all you like, but mention one hair on her head, and it's fucking war.

I stand, too angry to stay seated. "You want a cup of coffee?" I ask Harvey.

"No, thanks."

I march in the direction of the cafeteria and scroll through my phone. I turn the corner and call the Miles Media head lawyer.

"Christopher," he answers in surprise. "How are you?"

"Furious," I growl. "There is a story run in today's US *Ferrara News* about my girlfriend, and I want fucking blood," I spit. "I want a retraction, an apology, and if they dare run one more fucking story in regards to her . . . I'm taking them to court," I whisper angrily. "The images have been photoshopped and are complete and utter fucking bullshit."

"Calm down."

"I will not calm down," I half yell. "You fix this. You fucking fix this right now!"

"I'm on it."

I hang up in a rush. Adrenaline is pumping through my veins. The sky is so red that I can hardly see. I pace back and forth as I try to calm myself down. I've never been so fucking angry.

Average . . . what the actual fuck?

How dare they!

How dare they disrespect any woman with that derogatory term. But *my* woman . . . no fucking way.

My phone rings.

Jameson

"What?" I answer.

"I just saw it," he replies.

"You sort this fucking shit out," I fume as I pace. "I will not have her treated like this."

"We're already on it. Calm down."

"Calm down!" I cry. "*Ferrara* just drew a line in the sand. They're going to target her."

"We don't know that."

"Yes. We fucking do!" I yell. My heart is hammering in my chest. I'm so angry I can hardly even speak. "I'm about to get on a plane. Sort it out." I hang up in a rush.

I go to the window and stare out at the planes on the runway as I imagine the shitstorm we're about to fly into.

My god.

"Babe." Hayden's hand slides around my waist from behind. "Is everything all right?"

I turn and take her into my arms, and instantly I begin to relax. This woman is so calming and so beautiful, and fucking hell, whatever does she see in me?

"I'm so sorry," I whisper, "that . . ." I pause. "Please know that the story is an attack on me, not you. It's not personal."

Her eyes search mine. "Feels pretty personal."

I hug her and hold her tight, and I have no idea what to say to make this any better. "I'm on it," I reply.

"What does that mean?"

"I want a retraction."

Her face falls as she steps back from me. "So what you've effectively done is to make sure that everybody will know about the story now?"

"Hayden, they can't get away with writing a story like this. I won't stand by and let some idiotic woman write about you in this manner."

"How do you know it was a woman?"

"Because men don't think about women this way. We just don't."

"That photo was tampered with," she says as she looks up at me. "I don't have cellulite in my ankles. Nobody on earth does, not even elephants."

"I know. I'm so sorry. This is so appalling." I stare at her. My heart is in my throat as I wait for the impending explosion.

"This isn't appalling." She frowns. "What it is . . . is pathetic journalism on their behalf. I mean, if they called me a racist or a homophobe, I would be outraged and heartbroken." She shrugs.

421

"But . . . I have nothing to be ashamed about. I'm not a size two, and I'm not a supermodel. I'm completely okay with that."

I stare at the beautiful woman in front of me. Such a different species of female from what I've ever known.

"I mean, not my best shot . . . obviously." She widens her eyes. "Hideous, actually."

"How are you not upset about this?" I frown.

"Because I'm more than that. And if someone judges me about my looks, then it's a reflection of them and not me."

My god . . .

"Do you know how much I love you?" I whisper.

"Well, you better, because I'm just about to move to Bumfuck, London, to live with you."

I chuckle and take her into my arms, and we hold each other, and after a while, I feel my heartbeat slowly return to normal.

"My mom is crying." She sighs. "And our flight is boarding."

"God."

"You ready to go to Bumfuck, London?" She smiles up at me.

"Please tell me there's bumfucking in London."

"Keep dreaming." She smirks as she turns and walks off.

I stare after her . . . awed.

Hayden Whitmore just may be the strongest person I know . . . perhaps have ever met.

Calm and content, her nature is a force to be reckoned with.

Just when I think I couldn't love her any more, she goes and ups the ante.

I follow her out into the department lounge. With my heart breaking for her parents, I watch her kiss her mom and dad as they say their goodbyes.

I kiss her mom and shake Harvey's hand, and he gives me a wink as a gentle reminder of the conversation we had.

"I'll take good care of her." I smile, grateful that he has bestowed me with such a precious gift. "Goodbye, Mr. Whitmore."

"Goodbye, Christopher."

I take Hayden's hand, and as she waves to them over her shoulder, we start our new life.

Together.

HAYDEN

The car pulls into the underground parking lot, and I peer out the window in awe.

So many fancy cars all lined up.

We come to a stop beside the elevator, and the driver pops the trunk and hops out to retrieve our luggage.

"We won't be going out again tonight," Christopher tells him. "You may finish up."

"Yes, sir." He nods. "Would you like me to take your bags up for you?"

"No, I've got it. Thanks."

"See you in the morning." He turns to me with a kind smile. "Good night, Miss Whitmore."

"Good night." I smile. Oh, I like this driver. He's a nice person; I can tell.

Christopher takes his big backpack and swings it onto his back and goes to take mine, too, and I hold the strap. "I've got it."

"I'll carry it up."

"I am quite capable of carrying my own backpack, Christopher," I huff. "Don't insult my intelligence."

He chuckles and drops it at my feet. It lands with a thud.

"You could have passed it to me," I scoff.

"Wouldn't want to insult your intelligence," he mutters as he gets into the elevator. He turns to face the front with a mischievous look on his face.

I know that look.

I step in beside him and turn to face the front. "I suppose this apartment is going to be another dumpster fire."

He chuckles. "You could say that."

"And the bed?"

"Already been burned and a new one installed for your highness."

"So where are we sleeping?"

"The new one is ready and waiting to be corrupted with your forever-faithful servant."

"You've thought of everything." I smile.

He links his pinkie finger through mine, and we both smile as we stare at the doors. Such a simple and small gesture, but . . . it means so much.

"Leather couch, white bathrooms," I say.

He frowns over at me. "What do you mean?"

"I'm guessing that you have a leather couch and white marble bathrooms."

He smiles . . . he likes this game. "What makes you say that?"

"Because I know your taste."

"Oh." He raises an eyebrow. "Is that so?"

"Uh-huh."

"You want to bet on it?"

"Yep." I hold my hand out to shake his. "Fifty bucks."

His eyes twinkle in delight. "No, no, no, I only bet for things that I need."

"Such as?"

"Anal."

"What?" My eyes widen.

The elevator door opens, and he smiles over at me. "You heard me. I want to see how much of a gambler you really are." He leans down and puts his lips to my ear and whispers, "If you'll put your body on the line."

I bite my lip to hide my smile.

It's a test.

I roll my lips as I stare at him. This could backfire badly.

"All right . . . anal." I hold my hand out, and we shake on it.

He opens the door with an evil laugh, and as I put my hands over my eyes, I laugh. "Don't. I can't even look."

"Don't worry, I have lube," he teases as he pulls me through the apartment. My hands are still over my eyes.

"Stop it."

"Ta-da." He pulls my arms down, and we are in the most beautiful living room of all time. A chocolate leather couch sits proud as punch in the center of the room.

"Ha." I laugh. "I knew it."

"But . . . *are* the bathrooms white?"

I smile. I like this game too.

I turn and run up the stairs to find his bedroom as he chases me. I run down the large hallway and into the bedroom and stop dead in my tracks.

The air leaves my lungs, and my mouth falls open as I look around.

The bedroom is filled with red roses.

Vase after vase.

Beautiful roses with huge heads.

My eyes find his. "What's this?"

"Well . . ." He shrugs casually as he looks around. "If I'm going to fuck you up the ass . . . I want it to be romantic."

I burst out laughing, and his eyes hold mine as he laughs too. He takes me into his arms and kisses me softly.

"Is the bathroom white?" I murmur against his lips.

"No."

I pull out of his arms and walk into the bathroom. "Got you," I cry.

A white marble bathroom sits in all its grandeur.

"Fuck off." He screws up his face. "How did you know that?" He turns the shower on and slams me up against the tiles. His lips

426

take mine with hunger, and then he pulls me in under the water, clothes and all. We kiss, frantic and wild.

It's hot and wet . . . and perfect.

Like him.

With our lips locked, he pulls my wet shirt off over my head.

"Who brought the roses over?" I ask.

He unzips my jeans and slides them down. "Elliot."

I giggle as I step out of the wet pants. "You made your brother bring me flowers?"

"Yes." He kisses me. His tongue swipes through my open lips. "He's working with me on the romantic-anal thing. It's a two-man job."

I laugh out loud again. This man kills me.

He kisses me again, and as his clothes come off, we fall silent as we stare at each other.

His huge erection demands attention as it rests up against my lower stomach, and I take it in my hand and stroke him as we kiss. He's more himself here. I didn't realize he was quiet at my parents' until we landed in the UK.

His dark hair hangs over his forehead. His lips are big and soft, and damn. His large muscular body is dripping wet and with that waiting erection . . . just for me.

I'm in heaven.

He smiles darkly as he lifts me off my feet and pins me to the tiles. He wraps my legs around his waist and slides in deep.

My body ripples around his as he takes me over. This is what he does so well: dominates me . . . fucks me so deep that I can hardly remember my name.

We stare at each other, the water running over our heads, arousal screaming through my senses.

His dark eyes hold mine as he pulls out and slams in hard.

"Ahh," I cry out. The tiles are cold and hard on my back. Not that it matters now; when we are like this with each other, nothing else matters.

Brilliant and blinding *orgasm* is all that we can see.

He puts his two hands on my shoulders and pushes me up against the wall and steps back from me. "Lift your legs higher," he instructs me.

My eyes flutter closed . . . *fuck.*

I lift my legs, and he spreads his legs wide for leverage and lets me have it. Deep, punishing hits. The sound of the water slapping between our bodies is loud.

The friction burns from his heavy cock as it pounds me hard. *So good.*

His breathing is labored, and his eyes begin to roll back in his head. I smile triumphantly. This is when I love him the most.

When he is at my mercy, in this moment. I own him . . . and he knows it.

He grips my calf muscles as he holds me. I'm crumpled up against the wall like a piece of paper as he rides me hard.

And it's good . . . so fucking good.

"Oh . . . ," I moan. I try to hold it off, but I can't. I need it. I shudder hard as a freight train of an orgasm slams me.

"Fuck. Fuck. Fuck," he moans as he holds himself deep and comes in a rush. I feel the telling jerk of his body inside mine.

His eyes search mine, and I smile softly.

My tiger is tamed.

X

We lie on our sides in bed. The room is lit only by the lamp, and we stare at each other.

It's late.

For some reason, tonight feels like we crossed another barrier, jumped an invisible relationship fence. Hit another level. And I don't know if it's because we are in his main home or what it is . . . but something's different.

His barrier has come down a little more. Day by day, he's letting me in deeper.

And it's dangerous because I don't think it's healthy to love anyone the way I do him.

"I never thought I'd have this," he says softly.

I listen.

"I'd heard my brothers talk of it, telling me what it was like . . . but I honestly didn't believe in it."

"What didn't you believe in?"

"That someone could make me feel the way you do."

Emotion overwhelms me, and I smile as I kiss him softly. Our lips linger over each other's. A tenderness runs between us that's never been there before.

"I love you so much," he murmurs.

I smile against his lips. "Still working on that anal thing?"

He chuckles. "One hundred percent."

CHRISTOPHER

Buzz, buzz, buzz, buzz . . . my phone dances across the bedside table.

I roll over to turn it off and exhale heavily. Ugh, I haven't missed waking up to that sound.

Hayden mumbles sleepily, "You ready for your first day of work?"

"Not really." I sigh. I should be more excited, I guess.

She smiles as she kisses my chest. Our legs are a tangled mess. "I'll make you breakfast."

"It's okay. You stay in bed, babe."

"No." She sits up. "I need to get into a routine of some sort. I can't be staying in bed half the day like a sloth." She gets out of bed and puts her robe on. "And what does my man feel like to eat?" She ties the sash of her robe in a bow.

"A little bit of you wouldn't be bad." I grab her leg as she walks past me and pull her back onto the bed. I kiss her softly, our lips lingering over each other. "You want to come to work in my briefcase?" I ask.

"I wish." Hayden giggles. "You could get me out and play with me in your breaks."

I chuckle. "That's a good plan."

She kisses me quickly and stands. "Get up, Mr. Miles. You don't want to be late for your first day."

"I guess." I sigh.

Hayden disappears out of the room, and I hear her go downstairs.

I shower and shave and dress in a navy suit and white shirt. It feels so weird to be dressed like this again. My sabbatical is already becoming a distant memory.

Something that I did once upon a time.

"Breakfast is ready, babe," I hear Hayden call.

I smile. The drop-dead-gorgeous souvenir I brought home was *well* worth it, though. With Hayden in my life, I've never been so settled and happy.

I do up my tie and comb my hair, put on my watch and shoes, and stare at my reflection in the mirror. That's it . . . it's over.

Time to grow up and start my new life.

One with responsibilities and someone to take care of. I stare at my face as a twinge of sadness fills me.

Things will never be the same, from here on in . . .

"Christopher," Hayden calls. "Don't make me come up there and spank you."

I smile. "Coming, dear," I call.

"Don't patronize me."

"I wouldn't dare," I mutter to myself. I grab my briefcase and head downstairs.

Hayden is sitting at the kitchen counter; the heavenly aroma of omelet and coffee fills the apartment. The American news is on the television, and as she sits there in her robe, all disheveled and just fucked . . . a calm falls over me.

And suddenly all my fears disappear.

This is where I'm meant to be and exactly who I'm meant to be with.

London, my home. With my beloved, sweet girl.

Hayden raises her eyebrow. "Look at you being all hot CEO." She stands and runs her hand over my behind. "Meow."

She sits back down as my eyes hold hers.

"What is that look?" she asks.

"What look?"

"That twinkle in your eye."

I cut into my breakfast. "I have a lot to be grateful for."

"Like what?"

"Like omelets and coffee." I hold my coffee cup up to her in a salute with a wink.

She giggles. "Glad I can be of service, Mr. Miles." She holds her coffee cup up right back.

"What are you going to do today?" I ask as I cut into my omelet.

"Hmm . . ." She looks around the apartment. "I have no idea, to be honest." She shrugs. "I guess I'll putter around here, and then I might go for a wander."

I frown. "Where are you going to wander to?"

"I don't know yet."

"Your driver will take you anywhere you want to go."

"Or . . . I could just catch an Uber." She widens her eyes.

"Yes. You could," I agree. My natural instinct is to ask her to stay close to home, but I know I can't do that.

The story in the paper has ruffled me more than I care to admit. I know I can't keep her wrapped in cotton wool. If this is to be her home, she needs to find her own way. The mere thought of her not doing that makes me sick to my stomach.

We eat our breakfast, and I take her into my arms and kiss her softly. "Have a good day." She smiles up at me.

"I don't like the idea of not seeing you." I hug her tight. "Are you sure you're going to be all right here on your own?"

She giggles in my arms.

"Good grief, I'm pathetic," I mutter into her hair.

"Little bit." She pinches her fingers up in the air, and I grab her roughly on the behind and slam our hips together.

"You better fuck that out of me tonight," I warn her.

"Okay."

I kiss her softly and grab my briefcase. "See you tonight, babe."

I take the elevator downstairs and walk out to see my car waiting. "Good morning, Mr. Miles."

"Good morning, Hans." I get into the back of the car and stare out the window as we pull out into the traffic.

This all feels so . . . foreign. Even though I've been doing it throughout my entire adult life.

Those twelve months away felt like a lifetime.

As we sit in the London rush hour traffic, I dial my favorite number, and he answers on the first ring. "Hello, Mr. Christo."

His happy little voice brings a huge smile to my face. "How's my main man?"

✕

Forty minutes later the car pulls into the Miles Media building, and I get out of the car and peer up at the sleek and modern skyscraper.

MILES MEDIA

Hmm, it's so . . . huge.

I walk through the foyer and notice the marble and the guards and the sheer luxury of the building.

I catch the elevator to the top floor; the doors open with a ping, and I step out to the flitter of my stomach.

I'm nervous to be back.

Here early to start the day, I walk past the empty reception and down to my office.

433

My eyes roam over the couch and the drop-dead-gorgeous view, the large desk and fully stocked bar in the corner. A strange feeling washes over me.

Pride.

My family has built this business from the ground up, worked their fingers to the very bone, and I owe them a lot.

I've been given the opportunity of a lifetime . . . and damn it, I'm going to repay them for the privilege.

I turn my computer on with a new determination. I'm going to be the best version of myself that I can be. Work harder than ever before.

At the very least, I owe them that.

I open my email. We opened it back up over the weekend in preparation for my return today.

Six hundred and twenty-six emails.

Fuck.

I open my diary on my computer and see that I'm booked back to back with appointments for nearly the entire week. Zooms and conference calls with Paris and New York. Some running late into the nights.

Ugh . . .

I have a feeling that the first few weeks are going to be hectic hell while I catch up on everything. Elliot is here for the week with me, and then he leaves for a two-month vacation, which is only fair.

Then it's all on me.

I email Elouise, my PA.

Hi Elouise,

Great to be back!

Can you book me an appointment with Reynolds Jewels when my schedule permits please?

This week if possible.

Thank you.

Ps . . . and come and see me when you arrive!

Christopher.

I get up and make myself a coffee with a smile.
A diamond ring for my love . . .
Life is good.

Hayden

I walk around the apartment. It's big and grand and deathly quiet.

There are no sounds in this penthouse. No wind, no rain . . . no cows.

Nothing.

It's only eleven o'clock. It's like time has stood still. What am I supposed to do for the rest of the day? I've already done our washing and cleaned the apartment, not that I needed to. It was already spotless.

I pick up my phone, and my finger hovers over Christopher's name. Just a quick call?

No . . .

I need to let him work in peace. I can't call him every time I'm bored. I throw my phone onto the couch and go to the window and stare out over the city. It's pouring rain.

I was going to go for a walk or . . . to the shops to find a new dress for Friday night, but I don't fancy getting saturated, and I have no idea where an umbrella is.

There's no rush. I guess I can look around tomorrow, and I have the whole week to find a dress. How hard can it be?

I flop onto the couch and hold the remote to the television. Looks like it's a date with Netflix.

I flick through the movies. Now . . . what will I watch?

Wednesday

I walk through the shops on autopilot.

How do people actually like shopping? I would rather pull my teeth out than do this shit for fun.

My phone rings and I dig it out of my bag.

Miles Media

Ugh, Elouise.

I've spoken to Christopher's PA more than I've actually spoken to him this week. "Hi, Elouise," I answer.

"Hello, Hayden," she replies happily.

"What's happening?"

"Christopher asked me to call you."

Of course he did.

"Yes."

"He wanted me to let you know that he's got a Zoom meeting at six tonight, so he will be home late."

I roll my eyes. "Can you put me through to him, please?"

"He's in a board meeting now that will be running late into the afternoon. I can get him to call you between that and his Zoom, if you like?"

"No, that's fine." I exhale heavily. "Okay, thanks for letting me know."

"He also asked me to remind you that you have that meeting with Zoe this afternoon at two p.m."

"How could I forget?" I mutter dryly.

She laughs. "I don't envy you, that's for sure."

"Ugh, Elouise. How did I agree to this?"

"You'll love it. Zoe has been Christopher's personal shopper for many years; you're in safe hands. And don't forget you have that charity ball on Friday night."

Ugh . . . don't remind me.

"He's trying to help," she adds.

"Help me what? Go insane . . ."

"Buy up big, I say." She laughs. "Spend it all."

I chuckle. I do like Elouise. "Thank you."

"And Hayden . . ."

"Yes."

"Please call me if you need anything."

"I will." I smile. Christopher has Elouise on babysitting-Hayden duties. I swear the poor girl checks in with me twice a day.

"Have a good day."

"Bye."

I glance at my watch. An hour until I have to meet Zoe. I look around . . . I wonder where a bar is. I need wine for this shopping trip.

X

I sit in the bar along the window seat as I sip my wine. I've called my mom and Eddie, and I meet Zoe in half an hour.

I don't know what's going on with me, but time seems to have stopped in this city. I swear the days drag on forever.

"We've got her. There she is," I hear someone yell from out on the street. "Miss Whitmore."

Huh?

I glance up to see a flash, then another and another.

Almost blinding.

A large group of people clambers around as they take photos of me through the window. I duck and cover my face.

What the hell is going on?

438

Chapter 27

CHRISTOPHER

I bring up the spreadsheet on the large screen, and ten sets of eyes stare up at it. "What we need to do is focus our efforts onto the streaming service. When I looked over the results over the last twelve months, the one thing that's glaringly clear is that . . ."

My phone vibrates on the table . . .

Hayden

"So what you're saying is that you aren't happy with what we've been focusing on while you were away?" Henry asks.

My phone keeps vibrating . . .

I'll call her back when I've finished.

"Not entirely true, but to an extent I do agree," I reply. "If we change the tactic, we change the outcome."

I sit down at my computer as the discussion continues, and I discreetly email Elouise.

Hi Elouise.

Check in with Hayden please.

She just called and I can't answer.

"Here, I'll show you my projections if we change our route now." I stand and go back to the board.

Hayden

The phone rings out. "Damn it, Christopher, answer your fucking phone."

I hang up and dial his number again.

I'm hiding in the bathroom of the bar, my half-drunk glass of wine still back at the table. Photographers are gathered around the front doors as they wait to get their shot of me.

I'm in a panic.

This is a gross invasion of my privacy. I don't want another photo of me in circulation. The last one stressed Christopher out so bad that it took him three hours to calm down. These bastards are vile.

A waitress comes into the bathroom. "Hi."

"Are they still out there?" I ask her.

"Yep."

"Do you have a back entrance?"

"We don't," she says as she peers out the door at them. "I'm sorry."

"Okay." I nod.

My phone rings.

Elouise

"Elouise. Hi."

"Hello, Hayden," she says happily. "Are you okay, lovely? Christopher is stuck in a meeting."

"No. I'm not," I whisper. "I'm in a bar, and a group of photographers have found me and are waiting out front, and now I'm hiding in the bathroom," I splutter.

"Oh dear. Where are you? I'll get Hans to come and collect you now."

I put the phone down. "What's the name of this bar?" I ask the waitress.

"O'Brian's."

"What's the address?" God, I must sound stupid, but I was ambling down the street paying no attention.

She gives me the address, and I tell Elouise.

"Just wait there. Hans will call you when he pulls up out the front," Elouise says calmly.

I hear my angry heartbeat in my ears. This is all so overdramatic. And so . . . not me.

"It's okay, Hayden. Please don't let this worry you. It comes with Miles territory. In time, you will get used to it," Elouise says.

Not likely.

"Stay in the bathroom. Hans will be there soon."

Ugh, I hate this.

"Are you okay?" Elouise asks.

"Yep," I snap. I can't even hide how angry I am.

I stay in the bathroom, and twenty minutes later my phone rings.

Hans

"Hello," I answer.

"Hello, Miss Whitmore. I'm out the front."

I peer out the door to see the black Mercedes double-parked in the traffic.

"There's a security guard with me. He's coming in to get you."

My eyes well with embarrassed tears. *So dramatic.*

"Okay."

I peer around the corner again to see a big burly bodyguard get out of the car and walk into the bar, and I square my shoulders to prepare myself.

I walk out in a rush, and the security guard gives me a kind smile. "Hello, Miss Whitmore?"

"Yes."

"Let's go. Stay close." He turns and walks out of the bar, and I follow him like a child. Cameras flash, people call my name, and in a whirlwind of chaos I am ushered into the back of the waiting car.

The guard gets into the front passenger seat, and we drive off into the traffic.

"Imbeciles," Hans mutters under his breath.

A text bounces in from Elouise.

I've canceled your appointment with Zoe for this afternoon.
We will have to reschedule.
Let me know when suits.
X

I exhale heavily, great.

I can't even go shopping now.

That was the one thing that I was doing today . . . the *only* thing.

442

Now that's ruined too.

I stare out the window as I internally fume. How dare these fuckers chase me around town? Why don't they report on an issue that actually matters?

"Where would you like to go, Miss Whitmore?" Hans asks.

"Home, please."

Two hours later

My phone buzzes . . .

Christopher

"Hello," I answer.

"Babe, are you okay?" he stammers. "I was in a meeting and just found out what happened."

"I'm fine." I've calmed down now and am feeling stupid for letting it get to me.

"Are you sure?"

"Yep."

"They won't be able to sell the images. Everyone has been warned. I'm sorry that you had to deal with this alone."

"Don't apologize. It's not your fault."

"Do you want me to come home? I'll cancel the meeting I had with Paris for this afternoon."

"No." He can't come home every time I'm photographed. I know I have to learn to deal with this shit. "Finish your day. It's fine."

He hangs on the line. "Are you sure you're okay?"

"I promise."

"Just order in tonight; don't cook. I'm going to be late with this stupid fucking meeting."

"Okay."

"Why don't you go and get a massage or a pedicure . . ."

I roll my eyes. "Really?"

"I just thought . . ."

"You thought wrong. See you tonight." I hang up.

Idiot.

Because a massage or a pedicure is so fucking riveting. Does he even know me at all?

I throw the phone onto the couch and begin to pace. I'm so bored that I can hardly see straight. I want to be positive and love it here, but deep down I already know.

This isn't who I am.

This whole city-living life just isn't me.

I want to work, but then I don't want to commit to anything until after the three months. If we do decide not to live here long term, then I don't want to let anyone down.

What if we stay?

Hell . . . the thought of living here forever is traumatizing. No grass, no sun . . . not one thing to fucking do. I had all these hopes and dreams of opening my own animal husbandry business when I got back from traveling. I'd been working toward it for years. I was going to get an apprentice and perhaps hire a stable to work from.

But now what?

I walk to the window and look at the busy city way below . . . there are no animals here. Not a one.

Except for the paparazzi, of course.

I exhale heavily, disappointed that I feel this way. I want to love it. I want to support Christopher and be the good girlfriend that he deserves, but it's as if every day that I stay here, I feel like I lose a little more of myself. As if minute by minute I'm watching my hopes and dreams slowly drip down the drain.

If he had just told me who he was.

444

I know that I've said that I made peace with Christopher for lying to me, and I realize that he had a valid reason for doing it.

But deep down, I'm resentful. His life is chugging along just great, while mine has come to a complete standstill.

We don't have an equal exchange of power. It's all about him and *his* life and *his* job . . . and how I should fit into it.

What if I wanted him to fit into my life . . . could he do that? Of course not. It's not even an option, and I mean, it's ridiculous to even want that because he makes so much more money than me. Of course his job should come first.

The thought is depressing.

I fell for a simple cleaner and ended up with a workaholic . . . the two men I love are worlds apart.

10:00 p.m.

The movie is playing, but I'm not watching . . . I mean, I've never been one to watch a lot of television, but now that it's my only company, I'm beginning to really despise it.

I glance at the time on my phone: 10:00 p.m. . . . god, it's late. That must be some motherfucking long telecall to Paris. Poor Christopher, he's been at work since eight o'clock this morning. I hope he at least had something to eat before his meeting.

He works too hard.

I exhale heavily and hold the remote up and turn the television off.

I'm going to bed.

I close the automatic drapes in the apartment and watch as all the twinkling lights of London slowly disappear.

I brush my teeth and climb into bed. I smile as I smell the freshly washed linen.

At least I achieved something today.

I stare up at the ceiling as my mind wanders over the week ahead. I might go to a bookshop tomorrow and stock up.

I haven't read a book in a while. Maybe I'll read *War and Peace* and all the other books I've never had time to read.

It's the weirdest thing. When I was back at the farm, it felt like I no longer belonged there, like I'd grown out of it. But now that I'm here, this feels even more foreign.

I heard the horror stories of people having trouble settling back in one place after extended travel, but it's much worse than I imagined. Torn from a world of memories with no idea where I want my future forever home to be.

I exhale heavily. How the hell do you settle back down after a trip like that?

I need to come back to earth.

I doze for a while, and I feel the bed dip. "Baby," I hear Christopher whisper as he brushes the hair back from my forehead.

I smile and hold my arms out for him, and he lies on top of the blankets in his full suit and nestles his head into my chest. "I'm sorry I'm so late, sweetheart."

"That's okay." I kiss his forehead. "You must be exhausted."

"Hmm," he whispers as his heavy eyelids close.

"Did you have any dinner?"

He nods.

"What did you have?"

"A glass of scotch and nuts from my office minibar."

I smile into the darkness. "Your dinner is in the fridge on a plate. Put it in the microwave."

"Did you cook it?" he asks with his eyes still closed.

"No, it's takeout."

He smiles. "Good."

"Why is that good?"

"Because I don't feel bad if I'm too tired to eat it."

"Shower," I prompt him. He's going to fall asleep in his full suit.

"You want to have a shower with me?" He bites my nipple through my pajamas.

"No," I murmur. "I'm half-asleep."

"Party pooper." He drags himself out of bed and disappears into the bathroom, and I hear the shower running.

I smile. His aftershave wafts around the room, and everything is just better when he's home. I feel myself relax for the first time today.

Five minutes later he slides in beside me and takes me into his arms. He holds me tight. "I love you, baby," he whispers sleepily.

I turn my head and kiss him over my shoulder. "I love you too."

"Good night." He kisses me again.

We lie in comfortable silence for a few minutes. I'm nestled safely in his big strong arms. The best place in the world.

"You work too hard," I whisper.

But he doesn't answer . . . he's already asleep.

Friday night

The charity ball: my very first official engagement as Christopher Miles's partner.

I'm nervous and have put way too much effort into overthinking every little detail.

I blame Zoe, the personal shopper. She dragged me around the entirety of London looking for the perfect outfit for tonight. I think she's more nervous than me.

Per her instruction, I had my hair and makeup done, and now I'm about to get dressed. My clothes are laid out on the bed for me, and I hold the Spanx underwear up and look at it. It's tiny. Did Zoe get me the right size?

These pantie things look like they would fit a child.

Zoe's words from our shopping trip come back to me. *This dress needs good supportive underwear. Do not wear it without.*

Fine.

I walk into the bathroom and close the door. I don't want Christopher walking in while I'm struggling to pull these fuckers up.

I step into them and . . . oh hell, so tight. I struggle and breathe in as I slowly pull them up. I put my hands on my hips as I stare at the Lycra black underwear in the mirror. It looks like shiny short bike pants. Jeez . . . I guess there's no breathing tonight, then?

I put on the black lacy bra, the superboostiest thing I have ever seen. The girls are nearly at my neck. Surely people can't wear this shit every day, can they?

My honey hair is out and curled in big Hollywood finger curls, and my makeup is sultry, with red lipstick.

I walk back out into the bedroom and pick up my dress, and Christopher glances in as he walks past the bedroom door. He stops and puts his head back around the doorjamb. He's wearing a black dinner suit, white shirt, and black bow tie: classic black-tie porn. I've never seen anyone so handsome.

Delicious.

He frowns as he looks me up and down. "What's happening right now?"

I bite my lip to hide my smile. He means my underwear.

"I'm getting dressed," I reply. "I'll be ready in a minute."

He walks into the bedroom and circles me as he looks me up and down. "What . . ."

I put my hands on my hips as I wait for him to say it out loud. He sweeps his hand in the area of my Spanx. "What is this?"

"What's what?"

"Those gigantic underpants."

"Spanx."

"Hayden, when I look at those, the last thing I'm thinking about is spanking you."

I giggle. "No, silly, that's the name of them. They hold all your bits in, smooth everything out."

He raises an eyebrow as he keeps circling me, his eyes drinking me in. "Diabolical."

"What is?"

"Genius marketing," he mutters to himself.

"Huh?"

"They package grandma underpants with the promise of making a woman thinner, smooth, and rewarded with spanking." He nods as he contemplates the concept. "Brilliant. I need to hire the marketing head of this company. They've totally nailed it."

I laugh. Trust him to analyze the marketing plan. I put my hands on my hips. "It's what married women wear."

"I have to tell you, and I know I speak for all mankind"—he curls his lip—"not a huge incentive to walk down that aisle."

I giggle. "Get out. Let me get dressed."

He kisses me quickly and walks out of the room. "Take them off," he calls as he disappears up the hall. "*My* woman has curves."

I smile as I step into my dress. *I love that man.*

※

"Your seats are this way, Mr. Miles." The usher gestures. With my hand firmly in Christopher's, we follow him into the ballroom. I look around in awe . . . my god.

This place is spectacular.

A string quartet plays in the corner. Huge crystal vases of flowers, chandeliers hanging low, candles flickering on all the tables, creating a beautiful ambience. Everyone is in black tie and looking ever so glamorous. The room is abuzz with chatter and loud laughter.

Boy . . . this is full on.

I suddenly feel very out of my depth, like I don't belong here, nervous like never before. I grip Christopher's hand with white-knuckle force.

"It's fine, Grumps." He winks at me over his shoulder. "You look beautiful."

How does he always know exactly what to say?

I force a smile, and he leads me through to the table. "Hello." He smiles to everyone as he proudly presents me. "This is Hayden."

I feel my face blush. "Hello."

"This is"—he gestures around the table—"Margaret and Conrad, Eva and Mario."

I give a wave. Oh hell . . . this is so awkward.

"This is Edward Prescott and Julian Masters."

My eyes land on the last man . . . I've seen him before.

Where?

He gives me a sexy wink and raises his glass. "I told you we'd meet again, Hayden."

My eyes widen. No way.

He's the man who owned the yacht in Greece . . . what the hell? They're friends?

My mouth falls open in shock.

He and Christopher laugh out loud, and Christopher squeezes my shoulder blade. "You look like you saw a ghost, babe."

I laugh, half-embarrassed and not sure what to say.

"And this"—he smiles proudly—"is Elliot, my brother. Elliot, this is my Hayden."

Familiar warm eyes smile up at me.

Oh . . . he's like Christopher.

Elliot stands and kisses my cheek. "Hello, it's so lovely to finally meet you." His eyes linger on my face as he studies me, and I feel myself flush under his gaze.

He pulls out the chair beside him. "Sit next to me, Hayden."

Oh crap . . . do I really have to?

I fall into the chair beside him, and Christopher sits on the other side of me.

Christopher puts his hand protectively on my lap as the waiter fills our glasses with champagne.

"It's good to see you," Mr. Masters says from across the table. "How was the vacation?"

"Great." Christopher's eyes meet mine. "Brought home an amazing souvenir." He squeezes my leg.

"I see that." Julian smiles as he looks between the two of us. "How are you liking London, Hayden?"

"It's beautiful."

I glance up to see Elliot's eyes fixed firmly on me. He has his finger up along his temple and is studying me in great detail. I glance over to Christopher, who is now happily chatting away with the rest of the table.

Help.

I sip my drink. Eish . . . I feel like this is a test. Actually, that's not true. I don't feel it; I know it for certain.

"Are you here alone?" I ask Elliot.

"Yes, my wife is in Hawaii. She left last week with her brother, and I'm catching the first flight out in the morning."

"Hawaii. So beautiful." I smile.

"Have you ever been?" he asks.

451

"No. On my bucket list, though."

"We have a house there. Lucky enough to go every year for a couple of months."

"Oh, wow." I frown. "What made you choose Hawaii for your regular holiday vacation?"

"My wife lived there for a while and fell madly in love with the place."

I smile as I listen.

"It's a shame she's not here to meet you tonight. You'll love her. She's a lot like you."

Oh . . . how I wish she *was* here.

The table all falls into chatter while I look around the room in awe. I've never been somewhere so glamorous.

Beautiful women in beautiful dresses . . . and can we talk about the caliber of men here? If handsome was a place, this would be it.

What the actual hell?

Black tie sure does bring out the best in everyone.

"You coming to the bar?" Elliot asks Christopher.

"No, I'll stay here with Hayden." He picks up my hand and kisses my fingertips as he smiles over at me.

A trace of a smile crosses Elliot's face. "Who are you, and what have you done with my brother?"

Christopher laughs, and I do too. Does it make me a bad person if I'm glad he's changed?

) (

The night is a soiree of glamour.

People stop and talk to Christopher, commenting how relaxed and happy he looks.

And he . . . he plays the room like a pro.

All eyes are watching him. Everyone wants to talk to him. He laughs and jokes. The room is in the palm of his hand. Funny, charming, and sexy as all hell, Christopher Miles is London's darling *it* boy.

The longer I'm here, with the beauty and glamour, the more an underlying question in the back of my mind steps forward to the front.

What does he see in me?

I'm just a normal country girl.

I'm not gorgeous or glamorous with a high-flying job, and I certainly don't look like the beautiful model-like women who keep trying to make eye contact with him.

I'm like a fish out of water.

For the first time in my life, I feel something foreign crawl up and sit like a lead ball in my stomach.

Insecurity.

I know that there are others in the room who are wondering the same thing I am.

Why her?

Why has he chosen to settle down with someone so normal? Now that I know the life and people he's used to, I see why the sight of me causes such a stir. Why photographers are scrambling to get a shot and follow me everywhere. They're trying to work out what he sees in me. They're waiting to get the scoop for when we fall.

Stop it.

I sip my wine, disgusted by my thoughts. It's not healthy to think like this.

Christopher holds his hand out. "Do you want to dance, sweetheart?"

I smile, grateful for him.

"I do." He leads me onto the dance floor and takes me into his arms as we sway to the music. He kisses my temple, completely oblivious to everyone who is watching us.

"You look beautiful." He smiles over at me.

I force a smile.

How long will you believe that?

✗

I walk out the door of the shop to a whirl of paparazzi.

"Hayden, Hayden, this way," they all call.

I drop my head as I am ushered to the car by the security guard. He opens the door, and I get into the back seat and am whisked away. "Idiots," Hans sighs as we drive into the traffic.

I feel my heartbeat slowly return to normal.

I can't go anywhere now without being followed.

Hunting Hayden Whitmore has become a sport. I'm hounded night and day by photographers.

I had planned on having some lunch somewhere, but I can't.

What's the point?

I'll be a nervous wreck the entire time, knowing they are waiting just outside for me.

"Where would you like to go, Hayden?" Hans asks me.

"Home, please." I sigh.

His eyes meet mine in the rearview mirror, and he gives me a sad smile. "As you wish."

One month later

I sit cross-legged on the floor as I stare out the window. The sky is gray.

The clouds are full as I watch it come down.

Does it ever stop raining in this godforsaken place?

It has rained every single day that I've been here, and like a plant, I'm dying without the light.

The life is seeping out of me. A heavy blanket weighs on my shoulders, and I can't shake it off, no matter how hard I try.

Every day is the same.

I can't go out; I'm followed. I can't lie in the sun, because there is no fucking sun. I can't feel the earth beneath my feet because there is no earth.

All I do . . . is wait for Christopher to come home so that I can feel whole again.

Something is missing . . . everything is missing. But somehow everything is whole.

We're together. I'm with Christopher, the love of my life, supporting him and his important job. I should be happier than ever before.

But I'm not.

I find myself crying alone in the shower. Staring into space. My appetite has completely gone.

I'm sad to my bones . . . I can't shake it, no matter how hard I try.

I feel the loss of my life. Of who I was. The life I had.

I miss me.

I want to make my life here with my Christopher.

I love him more than anything. I would walk to the end of the earth if it meant that we were together . . . and it feels like I have.

But all he does is work, even on weekends. And I know this isn't his fault; this is what he does. He's trying his hardest. I know he is.

I need to snap myself out of this because I want to love it here. I want to feel excited to wake up. I want to support him and make friends, but as soon as I walk out that door, I'm followed by photographers, and it's all too hard . . . so I just stay home. It's easier that way.

But I feel lost in a concrete jungle.

I need the sun. To feel the warmth on my skin, the wind in my hair.

The grass beneath my feet.

Fresh air . . .

Cows.

My eyes well with tears, which then break the dam to slowly roll down my face. I angrily wipe them away. I need to stop this. Cut it out already. This isn't helping anyone, least of all me.

Buzz, buzz . . . buzz, buzz . . .

My phone sounds. I close my eyes, unable to answer it.

I know it's Christopher, and I know that he will hear the tears in my voice and come rushing home . . . just like he did yesterday.

No matter how hard he tries, no matter how much we love each other, he can't fix my problem.

I miss my home.

Chapter 28

CHRISTOPHER

I exhale heavily as I stare at my computer screen. I glance at my phone as it sits on the desk. I should call Hayden.

No.

You've called her already today.

I go back to trying to focus. The numbers all jumble on my screen.

Just a quick call.

No.

For fuck's sake, I'm not going to be able to focus until I know that she's okay.

I dial her number, and it rings out.

Hmm . . .

I text her.

Hi babes,
What's doing?

I put my phone to the side and look back to my computer screen. She'll call me back when she can.

I get back to work, and twenty minutes later I pick up my phone again. Why hasn't she called me back? I go to call her again . . . *Just stop it.*

Fuck.

I'm getting nothing done around here because I'm worrying about Hayden all the time.

Focus.

She says she's fine. I should believe her. I mean, how could she not be? She has the whole of London at her fingertips.

Of course she's fine.

My gut is telling me that something is off with her, but perhaps I'm looking for something that isn't there. I get back to work, and sure enough, ten minutes later I pick up my phone.

Call me . . . damn it.

Jameson and Tristan saunter into my office. "You ready to go to lunch?"

I exhale heavily. Where has the morning gone? I've literally achieved nothing.

Fuck. *I need to focus.*

My brothers are in London for the bimonthly board meeting.

"Yeah, I guess."

"What's wrong with you?" Tristan frowns.

"Nothing." I stand. "Let's go."

$$\displaystyle \bigwedge$$

Twenty minutes later we are seated in a bar close to the office. We've ordered, and I'm drinking mineral water.

"Not having a beer?" Jameson asks.

"No. I've got too much to do." I drag my hand down my face. "Ever since I got back, I'm achieving next to nothing."

Tristan smiles as he crunches a piece of ice from his water. "The vacation is officially over. Back to the real world, hey?"

"It's not even work; it's Hayden. The paps are giving her hell, and she hates the weather here."

"The weather?" Tristan frowns.

"It's pretty fucking dreary here lately. The sun is a special event ever since she arrived." I shrug. "I keep thinking that she's going to get used to it and adjust . . . but between you and me, I'm not actually sure she is."

"You going to move out of the city?" Jameson asks.

"No. Fuck that." I screw up my face. "I love the city. I hate being out of town, and besides, I asked her to give me three months before we do anything. There'll be times in my life that I need to live in a city, and it may not just be here. It could be anywhere. She needs to know what she's signed up for. I don't want to go to all the trouble to move and then it doesn't work out anyway."

They both frown and glance at each other.

"What?" I snap.

"She's on a three-month trial?" Tristan frowns. "Or are you?"

"Both, I guess, but that's how long I have to work long hours in London. After that we can discuss what we're going to do long term, but at this stage, with Elliot away, there's no way around it."

"And then with the next two weekends . . . ," Jameson adds.

"What about the next two weekends?" I frown.

"You've got the Paris team in town next weekend for training, and then the week after that we have a conference in Germany. So you technically won't have a day off at home for twenty-one days."

I pinch the bridge of my nose. "Fuck. Having someone depend on you is seriously a nightmare."

"Buy her a puppy." Jameson shrugs.

"Have a baby." Tristan smiles into his drink. "Then she'll be too exhausted to give a fuck if you are dead or alive . . . let alone where she lives."

"Not a bad plan, actually." I chuckle.

"Or if your dick has fallen off," Jameson mutters dryly.

"True story," Tristan agrees.

"Fuck that, then."

Our lunch arrives, and we eat in silence for a while.

"What are you going to do?" Jameson asks.

I shrug. "Nothing. She'll be okay, but if the sun would just come out for one minute, it would be very fucking helpful."

My phone beeps with a text. It's from Hans.

Hi Mr. Miles,
Not sure if I am overstepping.
I thought I would let you know that Hayden
has had a bad day.

I frown and text back.

What makes you say that?

A picture bounces back. It's a photo of Hayden in a park. She's sitting on the grass. Tears are running down her red face. She looks so lost and so forlorn.

So . . . unlike the happy Hayden that I fell in love with.

Her sadness seeps through the image, and I get a lump in my throat as I stare at it.

I stand. "I've got to go."

"What's wrong?" They both frown.

I hold my phone up and show them the photo, and their faces fall as they stare at it. "Fuck . . . ," Tristan whispers. "That doesn't look good."

"You think?" I throw my napkin on the table in disgust. "Bye, I'll call you later."

I march out of the restaurant on a mission. I call Hans.

"Hello, Mr. Miles."

"Where are you?"

HAYDEN

I sit and stare into space. The park bench is hard and cold and laden with impossible decisions.

I have this sinking feeling in my heart, but I don't know how to stop it. Every day I get up determined to be happy.

By lunchtime I'm in tears . . . and I'm not a crying kind of girl.

I've never had a reason to cry before, and I'm not even sure I do now.

Everything about our love is crystal clear and yet, in so many ways, messy and complicated.

I messed up, and the stupid thing is, I knew it at the time, but I didn't want to be the drama queen and cause a fight. But I should have. I should have fought harder to stand up for myself.

Looking back, Christopher should have come to London alone, let both of us get used to our surroundings before we jumped into the pressure cooker of living together in a big city.

It all happened so fast. Everything was just thrown at me, all or nothing from the very get-go.

Hindsight is a marvelous thing.

If only . . .

Christopher told me who he really was one minute before the car pulled up because he knew I wouldn't cause a scene in front of the driver.

It didn't sit well with me at the time, but I let it slide because I understood his reasoning for wanting to be anonymous, especially now that the press is hounding me day and night. I get why he needed that break from reality, and I respect him for taking it.

Now that I know him, it would have taken a lot of guts to do what he did.

He wanted to find someone who loved him for him. Mission accomplished: I love him.

With everything.

But what about my choices . . . and do they even matter anymore?

I had everything mapped out, and now my hopes and dreams are just . . . *gone.*

Christopher is the love of my life—I'm talking soul mate shit—but I know that to be with him I have to give up who I am.

For him to move to be with me . . . he would have to give up who he is.

There's no fucking winner. One of us has to lose everything in order for the other to be happy.

And I want it to be me. I don't want him to suffer like this . . . but it's harder than I thought it would be.

Lonelier.

I screw up my face in tears.

If I want to be my true self, then I can't stay living in a city. If I want a life with Christopher, then I have to stay.

It's not fair that I have to choose one over the other.

I can't lose either.

Tears slowly run down my face.

"Hey, babe," Christopher's voice says from behind me.

I turn, startled.

"Everything all right?" he asks.

I turn away from him and quickly wipe my eyes. Damn it, how did he know I was here? "Yep."

He sits down beside me and stares out over the park. "What's going on?"

"Nothing." I try to hide my tears. "I'm okay."

He raises his eyebrow.

I roll my eyes. "Don't."

We fall silent, and I troll my brain for the right thing to say.

"Hayden . . . you need to talk to me . . . I can't fix this if you won't talk to me."

Be honest.

"I think I'm going to go home to the States for a few weeks," I say softly.

"What?" He frowns. "Why?"

"You're so busy, and I . . . just need some fresh air . . . and . . ."

His eyes hold mine.

I steel myself to say the dreaded words out loud. "I'm struggling . . . and not entirely sure that city life is for me."

"My life is in the city, Hayden," he replies curtly.

My eyes well with tears. "I know."

"You said you would give it three months."

"I know I did."

"It's been only weeks. Of course you aren't settled in yet. Give it some time. You'll come around."

Come around?

He just doesn't get it.

"I don't want to come around, Christopher," I snap in frustration. "I'm thinking long term."

"Meaning what?"

"There's no way I could raise a family here in these conditions."

"What the fuck does that mean?" he barks angrily.

I shrug.

"A shrug?" he snaps. "You tell me you don't want to ever raise a family here, and then you answer it with a shrug? You've been here for two fucking minutes, Hayden."

"Don't get angry."

"How could I not?" He raises his voice. "These conditions happen to be the best of the best in London. You have a driver, you have a guard, you live in a forty-million-dollar penthouse and can do whatever you like, and it's still not fucking enough?"

"I don't have the cleaner I fell in love with, though, do I?" I snap back. "I hate this workaholic version of you. If I met you as you are now, we wouldn't even be together."

He sits back in the chair and gives me a sarcastic smile. "And there it is."

"There what is?"

"I wondered how long it would be until you threw that in my face."

My temper begins to rise. "Am I not allowed to bring it up? You're done with that topic, so that's the end of it? Is that how this relationship works? It's your way or the highway."

"Don't be fucking cute, Hayden. I don't like it."

"I beg *your* pardon." Adrenaline surges through my bloodstream. "I will not apologize for feeling let down by you. You brought this all onto yourself when you lied to me for twelve months, so don't you dare fucking sit there and defend your actions like I'm the one with the problem."

He rolls his eyes, and I see red.

"I'm going home to the farm for a while."

"No. You're not," he snaps.

"What do you mean, no, I'm not?"

"You told me that you would give it three months, and damn it, you *will* give them to me. You're having a bad day. Are you going to run back home to Mommy and Daddy every time you have a bad fucking day?"

Unbelievable.

"Proof that you are not fucking listening to a thing I'm saying," I yell.

465

"If you go home to that farm, then that's it," he yells.

"What?" I screw up my face. "What the hell does that mean?" I explode.

"Just what I said." He raises his chin in defiance. "I have to live in the city. It is nonnegotiable. If you choose not to give it a proper go, then . . ." He throws up his hands in defeat. "There's no fucking point. I'm not doing a long-distance relationship. It won't work."

"Why not?"

"Because I need sex!" he yells.

I sit back in my seat, shocked to silence.

Wow . . .

Reality hits home like a freight train, my heart splintering into pieces.

We really aren't going to be able to work through this. I get a lump in my throat. "If sex means more to you than my happiness . . . then I guess . . . this *is* goodbye."

He rolls his eyes. "Don't be so dramatic, Hayden. You know what I mean."

"Yes, I do." I stand. "I'm going home."

"*This* is your home." He stands in an outrage.

I roll my eyes. "It's just a few weeks. Who's the one being dramatic around here?"

"You're not going."

"You can't tell me that I'm not allowed to go home, Christopher. I won't stand for it."

"You said you would give it three months."

"I want to go home for a few weeks. It shouldn't be a big deal."

"No. You stay here, and we work through this together. I will not be held over a barrel every time you get homesick. You leave me, and that's fucking it."

What the hell?

I can't believe this. He would really rather we break up than go without sex?

Oh . . .

His silhouette blurs . . .

"Who even are you?" I whisper through tears.

"I'm the man who loves you."

"Are you sure about that?"

His chest rises and falls as he struggles for air.

"I'm going."

"Then"—he shrugs—"this is goodbye."

My eyes search his. "Just like that?"

"I can't drag this out. If you're leaving me without trying now, you will always leave me without trying. I can never move out of the city, Hayden. It's not who I am."

Oh no.

This really is it . . . my heart constricts in my chest.

We stare at each other, so close but a million miles apart.

"I love you," I whisper.

"Obviously not enough." He walks off.

"Are you not coming home to see me off?" I call after him.

"No." He turns back to face me, his cold eyes holding mine. "Goodbye, Hayden." He disappears through the park, and I drop back to the seat, shocked to my core.

Checkmate.

)(

I put the last of my things into my suitcase as it lies open on the bed, and I look around the bedroom.

Is this going to be the last time I see it?

Can't be . . .

No. We'll get through this. I know we will. We love each other too much not to be together. I glance at the time on my phone: 6:20 p.m.

Where is he?

I texted Christopher when I booked my flight and told him the time I'd be leaving. Don't tell me he's not coming home to see me off.

I know I could stay here for a while before I go, plan it better and leave next week or something, but with him working for the next three weeks straight, another day alone in that apartment is not something I can take. And besides, I'm angry at him for throwing the no-sex comment in my face. I know he just said it to try to shock me.

And it worked. He did . . . but not in a good way.

If anything, it's made me more determined to look after my own happiness. I would never say something like that to him in a fight. It surprised me that he would stoop that low. Actually, if I'm honest, I'm not surprised. Christopher has a way of railroading me into doing what he wants me to do. This time he took the wrong route . . . I won't be bullied with scare tactics. If he wants to sleep with someone else, he can go ahead.

I won't be here to pick up the pieces.

"Grumps," I hear him call from downstairs.

He's home.

I nearly run downstairs to find him in the kitchen. He's pouring two glasses of wine. My heart somersaults in my chest at the sight of him. In his perfectly fitted navy suit and crisp white shirt, he is the epitome of masculine perfection.

"Hi." I smile hopefully.

"Hi." He kisses my cheek and passes me a glass of wine. "We need to talk."

He takes my hand and leads me out to the living room, and we sit on the couch. I swallow the nervous lump in my throat, and I know this is it, the moment in time when we discuss our future.

His eyes hold mine. "How long have you been unhappy here?"

"I'm not unhappy with you . . ."

"Answer the question, Hayden," he replies flatly.

Be honest.

"Almost the whole time."

He raises an eyebrow and sips his wine.

"To clarify, I'm not unhappy with you and our relationship. I love you, more than anything."

"Not more than living in the country, though."

He's hurt.

"Chris, I just . . ." I hesitate, unsure what to say. I need all the facts in front of me. "Where do you see your permanent home being?" I ask. "Long term, like where do you see your children growing up?"

"Between London and New York."

"In apartments?"

"Yes, my apartments are bigger than most houses, Hayden."

"I know." I nod. "It's true; they are. And will you always work for Miles Media?"

"Of course I will; it's my family's business. I'll never leave the company."

"Oh." I sip my wine, unsure what to even say to that.

His future is set in stone.

"In a perfect world, where do you see yourself living?" he asks.

My eyes search his, and I don't want to say it out loud, because once I say it I can't take it back.

"Please, just be honest, Haze," he says softly.

"On the land."

"Where?"

"I don't know." I shrug. "Not necessarily my parents' farm, but something similar. I eventually want my own animal husbandry business. It's what I do, what I love, and I'm missing it so much."

I see the hurt flash through his eyes.

"Would you . . . ever live on a farm?" I tentatively ask. "Can you see yourself living in the country?"

"No."

"Would you ever try it?"

"No point. I already know that I would hate it."

We stare at each other as a realization begins to set in.

"What do you hate about the city?" he asks.

"Everything."

"Specifics."

"The pollution, the people, the chaos, the paparazzi. It's just so loud and on steroids. I don't feel myself here." I take his hand in mine. "And I desperately want to because I love you, but I already know that to be here, I have to give up who I am."

His haunted eyes hold mine.

"And maybe I should do that . . ." I shrug. "I just . . ."

"No." He cuts me off. "I don't want you to do that." He cups my face in his hand. "You're perfect the way you are. Don't change a thing."

My eyes well, and a tear escapes and rolls down my face. He wipes it away with his thumb.

"What does this mean for us, Chris?" I whisper.

His nostrils flare. "It means I have to let you go."

The lump in my throat hurts as I try to hold in my tears.

He kisses me softly. "I can't ask you to be someone you're not, Hayden. Because I know for certain that I can't change who I am."

Oh no.

"But I love you," I whisper.

His eyes well with tears. "And I will always love you."

He takes me into his arms and holds me tight, and the dam breaks, and I cry against his shoulder.

"But how . . . can two people be so in love and it not work out?" I sob.

"Because fairy tales aren't real."

I cry harder. "Don't say that."

"Deep down I always knew it."

I pull out of his arms. "I don't believe that." I begin to get panicked. He really is saying goodbye. "No. I'll stay. We'll work it out. We can do this," I splutter. "It will be okay."

"No, Hayden. We won't." He stands. "Get your things. I'm taking you to the airport. You will not be unhappy for one more minute because of me. I made a promise to your father that I would look after you, and this is me doing that."

"I don't want to go," I whisper.

"But you don't want to stay."

I sob out loud, and he walks from the room and two minutes later returns with my suitcase. "Come on."

I screw up my face in tears. "But we love each other."

"This is one of those cases where love isn't enough."

My heart constricts. *Oh no.*

"Get your things." He wheels my suitcase to the door and walks out into the foyer. I walk around the apartment, sobbing, as I find my handbag and everything I want to take.

The worst part about it is, deep down I know that he's right.

I have to leave, and he has to stay.

I take one last look around the beautiful apartment. It's always felt so cold and unwelcoming to me . . . and now I know why.

It's not my home.

I screw up my face and cry harder. I walk out the front door and get into the elevator.

Christopher is solemn and staring straight ahead. We ride down to the ground floor to the soft sounds of my sobs. He wheels my suitcase to the car and puts it into the trunk and gets in behind the wheel.

I cry all the way to the airport while he holds my hand in his lap, occasionally lifting it to kiss my fingertips.

We get to the airport, but instead of parking the car, he pulls into the drop-off parking bay. "You're not coming in?" I whisper.

His eyes well with tears. ". . . I can't."

"Baby . . ." I sob.

"Don't." He gets out of the car in a rush, and I know he needs this over with. He pops the trunk and gets my suitcase out.

We stare at each other. An ocean of heartbreak and sadness swims between us.

"I'll call you when I get there?" I whisper.

"Don't."

I frown.

"This needs to be a clean break."

Oh.

He takes me into his arms, and we stand on the street hugging, both in tears.

"I'll always love you," he whispers.

"I love you." I cling to him tight.

This can't be the end.

As if unable to stand it, he pulls out of my arms in a rush and gets into the car and, without looking back, pulls out into the traffic.

I stand on the sidewalk and through blurred vision watch the sports car disappear down the road. "Goodbye, my love."

Chapter 29

Time goes by so quickly . . . except when your heart is bleeding out.

Then every moment, every breath, every painful hour feels like an eternity.

It's been three weeks since Christopher dropped me at the airport.

Three weeks since my world fell apart.

And I would love to tell you that I'm healed and on my way back to being right, but I can't.

For there is no more sunshine.

My body lives here in the US; my heart lives in London . . . with him.

I think about him all the time, to the point that it's unhealthy.

I worry if he's taking care of himself, if he's eaten, and if he's working too hard . . . which I already know he is.

And I know I have to snap myself out of this, but how do you turn off your heart?

Is there a switch? Tell me, because I need to find it.

I drive the tractor as I look out over the green paddocks. It's dawn. The sun is peeping over the horizon as it rises for a new day.

And even though I know I belong here, every day is black to me. Darkness that comes from within.

The worst part about it is that the whole experience has changed me. I'm not even happy here at home on the farm now.

It's like everything I thought I wanted has shifted off center. All that I thought I was is wrong.

Nothing is making sense.

And I know I don't want to build a life in London . . . but I can't stand the thought of being here either. Maybe I should go somewhere new, start fresh, but where would I go?

Anywhere without him is a tragedy.

I know that there is no way around this. It is what it is.

He's a city boy; I'm a country girl.

The reason why we can't be together still stands. Nothing has changed.

My heart is still firmly broken.

CHRISTOPHER

The scalding-hot water runs over my head. If I stand under here long enough, the water will eventually run clean.

I need to wash this heartbreak off.

My hand is on the tiles as I lean against the wall, and I've hit an all-time low.

It's 3:00 a.m., and a new darkness has rolled in.

Regret.

And with it has come a deeper level of understanding of who I am.

Who I'm not.

I rest my forehead up against the tiles. My mind wanders to my sweet Hayden.

Where is she now?

Eventually I drag myself out of the shower and wrap a towel around my waist. I make my way downstairs and go through my Spotify list until I get to the song I need to hear.

I've had it on repeat lately. For just a moment . . . it makes me feel better, as if it brings me closer to the memory of being happy.

Closer to her.

It begins to play, and I drop to the couch to listen. This is Hayden's anthem. It was 100 percent written about her.

And to the haunting words of "Halo," by Beyoncé . . . I wallow in self-pity.

"So . . . what I'm saying here"—I point to the whiteboard—"is that the projection is way off."

Ten sets of eyes watch from around the board table.

My phone vibrates on the table, and I glance at the name. *Is it her?*

Tristan.

I ignore it.

I keep presenting. "So over on this spreadsheet—" I hold the remote to the screen and flick through to where I need to be.

My phone vibrates on the table, and once again, I glance at the name. *Is this her?*

Elliot.

Fuck off. Why are they all calling me this morning? I'm busy here.

I keep talking, and five minutes later my phone vibrates again.

Jameson.

Huh?

For fuck's sake, leave me alone, fuckers. I'm in the middle of something very important.

"If you go to recent years' trends—" I point to a graph, and there's a knock at the door.

"Come in."

Elouise comes in. "Christopher, Jameson is on line two. He said it's urgent."

I frown.

"He said to take it in your office."

"Hmm." I look around at the table. "My apologies. I have to take this. Let's have a ten-minute tea break."

"Sure," they all reply.

I walk out and storm down the hall. Fucking hell . . . I do not have time for this shit.

"Yes," I answer.

"Page four, *Ferrara News*," Jameson's voice growls.

"What?"

I open up the newspaper on my computer and drop into my seat.

A half-page photograph comes up.

Christopher Miles Breaks Miss Ordinary's Heart for a Supermodel.

There's a huge photo of Hayden in the park. I'm sitting beside her on the park bench. She's crying, and I look like I'm angry. Then beside it is a photo of me and Amira Conrad, a model who is dating one of my friends. I ran into her at the bar in a restaurant at lunch the other day. The photo is of me with my arm around her, snapped at precisely the moment I kissed her hello. I'm smiling at her, and she's smiling back at me. We look totally in love.

My blood boils.

"Are you fucking kidding me?" I whisper angrily.

"Any news from Hayden?" Jameson asks.

"Nope."

"This really doesn't look good."

"You think?" I explode. "Goodbye." I hang up and scroll through my phone. My finger hovers over Hayden's name . . . she might not even see the paper . . . and then . . . my heart sinks.

It doesn't matter even if she does.

We're over.

She doesn't want me . . . or my life.

One day I *will* have to move on, and so will she. My heart twists at the thought of some country bumpkin being able to give her the life that I couldn't . . . as much as I wish I could have.

I imagine her living on a large farm with heaps of wild and carefree kids and being happy, and I smile sadly. I want that for her. I want her to have everything she ever wanted. She deserves to be happy.

I put my phone back down.

My gaze goes to the window and London buzzing way down below. She's a million depressing miles away.

Buzz sounds my intercom.

"Yes."

"Are you coming back?" Elouise asks.

Shit . . . the meeting.

"On my way."

⋇

I sit at my desk and stare out the window. People are talking, coming and going, and things are happening, but my mind is a million miles away.

On her.

Always on her.

Six weeks is a long time. Too long.

It's not getting better; it's getting worse. There's a noose tightening around my neck that I can't shake. The only time I'm happy is when I'm talking to Eddie, but I haven't been able to reach him for a week now, and I'm getting worried. Why is his phone going straight to voice mail?

I glance at my watch. I might call the hostel to see when he's working next. I'll call Howard, the manager.

I google the number and dial as I begin to pace back and forth. "Hello, Barcelona Backpackers."

"Hello, can I speak to Howard, please?"

"Just a minute." I hear the line go through to an extension.

"Hello, Howard speaking."

"Howard," I reply, "it's Christo."

"Hey." He laughs. "How are you, man?"

"Good, good. How are you?"

"Same shit, different day. All fine here."

"Listen, sorry to bother you. I'm trying to get ahold of Eddie, but his phone isn't even ringing."

"Oh yeah . . . it got stolen."

"Oh." My heart sinks. I know how upset he'd be. "I wondered what happened. I've been calling and texting him, but no reply."

"No point texting," he replies casually.

"What do you mean?"

"Well . . . he can't read."

"What?" I frown.

"He can't read or write. You know that."

"That's ridiculous," I snap. "Of course he can."

"Christo . . . you know he's homeless, right?"

"What?" I whisper. "Are you serious?"

"Yeah," he replies casually. "No shit. He's an orphan."

I begin to hear my heartbeat in my ears.

"His parents are both . . . dead?" I gasp.

"His father took off before he was born, and his mother died in a car accident when he was eight, or something. No surviving grandparents or aunts or uncles. He was in the foster care system for a while but got put with assholes and ended up running away."

I drop to the chair at the desk, shocked to a horrified silence.

"But where does he sleep?" I whisper through a lump in my throat.

"In a deserted house around the corner from the hostel."

I stand. "Where is it?"

479

"It's almost directly behind the hostel. It's boarded up. You can't miss it."

I stay on the line, shocked to silence.

Dear god.

"Don't tell him I called, okay?" I ask.

"Yeah, okay."

"When is he working next?"

"Tomorrow night."

"Thanks." I hang up and stare at the wall in horror.

What the fuck?

Barcelona

The Uber pulls to the curb. "Just let me out here," I tell the driver.

I've never gotten on a plane so quickly. I don't know what I'm doing here, but I had to come.

I have to see him.

I walk around the corner and see the old deserted house.

I'm brimming with emotion; how can such a beautiful kid have such a horrible life and never tell me a word about it? I thought we were best friends.

I don't understand.

I see a flicker of movement, and I duck in to hide behind a bush. I watch as Eddie walks out of the house and up the street as if he doesn't have a care in the world. So brave and stoic.

Poor fucking kid.

I wait until he disappears around the corner, and I make my way up to the deserted house. It's dilapidated and barely standing. Two stories with a staircase running up the outside. The front doors and windows are boarded up, so I walk around the back and see an old broken door.

KEEP OUT
DANGEROUS CHEMICALS.

I tentatively push the door open, and it lets out a deep, loud creak. I peer in.

Darkness.

"Hello . . . ," I call.

Silence.

"Is anyone there?"

Silence.

I turn on the flashlight on my phone and push the door back and walk in. The floors are broken, and it's dark and musty. Holes are punched through the walls, and graffiti covers everything.

My stomach twists.

I shine the flashlight around. Where does he sleep?

I need to see.

I search all the rooms. It's worse than I thought.

Much worse.

My vision blurs, and I wipe my eyes so that I can see. I get to a room in the back, and I peer in, and my heart breaks.

A lone mattress is on the floor with a sleeping bag.

I walk over and look around. All the postcards I sent to him are carefully pinned to the wall like trophies. A laminated photo of Hayden strategically pinned in the center.

"Eddie," I whisper through tears. "My poor, poor Eddie."

I imagine him sleeping here in the musty dark.

All alone.

Nobody to care for him and make him feel safe.

I screw up my face. The reality of his situation is so raw and real.

Devastatingly sad.

I unpin the photo of Hayden; she's smiling and looks so happy and carefree; my heart constricts, and I sob out loud.

He misses her too.

"Who's there?" Eddie's voice barks.

I try to pull myself together and wipe my eyes. "It's me," I call.

"Who?"

"Christo."

He pushes open the door, and his face falls, and I can't help it: my face screws up in tears.

"Don't . . . ," he spits. "What are you doing here?"

"I came back for you."

He frowns.

"And I promise you on my life," I whisper through tears, "you'll never be alone again."

Chapter 30

His eyes search mine.

"Get your things," I tell him as I regain some composure.

"Why?"

"You're coming with me."

"To where?"

"London."

"What do you mean?" He frowns.

"I came to take you home."

"I am home."

"This is not your fucking home," I spit. "You belong with me . . . at least until you're older."

"Where's Hazen?"

My nostrils flare, and the lump in my throat hurts as I admit my failure. "We broke up." I hang my head in shame.

"Oh . . ." He steps forward and puts his hand on my shoulder. "It's okay," he says softly. He pats my shoulder. "It will work out."

It just makes me more unstable. How is he comforting me at a time like this?

Because he's Eddie . . .

"Come on, buddy, let's get the hell out of here," I blurt out in a rush.

He stares at me, completely confused.

"I'm asking you to come and live with me. Do you want to do that? I'll look after you . . . keep you safe."

He opens his mouth to say something and then shuts it as if stopping himself.

"Say it," I tell him.

"What would someone like you want me to live with them for?"

His silhouette blurs. "Because . . . I missed you."

His eyes widen. "You did?"

"Yes, fucker, I do," I snap. "You better have missed me."

He bites his bottom lip to hide his smile.

"Come on, get your things."

"Where are we going?"

"I don't know. We'll work it out." I throw up my hands in defeat. "Do you want these postcards?" I unpin one.

He stares at me, and I see the fear in his eyes. How many times has he been let down in his life?

"You can come back to Barcelona anytime you want . . . I promise. I'll bring you myself."

He stands still and looks around the room. "Could I bring my sleeping bag?"

The lump in my throat nearly closes it over, and I nod.

I have no words.

"Do you want these postcards?" I ask him.

"Yes, please."

I get to work in unpinning them.

"Can I bring my gas cooker?" he asks timidly.

With my back to him, I screw up my face. The tears won't stop. "Yep."

"And my flashlight?"

"Uh-huh . . . bring whatever you want."

He's killing me.

I wait as he meticulously packs up his life. Things that I would think are junk he treats like priceless treasures. I wait patiently, and fuck . . .

Plot twist of all plot twists. How is this happening?

With a few plastic bags, a little gas camping cooker, and a sleeping bag rolled into a ball, we walk toward the doors, and Eddie stops and looks around.

I wait, unsure what to say to make this moment less dramatic, but there is nothing to say.

It is fucking dramatic.

My tears . . . also dramatic, but I couldn't stop them if I tried.

The last few weeks, my emotions have come to a head, and I feel completely overwhelmed and out of control.

Eddie looks up at me. "Why are you crying?" he asks.

"I got something in my eye." I shrug, embarrassed. "You ready?"

He nods, and we walk out front, and while I order an Uber, he sits down on the concrete with all his things to wait.

"I have to book a hotel," I mutter to myself as I quickly go through the booking website.

"Aren't you staying in the hostel?"

"You aren't staying at the frigging hostel," I gasp. "No way."

"But I have to work tonight."

"No." I keep scrolling through the website. "You're never going there again."

"Christo, I have to work tonight. I'm not letting them down."

"I said no."

"I'm fucking working," he spits.

I look up, annoyed by his tone. "That's the first and last time you swear at me, do you understand?"

He hangs his head, and we fall silent for a while.

What do I do here? I'm completely out of my depth. If I push him before he trusts me, he's going to take off.

Fuck's sake . . . damn this kid and his good work ethic. "Fine. We will stay at the hostel so you can work. But we are getting private rooms, and if they don't have any, we are staying in a hotel."

"Fine." He sits there in a huff for a while.

"I'm going to call the hostel to get us some rooms, okay?"

He shrugs, full of attitude.

I call the hostel, and luckily, they have two deluxe en suite rooms available. We make our way around there, and I pick up the keys. We walk up the stairs to the top floor.

"This is us," I tell him as I open the door to his room.

His eyes widen. "We're staying here?"

"Uh-huh."

He quietly stands beside me, looking at every last detail in awe. "That must be some fancy school you teach at."

"Oh . . . yeah." I wince. "About that. I'm not a teacher."

He cuts me off. "I know."

"What do you know?"

"You're a cleaner."

Unbelievable.

"My family owns a company that makes newspapers."

He frowns.

"I'm kind of . . ." I shrug. "Well off."

"What do you mean?"

"I don't have to worry about money."

He stares at me blankly, unable to comprehend the concept.

"You'll see." I smile. "You can sleep in this bedroom."

His eyes flick to me in question. "Where will you sleep?"

"In the room down the hall."

"Oh." He twists his fingers, and I can tell that he's completely overwhelmed.

"Do you have a passport?" I ask him.

He shakes his head.

"Do you have a birth certificate?"

"What's that?"

Fuck.

"That's okay. We'll work it out." I glance at my watch. "You should get ready for work. You start in an hour."

He nods.

I walk into his bedroom and turn the shower on. "This is your bathroom."

"Are you sure we're allowed to use it? We're not going to get into trouble, are we?"

I fucking love this kid.

I smile. "Yeah, buddy, I'm sure. I paid for the rooms. It's okay."

"Okay." He twists his fingers as he looks around, completely lost.

"There's a towel here." I pass him the towel. "You can have a shower before you go down to work if you want."

"All right."

"You just use the soaps and shampoo in the little bottles. I'll wait outside." I walk toward the door.

"Christo," he calls.

I turn back.

"You don't have to look after me. I'm okay. Just because we're friends, you don't have to take me with you. That's not how things work."

"I know." I sit on the bed, unsure what to say, and I tap the bed beside me. He slowly sits down. "I know you'd be completely fine here. You're very brave and strong on your own." I look around the room as I try to think of the right way to put this. "But I kind of feel like we belong together . . . you know?"

His eyes hold mine.

"And . . . who knows?" I shrug. "Maybe your mom organized for us to meet."

His eyes well with tears as he stares at me.

"And I don't actually know what the hell I'm doing with a kid . . . so be patient with me, okay?"

He stays silent.

I put my hand on his knee. "We'll work this shit out together . . . you and me."

He looks down at my hand on his knee and slowly puts his hand over mine.

The first time we've touched.

The moment is tender and emotional and a turning point in both of our lives.

The lump in my throat is back, and he wipes his eyes, embarrassed.

"Anyway." I stand. "You have to go and serve those fuckers at the bar while I work out how to get you out of the country."

"How come you're allowed to say *fuck* and I'm not?"

"Because I'm the parent and you're the kid."

His eyes search mine as my words echo between us . . .

I'm the parent and you're the kid.

My heart free-falls from my chest, and in this moment, I know that life will never be the same.

For either of us.

Chapter 31

HAYDEN

The cry of a crow sounds in the distance, a peaceful song that sings to my soul.

There's no mistaking that I belong in the country. My return has only cemented how much I love my lifestyle.

If only . . .

This rocking chair has become my best friend.

When things get too much, which is often, rocking keeps me sane. Just like a baby, it soothes me until I feel better. In slow motion, the gentle rays of gold disappear over the mountain as the sun sets.

Six weeks without him.

Without a kiss, a hug, a private joke . . . love.

And some days fly by while on others I feel like I can hardly breathe.

Barely clinging to life.

I dial the number, and I wait. The voice recording answers.

The mobile phone you have called is switched off.

"Where are you, Eddie?"

I'm getting worried. I haven't heard from him for a couple of weeks now. We take turns calling each other, and it's his turn . . . but he hasn't called, and now he's not answering.

It's so unlike him. I can almost set my clock to the minute by how reliable his calls are.

I hope he's okay.

He is. Stop overthinking it.

Darkness falls, and the warm breeze blows over me, whipping my hair about my face and bringing a million beautiful memories home. I smile at the thought of my beautiful Christopher. I don't regret for a single moment falling in love with him, because now I know how it feels to be in heaven, when just for a while . . . he was mine.

I lean back in my rocking chair and pull the knit blanket over my legs as I relax into the night.

If only . . .

Ten days later

The plane touches down in Barcelona, and I watch the tarmac speed by through the window. I haven't been able to reach Eddie, and I'm really beginning to worry. I know that surely there's a reasonable excuse for why he's not answering his phone, but I can't relax until I've checked on him.

And besides, I needed an excuse to get out of town. The farm is making me feel claustrophobic.

Honestly, I don't know where the fuck I'm supposed to be at the moment. Everywhere feels wrong, and I'm hoping distance will give me some clarity.

I haven't started working again yet. Every time I go to commit to a position, something holds me back, and it's ridiculous, because

I really need to get my shit together. I'm twenty-six, and I don't even have a job.

Ugh . . .

I'm trying to be kind to myself. Once I'm over this heartbreak, things will be different, I'm sure.

I go through the motions and get off the plane, collect my luggage, and catch an Uber to the hostel, and as the car pulls up to the curb, I look out through the window in wonder. A million beautiful memories come flooding in.

There it is . . .

The hostel where we met.

The driver gets out of the car, interrupting my thoughts, and I tentatively get out.

I wasn't expecting this place to bring back so much emotion.

"Here you go, miss." The driver puts my suitcase down on the sidewalk.

"Thank you."

"Have a good night."

"You too."

He gets in and drives off, and I stand and stare at the hostel building. I don't even know if I want to go in now. Is being here going to undo all the healing I've been going through? Too bad . . .

I need closure. *Just go in.*

I wheel my suitcase in and up to reception. It's just before 10:00 p.m., and I know reception closes soon. The desk is unattended. "Hello," I call.

I can hear music and laughter coming from the bar area, and I smile. Nothing has changed around here.

"Coming," a female voice calls from the back office.

I wait patiently, and she eventually comes into view. "Sorry, I was on the phone." She smiles. She's new; I haven't seen her before.

"That's okay. I have a booking in the name Hayden Whitmore."

491

"Sure." She types into her computer. "Okay, you're in a private room for a week?"

"Yes."

She goes about scanning the keys and whatnot, and I look around at the familiar surroundings. There's no denying that this place makes me feel better.

"Actually, can you extend that booking to two weeks if possible?" I ask.

"Let me look." She types again. "Yeah, that's fine." She passes my key over. "Have you stayed with us before?"

"Yes." I smile.

"Great. You're on the top floor, room two oh nine. Take the stairs at the back of the corridor. The elevator is broken."

That damn elevator has never worked since I first came here over a year ago.

"Thank you. Do you know if Eddie is working in the bar tonight?" I ask her.

"No idea, sorry," she replies. "I've been too swamped. I haven't even been out there."

"Okay, thanks."

I walk up the corridor and lug my bag up the two flights of stairs as I smile to myself. Can't complain about the service at backpackers' hostels, because there is none.

I trudge up the corridor, find my room, and open the door. There's a double bed and a bedside table and a sink with a mirror over the top of it. It's clean and neat. I wish there were en suite rooms left. Oh well. It will be fine. "This will do nicely." I put my bag down and wash my face and put my hair into a high ponytail.

I change into a cool summer dress and make my way downstairs to the bar.

The music is loud, and people are dancing. Party lights are strung over the courtyard, and the place is pumping.

"Hey, baby." Some guy smiles as he looks me up and down. "Where you going?"

"Hi." I fake a smile and keep walking as I look for Eddie. *Ugh . . . nowhere with you.* I push through the crowd, and then I see him. He's serving a big group of guys, and he glances up. His face lights up, and without missing a beat, he runs out from behind the bar and nearly knocks me off my feet as he grabs me. "Hazen." He hugs me so tight. "You came back."

I laugh. "Of course I came back. I've been so worried. Why aren't you answering your phone?" I ask him.

His face falls. "It got stolen."

"Oh . . . baby." I can see how disappointed he is. "That's okay. You'll get another one soon." He seems to be giant now. "Have you grown six inches?" I laugh.

"Little bit."

I hold him at arm's length as I look him up and down. "Thank god you're okay."

He smiles goofily down at me. He's taller than me now.

"Look how handsome you are." I smile proudly.

He puts his arm around me, keeping me close. "Are you staying here?"

"Yes. You go back to work, and I'll see you later."

"You're not leaving, are you? Sit at the bar, and I'll get you a drink," he says hopefully as he pulls me out a stool at the end of the bar.

"Okay." I smile as I sink into the seat.

Eddie runs back behind the bar, makes me a drink, and puts it down in front of me. "Thank you."

"I finish at one," he tells me.

"I'll be in bed long before one, bubba."

He smiles goofily at me.

"What?"

"You called me bubba."

I swoon at the cuteness of this boy. "Of course I called you bubba. You *are* a bubba."

He laughs and goes back to serving. I pick up my drink and take a sip. I glance up and lock eyes with Christopher. He's sitting at the other end of the bar.

What?

We stare at each other, and he gives me a slow, sexy smile.

My heart somersaults in my chest as if in slow motion. He gets up and walks over to me.

"Grumps." He smiles softly.

"Hi."

He leans down and hugs me, and I close my eyes against his big strong shoulder. His aftershave wafts around me.

I miss him.

"What are you doing here?" he asks.

"I couldn't reach Eddie. I was worried. What about you?"

"Same."

We stare at each other as this beautiful familiarity falls between us. I gesture to the stools. "Sit down and have a drink with me."

"Okay." He pulls out his stool, and we both sit down. Nerves dance in my stomach.

Is this truly happening? What are the chances of running into each other on the other side of the world?

"How have you been?" he asks.

"Okay," I lie. "And you?"

He shrugs. "Been better."

Oh . . .

My eyes search his, and I just want to hug him and blurt out that I love him and beg him to take me back.

"When did you get here?" I ask.

"A week ago."

I frown. I thought he was stupidly busy?

"I found out that Eddie is an orphan and lives on the streets," he says softly.

"What?" I frown.

"He's all alone, Grumps."

My face falls as I look over to Eddie smiling happily as he serves someone. "Where are his parents?"

"Never knew his father, and his mother died when he was eight. No surviving relatives. He was in the foster care system but was put with assholes and ran away when he was eleven."

"Are you serious?"

He nods sadly.

"My god, poor Eddie."

"He can't read or write," he says softly.

My eyes well with tears.

"I'm taking him home with me."

"What do you mean?" I frown. He's making decisions about his long-term future without consulting me?

Because we're over.

"He's going to come and live with me in London." He shrugs. "That's if I can get him out of the country."

I stare at him, my mind a clusterfuck of confusion.

"He doesn't have a passport or a birth certificate. I've got my friend Sebastian Garcia helping me. You know, the one you met?"

I stare at him, so thrown by what he's telling me I can't even make a coherent sentence. "No?"

"He was on the yacht in Greece with Julian Masters."

Oh . . . the good-looking one.

"The one with the dark hair?" I ask as I act dumb.

"That's him. He's a politician in London and of Spanish descent. He's helping me with the red tape."

"Christopher . . ." I pause as I try to collect my thoughts. "You can't take him out of Spain. It's his home."

"Is it?" he replies with an annoyed tone. "He slept on a stained mattress on the floor, all alone in a deserted house. No plumbing, no electricity. Nothing. He had my postcards pinned to the wall with a photograph of you in the center. We are literally *all* he has, Hayden, and I can't leave him here. I won't."

I look over to Eddie serving a group of men at the bar, and I'm overcome with emotion. The lump in my throat hurts as I try to swallow.

Poor Eddie.

"Even if it's just until he's eighteen or nineteen and old enough to get a rental on his own," he says softly. "I can get him schooled to read and write so he at least stands a chance."

I nod as I listen, remaining silent.

There are no words for this situation. I'm completely shell shocked.

Christopher's eyes hold mine. "What are you thinking?"

I sip my drink and shrug. "Have you really thought about what this means for your future? A child is a lot to take on, Christopher."

"I know." He pinches the bridge of his nose. "But what am I supposed to do, Grumps?"

"I don't know," I whisper.

We sit in silence for a while.

"What does he think about all this?" I ask.

He shrugs. "He seems excited to come with me. I mean . . . what are his other options? Be scared every day that some fucker is going to steal his phone while he sleeps on the floor?"

Fuck.

I can't imagine being all alone. How frightening it must be for him. Christopher's silhouette blurs, and I quickly wipe my tears out of my eyes.

Christopher stares straight ahead. He looks like he has the weight of the world on his shoulders . . . and now I know that he does.

"You're such a good man, Christopher."

His eyes hold mine, and the air crackles between us. He slowly reaches over and tucks a piece of my hair behind my ear. "It's so good to see you, Grumps."

I've never needed to hug someone so badly in my life.

And I can't.

My heart beats faster, and I'm in information overload. Everything is different, but nothing has changed. Our fucked-up situation is still the same and yet now even messier.

There's a child.

I stand abruptly. "I should get going."

"What, where to?" He seems surprised.

"Bed. I'm . . . exhausted."

"Are you staying here?" He frowns.

"Yes."

"Me too." He gives me a soft smile. "I'll see you tomorrow, then?"

"Okay, bye," I blurt out in a rush. I need to get away from him right now.

This is all just too fucking much.

I catch Eddie's eye and blow him a kiss and make my way up to my room. I burst through the door and begin to pace.

What now?

CHRISTOPHER

I lie on the sand in the darkness. The distant thrill of partying sounds in the distance. The beach is quiet and deserted. There are a million things running through my mind.

Seeing her tonight . . .

It's unnatural not to touch Hayden . . . to hold her in my arms and tell her how much I need her.

I never believed in love. I thought it was a fantasy that only lonely people talked themselves into needing. I didn't think that it was possible to care for someone as much as I do her. And I know that we can't be together, and I know that it will never work out between us, but seeing her in the flesh has opened a wound . . . my heart aches for what it can't have.

Another moment in her arms.

I get a vision of her at the bar earlier tonight, so detached, so unlike the warm and gentle Hayden I know.

Seven weeks have dragged so slowly, and yet seeing her tonight, it's like she never left.

Everything feels the same, perhaps even stronger.

I'm completely and utterly fucked.

I stare up at the moon. So many nights Hayden and I would lie on this beach and dream about the future. But looking back now, it was her doing all the dreaming while I listened. I already knew my fate . . . I just never let on at the time. If only I was honest with myself and her, then I could have saved us both a lot of heartache.

Hindsight is a wonderful thing.

If only . . .

HAYDEN

I walk into the cafeteria with a new sense of purpose. A good night's sleep has worked wonders. I was so rude last night when Christopher told me his plans with Eddie. I wasn't supportive at all, but in my defense, I was in total shock.

Christopher taking on Eddie is the last thing I would expect, but after thinking on it all night, I'm not surprised. Christopher has the biggest heart of anyone I know.

Of course he would take him on. He adores him. And he's right: he can't leave him here all alone.

I catch sight of Christopher sitting at the back table. He's on the phone, and he gives me a wave.

Right . . .

I drop my shoulders, determined to be a better person, and I make my way over and sit down beside him.

Christopher smiles as he listens to the person on the other end of his phone call. "Right." He listens. "And there is absolutely no way to expedite this?"

He frowns and then drags his hand down his face. "Fuck . . ."

Is something wrong? "What's going on?" I mouth.

He rolls his eyes. "Thank you, I appreciate it." He listens again. "So I'll just wait to hear from you, then?"

I sit quietly as I listen in.

"Okay, thanks." He hangs up and lets out a deep sigh.

"What's wrong?" I ask.

"There's good news and bad news."

"Good first."

"I can get Eddie out of the country if I sponsor him as an employee rather than as a homeless child."

"Okay, well, that's good." I smile. "What's the bad news?"

"It's going to take a couple of weeks to organize the paperwork."

"Why is that a problem?"

"I have to be back at work. There's no way around it. I have meeting after meeting booked, and I can't cancel again, but then I can't leave him here alone either. If something happens to him, I'll never forgive myself."

"Oh . . ." I think for a moment. "I could stay here with him."

Christopher frowns.

"Yeah, why not?" I shrug. "I don't have to be back for anything. I'll just stay here with him, and you and he can keep working, and then when the paperwork is ready, you can come back and collect him."

"You'd do that for me?"

"Of course I'd do that for you. I'd do anything for you, Christopher."

"Really?"

"You're my best friend." I smile.

His face falls. "You've friend zoned me?"

"Babe . . ." I shrug as I put my hand over his on the table. "We started out as friends, and we will always be friends."

"But what about . . ."

"Our situation hasn't changed, and no matter how much we care for each other . . ." My voice trails off, not wanting to say the words out loud.

"You're right," he agrees. "We will never work. I do know that."

My heart drops. I was hoping he would tell me that there's a solution to our problem.

Nothing has changed.

"So when will you leave?" I ask to change the subject.

"Tomorrow."

"Oh."

His eyes hold mine.

"So soon?"

"Yes."

I nod, deflated. "Okay."

"I'll get you a nice apartment to stay in."

"No, we're okay here. Eddie can still work then, and it's not so different for him."

"Are you sure?"

"Yeah, of course." I smile. "You go back to London and do what you have to do. We'll be fine."

I want to blurt out that I don't care about my life plans anymore. As long as he is in them, then I can make do. But I know I can't. I made my bed, and now I need to lie in it.

"I'll be back as soon as I can for him."

For him.

"Okay." I force a smile. "He's a lucky boy to have you take him on."

"I'm the lucky one."

We stare at each other and . . .

Oh . . .

My heart aches for this beautiful man.

Eddie saunters into the restaurant like a rock star, and Christopher smiles and waves him over. "Eddie, my man."

"Hello, Hazen." He smiles as he sits down beside me.

"Good morning, bubba." I smile as I wipe the hair back from his forehead. He smiles down at me, and my heart melts. I do love this boy.

"Good news," Christopher tells him. "They are organizing the paperwork for you to come and stay with me."

Eddie's eyes widen in excitement. "They are?"

"They are." Christopher smiles. "But . . . it's going to take a little while."

"How long?"

"A few weeks, and I have work to do, so I'm going to go back to London."

Eddie's face falls.

"But Hazen is staying with you until I get back."

Eddie's eyes flick to me for confirmation.

"Is that okay?" I smile.

He bites his bottom lip to hide his smile. "And then are you coming to London with us?" he asks hopefully.

"Hazen doesn't live in London," Christopher answers for me. "She lives in the country."

"Oh." Eddie frowns as he contemplates the answer.

"You and I will have fun while Christopher is gone." I smile to try to reassure him.

He nods, and I can tell he's nervous that Christopher isn't coming back.

"He's coming back for you, Eddie, I promise."

Eddie's eyes search mine, and then he looks over to Christopher.

"Of course I'm coming back for you. I told you, we belong together," Christopher tells him.

Ouch . . .

I get a lump in my throat, and I push my chair out in a rush before I make a fool of myself. "I have things to do today. I'll see you both later?" I stand.

"Okay." Eddie smiles happily. "Bye."

"Bye." I leave the restaurant and walk out of the hostel into the street. I really don't have anything to do, but I do know that I can't stay anywhere in the vicinity of Christopher Miles. Onward and upward.

I need to stay strong.

Ж

I walk into the communal bathroom just at 11:00 p.m. There are a few showers going, but thankfully it's reasonably empty.

I left the hostel bar over an hour ago.

It's hard to be around him, especially when he won't even look at me. I'm suffering the slowest, most painful kind of fate.

I put my things down on the sink and take a long hard look in the mirror. An unrecognizable sad face stares back at me.

I've lost him.

I exhale heavily and walk into the cubicle and turn on the tap. I hang my towel over the hook and undress. I step in and put my head back under the hot water. I'm going to wash my hair to try to make myself feel better.

I step out of the water to grab my toiletries bag, only it's not on the shelf.

"What the fuck?" I brought it in. I know I did.

Damn it, I left it on the sink out there. I wrap my towel around me and open the cubicle door and come face to face with Christopher. He's naked, with a white towel around his waist. He's suntanned and rippled with muscle. His broad chest weakens me at the knees.

Before I can stop myself, I make an audible gasp. "What are you doing?" I stammer.

"Showering." His eyes drop down my body, and when they rise back to my eyes, they are blazing with desire.

You could cut the air with a knife.

Then he is on me. He slams me up against the wall and grabs a handful of my hair, dragging my head back so that my eyes meet his. "You need to fuck me."

The air crackles between us.

"I know."

His lips take mine, and I screw up my face against his. The kiss is wild, crazy, and filled with pent-up emotion.

Mostly hate for what we've put each other through . . .

He pushes me into the cubicle, slams the door shut, and then pins me to the wall.

We kiss like our lives depend on it. Emotional overload, and our teeth clash as we lose control.

He tears his towel off, and his large erection springs free. It hangs heavily between his legs, and I whimper as I feel it up against me.

Yessss!

He lifts me, spreads my legs open, and then, holding himself at the base, slides home in one sharp movement.

"Fuck yeah . . . ," he whispers.

We stare at each other as my body stretches to accommodate him.

Oh . . . I've missed him so.

He pulls out slowly and slides in deep. We do this a few times, and then he loses control and fucks me, hard and fast.

Angry.

The sound of our wet skin slapping echoes in the bathroom, and I see stars.

He's all-consuming as he takes me over, his teeth biting my neck, his hands cupping my ass, his cock stretching me wide open with deep, thick pumps.

But it's my heart that's in danger . . . it's free-falling from my chest, running down the drain with the water.

He's fucking me like he doesn't know me, as if we're strangers.

Maybe we are.

He holds himself deep, and I feel the telling jerk as he comes deep inside my body, and I screw up my face in tears. He never comes before me . . . never once has he done that.

He honestly doesn't care anymore.

He looks down at me, seeing my tears. His haunted eyes search mine.

"I can't do this," he whispers.

He pulls out and rushes from the cubicle. I hear his shower turn on, and I sob silently.

Alone.

He's washing me off him . . . for the last time.

Chapter 32

We stand in front of the hostel as we wait for the Uber. Eddie is chatting away happily, while Christopher and I are as awkward as fuck.

He won't even look at me, and all I can do is stare at his beautiful face, hoping to catch a glimpse of emotion.

Any emotion will do.

Last night's momentary brain snap has reopened the cut, and I'm bleeding out, in need of an urgent transfusion.

The car pulls up, and Christopher pulls Eddie into a hug. "Look after Hazen," he tells him. "I'll be back for you in a few weeks, and then we can start our new life in London."

Eddie smiles proudly up at his protector. "Okay."

Christopher's eyes find mine, and a wave of sadness hits me like a freight train. He hugs me and holds me close, cheek to cheek.

Don't go . . .

We cling to each other, both not wanting to say goodbye but knowing that we have to.

He pulls out of my arms and steps back. "I have to go."

I force a smile. "Safe travels."

"Call me if you need anything," he says.

I need you.

"Okay."

He messes up Eddie's hair. "See you soon, kiddo."

He gets into the Uber with a small wave, and the car pulls out into the traffic.

Eddie and I watch it disappear into the distance. My heart is dripping into a crying puddle on the floor.

Eddie turns to me, totally unfazed. "Want to go to the beach?"

I smile at his perfect innocence. "Sure."

CHRISTOPHER

I sit at my desk and stare into space.

I've never felt so low.

Not only have I lost the woman I love . . . I used her for sex.

And she knew it.

I had to. I couldn't help it. I had to dissociate so that I could go through with it.

In that moment I needed her body, and I couldn't bear needing her.

It was better if I pretended that we weren't breaking each other's hearts in the shower that night.

It was better that we pretended we didn't know each other.

So why does it feel so bad?

Like my whole world is coming to an end.

I regret losing her. I regret just fucking her more.

I only make love to Hayden Whitmore, nothing more and nothing less.

Why we went there, I don't know.

Maybe I'm broken now? Maybe casual sex is ruined forever?

I keep seeing the way she looked up at me, the heartbreak behind her eyes.

She knew. She knew that in that moment, she could have been anyone.

I only did it to try to protect my broken heart.

Didn't work . . .

I can't leave it like this. I have to apologize for being so cold.

The guilt is killing me.

I dial her number, and I close my eyes as it rings.

"Hello . . . ," she answers.

I get a lump in my throat, and I stay on the line, shocked that the sound of her voice can affect me so much. "Hi, Hayden," I eventually push out.

She stays silent, waiting for me to say something.

"Hayz." I try to articulate what I want to say. "I rang to apologize."

"For what?"

"My behavior in the shower that night."

Silence . . .

"I just . . ." My vision blurs with tears. "I had to block you out."

"Why?"

"Because I'm angry at you for breaking my heart."

"Chris . . . ," she says softly.

"And I feel terrible, and I can't forgive myself for it, and I know that's not how we are. You didn't deserve it."

"It's okay," she whispers, and I can tell that she's crying.

"I just . . ." I screw up my face. "I just miss you . . ."

"I know, baby. Me too."

This isn't helping anything. "I have to go," I blurt out.

"Christopher—"

"Goodbye." I cut her off before hanging up the phone.

I put my head into my hands. *Devastation* doesn't come close.

HAYDEN

I sit at breakfast and sip my coffee as Eddie tells me in great detail all about his shift behind the bar last night. "And then this other guy threw ice, and it started another fight." He continues on with the huge elaborate story.

I smile as I listen. I never realized how much of a chatterbox he is, or perhaps it's just that I'm only now noticing it because we are spending so much time together.

It's been two weeks since Christopher left, and it's been nice having one-on-one precious time with Eddie.

I glance at my watch. Christopher will call him soon. He does every morning, and at the end of their conversation, he will ask to speak to me.

And the five-minute conversation I have with him will make my entire day.

Our chats about nothing mean everything.

Like clockwork, my phone rings, and the name *Christopher* lights up the screen. I pass it to Eddie, and he smiles broadly and answers it. "Hello, Christo."

I watch as they speak, and Eddie talks, all animated, with a huge goofy grin. Christopher's calls make his day too.

I sit patiently and listen to them talk about the last twenty-four hours and what they did.

My turn.

Christopher chats away, and Eddie smiles as he listens.

My turn.

It's all I can do not to snatch the phone off him.

"Today?" Eddie says. "We're going to the fruit market, and then Hazen wants to buy a dress, so I guess I'll have to take her." He rolls his eyes as if it's a hassle.

I smile. The truth is he loves doing anything that's normal. Whatever we do together is fun for him.

Eddie holds the phone down. "Christopher says no white dresses."

I laugh. "Tell him about our reading," I mouth.

"Oh yeah." Eddie smiles excitedly. "Hayden and I started reading lessons. She's teaching me."

I hear Christopher's voice elevate louder. He likes the sound of that.

"And we bought some pencils, and we've been drawing in at the beach," he says proudly.

I smile as I listen in.

"And Hayden bought me some little-kid books." He rolls his eyes. "About baby animals and cars and stuff."

"Which you have already memorized," I tell him. "We have to go back to the beginning, remember?"

They chat and chat, and damn it, *my turn.*

Finally, Eddie holds the phone out to me. "He wants to speak to you."

My heart somersaults in my chest. "Hello."

"Hi, Grumps." His voice is deep and sexy. It instantly makes me feel warm and fuzzy. "How are you?"

Good now.

"I'm good, and you?"

"I'm okay."

We stay on the line as if we have a million things to say . . . but are unable to say them.

"How was your day?" I ask.

"Busy. I'm trying to get as much done as I can so that I can clear my schedule when he arrives."

"That's a good idea."

"I spoke to the embassy today. Looks like it will be another two weeks."

"Oh."

"Is that okay?" he asks.

"Can you fly over for a weekend to see us . . . *him*," I correct myself.

Shit.

"I can't, babe. I have to work."

Babe.

"Of course." I stay on the line, trying to think of something intelligent to say. "Have you been going out?" I ask nervously.

"I haven't been out since you left."

"You haven't?" I whisper.

"Out has nothing I want."

I smile. We stay on the line some more. There's a magic swirling between us when we speak now.

Deeper than sex, more special than love. An understanding that even we don't understand.

"I can't tell you how much I appreciate you doing this for me, Grumps," he says softly. "Maybe Eddie and I could come and visit you at the farm someday?"

"I'd like that."

My heart constricts . . . I want more than a visit.

"I should let you go," I reply.

"No, don't go," he splutters before catching himself. "I mean . . . sure, okay."

"You could call me tonight if you want?" I shrug.

"Really?"

"Uh-huh. I mean, Eddie is working . . . but . . . if you wanted to talk or . . . anything."

"I'll call you tonight."

I smile hopefully. "Goodbye."

"Bye."

We stay on the line, both waiting, and there're three words missing from our goodbye.

Three words I desperately want to hear.

"Speak tonight," he eventually says.

"Bye." I hang up, and Eddie rolls his eyes.

"What?"

"Why do you pull that face whenever you talk to him?" he asks.

"What face?"

"That gooey and gushy face."

"I do not," I scoff.

"Do so."

"Eat your breakfast." I point to his food. "We have coloring in to do."

My phone buzzes on the side table.

Christopher

I swear I'm like a groupie now. Even seeing his name light up on my phone sends me into overdrive. "Hi," I answer.

"Hi . . ." His voice is familiar and sexy and sends tingles up my spine. "How was my girl's day?"

His girl.

The smile nearly splits my face in two. "It was good. Better now."

Something's changed, and I can't tell you exactly what that is because I don't want to jinx it. I only know that our late-night calls have become softer, more intimate.

We don't talk about anything, and yet we talk about everything. Never once have we spoken about our relationship or where we stand, but the point is that we talk.

Every day.

He calls Eddie in the morning and talks to me briefly, but then he calls me late at night, and we talk for hours.

I miss us.

And I want to try again. I have so many regrets about how we ended last time. I should have stayed. I should have tried harder. I feel like the demise of our relationship was my fault, but I don't know how to tackle the subject. I keep hoping that he's going to bring it up, but he doesn't. The fact that we love each other has never been the issue.

However, our demographic situation is still the same. He loves the city life; I love the country. I don't know how to get around this. It's a huge issue. So I'm not sure if it's going to work.

Or if he even wants to try.

But his devotion to Eddie has set in stone what I already knew.

He's the one.

Christopher Miles is a very special person, and I don't know any man, let alone a playboy billionaire, who would put their hand up to adopt a homeless kid off the street. This is going to change his whole life, and he doesn't care. He's so selfless.

Caring and brave.

The thing is, I can see our future so clearly . . . the three of us.

It's perfect.

I just have to figure out how to get there.

"I've been thinking about what school Eddie will go to," he says.

"I'm not sure school is such a great option," I reply.

"What do you mean?"

"Kids are mean, Chris. He can't read or write. They will pick on him, and I feel like sending him to a snooty school is setting him up for failure."

"But he has to learn, Grumps. He can't not go to school."

"I'm not saying never. I mean at first. I think he should be homeschooled for a while."

"But how will he make friends?"

"He doesn't need friends; he needs a family. Friends will come later on, but at this early stage he needs to be protected. He's been through enough."

"Hmm, maybe . . ." He thinks.

"I could . . ." I pause, dreading his reaction. "I could come and help for a while."

"Meaning what?"

"I could stay and help you with Eddie."

"I don't want you to move here for Eddie, Hayden. If you move here, it has to be for me."

I close my eyes. My heart hammers in my chest.

Fuck.

Just say it . . .

"Christopher . . . I regret not trying harder," I whisper. "You were right. I should have stayed and worked through it with you. I feel like a massive failure."

He stays silent.

"I feel like I've ruined everything, and I don't know how to fix it."

"No, babe," he says softly. "It was my fault. I pushed you too hard."

515

"You didn't. You did everything right."

"What are you saying?" he asks.

"I'm saying I want another chance." My heart hammers in my chest, nervous about his reaction. "I'm saying that I'll . . ." I shrug. "I'll work harder on settling in, and the apartment will be great. I'll get used to it."

"I don't want you to have to get used to it."

"I *can't* get used to being without you," I whisper.

"Haze . . . ," he says softly. "Do you have any idea how much I love you?"

I screw up my face in tears. "I'm so sorry."

"Sweetheart, it's me that's sorry."

"So . . . I can come back?" I whisper hopefully.

"Of course you can come back. I love you; you know that."

I sob out loud as relief overwhelms me. "I love you."

"Now we just have to get this visa through so that we can be together."

I laugh through tears. "The three of us."

"Yeah." He smiles. "The three of us."

Four painfully long weeks later

The plane touches down on the tarmac, and Eddie excitedly smiles out the window. I can hardly contain my excitement.

I get to see him.

Everything feels different between Christopher and me now. Like we've been at war and in the trenches together and are now coming out the other side. I feel closer to him than I ever have, and that's saying something because we've always been close.

516

We decided that he would wait in London and I would bring Eddie home. There was no point in him flying all the way over here just to ride home in a plane together. He's been working super hard so that he's able to have some time off to settle Eddie in.

The plane stops on the tarmac, and we wait as everyone slowly gets off. It's early afternoon, and we make our way into the airport. Eddie is nearly jumping out of his skin, he's so excited.

Christopher is waiting by the door, and he laughs out loud when he sees Eddie and rushes him into a hug. I stand and wait patiently.

My turn.

He turns to me and gives me a slow, sexy smile, and my stomach flips. I know that look.

"Hi, Grumps."

"Hi."

He takes me into his arms and kisses me softly as he holds my face in his hands. "Come on, let's get you home."

Home.

He leads us out of the airport and into the parking lot. "How was the flight?" he asks Eddie.

"It was so great. You should see it from up there," he gasps.

Christopher laughs as he listens. Eddie's excitement is infectious.

"Where's Hans?" I ask as I look around.

"I drove."

"You did?"

"Uh-huh." He holds up the key, and the lights flash on a black SUV as it unlocks.

"Whose car is this?" I frown as I look it over.

"I thought it was time I bought a sensible car, now that Eddie is here."

Eddie's eyes widen, and his face nearly splits in two with excitement.

"Oh." I smile. "I'm impressed."

"In the back seat, kiddo," Christopher tells him. Eddie jumps in, and I get into the front, and we pull out into the traffic.

"You should see how fast the plane went while it was taking off," Eddie gasps from the back seat.

Christopher smiles. His eyes flick up to the rearview mirror to watch his excited face. "Yeah?"

"And we got food." He continues to talk at a million miles per minute.

"What did you get?" Christopher asks.

"Chicken something and then dessert. What was the dessert called, Hazen?"

"Chocolate brownie."

"Yeah, that, and it was so good I had Hazen's, too, because she was already full. And I had lemonade, and then the lady gave out hot towels, and I didn't know what you did with it, but you wash your face, in case you didn't know."

Christopher chuckles as he listens.

Eddie keeps chatting away and telling Christopher about every little detail about the flight, and I smile as I stare out the window.

This is a happy day.

※

An hour later we are still driving, and I look around, confused. "Where are we?"

"This is the back way. There's heaps of traffic through the city tonight."

"Oh, okay." I smile as I imagine Eddie's face when he sees Christopher's swanky apartment. I can't imagine how foreign this must all feel to him. Not that you would ever know it. He's so excited that he hasn't shut up.

We pull off the highway and drive up a country road. "This is a *real* back way." I frown as I look around.

"I'm just going to call in and pick something up from a friend. He lives out here."

"What are you picking up?"

"He has sons and has some things for Eddie. I haven't had time to call in and get them. I'll be quick."

"Oh, okay."

Weird.

We pull into a driveway, and a sign is hanging on a pole beside the gate.

BUMFUCK, NOWHERE

Huh?

I glance over to Christopher in question, and he smiles over at me with a sexy wink.

"Your friend called his property Bumfuck, Nowhere?" I frown.

"Uh-huh."

My eyebrows rise by themselves. "Now . . . I've seen it all."

Christopher chuckles, and we continue up the drive. The sun is just setting over the mountains, and all I can see is rolling green hills for miles. "Wow, it's beautiful out here."

"It is, isn't it?" Christopher says casually as he focuses on the road.

We drive and drive and drive. This is the longest driveway road of all time. "How big is his property?" I ask. "Must be huge."

Christopher shrugs. "I don't know, a couple of hundred acres, probably."

"Hmm."

We drive up a hill, and there's a huge big beautiful row of trees that leads to an old house. There are a few cars parked, and a man is sitting on the front steps.

Christopher waves out the window and gives a toot of his horn, and the man waves back.

Eddie and I peer in as our car pulls in around the huge circular driveway.

"You guys coming in?" Christopher asks.

"Um . . ." My eyes meet Eddie's. "Okay."

We tentatively get out, and the man walks down the front steps. "Hi, Hayden," he calls.

I frown. Do I know him? As he walks toward us, I see that it's Elliot, Christopher's brother. "Oh, hello." I smile. That's right: he lives in a country house. "How are you?"

He kisses my cheek. "It's so good to see you."

Christopher introduces Eddie. "This is Eduardo. This is my brother Elliot," he tells Eddie.

"Hey, buddy." Elliot shakes Eddie's hand.

"Your farm is beautiful," I gush.

"It is, isn't it." Elliot smiles. He leans up onto his toes as if excited. "Eddie, I want to show you something in the stables."

Eddie's eyes flick to me in question, and Christopher rubs his back reassuringly. "It's okay. Go with Elliot."

Elliot walks off, and Eddie tentatively follows. I watch as they walk off.

"I have something that I want to show you, Grumps." Christopher takes my hand and leads me up the stairs of the house. It's old and weathered and has an otherworldly feel.

"God, this house is beautiful." I smile.

Christopher opens the door, and my mouth falls open. The room is full of flowers, and lit candles are everywhere. My eyes flick to Christopher in question.

His big sexy eyes hold mine, and he takes my hands in his. "I realized something, Grumps."

"What's that?" I whisper as my heartbeat sounds in my ears.

"It doesn't matter where I live, because *you* are my home. As long as I'm with you, I'll be happy."

Oh . . .

He kisses me softly, his lips lingering over mine.

"I bought this farm for you."

"What?" My eyes widen as I look around. "You did?"

He drops to his knee and pulls out a ring box and flips it open. "Hayden Whitmore, you have taught me how to love somebody with all of my heart. I thought to be happy that I needed to be a diamond, but you showed me that it's okay to be coal, and you loved me just as I was. You didn't need me to be anything else. I was enough. I need to grow old with you, to love and protect you for all of my life. Will you marry me?"

My heart swells. *Is this happening?*

"I'll commute to work in London, and I know it's not your family farm, but—"

"Yes." I cut him off as I sink to my knees on the floor beside him. "Yes. Yes, yes." I laugh. "I'll marry you." I kiss him. Our kiss is tender and intimate, our lips lingering over each other's.

Perfect.

He slides the diamond ring onto my finger. It's a solitaire diamond set in gold.

Traditional and perfect.

"But you don't want to live on a farm," I whisper.

"I can't live without you. Bumfuck, Nowhere, is our compromise."

I giggle as we kiss. "We are not calling our farm Bumfuck, Nowhere, Christopher."

"Why not?" He kisses me again. "Hopefully there's going to be a lot of bumfucking going on here."

I burst out laughing. "You idiot."

Christopher's lips drop to my neck, and he walks me backward toward the couch. "We have approximately eight minutes before they get back."

I giggle and then look around. "Where has Elliot taken Eddie, anyway?" I ask.

"For a walk, just in case you said no."

I giggle. As if that would ever happen. I hug him tight as he bites my neck. "I love you so much."

A crash bang sounds on the porch, and Elliot and Eddie come flying through the front door. They slam it shut behind them. They look like they just saw a ghost and are panting and gasping for air.

"What's wrong?"

They glance at each other. "Nothing."

"Why did you run in the door like that?" Christopher frowns.

Elliot straightens his shoulders. "No reason. Just wanted to . . . join in the festivities."

"I said ten minutes." Christopher widens his eyes.

"I gave you fifteen." Elliot widens his eyes back.

"That was like two," Christopher gasps.

"Anyway, how did it go?" Elliot looks between us.

I hold out my hand with a goofy grin.

"Hayden and I are getting married," Christopher announces proudly.

Eddie's eyes widen, and Elliot laughs out loud. "Thank god for that!" He rushes me and pulls me into a hug. "Congratulations." He shakes Christopher's hand. "You old dog, you."

"Old dog?" Christopher mouths. "Really?"

Elliot shrugs. "Sounded good in my head, anyway. Congratulations. I'm going to leave your little family alone to let you get settled in."

Your little family.

"Thank you." I smile, grateful for him coming to watch Eddie.

"Dinner this weekend at my house to celebrate." He smiles.

"Sounds good." I wrap my arm around Eddie, and he looks up at me all adoringly.

Elliot opens the door and hesitates as he peers out into the darkness.

"What are you doing?" Christopher asks.

"Nothing," Elliot snaps. "Just . . . looking around."

"For what?"

Elliot holds his hands out and widens his eyes. "Things."

"What things?" Christopher frowns.

"We heard a growl in the bushes," Eddie says.

Christopher's eyes widen. "What kind of growl?"

"It was big," Eddie replies. "Huge."

"What do you fucking mean, a huge growl?" Christopher stammers. "Like what, like a bear?"

"Like a wolf."

"A wolf?" He gasps.

I burst out laughing. "Are you serious? There are no wolves in the United Kingdom," I scoff.

"Are you sure about that?" Elliot asks as he puts his hands on his hips. "It sounded pretty wolflike."

"Uh-huh." Eddie nods. "For real."

"Hmm, pretty sure." I get my phone out to ask Google.

"Anyway," Elliot replies, "Christopher, walk me to my car."

"What . . . me?" Christopher points to his chest in horror. "Why do I have to die too? Walk yourself to the fucking car. You're a big shot farm boy now. Handle it."

I roll my eyes. "Oh my god, you boys are pathetic. You deal with the biggest assholes every day at work and yet are scared of a tiny wolf?" I walk out the front door in a rush. "Come on, then."

Elliot follows me as I walk to his car. "You just need some lights out here. It's very dark," he justifies himself.

I look up to the house to see Christopher and Eddie peering around the doorjamb as if scared for their lives.

I giggle, and Elliot laughs too.

"Good luck living here with those two wimps," Elliot says as he kisses my cheek.

"Thanks." I wave him off and watch as his car drives away.

I walk over to the bush as I bite my bottom lip to stop myself smiling.

"What are you doing?" Christopher calls.

"Just checking things out."

"Check them out tomorrow, when it's light," he calls.

I walk into the bushes. Elliot is right—it *is* pitch black out here.

"Hayden . . . ," Christopher calls.

I crouch down and hide.

"Hayden . . . ," he calls. "The fuck is she doing out there?" I hear him ask Eddie.

"This isn't good," Eddie replies.

I hold my mouth to stop myself from laughing out loud.

"Hayden . . . ," Christopher calls. "This isn't funny . . ."

"Fuck, she's dead," Eddie says.

"Don't say *fuck*," Christopher replies. "Hayden . . ."

I giggle into my hand.

"Hayden!" he cries.

"Go and find her," Eddie snaps.

"Me! Why do I have to? You're supposed to be the tough one. Didn't you live on the fucking streets?"

"You said you're the parent," Eddie argues back.

524

"And when I find her, I'm going to smack her fucking ass." I hear him walk down the front steps in an outrage. "Hayden . . ."

I peer through the bushes to see him carrying a broom as a weapon, and I screw up my face to stop myself from laughing out loud.

He gets closer and closer.

"Hayden . . ."

I wait until he's right near me, and I jump out and scream as if something is chasing me. I run past him at full speed.

"Ahhhhhh," he screams as he sprints for the house.

"Ahhh," screams Eddie as he waits at the door.

Christopher runs past me into the house. It's the funniest thing I've ever seen in my life. I fall onto the front steps laughing so hard.

Christopher sticks his head around the door and glares at me, unimpressed with my joke. "I'm buying a wolf tomorrow, and I'm going to feed you to him, piece by piece."

The door slams shut, and I sit on the steps and look around the darkness. I hear the wind in the trees and the animals in the nearby forest. I can hear a stream bubbling in the distance.

It's peaceful and still. A sense of calm falls over me like never before.

I'm home.

CHRISTOPHER

"And these are your clothes. I wasn't sure what to get you, so I just got the minimum, and we can go shopping together for anything else you need."

Eddie sits quietly on the bed as I show him around his new bedroom.

"And through this wall will eventually be a bathroom, but it's not done yet. The house needs some work."

He smiles up at me as he watches me fuss.

It's been a big day. Flew across the world. Watched me get engaged. Nearly saw Hayden get eaten by a wolf.

"You okay, buddy?" I ask him. "You're very quiet."

He nods, and I can tell he's emotional.

"I hope you like it here. There's no wolves . . . I don't think?" I shrug. "At least I hope not."

He stays quiet, and I sit down beside him.

"What is it?" I ask.

His eyes search mine. "What if . . ." He stops himself from finishing the sentence.

I look at him, and I see a scared little boy who's lost everything that he loved.

"What if this doesn't work out?" I ask.

He nods.

"It will."

"How do you know?"

I think for a moment. "You know, Eddie, I've been thinking about this, and I've come to a conclusion."

"What's that?"

"A family isn't just the one you were born into. I told you before that I felt like we belonged together and that we met for a reason."

His eyes search mine.

"Hayden and I have been talking, and . . . if it's all right with you, we'd like to adopt you. We'll return to Spain with you whenever you want, but I want you in my and Hayden's family. The three of us. And one day there will hopefully be more children, and you will have your own brothers and sisters."

He stares at me, and I can see him imagining a future.

"It's not going to be easy, and there will be days when we'll all drive each other nuts, but I want you as my son."

His eyes well with tears.

"Would you like that?" I ask softly.

"Very much." He nods, and I pull him into a hug and hold him tight.

"Thank you, Christo," he whispers into my shoulder. "Thank you so much."

I smile as I hold him. "Call me Dad."

THE END

Thank you to my wonderful readers. I'm thrilled to announce *MILES EVER AFTER*: the book of extended epilogues for the Miles High series.

READ ON FOR AN EXCERPT OF

MR. MASTERS

PROLOGUE

Julian Masters

ALINA MASTERS
1984–2013
WIFE AND BELOVED MOTHER.
IN GOD'S HANDS WE TRUST.

Grief. The Grim Reaper of life.

Stealer of joy, hope and purpose.

Some days are bearable. Other days I can hardly breathe, and I suffocate in a world of regret where good reason has no sense.

I never know when those days will hit, only that when I wake, my chest feels constricted and I need to run. I need to be anywhere but here, dealing with this life.

My life.

Our life.

Until *you* left.

The sound of a distant lawnmower brings me back to the present, and I glance over at the cemetery's caretaker. He's concentrating as he weaves between the tombstones, careful not to clip or damage one as he passes. It's dusk, and the mist is rolling in for the night.

I come here often to think, to try and feel.

I can't talk to anyone. I can't express my true feelings.

I want to know why.

Why did you do this to us?

I clench my jaw as I stare at my late wife's tombstone.

We could have had it all . . . but, we didn't.

I lean down and brush the dust away from her name and rearrange the pink lilies that I have just placed in the vase. I touch her face on the small oval photo. She stares back at me, void of emotion.

Stepping back, I drop my hands in the pockets of my black overcoat.

I could stand here and stare at this headstone all day—sometimes I do—but I turn and walk to the car without looking back.

My *Porsche*.

Sure, I have money and two kids that love me. I'm at the top of my professional field, working as a judge. I have all the tools to be happy, but I'm not.

I'm barely surviving; holding on by a thread.

Playing the façade to the world.

Dying inside.

Half an hour later, I arrive at Madison's—my therapist.

I always leave here relaxed.

I don't have to talk, I don't have to think, I don't have to feel.

I walk through the front doors on autopilot.

"Good afternoon, Mr. Smith." Hayley the receptionist smiles. "Your room is waiting, sir."

"Thank you." I frown, feeling like I need something more today. Something to take this edginess off.

A distraction.

"I'll have someone extra today, Hayley."

"Of course, sir. Who would you like?"

I frown and take a moment to get it right. "Hmm. Hannah."

"So, Hannah and Belinda?"

"Yes."

"No problem, sir. Make yourself comfortable and they will be right up."

I take the lift to the exclusive penthouse. Once there I make myself a scotch and stare out the smoke-glass window overlooking London.

I hear the door click behind me and I turn toward the sound.

Hannah and Belinda stand before me smiling.

Belinda has long, blonde hair, while Hannah is a brunette. There's no denying they're both young and beautiful.

"Hello, Mr. Smith," they say in unison.

I sip my scotch as my eyes drink them in.

"Where would you like us, sir?"

I unbuckle my belt. "On your knees."

Chapter 1

Brielle

Customs is ridiculously slow, and a man has been pulled into the office up ahead. It all looks very suspicious from my position at the back of the line. "What do you think he did?" I whisper as I crane my neck to spy the commotion up ahead.

"I don't know, something stupid, probably," Emerson replies. We shuffle towards the desk as the line moves a little quicker.

We've just arrived in London to begin our year-long working holiday. I'm going to work for a judge as a nanny, while Emerson, my best friend, is working for an art auctioneer. I'm terrified, yet excited.

"I wish we had come a week earlier so we could have spent some time together," Emerson says.

"Yeah, I know, but she needed me to start this week because she's going away next week. I need to learn the kids' routine."

"Who leaves their kids alone for three days with a complete stranger?" Em frowns in disgust.

I shrug. "My new boss, apparently."

"Well, at least I can come and stay with you next week. That's a bonus."

My position is residential, so my accommodation is secure. However, poor Emerson will be living with two strangers. She's freaking out over it.

"Yeah, but I'm sneaking you in," I say. "I don't want it to look like we're partying or anything."

I look around the airport. It's busy, bustling, and I already feel so alive. Emerson and I are more than just young travellers.

Emerson is trying to find her purpose and I'm running from a destructive past, one that involves me being in love with an adultering prick.

I loved him. He just didn't love me. Not enough, anyway.

If he had, he would have kept it in his pants, and I wouldn't be at Heathrow Airport feeling like I'm about to throw up.

I look down at myself and smooth the wrinkles from my dress. "She's picking me up. Do I look okay?"

Emerson looks me up and down, smiling broadly. "You look exactly how a twenty-five-year-old nanny from Australia should."

I bite my bottom lip to stop myself from smiling stupidly. That was a good answer.

"So, what's your boss's name?" she asks.

I rustle around in my bag for my phone and scroll through the emails until I get to the one from the nanny agency. "Mrs. Julian Masters."

Emerson nods. "And what's her story again? I know you've told me before but I've forgotten."

"She's a Supreme Court judge, widowed five years ago."

"What happened to the husband?"

"I don't know, but apparently she's quite wealthy." I shrug. "Two kids, well behaved."

"Sounds good."

"I hope so. I hope they like me."

"They will." We move forward in the line. "We are definitely going out at the weekend though, yes?"

"Yes." I nod. "What are you going to do until then?"

Emerson shrugs. "Look around. I start work on Monday and it's Thursday today." She frowns as she watches me. "Are you sure you can go out on the weekends?"

"Yes," I snap, exasperated. "I told you a thousand times, we're going out on Saturday night."

Emerson nods nervously. I think she may be more nervous than I am, but at least I'm acting brave. "Did you get your phone sorted?" I ask.

"No, not yet. I'll find a phone shop tomorrow so I can call you."

"Okay."

We are called to the front of the line, and finally, half an hour later, we walk into the arrival lounge of Heathrow International Airport.

"Do you see our names?" Emerson whispers as we both look around.

"No."

"Shit, no one is here to pick us up. Typical." She begins to panic.

"Relax, they will be here," I mutter.

"What do we do if no one turns up?"

I raise my eyebrow as I consider the possibility. "Well, I don't know about you, but I'm going to lose my shit."

Emerson looks over my shoulder. "Oh, look, there's your name. She must have sent a driver."

I turn to see a tall, broad man in a navy suit holding a sign with the name Brielle Johnston on it. I force a smile and wave meekly as I feel my anxiety rise like a tidal wave in my stomach.

He walks over and smiles at me. "Brielle?"

His voice is deep and commanding. "Yes, that's me," I breathe. He holds out his hand to shake mine. "Julian Masters."

What?

My eyes widen.

A man?

He raises his eyebrows.

"Um, so, I'm . . . I'm Brielle," I stammer as I push my hand out. "And this is my friend, Emerson, who I'm travelling with." He takes my hand in his and my heart races.

A trace of a smile crosses his face before he covers it. "Nice to meet you." He turns to Emerson and shakes her hand. "How do you do?"

My eyes flash to Emerson, who is clearly loving this shit. She grins brightly. "Hello."

"I thought you were a woman," I whisper.

His brows furrow. "Last time I checked I was all man." His eyes hold mine.

Why did I just say that out loud? Oh my God, stop talking. This is so awkward.

I want to go home. This is a bad idea.

"I'll wait over here." He gestures to the corner before marching off in that direction. My horrified eyes meet Emerson's, and she giggles, so I punch her hard in the arm.

"Oh my fuck, he's a fucking man," I whisper angrily.

"I can see that." She smirks, her eyes fixed on him.

"Excuse me, Mr. Masters?" I call after him.

He turns. "Yes."

We both wither under his glare. "We . . . we are just going to use the bathroom," I stammer nervously.

With one curt nod he gestures to the right. We look up and see the sign. I grab Emerson by the arm and drag her into the bathroom. "I'm not working with a stuffy old man!" I shriek as we burst through the door.

"It will be okay. How did this happen?"

I take out my phone and scroll through the emails quickly. I knew it. "It says woman. I knew it said woman."

"He's not that old," she calls out from her cubicle. "I would prefer to work for a man than a woman, to be honest."

"You know what, Emerson? This is a shit idea. How the hell did I let you talk me into this?"

She smiles as she exits the cubicle and washes her hands. "It doesn't matter. You'll hardly see him anyway, and you're not working weekends when he's home." She's clearly trying to calm me. "Stop with the carry on."

Stop the carry on.

Steam feels like it's shooting from my ears. "I'm going to kill you. I'm going to fucking kill you."

Emerson bites her lip to stifle her smile. "Listen, just stay with him until we find you something else. I will get my phone sorted tomorrow and we can start looking elsewhere for another job," she reassures me. "At least someone picked you up. Nobody cares about me at all."

I put my head into my hands as I try to calm my breathing. "This is a disaster, Em," I whisper. Suddenly every fear I had about travelling is coming true. I feel completely out of my comfort zone.

"It's going to be one week . . . tops."

My scared eyes lift to hold hers, and I nod.

"Okay?" She smiles as she pulls me into a hug.

"Okay." I glance back in the mirror, fix my hair, and straighten my dress. I'm completely rattled.

We walk back out and take our place next to Mr. Masters. He's in his late thirties, immaculately dressed, and kind of attractive. His hair is dark with a sprinkle of grey.

"Did you have a good flight?" he asks as he looks down at me.

"Yes, thanks," I push out. Oh, that sounded so forced. "Thank you for picking us up," I add meekly.

He nods with no fuss.

Emerson smiles at the floor as she tries to hide her smile.

That bitch is loving this shit.

"Emerson?" a male voice calls. We all turn to see a blond man, and Emerson's face falls. Ha! Now it's my turn to laugh.

"Hello, I'm Mark." He kisses her on the cheek and then turns to me. "You must be Brielle?"

"Yes." I smile then turn to Mr. Masters. "And this is . . ." I pause because I don't know how to introduce him.

"Julian Masters," he finishes for me, adding in a strong handshake.

Emerson and I fake smile at each other.

Oh dear God, help me.

Emerson stands and talks with Mark and Mr. Masters, while I stand in uncomfortable silence.

"The car is this way." He gestures to the right.

I nod nervously. Oh God, don't leave me with him.

This is terrifying.

"Nice to meet you, Emerson and Mark." He shakes their hands.

"Likewise. Please look after my friend," Emerson whispers as her eyes flicker to mine.

Mr. Masters nods, smiles, and then pulls my luggage behind him as he walks to the car. Emerson pulls me into an embrace. "This is shit," I whisper into her hair.

"It will be fine. He's probably really nice."

"He doesn't look nice," I whisper.

"Yeah, I agree. He looks like a tool," Mark adds as he watches him disappear through the crowd.

Emerson throws her new friend a dirty look, and I smirk. I think her friend is more annoying than mine, but anyway . . . "Mark, look after my friend, please?"

He beats his chest like a gorilla. "Oh, I intend to."

Emerson's eyes meet mine. She subtly shakes her head and I bite my bottom lip to hide my smile. This guy is a dick. We both look over to see Mr. Masters looking back impatiently. "I better go," I whisper.

"You have my apartment details if you need me?"

"I'll probably turn up in an hour. Tell your roommates I'm coming in case I need a key."

She laughs and waves me off, and I go to Mr. Masters. He sees me coming and then starts to walk again.

God, can he not even wait for me? So rude.

He walks out of the building into the VIP parking section. I follow him in complete silence.

Any notion that I was going to become friends with my new boss has been thrown out the window. I think he hates me already.

Just wait until he finds out that I lied on my resume and I have no fucking idea what I'm doing. Nerves flutter in my stomach at the thought.

We get to a large, swanky, black SUV, and he clicks it open to put my suitcase in the trunk. He opens the back door for me to get in. "Thank you." I smile awkwardly as I slide into the seat. He wants me to sit in the back when the front seat is empty.

This man is odd.

He slides into the front seat and eventually pulls out into the traffic. All I can do is clutch my handbag in my lap.

Should I say something? Try and make conversation?

What will I say?

"Do you live far from here?" I ask.

"Twenty minutes," he replies, his tone clipped.

Oh . . . is that it? Okay, shut up now. He doesn't want a conversation. For ten long minutes we sit in silence.

"You can drive this car when you have the children, or we have a small minivan. The choice is yours."

"Oh, okay." I pause for a moment. "Is this your car?"

"No." He turns onto a street and into a driveway with huge sandstone gates. "I drive a Porsche," he replies casually.

"Oh."

The driveway goes on and on and on. I look around at the perfectly kept grounds and rolling green hills. With every meter we pass, I feel my heart beat just that bit faster.

As if it isn't bad enough that I can't do the whole nanny thing . . . I really can't do the rich thing. I have no idea what to do with polite company. I don't even know what fork to use at dinner. I've got myself into a right mess here.

The house comes into focus and the blood drains from my face.

It's not a house, not even close. It's a mansion, white and sandstone with a castle kind of feel to it, with six garages to the left.

He pulls into the large circular driveway, stopping under the awning.

"Your house is beautiful," I whisper.

He nods, as his eyes stay fixed out front. "We are fortunate."

He gets out of the car and opens my door for me. I climb out as I grip my handbag with white-knuckle force. My eyes rise up to the luxurious building in front of me.

This is an insane amount of money.

He retrieves my suitcase and wheels it around to the side of the building. "Your entrance is around to the side," he says. I follow him up a path until we get to a door, which he opens and lets me walk through. There is a foyer and a living area in front of me.

"The kitchen is this way." He points to the kitchen. "And your bedroom is in the back left corner."

I nod and walk past him, into the apartment.

He stands at the door but doesn't come in. "The bathroom is to the right," he continues.

Why isn't he coming in here? "Okay, thanks," I reply.

"Order any groceries you want on the family shopping order and . . ." He pauses, as if collecting his thoughts. "If there is anything else you need, please talk to me first."

I frown. "First?"

He shrugs. "I don't want to be told about a problem for the first time when reading a resignation letter."

"Oh." Did that happen before? "Of course," I mutter.

"If you would like to come and meet the children . . ." He gestures to a hallway.

"Yes, please." Oh God, here we go. I follow him out into a corridor with glass walls that looks out onto the main house, which is about four meters away. A garden sits between the two buildings creating an atrium, and I smile as I look up in wonder. There is a large window in the main house that looks into the kitchen. I can see beyond that into the living area from the corridor where a young girl and small boy are watching television together. We continue to the end of the glass corridor where there is a staircase with six steps leading up to the main house.

I blow out a breath, and I follow Mr. Masters up the stairs.

"Children, come and meet your new nanny."

The little boy jumps down and rushes over to me, clearly excited, while the girl just looks up and rolls her eyes. I smile to myself, remembering what it's like to be a typical teenager.

"Hello, I'm Samuel." The little boy smiles as he wraps his arms around my legs. He has dark hair, is wearing glasses, and he's so damn cute.

"Hello, Samuel." I smile.

"This is Willow," he introduces.

I smile at the teenage girl. "Hello." She folds her arms across her chest defiantly. "Hi," she grumbles.

Mr. Masters holds her gaze for a moment, saying so much with just one look.

Willow eventually holds her hand out for me to shake. "I'm Willow."

I smile as my eyes flash up to Mr. Masters. He can keep her under control with just a simple glare.

Samuel runs back to the lounge, grabs something, and then comes straight back.

I see a flash.

Click, click.

What the hell?

He has a small instant Polaroid camera. He watches my face appear on the piece of paper in front of him before he looks back up at me. "You're pretty." He smiles. "I'm putting this on the fridge." He carefully pins it to the fridge with a magnet.

Mr. Masters seems to become flustered for some reason. "Bedtime for you two," he instructs and they both complain. He turns his attention back to me. "Your kitchen is stocked with groceries, and I'm sure you're tired."

I fake a smile. Oh, I'm being dismissed. "Yes, of course." I go to walk back down to my apartment, and then turn back to him. "What time do I start tomorrow?"

His eyes hold mine. "When you hear Samuel wake up."

"Yes, of course." My eyes search his as I wait for him to say something else, but it doesn't come. "Goodnight then." I smile awkwardly.

"Goodnight."

"Bye, Brielle." Samuel smiles, and Willow ignores me, walking away and up the stairs.

I walk back down into my apartment and close the door behind me. Then I flop onto the bed and stare up at the ceiling.

What have I done?

✕

It's midnight and I'm thirsty, but I have looked everywhere and I still cannot find a glass. There's no other option; I'm going to have to sneak up into the main house to find one. I'm wearing my silky white nightdress, but I'm sure they are all in bed.

Sneaking out into the darkened corridor, I can see into the lit-up house.

I suddenly catch sight of Mr. Masters sitting in the armchair reading a book. He has a glass of red wine in his hand. I stand in the dark, unable to tear my eyes away. There's something about him that fascinates me but I don't quite know what it is.

He stands abruptly, and I push myself back against the wall.

Can he see me here in the dark?

Shit.

My eyes follow him as he walks into the kitchen. The only thing he's wearing is his navy-blue boxer shorts. His dark hair has messy, loose waves on top. His chest is broad, his body is . . .

My heart begins to beat faster. What am I doing? I shouldn't be standing here in the dark, watching him like a creep, but for some reason I can't make myself look away.

He goes to stand by the kitchen counter; his back is to me as he pours himself another glass of red. He lifts it to his lips slowly and my eyes run over his body.

I push myself against the wall harder.

He walks over to the fridge and takes off the photo of me.

What?

He leans his ass on the counter as he studies it.

546

What is he doing?

I feel like I can't breathe.

He slowly puts his hand down the front of his boxer shorts, and then he seems to stroke himself a few times.

My eyes widen.

What the fuck?

He puts his glass of wine on the counter and turns the main light off, leaving only a lamp to light the room.

With my picture in his hand, he disappears up the hall.

What the hell was that?

I think Mr. Masters just went up to his bedroom to jerk off to my photo.

Oh.

My.

God.

⋈

The Mr. Series is complete and available on Amazon in Kindle Unlimited.

Mr. Masters

Mr. Spencer

Mr. Garcia

Thank you so much for taking the time to read *The Do-Over.* Your support means EVERYTHING!!

ACKNOWLEDGMENTS

There are a million people I need to thank. There is never enough room on the page.

To my beautiful mum, thank you for reading everything I write a million times. You are the best beta reader, the best mum, and the very best friend.

To Kellie, the most wonderful PA who runs SWAN HQ, thank you for everything you do to make everything run so smoothly. I love you!

To my amazing beta team and friends, Lisa, Rena, Nadia, Rachel, Nicole, and Amanda, thank you for putting up with me. I adore you all.

To my incredible team, Lindsey Faber and Victoria Oundjian.

To Amazon for providing such a wonderful platform for me to publish on.

To my amazing girl gang, the Swan Squad, thank you for giving me a safe place to hang out and have fun in internet land. You really are the best friends.

To my Cygnet girls, you are a blessing that keeps on giving. You amaze me every day.

To my family, thanks for putting up with my workaholic ways. One day we will sit on a beach for longer than two hours, I promise.

I love you all so much,

Xoxoxo

And to you!

My amazing readers.

You make my dreams come true. There aren't enough words to express my gratitude to you for picking up my books. With all of my heart,

THANK YOU XOX

ABOUT THE AUTHOR

T L Swan is seriously addicted to the thrill of writing and can't imagine a time when she wasn't. She resides in Sydney, Australia, where she is living out her own happily-ever-after with her husband and their three children.